P9-DHH-170

CONTAGION

BOOK I OF THE DARK MATTER TRILOGY

TERI TERRY

Charlesbridge
TEEN

Published by Charlesbridge
85 Main Street, Watertown, MA 02472
(617) 926-0329 • www.charlesbridgeteen.com

First published in 2017 by Orchard Books
An imprint of Hachette Children's Group
Part of the Watts Publishing Group Limited
Carmelite House
50 Victoria Embankment
London EC4Y 0DZ
An Hachette UK Company
www.hachette.co.uk
www.hachettechildrens.co.uk

Library of Congress Cataloging-in-Publication Data
Names: Terry, Teri, author.
Title: Contagion / by Teri Terry.
Description: Watertown, MA: Charlesbridge, 2019. |
Series: Dark matter trilogy; book 1 | "Orchard Books." |
    "First published in Great Britain in 2017 by The Watts Publishing Group"—Copyright page. |
Summary: A deadly, mysterious epidemic is sweeping the country, and young kidnap victim
    Callie is one of the few who survived infection, only to be sacrificed by her captors at a
    secret lab working with antimatter; her older brother Kai is desperate to find out what hap-
    pened to her—his best hope lies with Shay, the girl who last saw Callie alive, and together
    they will seek answers, even if it means evading soldiers and crossing the quarantine zone.
Identifiers: LCCN 2018025620 (print) | LCCN 2018040192 (ebook) |
    ISBN 9781632898104 (ebook) | ISBN 9781580899895 (reinforced for library use)
Subjects: LCSH: Epidemics–Juvenile fiction. | Missing persons–Juvenile fiction. | Memory–
    Juvenile fiction. | Antimatter–Juvenile fiction. | Dystopias–Juvenile fiction. | Identity
    (Psychology)–Juvenile fiction. | Brothers and sisters–Juvenile fiction. | Science fiction. |
    Great Britain–Juvenile fiction. | CYAC: Science fiction. | Epidemics–Fiction. | Missing
    children–Fiction. | Memory–Fiction. | Antimatter–Fiction. | Identity–Fiction. | Brothers
    and sisters–Fiction. | Great Britain–Fiction. | LCGFT: Science fiction.
Classification: LCC PZ7.T2815 (ebook) | LCC PZ7.T2815 Co 2019 (print) |
    DDC 813.6 [Fic] –dc23
LC record available at https://lccn.loc.gov/2018025620

Printed in the United States of America
(hc) 10 9 8 7 6 5 4 3 2 1

Display type set in S&S Amberosa Sans by Gilang Purnama Jaya
Text type set in Stempel Garamond by Adobe
Printed by Berryville Graphics in Berryville, Virginia, USA
Production supervision by Brian G. Walker
Jacket and map art by Sarah Richards Taylor
Designed by Sarah Richards Taylor

In memory of Sue Hyams,
whose story ended too soon

SCOTLAND

ORKNEY ISLANDS

KIRKWAL

STORNOWAY

WESTERN ISLES

SKYE

INVERNESS

ELGIN

ABERDEEN

MULL

KILLIN

CALLANDER

DUNDEE

NORTH ATLANTIC OCEAN

STIRLING

NORTH SEA

ISLAY

★ EDINBURGH

GLASGOW

ARRAN

NORTH CHANNEL

DUMFRIES

NORTHERN IRELAND

ENGLAND

NEWCASTLE UPON TYNE

SHETLAND ISLANDS

UNST

YELL

SULLOM VOE

LERWICK

MAINLAND

10 km

0   10 Miles

100 km

0   100 Miles

PROLOGUE

XANDER

DESERTRON, TEXAS

1993

Eroooo . . . eroooo . . . eroooo . . .

Alarms reverberate through my skull, high-pitched and insistent. I scramble out of bed. Disbelief fights reality: how do you think the unthinkable? The fail-safes have failed. This is really happening.

We run.

Henri barks orders; Lena and I rush to comply. My hands are shaking on the controls, fear and adrenaline rushing through my body, but we've nearly finished the manual shutdown now. It'll be all right, we'll be all—

BANG

Waves of sound knock us off our feet. *Intense* cold. Shards of metal fly toward us, and worse.

Much, much worse.

It gets out.

It finds us.

There is pain.

PAIN
PAIN

Screams mingle and join to become one—Lena's, Henri's, mine. Three sing together in the perfect pitch of agony.

But then my voice fades away. A duet of pain is left behind.

Cells, tissues, and organs are destroyed from the inside out, a chain reaction that rips them apart. A brief moment of lucidity at the end shows what could have been, before Henri and Lena—friends, colleagues, brilliant scientists, both of them—slip away. *Lena, my Lena.* Dead.

I survive. They're gone, but their last moments are imprinted inside me, forever.

No one notices how I am changed—the things I've lost, the skills I've gained. Part pleasure, part curse.

My new senses register waves I liken to sound and color; they come from all things—inanimate, animate, human. *Especially* human.

Each man, woman, and child has their own unique pattern that emanates from them without their knowledge—more individual than fingerprints, more telling than thoughts or actions. It's as if I can see their very *soul*. Their Vox, I call it—a voice they do not know they have.

But I do. And with knowledge comes power.

And I want *more*; always more.

To know all that can be known.

First came the accident. Then came the plan . . .

PART 1

THE STRAY

The state of Schrödinger's cat is not the paradox
he thought. If the finite, observable world is left
behind—and the infinite accepted—the cat
may live and die, both at once.

—Xander, *Multiverse Manifesto*

CHAPTER 1

SUBJECT 369X
SHETLAND INSTITUTE, SCOTLAND
Time Zero: 32 hours

THEY SAY I'M SICK, and I need to be cured. But I don't feel sick. Not anymore.

They wear shiny jumpsuits that cover everything, from their shoes to the paper hats that hide their hair, making them look strange and alien—more Doctor Who villains than anything human. They reach hands to me through heavy gloves in the transparent wall, push me into the wheelchair, and do up the straps that hold me in it tight.

They wear masks, as do I, but theirs stop air getting to them from outside, in case whatever it is they are afraid of makes it through the wall, the gloves, and the suit. They can still talk in murmurs behind an internal breathing thing, and they think they can choose for me to hear what they say, or not, by flicking a switch. They shouldn't bother; I can hear enough. More than I want to.

My mask is different. It stills my tongue. It lets me breathe but stops me from speaking—as if any words I might say are dangerous.

I don't remember coming to this place, or where I came from.

There are things I know, like my name is Callie, I'm twelve years old, and they are scientists searching for answers that I may be able to give. When things have been very bad, I've held on to my name, saying *Callie, Callie* over and over again inside my head. As if as long as I can remember my name, all the forgotten things don't matter, at least not so much. As long as I have a name, I am here; I am me. Even if they don't use it.

And the other thing I know is that today, I'm going to be cured.

My wheelchair is covered in a giant bubble, sealed all around with me inside, and a door is opened. Dr. 6 comes in and pushes my enclosed chair out through the door, while Nurse 11 and Dr. 1 walk alongside.

The others seem awed that Dr. 1 is here. Whenever he speaks—his voice like velvet, like chocolate and cream and Christmas morning all together—they rush to do as he says. He is like me—known only by a number. The others all have names, but in my mind I number them. They call me Subject 369X, so it only seems fair.

I can walk; I'd tell them, if I could speak, but I'm wheeled along a corridor. Nurse 11 seems upset, and turns. She walks back the way we came.

Then we stop. Dr. 1 pushes a button in the wall, and metal doors open. Dr. 6 pushes me in. They follow and the doors close behind us, and then another opens, and another, until finally they push me into a dark room. They turn and go back through the last door. It shuts with a *whoosh* behind them, leaving me alone in darkness.

Moments later, one wall starts to glow. A little at first, then more, and I can see. I'm in a small square room. No windows. Apart from the glowing wall, it is empty. There is no medicine. There are no doctors, needles, or knives, and I'm glad.

But then the cure starts.

I'd scream if I could make a sound.

Callie, Callie, Callie, Callie . . .

CHAPTER 2

SHAY
KILLIN, SCOTLAND
Time Zero: 31 hours

I SHRINK DOWN behind the shelves, but it's too late—they saw me.

I bolt to the left, then stop abruptly. Duncan stands at the end of the aisle. I spin around the other way—again, too late. His two side-kicks, the ones I'd seen over the shelves, are there now. Not good: no one else is in sight.

"Well, well. Look, guys. If it isn't *my Sharona*." Duncan swaggers toward me while the other two start to sing the song, complete with pelvic thrusts. Nice touch. I'd hoped when I moved to Scotland last year that they wouldn't find out my real name. I'd hoped that if they did, they wouldn't know the song. I mean, how old is "My Sharona," anyway? About a million years? But as if I wasn't weird enough already, someone found out, and someone else played it on the school bus. And that was it for me.

"How about it, baby?" Duncan says, and guffaws.

"Just as soon as you grow one, loser." I scowl and try to push past him, but it was never going to be that easy, was it?

He grabs my arm and pushes me against a shelf. I face him, make myself smile. Duncan smiles back, surprised, and it makes me angry, so *angry* that I'm letting him get to me—letting myself be scared of this idiot. I use the fear and the anger to draw my knee up and slam it between his legs, hard.

He drops to the floor in the fetal position and groans.

"Well, my mistake. I guess you have one after all."

I run for the door, but an old lady with a walker is coming through it just as I get there. I cut to the side to avoid knocking into her and slam into the wall.

The guy behind the cash register by the door glares, and I turn, rubbing my shoulder, and realize I've knocked the community bulletin board to the floor. I glance back, but there's no sign of them; Duncan's friends must still be helping him up off the floor.

"Sorry, I'm sorry," I say, and bend to pick it up and lean it against the wall. As I do, a few notices that have come loose flutter to the floor, but I've got to get out of here.

That's when I see her.

That girl.

She's staring up at me from a paper on the floor.

Long, dark, almost black hair. Blue eyes, unforgettable both from the striking color that doesn't seem to go with her dark hair and the haunted look that stares at me right from the page—the same way she did that day. Not a trace of a smile.

I hear movement behind me, shove the paper in my pocket, and run for the door. I sprint across the road to where I locked my bike and fiddle frantically with the lock; it clicks off. I get on my bike just as they're nearing and pump the pedals as hard as I can. They're getting close, a hand is reaching out; they're going to catch me.

Fear makes me pick up speed, just enough. I pull away.

I glance back over my shoulder. His sidekicks have stopped running; they're wheezing. Duncan follows more slowly behind.

In case they have a car and cut me off, I don't go straight home. I veer off road to the bike path and then take an unmarked branch for the long, twisty hill through the woods: up, up, and more up.

The familiar effort of biking miles settles my nerves, makes what happened begin to fade.

But honestly, what was my mother thinking, naming me Sharona? Not a thought I am having for the first time. As if I didn't stand out enough with my London accent and knowing the kind of stuff I should hide at school but too often forget to, like the crazy way quantum particles, the teeniest tiniest things in existence, can act like both waves *and* particles at the same time, and—my current favorite—how the structure of DNA, our genetic code, is what makes my hair dark and curly and Duncan such a jerk. And as if calling me Sharona wasn't bad enough, Mum will tell anyone who'll listen why I got the name from the song. How I was conceived in a field at the back of a Knack concert.

No matter how I try to get everyone to call me Shay, even my friends sometimes can't resist *Sharona*. As soon as I'm eighteen—in a year, four months, and six days—I'm legally changing my name.

I stop near the top of the hill. The late-afternoon sun is starting to wane, to cool, and I need to go soon, but I always stop here.

That's when I remember: the girl. The paper I'd shoved in my pocket.

It was here, almost a year ago, that I saw her. I was leaning against this same curved tree that is just the right angle to be a good backrest. My bike was next to me, like it is now.

Then something caught my eye: a moving spot, seen below me now and then through gaps in the trees. I probably only saw her as soon as I did because of the bright red of something she was wearing. Whoever she was, she was walking up the hill, and I frowned. This was *my* spot, picked precisely because of the crazy hill that no one wants to walk or bike up. Who was invading my space?

But as she got closer I could see she was just a kid, much younger than me. Maybe ten or eleven years old. Wearing jeans and a red hoodie, with thick, dark hair down her back. And there was something about her that drew the eye. She walked up the hill at a good pace, determinedly, without fuss or extra movement. Without looking around her. Without smiling.

When she got close, I called out, "Hello. Are you lost?"

She jumped violently, a wild look on her face as her eyes hunted

9

for the source of the voice.

I stood up, waved. "It's just me; don't be scared. Are you lost?"

"No," she said, composed again, and kept walking.

I shrugged and let her go. At first. But then I started to worry. This path leads to a quiet road, miles and miles from anywhere, and it's a long walk back the way she came. Even if she turned around now, it'd probably be dark before she got there.

I got my bike, wheeled it, and followed behind her on foot. Ahead of me she stopped when she reached the road and looked both ways. Right led back to Killin—this was the way I generally went from here, flying down the hill on the tarmac. Left was miles to nowhere. She turned left. I remember thinking, *She must be lost. If she won't talk to me, I should call the police or something.*

I tried again. "Hello? There's nothing that way. Where are you going?"

No answer. I stopped, leaned my bike against a tree, took off my pack, and bent down to rummage around in it for my phone. My fingers closed around it just as a dark car came from the direction of Killin. It passed me, slowed, and stopped.

A man got out.

"There you are," he said to the girl. "Come."

She stopped in her tracks. He held out a hand; she walked toward him but didn't take it. He opened the back door and she got in. The man got into the driver's seat, and the car pulled away seconds later.

I remember I felt relieved. I didn't want to call the police and have to talk to them and get involved. Mum and I were heading out the next morning for our summer away, backpacking in Europe, and I still had to pack. But I was uneasy too. It was weird, wasn't it? That was a long walk for a kid that age, all on her own. The way he'd said, "There you are," it was like she'd been misplaced. Or had run away. And if she'd really been lost, wouldn't she have smiled or seemed happy when she'd been found?

But how many times would I have liked to run away from home at that age? Or even now. It wasn't my business.

I biked home and forgot about it.

10

Until today.

I take the scrunched paper out of my pocket. It's dusty, like it's been hanging on that board forever. I smooth it out and draw in a sharp breath. It's definitely her, but it is the words above her image that are making my stomach twist.

Calista, age 11. Missing.

She's *missing*? I feel sick. I lower myself down to sit on the ground and read the rest of it. She's been missing since last June 29: almost a year ago. She was wearing—I swallow, hard—a red hoodie and jeans when last seen, just miles from here.

Oh my God.

When *exactly* did I see her? Was it before or after she went missing? I think, really hard, but can't come up with a date. I know it was around then—we break early for summer in Scotland. Mum and I had left the week after school finished, but I can't remember what day.

She couldn't have been missing yet, could she? Because we'd have heard about it if we'd still been at home. It would have been all over the news.

Underneath her photo are these words: *If you think you've seen Calista, or have any information about her disappearance at all, no matter how minor it may seem, please call this number. We love her and want her back.*

CHAPTER 3

SUBJECT 369X
SHETLAND INSTITUTE, SCOTLAND
Time Zero: 30 hours

THERE IS *PAIN*, like no other pain before. It sears not just flesh but every thought and feeling from my mind, leaving only one word behind: *Callie, Callie, Callie.* Naming myself to try to hold on to who I am, but all I am is pain. Flames eat my skin, my lungs, every soft part of me.

And then, abruptly, the pain stops. The flames carry on, and I'm above myself now. I see my body and the chair. The fire must be so hot; even my bones burn. Soon they are rendered to ash along with the rest of me.

Am I dead?

I must be. Right?

I stand in fire and feel no pain. Living things can't do that. I hold out a hand, and I can see it—it soothes my eyes, cool darkness in the midst of an inferno. I look down: my legs are there, dark and whole.

After a time the flames stop. Shimmers of heat fade away, and the brightness of the walls fades.

I explore the walls, every inch, the floor and ceiling too, but there is no way out of this place. I lie on the floor and stare at the ceiling; then, bored, I lie on the ceiling and stare at the floor. Gravity doesn't seem to apply to whatever I am now. But if I were a ghost, I could sail through the walls, couldn't I? And get out of here. But no matter how I push, I can't get through. The walls are of metal, many feet thick.

CHAPTER 4

SHAY
KILLIN, SCOTLAND
Time Zero: 29 hours

"I'M HOME," I YELL, kick off my shoes, and start for the stairs, breathing hard. No phone on me today; I'd pedaled home as fast as I could.

Mum comes into the hall. "So I see. Have you been forgetting the milk again?"

"Uh, not exactly," I say, not wanting to get into a long explanation when something else can't wait.

"Honestly, Sharona, for someone who is supposed to be so smart, I don't know what is in that head of yours sometimes."

"*Shay*. Please, call me Shay."

She rolls her eyes, laughs, then looks at me more closely. "Is something wrong?"

For all that she drives me crazy, Mum is good at that kind of stuff. Like the hippie throwback that she is, she's standing there in some sort of long skirt. Her dark hair is curly like mine, but where mine is cropped at my shoulders, hers hangs down to my waist, and there are long strings of beads around her neck. She's one to talk about forgetting things; half the time she'd forget to eat if I didn't remind her. But she notices the important stuff.

"Yes. Something's very wrong."

"Is it those boys bothering you again?"

"No. Well, not really. It's this." I pull the crumpled paper out of my pocket. She smooths it out, reads it. Looks back at me with a question in her eyes.

"I saw her; I saw this girl. I have to call them."

"Tell me." So I tell her the whole story, everything, while she draws me into the kitchen and makes a special herbal tea that is supposed to be good for nerves. It tastes pretty strong.

"Are you *sure* it was this girl? That was a long time ago: were you paying attention? Are you really sure?"

"Yes."

"This isn't one of those crazy stories your friend Iona reports on her blog, is it, Shay?" she says hesitantly. "You're not getting confused between one of them and this, are you?"

"Of course not!"

"I just had to make sure. I believe you."

"What day did we go away last year?"

She frowns, thinking. Then she rummages in a bottom drawer and holds up last year's calendar. She opens it, and . . . her face falls. "It was the thirtieth of June."

"So the day I saw her was the twenty-ninth—the day it says she went missing."

"Do you want me to call them?"

I shake my head. "No. I'll do it."

She gets the phone and holds it out.

I dial the number, hands shaking a little. If only I *had* called the police that day; if that car had been a minute later, I would have. But was it even after she went missing that I saw her? Maybe that man I saw was her dad. Maybe she went missing later that day, and nothing I could have done would have changed anything.

It rings—once, twice, three times, four times. I look at Mum, shake my head. Finally it picks up.

"Hello. Sorry we can't answer just now, please leave a message at the beep." A warm male voice and a posh English accent, with a touch of something foreign.

"It's a machine," I hiss to Mum, wondering what to say.

Beep.

"Uh, hi. I saw this flyer in a shop. About a girl named Calista. And—"

"Hello, hello? This is Kai Tanzer. I'm Calista's brother. Do you know where she is?" His voice is the one from the machine; his words come out in a rush, full of hope. Without even knowing who he is or anything about him, I hate to crush that hope.

"No, I'm sorry. I don't know where she is. But I saw her."

"Where? When?"

"It wasn't recently. I just found your flyer today, but it was on the twenty-ninth of June last year that I saw her, the day it says she went missing." A flyer that was pinned to a shop board I must have walked past a hundred times since then and not noticed. "It was late afternoon. She was walking and got into a car with a man. I thought it was her father." Did I? Did I *really*, or am I just covering for the fear that if I had questioned what was going on, I could have stopped something happening to her?

"Oh. I see." There is pain in his voice. "She was missing in the morning, so this was after. Do you remember what he looked like?"

"I think so."

"Where are you?"

"Just outside Killin, in Stirlingshire. Scotland." I give him our address, tell him the single-track road to follow, explain the hill and our lane, with the signpost to *Addy's Folly*.

"Wait. Right there. I'm coming to talk to you. Don't go any-where—do you promise?"

"I'll be here."

"It'll take me about two, maybe two and a half hours to get there. What's your name?"

"Shay."

The line cuts off.

16

CHAPTER 5

SUBJECT 369X

SHETLAND INSTITUTE

Time Zero: 28 hours

TIME TICKS SLOWLY BY.

Finally something moves. A door starts to open on one of the walls, and I shrink into a corner of the room. Suited figures come in.

They ignore me, and after a while I come out of my corner. I wave my hands in front of one of their faces; no reaction.

They have instruments and are testing the ash on the floor, taking little scoops and putting it in some sensor. They seem happy, and out comes a broom. That's a little low tech. They sweep what is left of my body into a pile and then pull in a silver piece of equipment, attach a nozzle, and then . . . oh. It's a fancy vacuum cleaner. They vacuum me up.

Just like that. Gone.

They take the bag out of the vacuum cleaner and write "Subject 369X" on the bag.

And now I'm angry. *So angry.*

"It's Callie!" I shout.

They stop, uneasy. Look at each other, then shrug and continue to gather up their equipment. They start out the door with me close behind. I don't want to get trapped in this empty place.

Their reaction said that they could hear me, at least a little. Whatever I am now, my mask is gone—I can talk, and it's been so long since I've had a voice that finding it makes me happy.

I can sing! I begin a song one of the nurses sometimes sang when I was in bed, sick, and one of the techs starts to whistle along in time.

CHAPTER 6

SHAY

KILLIN, SCOTLAND
Time Zero: 27 hours

"**ARE YOU SURE** you don't want me to stay?" Mum says, and hovers uncertainly by the door.

"No, as I've told you the other ninety-nine times you asked me: *go*. I'll be fine."

"You'll call if—"

"If what? He's an ax murderer? I'm not sure it'd work if I said, 'Excuse me, could you please put your ax down while I call my mother?'" She gives me a look. "It'll be fine. You've got his name and number, right? Go."

She leans over, kisses the top of my forehead. And walks out the door.

Part of me wants to call her back, but I quash it down. Sixteen—not far from seventeen—is far too old to want to hide behind my mother. Why am I so nervous?

I sigh and flop on the sofa, leaning against Ramsay, my giant plush polar bear. "Be honest, at least to yourself, Shay." I say the words out loud in the quiet house, and the sound of my own voice makes me jump. What has me wound up is that when he hears the whole story, all that I saw, all that I *didn't* do, he might think it's my fault, that I could have saved his sister from whatever has happened to her.

Maybe there is a little voice inside me that thinks the same thing. A chance meeting with a stranger almost a year ago wouldn't normally have stayed with me—there'd have been no reason to give it enough attention to remember it. That's the real reason I remember her so clearly: it felt wrong, didn't it? And I did nothing.

Time ticks slowly past. Finally there is a distant rumble outside, and I get up, pull the curtain aside to look. The sun is just about to dip behind the mountain when a motorcycle rounds the corner. For a second the big bike and rider, dressed in black, are outlined in a bright halo from the sun. Then all is darkness.

I open the front door just as he's pulling off his helmet. He runs his fingers through his hair to pull it away from his eyes.

"Shay?" he says. "I'm Kai." He takes off his gloves and holds out a hand; he takes mine, and holds it in his. His eyes are locked on mine—intense, wanting, *needing* something from me—and I can't look away. Hazel eyes, with gold around the pupils blending to green.

I blink and let go. "Come in," I say, and step inside. He follows. "Would you like a cup of tea, or—"

"No. No, Shay. Tell me what you saw. Please." There is tension and anguish in his voice. His sister, his little sister, has been missing for almost a year. How must that feel? I have to tell him exactly what happened, not try to cover for myself in any way.

"Of course. I'm sorry."

He follows me in, and I point him to a chair and sit on the sofa. He pauses, unzips his bike jacket, and takes it off. He's tall, with wide shoulders. Sun-streaked hair that is somewhere between blond and light brown. Probably a year or two older than me, and what my friend Iona would call *pure dead gorgeous*. He sits down and faces me, quiet and still. Waiting for me to speak.

"Okay. I'd been biking in the woods, and there's a place I always stop. It was late in the afternoon. I know it was the twenty-ninth of

June, because we went away for the summer the next day. Otherwise I'm sure I'd have heard she was missing."

He nods, his eyes intent.

"I could see someone walking up the path below. A girl. She had jeans on and a red hoodie. It's a steep ride and a long walk from town, and I almost never see anybody up there. So I was watching her get closer, wondering who it was."

He reaches into his pocket, takes out a photo. "And you think it was my sister, our Calista?" He holds it out to me.

I take it in my hand. It's a different photo from the one on the flyer, but there's no doubt: the long dark hair, those blue eyes, a faint quizzical look. I nod. "It's her. I'm sure of it."

"Even after all this time?"

"Yes." I hesitate, not really wanting to go there, but needing to at the same time. "It's kind of this thing I can do. If I'm paying attention, my memory is photographic. I remember stuff."

"All right; go on. And then?"

So I tell him the rest. How she said no when I asked if she was lost, and I followed her. How a car stopped on the road and a man got out, and she got into the car.

"Describe him to me."

"He looked ordinary. Sorry, I know that isn't helpful. Short hair, a bit balding. Average height. Maybe forty-something. If I think about it for a while, I might come up with more detail."

He frowns. Shakes his head a little.

"I'm so sorry. I wish I'd made her talk to me, or called the police, or done something. Anything."

He looks up and sees my face; his softens. He shakes his head. "Whatever has happened to my sister, it isn't your doing. I just thought—well." He reaches into his pocket again and takes out another photo. "I thought it might have been this man." His glance at the image says more than words: he *hates* him.

I take the photo. Of an older man, with longish, silvery-gray hair, lots of it. Piercing blue eyes, movie-star looks—or presence, or something, even just in a photograph. He is vaguely familiar, as if he'd been in a film I've seen and then forgotten. But it's not the man I saw with Calista. "It's not him. He's nothing like him."

"Are you sure? Are you really sure?"

Because I know he wants me to, I look again, *really* look. And it's weird, but there definitely is something about him that triggers some memory inside. But not quite as he is in the photo. Not with silver hair? I frown, trying to find the memory, then shake my head; this isn't what Kai wants to know. "It's not the man I saw with your sister." I look back at Kai. "Who is he?"

"He was my stepfather. Mum divorced him a few years ago."

"And you think he'd take your sister?"

"He would do *anything* to hurt mum. Will you come with me to talk to the police, to tell them what you saw?"

"Of course."

"Can you show me where you saw her?"

I nod. "Yes. It'll have to be in daylight."

"I'll come back tomorrow."

The fierce energy that had me caught so intently in his gaze is fading. He looks drawn, tired.

"Where have you come from today?"

"Newcastle."

"You don't sound very Geordie."

He half smiles. "No. We've only lived there for about five years; before that, many other places. Germany originally. You don't sound very Scottish . . . ?"

I shake my head. "I'm not. Well, my mum is. She's from around here, but we moved from London over a year ago. Her Aunt Addy died and left her this house, so I got dragged to the middle of nowhere, and—" I stop abruptly when I realize I'm babbling. *Shut up, Shay. He doesn't want to know about your pathetic family dramas.*

"I'd best get going." He stretches and reaches for his bike jacket.

I hesitate. I know what Mum would do if she were here.

"Newcastle is a long way to ride tonight and back tomorrow. The sofa is free if you want it."

"Complete with company?" he says, and heat climbs in my cheeks.

His eyes move to Ramsay the bear and back again, and he grins. Laughter is in his eyes as if he knows what I thought he meant, as completely stupid as it could be to think he'd want anything to do with me.

"Well, you'll have to ask Ramsay about that. He might prefer solo on the chair."

"Don't you need to check with your parents?"

"It's just me and my mum. She's at work at the pub and will be back in a few hours. Besides, she'll be fine with it."

His smile falls away, like it is an expression that rarely settles on his face for long. "That reminds me. I'd better call my mother and tell her what you've said."

He slips outside. I can hear him speaking in another language—they're from Germany, he said; it must be German. The words have no meaning to me, but his voice is music. When he speaks English, the deliberate way he frames words is almost textbook perfect. No trace of Newcastle or anything else to place him.

I text Mum. He's here and hasn't murdered me. Can he have the sofa tonight? Wants me to show him where I saw his sister tomorrow and talk to the police.

She texts back in seconds, so quick I know she had her phone in her hand, waiting for word from me. Of course. Make him some dinner. Are you okay on your own? Is he nice?

His voice still sounds like music outside in the darkness; sad music now, like the scene in the opera where everything goes wrong. Is he nice? Not like puppies are nice. There is something deeply unsettling about the intensity of his eyes—a sense that he has too many demons inside him.

He comes back in, stands awkwardly in the doorway. The anger has been replaced by sadness, one so deep it isn't something I've ever felt in my own life. I wish I had something to tell him that could take it away.

I text back: Yes.

CHAPTER 7

CALLIE
SHETLAND INSTITUTE
Time Zero: 26 hours

I FOLLOW THE WHISTLING TECH and the vacuum bag marked Subject 369X down corridors, through doors. Every one has a double locking mechanism, so you go through one door, wait for it to lock behind you, then go through another door. I stay close to them so I don't get trapped.

But then one door doesn't lead to another. Instead, when we go through it, we are in a room with benches and fancy equipment—some sort of science lab? There are two scientists there, also suited up like the techs in shiny jumpsuits.

The whistling tech stops whistling. "Got another one for you, doc," he says, and one of the scientists gets up and takes the bag with 369X on it.

"Ah yes, the *X* girl," he says. "How interesting."

The techs leave; I stay in the lab, stay with my bag. One of the scientists takes it. He opens a door at the back and steps into a room. I follow. Where his breath exits his suit there is white mist. It must be a cold room, not that I can feel it, and it's huge. Inside are bags hanging on a sort of conveyor belt thing from the ceiling by hooks, all like my one. All with numbers.

He presses a button near the door, and the conveyor moves on a track—like at a dry cleaner's. Bag after bag goes slowly by. Then it stops. There is an empty hook between 368 and 370; he hangs my bag there.

Were all these bags once people, like me? With *names*, not numbers. I'm not 369X. I'm not!

I will never, ever be a number again.

I AM CALLIE!

CHAPTER 8

SHAY
KILLIN, SCOTLAND
Time Zero: 25 hours

MY BLANKETS ARE PULLED AROUND ME, but I'm not sleepy.

Mum came home early. She said it was quiet at work, but I doubt that was true.

But I was glad when she got here. We'd already had dinner—pasta, the only halfway decent thing I can make—and Kai had been polite, said it was good, and generally spoke when spoken to. He answered my pathetic attempts at conversation enough for me to know that it is just him and his mum in Newcastle, that he finished his A levels this year and should go to university after the summer. The way he said *should* sounded like he wasn't going to go. That his mum is some kind of doctor and does research. And he even helped me wash up. But I could tell he didn't want to talk, that he wanted to be alone. Even though it was early for a Friday night, I was about to fake a yawn and escape upstairs when Mum got home. But it still rankled when she pretty much sent me to bed like a child.

Below, voices rise and fall—a murmur, not words I can make out. Just Mum mostly, and his short replies.

So he won't even open up to Mum?

I'm surprised. Whenever somebody has a problem—a broken heart, a death in the family, a bad hair day, whatever—they seek her out. That's why they love Mum at the pub: people come in to talk to her and have a few drinks while they do. She says it's all about how you listen.

After a while their voices have stilled. The house is silent, dark. It's taken me a long time to learn to fall asleep in complete silence. After London traffic, sirens, and people singing or shouting at all hours in the street below, the silence of this isolated house is deafening.

What I must try to do now is this: I *must* remember. If I can picture the moment I saw Calista clearly in my mind, maybe there will be something that will help.

As I told Kai, my memory is photographic, but only if I'm paying close attention. And I must have been, to recognize Calista from a photo so readily. The trick is retrieving the memory after so much time—finding the links that will lead me there. Then I'll be able to study it in detail, as if my memory is a video I can watch—one I can pause, rewind, and go over again and again.

Think, Shay, think . . .

CHAPTER 9

CALLIE
SHETLAND INSTITUTE, SCOTLAND
Time Zero: 24 hours

MY FAULT. I should have followed the scientist out of the cold room, but I was so *angry* I didn't realize he was leaving until the door clanged shut. Then the lights dimmed, and I was alone.

I press myself against the walls, the door, the floor, even the ceiling, but it's no good. The room is completely sealed. What is the point of being a ghost if you can't even pass through walls?

I look around me, and hanging everywhere are bags. Like mine. I'm uneasy. If they are all full of the ashes of dead people too, are they ghosts like me? Where are they all? How many are there?

So many.

Panic is starting inside. Breathe in and out and count to ten—that's what they used to say when I panicked. Try to stop it before it really gets started. But how do you do that when you don't breathe anymore?

I'll count. Count the bags, from the beginning.

I follow the overhead conveyor around to the start, find a bag labeled number 1, and begin: 1, 2, 3, 4 . . . 99, 100, 101 . . . 243, 244, 245 . . .

I count and count. They go all the way up to 368, then me: 369X. Then they carry on: 370, 371, 372, and on, up to 403. Many empty hooks wait past that. Why are there so many bags in place past mine? I must have been behind schedule.

None of the others have Xs on them; just numbers. What does the X mean?

Over four hundred dead people hang in this room.

Including me. My ashes hang, just there.

I'm dead. They're dead.

Where are their ghosts? Will they come out in the night?

Is it day or night right now? I don't know.

I'm scared. I roll myself into a little ball and throw myself at the door.

"Let me out!" I howl, and I do it again, and again, and again.

The panic and rage are growing, more and more, becoming a wave of heat that washes over me, and then—

Beep-beep. Beep-beep.

A faint alarm is sounding. Is it somewhere outside this door?

Beep-beep. Beep-beep.

A moment passes, and then the door starts to open. I throw myself through it while it is still moving, straight into the scientist who hung me up in there before.

He stops in his tracks. There are two technicians behind him; they push past him with an impatient look and go in.

"I don't understand why the temperature was rising," one of the techs says, after checking some dials and screens. "It's correct now. All the settings are correct. Everything is working just the way it should."

"It's weird, though," the scientist says. "When I opened the door, it felt like a blast of heat in my face."

The tech turns to look at the scientist. "The temperature sensors are all normal now. And you can't feel external temperature changes when you're in your biohazard suit. You know that."

The scientist draws himself up. "Well, just keep an eye on it tonight," he says, and stomps away to the door of the lab.

I follow quickly behind him; I'm getting out of here. I slip through the door, close on his heels—leaving all the bags of ashes of dead people behind.

Including mine.

CHAPTER 10

SHAY
KILLIN, SCOTLAND
Time Zero: 23 hours

IT IS LATE AT NIGHT when I finally find the way to my memory of that day and replay it all in my mind, as if it were happening *now*:

The sun shines, but it is cool in the shade of the wood.

I'm watching her—dark hair, red hoodie—catching glimpses through the trees below. She walks closer and closer.

I want to yell out to her to wait for me there. Tell her to get on the back of my bike, that I'll double her back down and take her to the police, or call Kai. But I can't go back in time; I'm paralyzed, stuck. Forced to relive what happened.

Exactly as it happened.

She's nearly reached me.

"Hello, are you lost?"

"It's just me; don't be scared. Are you lost?"

She turns. Her eyes are blue, yes, but not a boring medium-blue like mine—hers are so dark they are almost violet. There is a shaft of sunlight through the trees where she stands, and something glints and sparkles around her neck. A necklace, with a pendant. I squint; she moves a little out of the sun. A pendant, something like a starburst—but not quite that. It's like nothing I've ever seen before, yet it reminds me of something at the same time.

"No," she says, turns, and keeps walking.

Again I want to run after her, but I'm frozen. She is almost out of sight before I can finally move again and follow her to the road above. Just as I did that day, I bend down to find my phone in my backpack.

Really call the police this time, Shay. Do it!

The car comes.

It's black, with four doors—a shiny Mercedes with tinted windows. I squint at the license plate, but from where I am, kneeling down by my backpack, it's mostly blocked by green growing things on the side of the road. I can only see the tops of the letters and numbers. Not enough to work them out.

A man gets out of the car.

"There you are," he says. "Come." He is half turned away; I can't see his face very well. Thinning hair, bald on top. Dark, not gray. His height is hard to judge from my position, but perhaps five foot ten or so.

She goes to him, gets into the car when he opens the door, into the back seat.

He turns to get into the driver's seat, and he looks this way for a split second. I drink in the details. The barely controlled anger in wide-set, brown eyes; a small scar by his left eye, red and a bit puffy around his right eye, as if he'd recently been hit and would have a black eye tomorrow; a glint of gold at his neck.

There is someone else in the front seat—turned away—and I can't see anything beyond the form through the tinted windows. Just an impression of height; of strength. Another man?

The car pulls away, and then is gone.

CHAPTER 11

CALLIE
SHETLAND INSTITUTE, SCOTLAND
Time Zero: 22 hours

I FOLLOW THE SCIENTIST down one hall, then another. We reach a junction with double security doors. He swipes a pass to get them to open. I stay close; I don't want to get trapped between two sets of doors until someone else comes by.

We reach another door, and he lines his eye up with a device alongside it and looks inside. The door slides open. I follow close behind; the door has slid shut behind us before I realize we're in an elevator.

I *hate* elevators. I hate being confined anywhere, but elevators are the worst. I'm shaking, rolling myself up in the corner, but it isn't just from being in this elevator. It is this *whole place*. All the long corridors, labs, everywhere I've been, there are no windows. Not anywhere. I want *out*! I long to see the sun, the sky, a few trees, or even a half-dead city garden with graffiti scrawled on the walls.

We're in the elevator a long time. Are we going up, or down? I have no feeling of movement, and there are no floor numbers lit up over the elevator door to help.

Finally the door opens again. The scientist steps out, me still his shadow, into a weird tunnel of hanging plastic sheets. He steps through jets—first of water, then of some gas—and then through a section with weird, bluish lights. It's kind of like he's walking through an automatic car wash. Afterward he takes off his suit, helmet, the works, and puts it all through a hatch. Under everything he looks less like a space alien and more like a grumpy old man in creased trousers and shirt.

He smooths his hair with one hand and finally eyeballs a device by another door. It swings open, and we step into a large room.

We're in an open space, at last—even if there are no windows—and my panic eases. There are people, and none of them are suited. They wear ordinary clothes; some wear quite fancy skirts and business suits, some wear white jackets over their clothes, and some are in work-type clothes with boots.

There are huge monitors all along a wall, and rows of desks with computers all facing the monitors. There is a hum of voices, excitement.

"Ah, there you are. I was starting to think you weren't going to make it down in time for all the fun," a woman in a white coat says to the scientist I followed.

"I was delayed," he answers. "There was a temperature alarm in the vault. I haven't missed it?"

"No. T minus two minutes to beam," she says.

Gradually the voices in the room quiet down. A big digital clock over the monitors counts down sixty seconds. When it nears zero, the whole room is completely silent.

3 . . . 2 . . . 1 . . .

And everyone seems to be holding their breath, staring at a screen in the center.

Then there is a faint *beep*; a brief glow of a bright light in the center of the screen.

Everybody cheers. They start talking excitedly, shaking hands. They seem to be congratulating each other. Snatches of conversation filter above: *Another success . . . Always a thrill . . . We've done it again . . .*

All for a blip on a screen?

There are a few worried faces to one side watching some other computer screens. A heated discussion breaks out, and I drift over to listen.

"See? We're fine. No need for a shutdown. Specs for another five runs before—"

"Delay collision. Check sector 24."

"It's not necessary. The readings show that—"

"Just do it."

Some of the people in work gear go through a door. Curious, I slip behind them.

They walk down another endless corridor, muttering and cursing to each other. Whatever they've been sent to do, they're not happy about it. There are hatches in the floor. They walk on and on and then finally stop at one of them.

A worker bends and twists the hatch open. He mutters under his breath about how this shouldn't be done during beam. The other worker's eyes are wide. They drop through the hatch to a ladder and climb down, down, down.

I float past them.

Where the ladder ends below, there is another curved tunnel—a much bigger one. This one has a huge structure inside it that follows the tunnel, like a giant metal earthworm that burrows in the earth—round, with equipment attached around it at intervals all along its length.

I'm drawn to it, and I drape myself on top of the massive worm, listening. Is there a musical hum inside? This has something to do with me; what or how, I don't know.

The two men emerge from the hatch and start checking some equipment under the worm. I leave them behind and fly along the top of it, on and on and on, as fast as I can go, past endless numbers of hatches like the one we came through. In a few places there are big rooms with even more weird-looking science junk and people inside. Around and around I go, again and again. I'm nearly past one of those rooms when a voice floats up.

It's a woman's voice, with a particular biting tone. One I know. I home in on her voice and stop.

It's Dr. 6—the one who pushed my chair when they took me to be cured. I've never seen her before, not really—only in a suit—and it seems weird to see someone in the flesh after they've always been mostly hidden.

She's walking toward a door now, a few other people behind her, and as drawn as I am to the worm, somehow I have to follow her.

Once through the door they stop. They put on biohazard suits, and the brief glimpse I had of them as real people vanishes behind visors and plastic.

They go through doors and more doors: security doors with that same sort of eye device the scientist used earlier. As I follow, a twisted, sinking feeling grows inside me. I wish I'd stayed in the tunnel, flying around and listening for the hum deep inside the worm.

There's something about where they are going that I don't like. Still they walk. I could stay behind but might get trapped in this narrow corridor.

My dread grows.

CHAPTER 12

SHAY
KILLIN, SCOTLAND
Time Zero: 21 hours

MY MIND ECHOES with the detailed memory I finally found and relived. Calista, the woods, the car, the man—there was something about him. He was *not* a nice guy. I shiver.

I grope around in the dark until my fingers touch the cold shape of my phone. I hit the button and blink at the bright screen: it's 3:00 a.m.

The quiet gets to me. I get up and walk slowly and carefully. Any little noise I make sounds like a megaphone in the stillness.

I start to head down to make a hot drink, but then remember Kai asleep on the sofa downstairs.

Alone in the dark.

What if he wakes up and his eyes find me as I slip past to the kitchen? What if his sorrow is too deep to bear alone? What if, now, in the quiet and the dark, he finally wants to talk? To *me*. And what if . . .

Get a grip, Shay. I sigh.

I retreat back up the stairs for a glass of water instead. When I turn the bathroom faucet on, I flinch when the pipes rattle and bang.

Instead of the whole glass, a sip will have to do. I am *so* not flushing the toilet.

CHAPTER 13

CALLIE
SHETLAND INSTITUTE, SCOTLAND
Time Zero: 20 hours

ONE LAST DOOR. The corridor ends. I have to follow Dr. 6 and the others through it or stay out here, trapped between two sets of doors. It is about to swing shut when I decide in a panic against being alone and throw myself through the gap.

When I see where we are, I try to scrabble backward, but it's too late. The door is shut.

I close my eyes, but it's no good. I can see it with my memory when my eyes are shut, and that is even worse. I open them and look around a room that I've only ever seen from the other side.

It's big and square, and all around three of the walls are windows. Thick windows, looking into small spaces. More like little cells than rooms.

Inside each cell is a scared face. They belong to people of all ages, from children to teens to old people. Each one is strapped tight to a stretcher.

On this side, doctors and nurses bustle about. There are monitors, equipment.

"Sedative section one," Dr. 6 says. Along one side of the room, the scared faces still, relax, then slacken. Their eyes close, but now I'm screaming, *Stop this! Let them go!*

They didn't use sedatives when I was in one of those little rooms. I screamed and screamed, way before anything even happened. They didn't know I couldn't be in small spaces like that.

There are weird hands that go through the wall under the windows. Each of the section one cells now has a nurse or doctor controlling the hands.

When I was in there, even though I was strapped down tight, they still had trouble injecting me. I was so scared.

The needle not like any other needle.

The pain not like any other pain. Until the pain of the cure, I'd have sworn it was the worst pain there could be in the world.

Maybe they've started using sedatives now because they don't like listening to the screaming?

I roll myself into a little ball away from the windows, away from the needles, away from the pain.

But the memory won't let me go.

CHAPTER 14

SHAY
KILLIN, SCOTLAND
Time Zero: 19 hours

A SMALL ROOM. A girl with dark hair. She's crying; she's alone.
She looks up, blue eyes shiny with tears. She stares and her lip curls back.
"You could have helped me, but you didn't. You couldn't be both-
ered."
"No, no, that's not true. I—"
"It is true, and you know it is. I'm dead, and it's your fault."
"No!"
"Kai will work it out. He will. And then he'll hate you, like I do."

A cry is rising in my throat. I twist, and the pull of the sheets around me brings me back, to here, to now.

Alone. In bed; in *my* bed.

That wasn't real; it was a nightmare.

Is Calista really dead?

Is it my fault?

It can't be true.

Can it?

CHAPTER 15

CALLIE
SHETLAND INSTITUTE, SCOTLAND
Time Zero: 18 hours

FINALLY A DOOR OPENS: a group of nurses comes in. Some of the nurses who were here say hello to them, goodbye to others, and go out through the door. I bolt after them.

There are a dozen or so of them, chatting and laughing like they didn't just cause severe pain; didn't just cause dozens of deaths, slow and painful. Or maybe they're just trying to forget.

I hate them.

They go on through many corridors and security doors until finally they stop at a door. Two go in, and the door shuts. Minutes later it opens again, and another two go in. This time I go with them.

They pass through one of those car wash things like the scientist I followed earlier, then finally take off their suits. They look ordinary, not like mass murderers.

When they get to the door at the end, it won't open.

"Please wait," a voice says, echoing in the space.

The nurses exchange a glance. "Wonder what it is this time?" one of them says.

The other one frowns. "I know somebody in tech down below. He heard somebody collapsed in the control room. What if there's been a real breach this time?"

"I'm sure it was just something normal, like indigestion or appendicitis. You know how careful they are; it can't get out."

Someone collapsed? Maybe she's wrong. Maybe all their jumpsuits and precautions aren't enough, and one of them caught whatever it is they're injecting into people.

I hope so.

"No, it's not just that," the other answers. "They've quarantined the control room; that's why he knows. No one can get in or out."

CHAPTER 16

SHAY
KILLIN, SCOTLAND
Time Zero: 17 hours

TOO MANY HOURS OF BEING AWAKE, being quiet, and not flushing the toilet have caught up with me. I just don't care anymore what Kai hears.

But I run the shower before I flush. Just in case.

It's only 7:00 a.m. when I tiptoe down the stairs to sneak past the sofa to the kitchen, but he isn't there. Instead, Ramsay the bear is tucked underneath the blanket with his head on the pillow. Sweet.

I peer into the kitchen: no sign of Kai.

He hasn't left, has he?

No, why would he?

I look out the window; his bike is still there. And then I spot Kai on the bench at the end of our garden. I slip on some shoes and step through the door.

He's facing away, not moving. His hair has golden streaks through it that catch the morning light. Is he lost in the view? Most people *ooh* and *ahh* if they haven't seen it before. From here you can see over the trees to Loch Tay below us, a glistening blue that stretches miles in both directions. If you turn the other way, Ben Lawers and other peaks are stark above.

I walk toward him; he turns at the sound. He smiles.

"Hi," I say. "Up early?"

"Didn't sleep very well."

"Sorry, was it the sofa?"

"No, not at all." He shrugs. "Just couldn't sleep."

"Me neither."

I sit next to him and look across the loch. On a sunny, still morning like today, the water is glass, the world above—trees, hills, mountains—reflected within it in perfect detail. If I could see well enough from this distance, I'm sure there'd be perfect replicas of the two of us in a watery world.

Then Kai shakes his head. "I can see why people come here, but it just makes me think of what is missing." He stands abruptly and turns away from the loch.

CHAPTER 17

CALLIE
SHETLAND INSTITUTE, SCOTLAND
Time Zero: 16 hours

THE DOOR FINALLY OPENS, and the two nurses walk through to a square room, me close behind. A suited technician checks their temperatures and asks how they feel. They're told they must sit and wait an hour and have their temperatures taken again.

They sit and complain about being hungry and missing the start of some movie they want to watch.

Finally their temperatures are taken again, and a door opens on the other side of the room.

They go down a corridor to a cafeteria; dinner is underway. There are tables, large and small, and groups of people in twos or threes or many more, talking, laughing, eating, or finished and just hanging out. There are some grumpy, worried faces in a clump; a heated, whispered conversation that I can't hear. Overall, it doesn't seem much different from a small school cafeteria at lunchtime, except the food looks better and the chairs more comfortable.

There is a loud clattering.

A woman has tripped, her tray of food spilled on the floor.

Someone goes to help her. The woman who fell looks familiar. Ah, yes, she was the woman with a white coat who spoke to the scientist in the room with all the monitors and asked him why he was late.

If that was the control room . . . I thought the nurse said they were quarantined? She must have left before that happened.

She looks a little pale.

CHAPTER 18

SHAY
KILLIN, SCOTLAND
Time Zero: 15 hours

"HAVE YOU BEEN ON A MOTORCYCLE BEFORE?" Kai asks.

"No. Well, only a moped."

Kai opens a storage box on the back of his bike and pulls out something red: a helmet.

He holds it out. "See if that fits."

I tug it over my head and get the angle a little wrong. Kai catches it in his hands, straightens it. Tucks my hair around.

"Comfortable?" he asks.

"It's fine." I hesitate. "Was this hers? I mean—"

"Was this Calista's helmet? Yes. Red was her favorite color. Her hair was dark, like yours. Though hers was—"

"Long and straight. Not this mess—I got the wrong copy of the curly hair gene." Just in time I stop myself from telling him about the genetic studies that one day may sort out my hair without hours spent using straighteners—because who has time for that?

"But it suits you." He catches a curl around his finger where my hair spills out under the helmet. Then, like he realizes what he's done, he yanks his hand away so fast that my hair springs back.

He gets me to tuck my jeans into my heaviest boots, which he'd told me to wear, and shows me how to get on the bike. Where to hold on.

And then we're off.

He's going slower than I bet he usually does to start with, but the feel of speed, of the road underneath us, has my blood singing. All too soon we've done the distance that would take half an hour on my bicycle.

He slows as we near the main street of Killin with its few shops, cafés, churches, and pubs—what passes for civilization here. The sky is clear blue; the early morning sun reflects and shimmers on the surface of the river as it tumbles over the Falls of Dochart. The mountains and trees above are lit up with a glittering halo. It's a warm spring day, but snow still lines the peaks above.

Okay, so this place is pretty beautiful on days like this. But sometimes I wish there were enough people around to feel anonymous. Here, everyone knows who is local, who is a tourist. And who is neither: me. Despite having a Scottish mother, I'll always be marked as alien.

We pass a few girls from my school, out early for a Saturday, and I can feel eyes following us as Kai pulls in to park by the side of the road. At least, for a change, the thing they're noticing about me—the topic for dissection on the bus to school on Monday—is tall, blond, and handsome.

"Was that all right?" Kai asks as I take off my helmet.

"I loved it!" I can feel my eyes sparkling.

"Another time I'll take you on a proper ride where we can put on some speed."

My stomach does a weird flip. "I'd like that," I manage to say.

He turns to put the helmets in the storage box on the back of his bike. An odd look crosses his face, as if he wishes he hadn't said it. He was just being polite, wasn't he? He didn't really mean it. I try not to mind that he didn't—he's got enough to deal with just now.

"Now, where does this path start?" he asks.

"Come on. I'll show you," I say, and we cross the road and walk over the bridge by the falls. As always I listen to the music of the water and don't speak again until we're across and starting down the lane below the pub. "Why was your sister here—where was she staying?"

"She was with our mother, at our vacation house. It's one of a group of them on the south side of the loch." He gestures toward Loch Tay, not visible here through the trees. "Sorry, I guess I could have stayed there. I don't like going there anymore."

"That's understandable—don't worry about it." I know the place he means; there are a half dozen very, very expensive houses there, all barely used vacation homes. And while they may be reasonably close by boat, they're a long way around the shores of the loch. "That'd be a long walk to here. There are no paths most of the way; much of it is by road. Unless she was on the water?"

"She liked to go out on the loch when we were here, and often went alone even though she wasn't supposed to. But our canoe was still at the house."

"Even assuming she walked that far, it's unlikely she wouldn't have been seen somewhere along the way. Everyone here knows everybody; who belongs, who doesn't. She would have been noticed for sure."

"That's what the detective said. So he thought she must have wandered off into the woods. Or been taken from the house."

"What about your mum—did she hear or see anything?" He's silent a moment. "I'm sorry if I'm asking too many questions," I say, then stop walking and gesture to the rough lane. "Here's where we join the bike route. Then farther along there is an unmarked branch that veers up; that's the way we go."

We continue, and as we walk I glance sideways at Kai. His face is closed, carefully contained, like he is scared to let anything of himself out.

"I'm sorry," he says, finally breaking the silence. "It's fine to ask questions. It's just difficult to talk about. No, our mother didn't hear anything. She got up late in the morning, and Calista was gone. Mum wasn't alarmed—thought she'd gone for a walk, or on the loch. But time passed. She checked; the canoe was still there. She started to panic and called the police. They assumed Calista had merely gotten lost on a walk. Searches were arranged. They carried on for days. No sign of her was ever found."

"Do they think she just got lost, and . . ." My words trail away. I don't know how to finish the sentence.

"That seems to be the police's main theory. That she was lost, or hurt. That her body will be found one day in the woods." He flinches when he says *body*.

"But you don't believe that."

"No. I was sure something else had happened to her. She wasn't the kind of person to get lost; she was sensible for her age and had a good sense of direction. But there was nothing, no proof of anything else. Without it—well." He shrugs. "I think the police had a theory they liked, so they gave up."

"But now you know I saw her."

"Yes. Now they *must* look at her case again." He says it with cold determination.

We walk on in silence. Kai had been so excited when I called; his hopes so dashed when he realized how long ago it was that I saw Calista.

But now they know she didn't just wander away and get lost. Now the police have to try to find her again. This is his new hope.

CHAPTER 19

CALLIE
SHETLAND INSTITUTE, SCOTLAND
Time Zero: 14 hours

BORED WITH WATCHING EVERYONE EAT FOOD I CAN'T HAVE, I follow some other people through a door when they leave, and explore. There's a library and a movie theater. Individual rooms, like hotel rooms but more lived-in looking. Again, there are no windows, no clue if it is day or night. And there is no guessing by what people are doing: some are settling down to sleep, some are just getting up, others are arriving.

I'm wandering down another corridor when I hear someone singing—a voice I recognize.

The sound is faint; I home in on it, follow it. It comes from behind a closed door, but this is an ordinary one with a crack along the bottom. I flow under the door to the other side.

She's still singing. That's how I recognized her: Nurse 11. I wouldn't have been able to from her face because there was never much of her that I could see in her suit. Now she's in a nightgown, brushing her hair, singing along to quiet music.

She was nicer than some of the nurses and doctors. She was the one who sang to me when the pain was so bad. And the one who wouldn't go with the doctors when they took me for their cure.

I stand there and watch her. Her face looks kind.

She turns off the music and gets into bed. There's a book beside her, and she picks it up and starts to read.

There are pictures on her wall: children. Most are teenagers, older than me, but there is one girl who is younger than the others, probably about my age, twelve or thirteen. I stare at the photograph. Nurse 11 is smiling in this one, her arm half around this thin, pale girl who stares at the camera.

How could she work here and let them do things to me that she'd never let anyone do to this girl?

Anger twists inside me. She couldn't go with the doctors to my cure because she didn't want to think about what they were doing to me. That's it, isn't it?

There is a *beep-beep* through a speaker on the walls. She puts her book down and listens.

"Attention, please. This is not a drill. Go to your meeting points immediately and follow decontamination procedure one. Do not leave them unless told to do so."

CHAPTER 20

SHAY
KILLIN, SCOTLAND
Time Zero: 13 hours

WE'RE ON THE UNMARKED PATH NOW, and it gradually gets steeper. I'm used to it, and Kai isn't breathing any harder than I am.

Like he feels my eyes on him, he turns his head and smiles. "You go up this on a *bicycle*?"

"Yes."

"Do you walk parts of it?"

"I used to. Not anymore." I grin.

"Why?"

I hesitate, then answer truthfully—surprised that I do. "It's not like there's much else to do around here, but that isn't the reason. Pushing myself makes the world go away."

He nods as if that makes perfect sense.

We keep going. The sun climbs higher in the sky as we zigzag up the slope. Light dapples through leaves above to make moving patterns on us, on the path. Then there's a stretch where the sun breaks through and is warm on our faces.

I pause. "I think this is about where she was when I first spotted her. I was a bit farther up, and I saw something red moving below me through the trees. It was unusual to see anyone here; it's not a marked trail. So I kept watching and wondered who it was."

We walk on until we get to my place.

"This is where I was when I saw her. I always stop and lean against the bent tree there." I point.

"Could you pretend to be her? Go where she was when you saw her, and I'll stay here and be you?" he says. I hesitate. "Please."

"All right."

Kai settles himself against my tree. I walk back to where Calista would have been when I first saw her.

And I'm Calista. I remember how she moved, and I walk back up the path like her. Kai remembers what I told him I had said, and he says the same words. I jump and turn at the sound of his voice like she did; calm when I see him as me. Keep going. Say "no" when he asks again if I'm lost.

I walk up the path, and he follows behind. He catches up when I reach the road.

"There is something about you; some way of moving, the dark hair, I don't know. For a moment I could imagine you were my sister." The closed look he had before is replaced by pain, so stark and real that to see it makes me flinch.

"I'm sorry I didn't stop her, didn't make her talk to me. If she'd gotten away from somebody, why wouldn't she talk to me? I don't understand. But I should have done something *more*. And if only we hadn't gone away the next morning—I'd have heard she was missing and gone straight to the police."

"Don't blame yourself. I'm the one that should have been there. I should have been with them. Mum wanted me to go, but I was too busy with my friends," Kai says, the torture inside him plain on his face. He blames himself, just like I have been. But neither of us is to blame, are we?

We weren't driving the car that took her away.

CHAPTER 21

CALLIE
SHETLAND INSTITUTE, SCOTLAND
Time Zero: 12 hours

THIS IS NOT A DRILL.

Everywhere there are scared faces. Hurrying feet. The click of locking doors.

And then there is a new sound: many voices, high-pitched and panicked.

I follow the sound. It seems to be coming from the movie theater.

The lights are on; the movie is still running on the screen, ignored.

The woman who fell in the cafeteria is lying on the floor by the back row. Trembling, moaning. Suited people are by the doors and won't let anybody out. There are angry faces, terrified faces, and people pulling away as far as they can and piling into the front of the theater. The two nurses I'd followed earlier are here. One of them is crying. The other has beads of sweat on her brow.

"I don't feel very well," she says.

She collapses, and her friend screams.

CHAPTER 22

SHAY
KILLIN, SCOTLAND
Time Zero: 11 hours

THE RAW EMOTION that Kai's eyes held before is gone. His jaw is clenched, like hiding it costs him effort.

"It's not your fault, any more than it is mine." I say the words because they have to be said. He nods, but I can see he doesn't believe me. With his shields up again I'm not sure the meaning of the words even gets through to Kai.

We walk down the hill back to Killin in silence.

CHAPTER 23

CALLIE
SHETLAND INSTITUTE, SCOTLAND
Time Zero: 10 hours

SOMEONE HAS FOUND THE SWITCH and turned off the movie that had been running on the cinema screen. No one was watching it anymore, but now their fear is louder.

Now they can hear the woman in the back row screaming in pain.

Suited figures collect the nurse who collapsed next to her friend at the front of the cinema and put her near the other sick woman at the back. Her friend doesn't go with her.

Soon she'll be screaming too. They both will.

CHAPTER 24

SHAY

KILLIN, SCOTLAND
Time Zero: 9 hours

KAI GETS UP FROM OUR TABLE when he sees the policeman we are waiting for nearing the café. They shake hands, say a few words, and walk back over to me.

"Pleased to meet you. I'm Dougal. Shay, is it?" He is dressed in ordinary clothes. He holds out a hand, shakes mine, and then sits in the empty seat opposite, next to Kai's.

"Yes. I'm Shay."

"Now, I hear from Kai that you think you saw his sister the day she went missing."

"I don't *think* I saw her; I saw her."

"And that you didn't come forward before because you went away the next day and didn't know she was missing."

He smiles and his demeanor is friendly, but there is something about him I don't like.

"That's right." I exchange a glance with Kai. Dougal sits down, orders a coffee. The waitress comes back to clear the remains of our late lunch from around us; I push my phone out of the way to the corner of the table.

Dougal takes out a little recorder thing and holds it up. "Is it okay with you if I use this?"

I shrug. "Fine."

He turns it on and says his name, where we are, and the date and time. He looks at me. "Please state your full name."

I glance at Kai and sigh. "Sharona Addy McAllister. Known as Shay."

"All right then, Shay. Tell me what you saw on the twenty-ninth of June last year."

So I tell him the whole story, with every little thing I can remember—especially about the man I saw and the car. Which, since I relived my memory over and over again late last night, is a lot. I even draw the top of the license plate of the black Mercedes on a napkin, though I'm not convinced they'll be able to work it out from so little.

When I'm finally done, Dougal stops the recorder. He's looking at me strangely. Kai is staring a little as well, and I realize I hadn't told him all the extra things I remembered last night.

"That's a lot of detail," Dougal says finally.

"It's all true."

"Is it?" He's skeptical. Even Kai is looking at me like he's starting to wonder.

"I have a type of photographic memory. It's a bit selective, so I don't remember everything." I pick up the menu and hold it up. "Like I don't remember this word for word, because I wasn't paying that much attention to it."

"Yet you remember all that from almost a year ago." He doesn't believe me. I can tell he doesn't.

"Fine. Let me show you."

I look around us. The rest of the tables are empty now; the waitress is pretending to read a novel. She's sitting close enough to us to listen, and she hasn't turned a page anytime recently.

"Excuse me. Can I borrow your book for a sec?" I ask her.

She hands it over, and I look down and groan. *Fifty Shades of Grey*. That figures, doesn't it?

"Pick a page, any page, then show it to me," I say to Dougal.

He shrugs, flips it open, and hands me the book.

I glance at it for a split second—paying the right sort of attention. Then I give it back to him, still open, and point to the top of the page. Holding the image of the page in my mind, I start to read. Word for word. When I get to the third paragraph, things are starting to go very *Fifty Shades*, and thankfully he holds up a hand to tell me to stop. Color is rising in my cheeks.

I hand the book back to the waitress. Her mouth is hanging open. That'll be all over town today and school by Monday. I sigh.

Dougal is tapping the table with a pen. "Right. Okay then, we'll look into this. See if anyone can make sense of the license plate also." He takes my napkin drawing. "If we find out anything, we'll be in touch with you and your mother, Kai," he says, and shakes Kai's hand, then mine. He heads for the gate.

Kai is looking at me, eyes a little wide.

I sigh. "Okay, so now you know I'm a freak."

"No. I think you are clever, amazing, and wonderful!" Kai grabs my hand, pulls me out of my seat, and hugs me.

His T-shirt is warm and soft against my cheek, the *th-thump* of his heart beating under it. I breathe him in and pay attention to every sensation: *this*, I will remember.

He lets go, and I pull away, standing there awkwardly.

"I hope you find her," I say. "I hope she's okay. Will you let me know?"

"Thank you. And of course I will, *Sharona*."

I roll my eyes. "You've got both my secrets now."

"If you've only got two, that's not so bad. But I'll tell you one of my secrets. It's only fair."

"What?"

He leans in closer. "My first name is really Geordie. You see why I go by my second name, Kai, now?"

I stifle a laugh. *Geordie*: a name used for people from Tyneside— the area around Newcastle—with that thick northern accent. "So you were Geordie the Geordie."

"Five years ago, when we moved to Newcastle, you wouldn't believe how many fights I got into because of having that name with the wrong accent. But I'll keep your secrets if you keep mine."

"Deal. And now I've got to go. Mum's waiting for me."

"Goodbye, *Shay*. Thank you again." His eyes are warm.

Somehow I pull mine away from his. Walk through the other tables and out the gate.

I glance at my watch. Mum had said to meet her at work and that she'd take me home. She might be wondering what's happened to me by now, but I never said when I'd get there, so there's no real rush. I want to be on my own for a while. Instead of going left up the road to her pub, I head right and for the park.

I glance back just before the café garden is out of sight. Kai is still standing by our table, watching. He holds up one hand. I wave in return, looking at him instead of where I'm going, and almost walk into one of the stone pillars at the park entrance. I hastily take a few more steps and look back again. He's gone from sight.

Maybe he didn't see that graceful moment.

Yeah, right.

I walk across the park, then hesitate by the wooden steps over the fence at the back. It leads to a hill path, one of my favorites on foot and steep enough to put most people off: somehow I don't want to be around anyone right now. I climb the steps over the fence and cross the field beyond it to another fence, another set of steps, and enter the oak woodland. The path climbs steeply, but for once I'm not pushing myself; I walk slowly. I'm back in that moment when Kai hugged me.

Crazy, Shay. Our emotions were high because of Calista, and he was just thankful I gave him this hope to hang on to. That's all it was.

But I'm holding the moment to myself; lost in it. A smile on my lips, remembering—

Hands grab my shoulders roughly from behind.

"Well, look who I've found, all alone. It's just the two of us this time, *my Sharona*."

CHAPTER 25

CALLIE
SHETLAND INSTITUTE, SCOTLAND
Time Zero: 8 hours

SOON IT'S NOT JUST IN THE MOVIE THEATER that people are screaming in pain. I wander down the corridors, into rooms, following the sounds of distress. People are sick everywhere.

They're all going to die, and I'm glad. All these nurses, doctors, and techs, injecting people, watching and taking notes while they die; burning people to ash, vacuuming up what is left and hanging the bags in an endless room of death. They deserve it.

And the scientists and everyone down below us too. I don't know how they're involved in all this, but they must be. Some are quarantined in their control room—isn't that what the nurse said? Though they did that too late: that woman who fell must have left before they stopped letting people out, and she was the first one here who was ill. She must have brought *it* along with her.

There is panic everywhere. There is lockdown between sections, people trying to contain what can't be contained. Many who aren't already sick are suited now, but there don't seem to be enough suits to go around. They're all scared, even the ones with suits; waiting to see if they got theirs on in time. If they will live or die.

They may deserve this, but who is it that made it all happen, from the very beginning? Who set this place up, decided they'd infect people like me with *it*, and watch them die?

It must be Dr. 1. He's the one they all bow down to. Is he here? If he is, he's the one who deserves this most of all. I want to watch him die. But where is he?

Who might know? There are a lot of people in the cafeteria, but no one is eating now. There is fear all over their faces, and none of them are wearing suits.

I drift around, listening. If he's here I might not recognize him, as he's always been in a suit; all I know for sure is that he's tall. But I'd recognize his voice, for sure—like velvet.

Some are silent, sitting alone. Blank eyes staring straight ahead, like they've been switched off.

Some huddle together in twos and threes. Either crying and talking in low voices, or agitated and loud.

"I never told him, I should have told him. He won't know what's happened to me . . ."

"What's going on? Why won't they tell us what's going on?"

"It's my granddaughter's twelfth birthday next week; I've got time off. We were going to go to Harry Potter world before her next round of chemo. I won't see her again now, will I? I'll never be able to tell her why I've been away and what we were doing here. We've failed. We haven't found the cure."

I stop, abruptly, at the last one. I recognize that voice and the rest of her too: it's Nurse 11. Was her granddaughter the pale girl she was with in her photo?

"Her next round of chemo," she said. Her granddaughter must have cancer, and she wants to cure her—is that what they are doing here? Experimenting on people to try to find a cure for cancer?

There's a commotion by the door. Three more people are pushed into the room, and the doors shut behind them.

They turn and bang on the doors. "Let us out!"

A few others walk over to them. "What's going on out there? Why aren't they telling us?"

"The intercom has failed. They're rounding up those who aren't ill and bringing them here. The rest get hauled off somewhere else."

Everyone looks around them as if doing a headcount, trying to work out who is missing.

"But what happens if somebody gets it in here, what then?"

"What do you mean *if*? More like *when*."

"This is crazy. They can't lock us up together like this. It's more likely to spread. If anyone in here has it, we'll all get it."

"But they have to quarantine everyone. What if it gets out?"

"But what about us? Why aren't there enough suits to go around?"

"They think we've all got it already. That's why they're doing this."

"Where is he? Where is Dr. 1?"

The last was said by an angry woman in a voice that carries, and the rest of them look nervous, like that isn't something that should be said out loud.

So, he's not in here. And none of these people know what is going on, that's clear. I slip out through the crack under the door.

There are guards on the other side of it now. With actual *guns*. They weren't here when I went in before. They're suited, but their suits look different. Heavier. They're talking to each other, but I can't hear what they're saying.

There is banging on the door again from the inside.

There is some sort of exchange between the guards. Then one of them gestures to another.

"Stand back and we'll open the door!" he barks, his voice plain now.

The ones with guns come closer and arrange themselves in a semi-circle around the door.

The first one opens the door.

"What's the problem?"

A barrage of shouts greets him, but he doesn't want to listen.

He holds up a hand, and somehow his voice gets louder than theirs. He must have a megaphone built into his suit. "Yes, I know: we're all trapped underground, and some of us are dying. We're doing what we can to contain the spread. You'll have to wait in here for now."

"What about Dr. 1?" a man shouts. "Where is he? Is he even on the island?"

The guard turns and looks at him slowly, like he's weighing his response. His hands tighten on his gun. But then he shrugs. "Wish I bloody knew. Now! Get back in, sit down. Chill out, because we've got a temperature scanner on the room. If anyone's temperature reading goes up, well . . . you'll be *removed*. Be thankful you're in here and not where you'd be taken then."

They quiet down, and the doors are shut.

The guard who spoke turns. One of the other guards must say something, as he looks at him and shrugs again. "They've been trying to reach him, but communications aren't working. Someone was sent up to check if he's at his house above, but they never reported back. Maybe he bolted, or—" Then, like he realizes he's forgotten to turn off his external speaker, his voice suddenly goes silent even though his lips, behind his mask, are still moving.

Well. We're on an island?

Island means the sea is all around. Open and wide as far as eyes can see, and now I'm even more desperate to get out of this place, to hear waves crash, smell salty air. A trace of a memory from long ago grips me: of the sea—of a holiday. Of someone tall holding my hand as I stand, barefoot, sand squidgy through my toes. Squealing and laughing as cold waves splash my feet and ankles.

Can I even smell or feel the sea anymore, as what I am now?

I have to know.

And if Dr. 1 is out there, all the more reason to go.

Let me out!

CHAPTER 26

SHAY
KILLIN, SCOTLAND
Time Zero: 7 hours

I TWIST AND STRUGGLE but can't get away. Duncan's too strong when I haven't got the element of surprise on my side.

"Now, Sharona, you really hurt me the other day. Hurt my feelings too; pretending to be nice, and then look what you did to me."

"I'm sorry. Let me go!"

"Are you really sorry? I doubt it. You're going to have to *show* me that you're sorry. Kiss me like you mean it, and then maybe I'll let you go." And he tries to twist me around, his breath hot on my neck.

And I'm struggling uselessly, scared, a scream working its way up inside, but I can hardly breathe with his arms crushing my chest, and anyhow no one is anywhere near to hear me.

That's when I remember that I'm wearing boots. I stomp back on his foot, hard, with one heavy boot. While he's still crying out in pain, I kick backward with the other boot into his shin.

He lets go.

I spring around, fists up.

But it's Kai who's got him, who's pulling him away. Kai punches him hard once, and again, and again, and Duncan slumps to the ground, moaning, hands and arms covering his head.

Kai grabs his shoulder with one hand and pulls him to his feet. His other hand is a fist that is ready to hit again. Blood and tears are running down Duncan's face.

I grab Kai's fist with both of my hands. "That's enough, Kai!" He turns to me, wild-eyed, like he can't really see me.

"That's enough!" I say again. "Let him go."

Gradually Kai's eyes focus in on my face; his breathing steadies. One hand is still gripping Duncan's shoulder. He relaxes his fist and turns to Duncan.

"Listen to me. If you *ever* go anywhere near Shay again, I'll kill you. Do you understand?"

Snot and blood are dribbling down Duncan's face from his nose. "Yep. Keep away from Shay. Got it."

Kai lets go of Duncan's shoulder, and he runs.

"Are you all right?" Kai says, and now he's trying to hug me again.

But I don't want anyone's hands grabbing me, touching me, right now, not even Kai's; I push him away. "I can take care of myself. I had him on the ropes."

"Did you?" He reaches down and pulls at my collar. My shirt is ripped from when I was trying to get away from Duncan's hands. These are memories I don't want to keep, but every little tiny bit of it starts to replay in my mind, and now I'm shaking.

Kai holds out my phone. "You left this on our table; that's why I followed you. I only just saw which way you went across the park. Thank God I did. Let's call the police."

"He'll have you up for assault if you call them. Besides, I think you punished him enough."

"If you hadn't stopped me, I think I really could have killed him." Kai's hands are hanging helplessly by his sides, as if he's afraid of them. He looks up. "It was like you were Calista, and I could save you. But I wasn't there to save her." His eyes go glassy, welling up. As if they are linked, mine do too.

This time it is me who reaches for Kai. We hold each other and cry. And the way he fights against it, his shoulders shuddering, I know he doesn't allow himself to do this often.

Not often enough.

After a while Kai takes me home on his bike. I cover my ripped top with his jacket.

When we get there I call Mum, tell her Kai brought me home.

And Kai waits. He promises he won't leave until Mum gets home.

I throw my ripped top in the trash and take a shower—scrub and scrub, washing Duncan away—and even though I know Kai is out there, that no one could get past him, I keep feeling like this could be the shower scene out of *Psycho*. Nervous and jumpy, I get soap in my eyes, trying to watch the door all the time even though I locked it.

I hurry and throw on jeans and a sweater, not wanting to be alone, wanting to rush to Kai. To feel safe.

CHAPTER 27

CALLIE
SHETLAND INSTITUTE, SCOTLAND
Time Zero: 6 hours

NOT KNOWING WHAT ELSE TO DO, I stay with the guards by the door. They must be the ones who know things. One of them is watching a control panel, and on it a button starts flashing red; then another.

They open the door. The people who were yelling earlier look more subdued now. A few of the guards go in, holding up some sort of scanner thing. They stop next to a few people, speak to them. One of them is Nurse 11. They are told to stand up and follow the guards out. One of those selected protests, and they grab his arms, drag him along with them.

Everyone shrinks away from them as they walk out. I follow them. They're not taking them to the movie theater, where the first sick people were. Instead they open the door to a large open space—it's got basketball hoops at either end, courts marked out on the floor. It's the gym.

People are lying on the floor. Some are still, silent. Some are writhing, screaming. The ones with Nurse 11 that just got pushed through the door shrink away in horror. They don't feel sick yet, at least not much; they've just got a temperature.

But Nurse 11 walks into the room. She clucks under her breath. "Where are the doctors?" she says.

Someone who is shaking on the floor hears her. "Th-th-the last one just died."

Nurse 11 turns, bends down to the woman who spoke. "Jan?"

Jan's eyes are closed now; she's shaking and moaning.

Nurse 11 goes to the door, bangs on it, and yells out, "We need pain relief. Get me some morphine and syringes."

"There's none left" is the answer called through.

As if that was the last thing they couldn't bear to hear, the crying and screaming goes up a notch.

All these people lying on the floor deserve what they've got.

So many people.

Crying out in pain, shaking, just plain crying. The distress and agony leak out from them into the room, filling it like it is a separate living thing, one growing bigger and bigger while they get smaller and more insignificant.

Except for the lucky ones.

They're still. They're dead.

This sickness escaped and caught those who inflicted it on others. But who made this thing happen on purpose in the first place? *Why?*

Nurse 11 may have come here because she wanted to find a cure for cancer for her granddaughter, but I bet that isn't the only reason Dr. 1 set this place up. Anyone who found a cure would be rich—richer than pop stars. Richer than professional athletes. Richer than royalty.

I shrink away from all the concentrated agony. I'm getting out of here. I rush for the door, but then stop.

Nurse 11 has started to sing, like she used to sing to me. Others, those who can, join in and sing with her. And as their voices rise in the room, the pain monster settles down, at least a little.

Who is this woman, who one minute comforts the sick, and another minute deliberately infects others and ends their lives?

71

I shake my head. I don't understand her. I don't understand how I feel either, but something inside me wishes she wouldn't die.

But she will, and I don't want to watch it happen. I don't want to see any of this anymore. I slip back under the door, past the guards.

I hope someone is left to sing to her.

CHAPTER 28

SHAY
KILLIN, SCOTLAND
Time Zero: 5 hours

WHEN I GET TO THE FRONT ROOM, hair a mess of wet curls from the shower, I'm suddenly shy. I hesitate by the door. Kai is on the sofa, next to Ramsay, looking lost and alone. He gives me a ghost of an uncertain smile.

He hesitates, then holds out a hand. I cross the room, feeling awkward with his eyes on me, and sit next to him, close—too close? I start to pull away a little, but then his hand finds mine. As his warm fingers wrap around mine, some new feeling wraps around inside me, even warmer.

"Are you all right?" he asks. His eyes search my face.

"Yes," I say, and Kai raises an eyebrow, as if he can see through what I'm hiding. "Ish," I add. What I don't say is that now that I'm here, sitting next to him, with him holding my hand, the nervous weirdness I had before is gone, and I am all right. More than all right.

"I want to apologize," he says.

"What for?"

He shakes his head, as if the words aren't there. But I wait, saying nothing.

"For losing control," he says finally. "Both of my temper, and . . ." He shrugs, doesn't finish the sentence.

"While I appreciate you punching that loser, once was probably enough."

"I know. While I am here, calm, I know this." He frowns. "But somehow, inside, I was confusing you and my sister; what happened to her, and today."

"I'm not a child, you know. I can take care of myself."

"Sure you can." He grins, a trace of a twinkle in his eyes. "I saw you stamp on his foot in those boots you were wearing. Once the fear wears off, I bet he can't walk."

"Just now you were going to add something else?"

"Sorry about *after*, also."

I'm puzzled, but then it clicks. "What, for *crying*, is that what you mean? For being human?"

"Yes, that's it. Far too much of being human. I must put a stop to that." A trace of humor is back in his eyes.

"Being human means having feelings. You can't bottle them up, or they explode. As Duncan found out."

"Is that his name?" I nod. "Do you think he'll leave you alone now? You'll let me know if he causes any problems?"

"He's a coward; he won't go anywhere near me after what you did to him." *I hope.* But if he has enough imagination to come up with them, I'm sure there are other ways he can be a nightmare at school. I shake my head. "Let's not talk about him anymore."

"What do you want to talk about?"

I hesitate, somehow knowing there is one person he needs to talk about more than anything else, even if he doesn't want to. "Please, Kai. Tell me about your sister."

CHAPTER 29

CALLIE
SHETLAND INSTITUTE, SCOTLAND
Time Zero: 4 hours

THERE IS A LOUD BANGING down the hall: gunshots?

There is *screaming*—a sort that is somehow different from that of the sick. More surprised; cut off quickly.

More gunshots.

I follow the sound. It leads back to the cafeteria. The doors have been thrown open; a guard is on the ground, a knife sticking out of him. His suit is ripped open, blood leaking out around the blade.

But even more of the people from the cafeteria lie bleeding and still on the ground.

Two guards are there, guns trained on the few left inside. Where are the rest of them?

I follow the sound—running feet. Yelling. More gunshots. Another body lies on the floor, and another. I pass running guards—they are chasing half a dozen or so people, who round a corner and almost run into another group of guards. Their feet backpedal in haste, but now they're trapped between the two groups of guards. They raise their hands over their heads to surrender, but there are gunshots, screams. They fall to the ground.

Why are they killing each other?

I feel sick, like I could be sick over and over again until nothing could come up, but I can't even throw up anymore.

Why kill each other when so many are already dying?

I have to get out of here. *I have to.*

I fly away from the bleeding and dying, up and down every corridor I've already been up and down, looking for a way out.

But everywhere I go, it's a dead end.

What if everyone in here dies, and I'm sealed in with all the bodies and ghosts, forever?

There must be a way out.

CHAPTER 30

SHAY

KILLIN, SCOTLAND

Time Zero: 3 hours

KAI HESITATES, and I'm afraid he'll refuse. But then he begins. Halting at first, then with more and more animation, he tells me how Calista was born early; tiny, like a little doll. How his name was her first word. How she drove him crazy, following after him everywhere as soon as she could walk. How she loved reading and hated sports but still made their Mum take her to his soccer games, even if she sat there with a book on her knees.

How much he loved her.

Once he starts it's like he can't stop.

And the whole time he talks, he holds my hand like a lifeline.

CHAPTER 31

CALLIE
SHETLAND INSTITUTE, SCOTLAND
Time Zero: 2 hours

KABOOM!

The explosion is loud, like a million cracks of thunder at once. The very earth shudders, as if it doesn't like this place any more than I do.

The screaming is quiet by comparison.

And like the explosion knocks some sense into me, I finally work it out. The place those people were running to when they were shot? There were guards there. What were they guarding? Those people wanted to escape. They must have been running there because that was the way out!

I don't want to go back there. I don't want to see the blood and the bodies.

But I have no choice.

CHAPTER 32

SHAY
KILLIN, SCOTLAND
Time Zero: 1 hour

AFTER A WHILE KAI IS SILENT, but it's not like the locked-down silence from this morning, when he couldn't talk about anything real. This time it is because he has finally said all that he needed to say.

The clock ticks, a breeze ruffles leaves outside. Kai lets go of my hand, but before I can feel the loss of it his arm is around my shoulders.

My head is against his shoulder, then snuggled a little closer, against his chest, but it's not awkward or uncomfortable, or wondering what could or should happen next—it's being still, here, now, as if this is where I was always meant to be.

My eyes close, the lack of sleep last night catching up with me no matter how much I want to stay in this moment.

His heart beats, *th-thump*, *th-thump*, against my ear, and I'm warm, sleepy, drifting between awake and asleep as his hand gently strokes my hair.

CHAPTER 33

CALLIE
SHETLAND INSTITUTE, SCOTLAND
Time Zero: 40 minutes

THE BODIES ARE STILL THERE, but they've been pulled to one side. Piled up. The guards are gone.

Did they run out on everyone?

If they did, they shut the door behind them. It's sealed, tightly sealed. I search every part of it, but there is no gap, no way through.

Smoke is filling the corridor. Footsteps pound on the floor, coming this way.

More people from the cafeteria? They try the door, but they can't open it. It's locked.

"We need to blast it," one of them says. They're all coughing from the smoke.

"Maybe one of the guards had a gun," another one says, and a few of them run back the way they came to check the bodies.

They return. One of them has a gun in his hands and shoots wildly at the door. Then he steadies his aim and shoots again and again, until finally he blasts the lock mechanism. "Try it!" he says.

Another one pushes at the door. It opens, and they rush through. I zoom past them, but the corridor on the other side of it soon branches off, and I don't know which way to go. I have to wait for them and follow.

But some are falling to the ground.

Some keep going, coughing, staggering in thickening smoke.

They go up to one last door.

It's an elevator?

They force the doors open, but the elevator isn't there.

CHAPTER 34

SHAY
KILLIN, SCOTLAND
Time Zero: 20 minutes

"HELLO," MUM SAYS, and I'm instantly awake.

She stands in the doorway, her eyes open wide. Part of me wants to jump up and pull away from Kai, and another part doesn't.

Kai's arm tightens around my shoulders for a moment, then he takes it away.

He'd said he'd wait with me until Mum got back from work, that he'd have to go home then. And he did wait, even though she was late, and I fell asleep.

Mum doesn't say anything about us being so close on the sofa, about it being almost midnight.

She leaves while we say goodbye.

"Thank you for listening, Shay," Kai says. His eyes are warm; there is more, I don't know, *peace* there than I have seen before. He leans forward, puts his arms around my shoulders; mine slip around his waist. He holds me for a moment. He pulls away, and now a slight frown lurks between his eyes. "You'll call if he—"

"Yes," I say, cutting him off, not wanting to lose this moment to Duncan. "Are you sure you're okay to ride back this late?"

He touches my chin. "Is this worry for me?" He smiles. "I'll be fine. Give me your number, and I'll text when I get there." He gets out his phone and enters the numbers as I tell him.

He leans down and quickly kisses my cheek: a feather touch. His lips are soft, his breath warm; his cheek, against mine, scratchy now with a shadow of stubble. And I *want* to turn my face, reach up with my hand into his hair and kiss him, kiss him properly. Everything is tumbling inside; my blood is rushing to my arms and hands and everywhere, making them too heavy to move. I'm frozen, and even though I can't move, the moment is perfect.

Then all the emotion of the last day or so crashes in on me. My eyes are welling up. So much has been crammed into such a short time that I feel like I've aged, like I'm older than the girl who got up yesterday morning. His sister, missing; going on the walk together, and reliving seeing her that day; finding hope in the police renewing efforts to look for her again. Duncan; the way Kai rushed to save me; the way he couldn't stop. His tears, and mine; all the things he told me, holding my hand; his arm around me, and his beating heart as I drifted to sleep.

And now he's saying goodbye.

But he doesn't see the tear that spills on my cheek. He's turned, putting on his jacket and helmet to leave. I hastily wipe it away.

CHAPTER 35

CALLIE
SHETLAND INSTITUTE, SCOTLAND
Time Zero: 5 minutes

THERE IS ANOTHER EXPLOSION, long and rumbling.

It's not under us this time—it's in the distance—but it comes with waves and waves of sound. Even more than the first one.

Those I followed are collapsed on the floor now. Some call out for help, but who to? Some are crying. Some are still and silent.

I fly up the elevator shaft, leaving them behind. Up and up and up, until I can't hear the crying below anymore.

The shaft is rocked again and again by smaller explosions.

When I finally reach the top, the elevator is there, blocking my way.

No! Let me out!

I spread myself thin over the bottom of the elevator and the walls, hunting, searching . . .

And I find it. A crack in the wall by the floor of the elevator. I don't know if it was always there, or if something was shaken free by the explosions.

But then there is a *whoosh* below.

The very air seems to claw and pull, dragging me back the way I came, back down into the depths. I scrabble uselessly at the walls, falling, falling, until a rush of heat slams into me and forces me back up. A ball of fire: a wall of flame.

Immersed in fire, I find the crack again. Is it big enough? I make myself small and thin, and start to push through the crack. The flames are all around me. The metal is warping; the crack gets smaller. I pour myself more and more through the crack. There is pain from the heat of the fire now, and it is getting stronger—*pain* like the cure, tearing and burning. The first time I've felt pain or anything else since I was cured.

I've survived flames before, but is it too much when I'm spread thin like I am now? I need to roll into a ball, get out of here fast—or it could destroy me.

I don't care if it does; anything would be better than being trapped underground.

But then, all at once, I've escaped. I'm through!

Into a . . . house? No—a barn. It looks like an ordinary sort of barn: stone and wood, somewhat falling down.

The elevator was hidden behind bales of straw; they're burning now, flames shooting up.

And across the room, a door stands open.

A door to . . . outside?

There is fresh air. A moon hangs in the sky, but it isn't dark enough to be night.

I rush for the door.

CHAPTER 36

SHAY
KILLIN, SCOTLAND
Time Zero: 2 minutes

MUM COMES BACK IN. She stands with her hand on my shoulder, like she knows I need it to be there. We watch through the window as Kai's bike disappears up the road. Will I ever see him again?

I'm not cold, but the hairs on my arms and neck stand on end, and I shiver. Somehow the world feels like more of a dangerous place than it used to, even just a day ago. For reasons I can't explain, I worry for Kai, for me, for everyone I care about.

Goodbye, Kai, I whisper inside. *Stay safe. Come back to me one day.*

CHAPTER 37

CALLIE
SHETLAND INSTITUTE, SCOTLAND
TIME ZERO

I FLY THROUGH THE DOOR AND OUT.

The barn burns behind me. There are rumbles in the earth below. The sky glows red in the distance.

But I don't care.

I'm swept up with overwhelming joy and run on the grass, away from the barn and the flames. Spinning somersaults high through the air, in weird half-light that is more night than day.

I'M FREE!

PART 2

THE APPLE

Discovery is rarely a planned thing.
A mistake, intelligently observed,
can open a multiverse of possibility.

—Xander, *Multiverse Manifesto*

CHAPTER 1

SHAY

"**WAKE UP**. Please wake up, Sharona."

Mum's voice is insistent, but my head is groggy and thick after so little sleep. A thrill rushes through me as I remember *why* I'm so tired; I'd stayed awake, waiting for my phone to beep. And it did. Kai had texted: Dear Shay, I'm home safe. Take care. Kai. And I'd hugged his words inside, reading them over and over again, before I let myself drift to sleep.

"Shay?" Mum says again, and I open one eye. It's still dark. And isn't it Sunday . . . ?

I sit up, awake in a rush. "What is it? Is something wrong?"

Mum stands in my bedroom doorway, still in her clothes from last night. "Come see the news. Something's happening in Shetland." There's an edge of distress in her voice that makes me rush to rub my eyes, pull on a robe, and stumble down the stairs after her to the TV. Her brother Davy lives in Shetland, he and his wife and three kids—my cousins.

She holds out a hand; I sit on the sofa next to her and cuddle up.

The images moving on the screen are like a scene out of a disaster movie. This can't be real, can it? But it is.

Flames shoot high into the sky. The very ground appears to be burning. Buildings are in flames, the whole scene lit strangely by red fire against the Shetland night sky. I reach for Mum's hand.

"Have you called?"

"I tried. The phone lines are down. Davy's not answering his cell."

"What's happened?"

She shakes her head. "The oil terminal at Sullom Voe has exploded; fires have spread. They don't know why. Or they're not saying," she says, her voice thick with unshed tears.

We watch the coverage through what is left of the night. Is it an act of terrorism? A terrible accident? The reporters speculate. They know there was a massive explosion, and the oil stores on the island—oil delivered by sea or fed there by pipelines from North Sea rigs to one of the largest terminals in Europe—are up in flames. Safety features designed to contain and isolate sections of the pipeline didn't work. Rigs are burning too.

And the unusually lovely, dry weather they'd had there in recent weeks has made everything like tinder. Even the grass burns. The scale of it all is beyond anything that can be coped with by resources on the island. The only answer is evacuation.

There is an emergency call out to ships in the area to come to the islanders' aid. Our eyes are fixed on the screen, hour after hour. The sun comes up, and still we're watching, willing our family to be shown getting on a boat, or in a helicopter. Fishing boats and others of all sizes—even a cruise ship—help in the evacuation, and our eyes search the faces.

We don't see them.

CHAPTER 2

CALLIE

THE JOY OF BEING FREE from that underground place doesn't distract me for long. The guards said that Dr. 1 has a place on the island—that when communications failed, someone had been sent up to check if he was there.

Did they make it out before the fire stopped them?

The elevator was at the top. Unless they were trapped inside it, they got out.

How can I find them?

I rush back to the burning barn, the one with the hidden elevator. It's almost completely destroyed now. I soar high into the air for a better look. All around me, things are burning; smoke makes it hard to see. Fire is spreading along grass and scrub from here too, but most of it comes from another place, across water—where the sky was glowing red when I first came out. It's not just a red glow anymore: flames are high against the sky. It's spreading and growing. Was this from the other explosion we heard?

Focus on Dr. 1.

There isn't a road that leads to the barn; there are only fields, footpaths. I swoop down low through the burning grass: there are no tire marks that I can find. If they sent somebody on foot, Dr. 1's place can't be too far away.

I sweep through the air in ever-widening circles from the barn. There are no trees and the ground is bleak, rising into craggy hills with weirdly colored stone, almost red in the half-light. Not easy to climb, so they probably went the other way. I drop to lower ground, and finally something white on the ground catches my eye.

There. A man lies awkwardly on a path. He's wearing a white jacket like some of them wore under their suits underground. I stop next to him. There's no fire in this area, at least not yet. I don't think the smoke here is thick enough to have made him collapse.

Sweat is pouring out of his skin. His lips are moving; he's mumbling. His body shudders—once, twice, and again—with convulsions.

He's got *it*. He won't live for long.

How am I going to find Dr. 1 without him?

Defeated, I sigh and sit on the ground next to him. He mumbles again and half opens his eyes, then he opens them wide all the way and stares—right at me.

Can you see me? I ask.

"What are you?" he whispers.

I'm a ghost.

"Am I dead?"

No. But you're not far off. Maybe that's why you can see me.

He sighs. "I thought so."

Where is Dr. 1?

"Don't know," he says, and his eyes flutter closed.

Wait; stay with me. Where is his place? I'll go see if he's there.

Even though I'm a ghost, he seems to find this reasonable. He mumbles about a white house with water all around—like the bastard knew fire would be an issue one day, he says. Not quite a separate island, he says when I ask; it's connected by sand, near the ruins. He coughs. His house is on the other side, looking out to sea. It's the only house; it has a big telescope, he adds.

And then he dies.

I follow the path his body lies on, in the direction away from the barn. There is another glow in the sky now: the sun is starting to come up. It's not as bright as the flames that shoot into the sky, but it still helps me see the way. The path branches a few times, and I have to go first one way, then come back and try another—searching for a house surrounded by water.

I spot what looks like a separate small island, but when I get closer I see it is connected to this one by a thin strip of land that is mostly sand. There are ruined buildings near the sand on the other side: is this the place?

I sweep up into the air and follow the coast around. And there, facing away from the flames on the seaward side, is a white house. It is about as far away from the fires as it could be, here on this not-quite-an-island.

It looks expensive: Dr. 1 must have money.

It also looks dark, empty, cold. I go in through the chimney and check every room of the house. There are two bedrooms upstairs; the beds are neatly made and empty. Downstairs is open plan with a big fancy kitchen—no dishes in the sink—and plush sofas, bookshelves, and a desk. A conservatory at the back of the house looks out to sea and has a big object under a dust cover. If that is a telescope, this must be Dr. 1's house.

Where could he be if he's not here, and he wasn't underground?

His desk is huge, with books and folders on shelves above; drawers underneath that tantalize. There may be answers to where he's gone, but I can't open the drawers or lift folders from the shelves. I'm *useless*.

I go back up through the chimney, resolved to check the whole island.

The sun is up properly now. I skim above ground fast, back over the spit of sand and past the now burned-out barn and hills of red stone. This part of the island is connected to others, including the part over the water that is still a wall of flame. It covers a huge area; as I watch, there is another explosion, and it shoots even higher. If he was that way, he's dead.

I follow the coast around. The island is big and sprawling, with fingers stretching out in different directions. There are pockets of fire all over the place, wherever there are houses—almost as if whatever was burning and exploding was connected to all the houses. Fire is spreading from these areas onto grass and scrub; fires are growing and reaching for each other.

So much has been destroyed. Everywhere I look seems to be either black and smoking, or still burning. The biggest town is by the sea, and flames shoot into the sky from buildings along the waterfront.

People are gathering in a few places away from villages and towns, in coves where small boats can reach them. I drop down to stand among them, and walk down rocks and sand to the water's edge. Waves lap at my feet, but they're not cold or wet. I stare out at the sea. The wild blue green of it is beautiful, but I can't smell the salt.

If I close my eyes, I feel *nothing*. Nothing tells me where I am.

I want to yell and scream and make all this not be real. I wrap my arms around myself, trying to hold it in—this panic that washes through me like the sea washes against the rocks. The sea I loved, that now I can't smell, feel, or taste.

I sit on a rock, and watch. Small boats are going back and forth from larger boats to the shore. People wait to get on them and leave this place; people who are dazed or crying, burned, injured. Some aren't moving and are carried, dead or dying.

There are helicopters whirring about, some with cameras. Some scoop water from the sea and empty it where fires burn. Others take injured people away.

And with all this suffering around me, I feel numb. I'm dead inside to match my dead outsides—a bag of ash in a burned-out lab underground.

How I am now is Dr. 1's fault.

Where is he?

I leave my rock behind, and everywhere people move, I search for Dr. 1. I've never seen his face, not really—just a shadow of it behind his mask. But I know he's very tall; I know the way he stands, the way he walks, like he is the one that must be noticed. I've never seen a king, but that is how I imagine a king would walk. And I know his voice. I look, and listen, but nowhere is anyone who could be him.

He might have died in the fires. If he didn't, he's not on the island, so I must leave it.

Another boat stops by a beach; more people are helped into it. Some are carried, some walk. I go with them.

We rock on the sea in our small boat, heading toward another one; it's huge. It looks like one of those fancy cruise ships rich people sail about on. We start to pull in alongside, but I don't wait. I float up, along a gangway thing, through a door.

I follow the sounds of people, along a hall and up some stairs to a big open area that goes up and up, through all different levels of the ship. It is like a makeshift hospital in Disneyland—people with burns scream in pain under chandeliers and glass stairs.

There seems to be just one doctor, and a few nurses. They look panicked, like they'd like to jump into the sea to escape.

A man walks toward one of the nurses. He's pale; sweat pours from his brow. He slumps and falls to the deck.

CHAPTER 3

SHAY

THE PHONE FINALLY RINGS.

Mum rushes to it so fast she almost trips, and I'm along at her heels.

"Hello? Hello?"

Her face breaks out in a smile, and she gives me a thumbs-up.

"Thank God. Yes. All okay?" A pause. "Come to us. We'll make room." Another pause. "Well, the offer is open. Okay, yes. Love you, Davy. Bye."

She hangs up the phone, stands there, head down, saying nothing.

"Well? Tell me!" I say.

But she can't answer. She's been dry-eyed all these hours, and now she's crying.

"Tell me!"

She draws in a shuddering breath and looks up. "They're all fine. Little Shona has broken a leg falling over in the rush to get away from the fire, and Davy thinks their house was completely destroyed. But they're all fine."

"And? Aren't they coming here?"

"No." She frowns through her tears. "He said he couldn't talk for long, that others were waiting to use the phone. He said something about needing to stay in Aberdeen for now. I can't imagine why. He's always hated it there."

"Well, apart from a broken leg, they're all right. That's the important thing, isn't it?"

"Yes. Of course." She's still crying, holding on to me.

We eat something and lie down. Together, in Mum's bed, her hand clinging tight to mine even as she sleeps.

CHAPTER 4

CALLIE

SO THIS IS ABERDEEN.

I wander around the dock area first. There is a procession of ambulances, sirens wailing as they hurtle toward us. Doctors and nurses sort out who must go first, but they don't look like the doctors and nurses from underground: they look like they really care about the people they're trying to help.

I've had enough of screaming and pain, of the ill and the dying. I want to get away. There is no one I've seen that I recognize from underground, but they were all suited up when I knew them, so they'd be hard to pick out. Dr. 1 could be anywhere; more than that, he could be *anyone*. If he wanted to blend into the crowd to get away from this place, he could disguise how he walks and go right past me, and I'd never know it. There's no point hanging around here.

And the city is mine to explore.

There are loads of big impressive buildings away from the screaming: sort of white or off-white, made of something like stone. The sun is low in a clear sky now, and where it glints off the buildings they are sprinkled in silver fairy dust.

I wander down streets of shops and restaurants. Is it possible to be hungry when you can't eat? I think I am. I watch people eating dinner in cafés and wish I could try things. They wouldn't see me; I could just grab things off their plates, have a bite, keep it if I liked it. But of course I can't even pick anything up.

There's a family in a pizza place. A picture-perfect mum, dad, and four children—from a baby to a boy about my age. I sit at the table with them and play pretend: that they are my parents, my brothers and sisters.

But it doesn't feel right or real, not for long. It's getting dark now, and I leave. *None* of this feels right, these well-dressed people out for dinner, smiling and talking to each other. Instead I wander away, down darker streets.

Below a bridge, a group of teenage boys passes a bottle around. A girl is with them; they pass her the bottle and laugh when she gags.

I feel more at ease here and stay a while to think.

What next? I can go anywhere, see anything. No one can catch me, no one can stop me. They can't even see me. The only person who could was that man on the island who was dying.

Unable to stop myself from trying again, I wave my hand in front of the girl's eyes; nothing registers. She lolls to one side, then wobbles as she tries to sit up straight again. One of the boys helps her and puts an arm around her shoulders. She's getting drunk. Are they getting her drunk on *purpose*?

The one with his arm on her shoulders starts kissing her, and now I'm *furious*. That is just so wrong.

Stop it! I scream at him, as loud as I can. And he stops, a puzzled look on his face. His friends laugh at him, and another one of them reaches for the girl, pulls her toward him.

Angry heat rushes through me, intense and wild. I throw myself at him, into him.

The other boys scream, get up, start to run, the girl staggering behind them.

There's a rush of heat, of flames.

The boy screams. Flames erupt from inside him and he burns *everywhere*, at once.

He stands, staggers for the water's edge, but fire consumes him before he reaches the water.

He falls.

CHAPTER 5

SHAY

THE SCHOOL BUS is approaching before Duncan appears, as if he'd hung back, around the corner, until he saw it coming.

He's on crutches? So I really *did* have him on the ropes. My boot must have done a good job on his foot.

He avoids my eye. His nose is taped and his face is a mess of bruises, and everyone crowds around him. He starts telling a crazy story about how he interrupted some burglars robbing his house and that he gave worse than he got. Everyone cheers.

Huh. As if he's testing me, to see if I'll contradict him, he glances over from across the bus after we get on. One eyebrow—the not-swollen one—raised. I sort of half nod.

The guy is a total lowlife; absolutely true. He's been bugging me ever since I got here, and getting worse.

But what Kai did to him still shocks me. If he hadn't half killed him, we could have called the police and maybe gotten that jerk chucked in a cell. As things are, I almost feel like he has something on me. I don't like it.

"Shay?" I turn. It's Amy—not a friend. She's smiling.

"Yes?"

"So, who was that lad you were with on Saturday? He was cute."

Many eyes turn my way now.

"None of your business."

She smiles sweetly. "Well, I heard you were making up some big story that you saw that girl who went missing last summer and that she was his little sister. That's going to extremes to get a boy, isn't it?"

I keep quiet, face like stone.

"And I also heard you've got some kind of *genius* memory." She titters along with her friends, and they just seem so childish with Calista being missing and what happened on Shetland. Don't they even care what happens outside of their own little corner of the world? At least they've decided not to believe what they heard about my memory. Somehow I'd rather they thought I was a liar than a freak.

The bus stops again, and Iona and others get on. She sits next to me, an eyebrow raised.

"Tell me: whatever has happened to Duncan?"

"Well. He *says* he interrupted some burglars at his house and chased them away."

"Oh, does he? What a load of shit." She looks at me closer. "There's got to be more to this story, and I have a feeling you know it."

I shake my head.

"I'll use my investigative skills to get it out of you later."

Iona pulls the newspapers out of her bag. Obsessed with being a journalist, she always reads them on the long bus ride to school in Callander. I pounce on one of the papers with more enthusiasm than usual, hoping there'll be something new on Shetland.

She sees where I'm looking. "It's beyond terrible," she says.

"My uncle lives there. We didn't know if they were okay for most of yesterday until he called from Aberdeen."

"Ah, poor you," she says, and squeezes my hand. "I thought you looked a little upset."

We pore over the photos of Shetland, covering most or all of the front page of every paper. I hunt through the words, but there is only speculation. No answers.

"What the hell happened?" I say.

Iona shrugs. "They say they don't know. The authorities must know something by now; what is it they don't want to admit?"

Sharing the corner of one front page: "Boy Dies of Spontaneous Combustion." I mean, really? How can they print such nonsense alongside the real tragedy that is Shetland?

Iona is tsk-tsking under her breath.

"What?"

She holds up a back page. "It's this group of weirdos. Seeking planning permission to build what they've already built: some sort of commune up Rannoch Wood way. It's part of a network springing up all over the US and Europe. Other places too."

I peer over her shoulder. "What are they? Religious weirdos, or just general-purpose ones?"

"They call themselves *Multiverse*. No one seems sure what they're about; they keep to themselves and don't cause problems. My sources tell me they worship truth."

I've stopped reacting when Iona refers to *her sources*. There are networks she taps into, mostly people with too much time on their hands who lurk on the internet. Much of what they say is garbage, but every now and then she hears something real before it hits the news.

"Well, I guess worshipping truth is okay."

"Yeah, but whose truth?"

"That's too much for my brain on a Monday morning, Iona."

She flips back to the front section of the paper in her hands and passes it to me. "This one has more on Shetland."

I take it from her. There are bodies waiting for identification or for relatives to be notified. Some areas haven't even been checked yet. There are heartrending lists of the missing: whole families, presumed burned in their sleep. I wonder if any are people I'd passed in the street when we were visiting my uncle, if any are their friends.

And there is a list of the confirmed dead, some with photos.

Near the end is one I really didn't expect to see.

"It's him!" The shock makes me say it out loud without meaning to.

Iona looks up. "It's who?"

I fold the paper around the square and stare at the small photo carefully. I have to be right about this; there is no making a mistake, not on something so important.

Iona studies his face alongside me. "Looks like a mean guy."

Receding hair. A small scar by one eye. A belligerent look. There's no swollen eye or shiner, but that was a year ago, after all, and who knows when this was taken.

It's him; I'm absolutely sure of it. The man who drove away with Calista.

I hunt through my bag but can't find my cell. "Call my phone?" I ask Iona.

She rolls her eyes. "What have you done with it this time?" She calls it, but there is no ring inside any of my pockets or my bag.

"It must be at home," I say. Iona holds her phone out to me with a resigned look.

"Thanks, you're the best."

She pulls it away when I reach for it. "There's a condition. You have to tell me what's going on."

I glance around us. It may look like they're all ignoring us as usual, but there are ears everywhere. "Not here—later."

"Fine." She gives me her phone. I remember Kai's mobile number—of course I do. I paid particular attention when he texted me that he'd gotten back to Newcastle on Saturday night.

It rings three times, four times, then . . . "Hi, this is Kai. Leave a message!"

Damn. I bite my lip. "Hi, it's Shay. I'm using a friend's phone. In today's *Herald*, page two, the third from bottom left, see Brian Daugherty? It's him. The man I saw with your sister. You can reach me on this number until four p.m., or I'll be home and have my phone after about five thirty. Bye."

Iona raises an eyebrow. "So, then. Is there something else you want to ask me?"

"Is it okay if I keep your phone today?"

"Is there any guarantee you won't lose it?" She shakes her head and sighs. "Yes, you can have it. But you're in deep shit if you lose it."

CHAPTER 6

CALLIE

I **WATCH THE SCENERY** go by through the train window. Once I'd really thought about it, it was obvious what I should do and where I should go. *Home.* Newcastle. I found the train station in Aberdeen and listened to people until I worked out what to do. I found the right platform from the signboards and got on a train to Edinburgh. There I changed to this one to Newcastle.

It took me a while to find an empty window seat. After what happened last night under the bridge, I don't want to sit too close to anybody in case they go up in flames. That was so *weird*. Maybe it had nothing to do with me. Maybe it was just that boy's moment to spontaneously combust—some sort of act of God. It's not like he didn't deserve it.

Beyond knowing I need to get to Newcastle, I'm confused; my memory seems weird and splintered. Some things are there, like when I could remember how much I loved the sea, how the water felt splashing on my feet—something I can't feel anymore. But others aren't. No matter how hard I concentrate, I can't think where we lived. I can't picture the house, or my room, or anything in it.

I can see my brother, Kai, in my mind, and my mother too, but they're sort of flat. Like something is missing, but I don't know what.

And that's about it.

Whatever they did to me in that place in Shetland has messed me up. Duh—very true, since I'm dead. But beyond that, as well; my memory is like cheese with holes in it. Or worse, cheese with holes in it that has been grated, then mixed up out of order.

Can I put it back together?

And where am I going to go when the train arrives in Newcastle?

I try to relax, to let my mind float, to see if anything will come to me. If I can't remember where we lived, is there some other place I could find my family?

Kai played soccer, but I don't remember where.

How about Mum? She's a doctor. Yes, that's it—a doctor! And she works at the university.

What university? Well, how many can there be in Newcastle?

I guess I'm going to find out.

The more I want to remember, the more it seems to slip away like the countryside out my window, and I get sadder and sadder. I want to cry but I have no tears, and somehow that makes it worse. There's no way to let it out.

Rain starts to fall, and there is a whisper in my mind, a forgotten voice—*tears from heaven*. Rain is tears from heaven. Who used to say that?

Maybe heaven is crying for me because I can't, not anymore.

CHAPTER 7

SHAY

IONA'S PHONE VIBRATES in the middle of math. I peer down under the desk. It's Kai.

I raise my hand, show the phone I shouldn't have on in class. "I'm sorry, Miss. It's my relatives from Shetland. I have to take it."

She nods, sympathy in her eyes. Guilt twists at my lie as I race for the hallway, but this is important—and not something I want to explain in front of the class.

"Hello, hello?" I say, afraid he'll have hung up by now.

"Shay. It's Kai." His voice is warm and eager, and a thrill rushes through me to hear him say my name. "I've got the paper. You're sure that it's him, this Brian Daugherty?"

"Yes, completely sure. It's him."

"All right. I'm calling Detective Dougal. Are you able to meet if he wants to see you?"

"Of course."

"What number should I reach you on?"

"Uh, this one, for now," I say, with a mental *sorry* to Iona. "I'm not sure where my phone is. I'll text you when I find it."

"What if you really need it one day? Promise me you'll find it, and keep it with you."

Even though the words sound like Mum, the concern in his voice warms me.

"I will. I promise."

CHAPTER 8

CALLIE

BY THE TIME THE TRAIN PULLS INTO NEWCASTLE, I've formulated a plan. Of sorts.

I've gone up and down the train, looking for passengers the right age to maybe be university students. I listened to one group, then another, until I found one talking about some party in Edinburgh they're coming back from and trying to come up with a good excuse for missing a seminar this morning.

They set off on foot from the station, and I follow, looking all around us—hungry to recognize this city as mine. They stop across the road for coffee, and while I wait I spin up and down the road, but nothing is familiar.

The day has turned gray; gray sky, gray streets. It starts to drizzle, and when they emerge with their coffees, they hurry on.

We walk up a long street, shops on both sides, and down more streets, and it starts to rain harder.

Then finally we round a corner, and I see the sign: The University of Northumbria.

Where would Mum be? She's a doctor—Dr. Tanzer. So is there a medical school? But then I'm gripped by confusion, as one of the students says something about Dr. So-in-So in the English department. Is Mum a doctor-doctor, or a doctor in something else? How can I not know this? My guts—or where they'd be if I had any—swirl in rage and panic.

I stop following the students and drift into one building, then another, hoping something will feel familiar, will guide me to where I want to go. But nothing. Maybe I never came here.

Nothing seems medical, and I float around, building to building, in increasing circles. That's when I see another sign across the road: Newcastle University.

No way. Are there *two* universities, across the road from each other?

Soon I see that this one is even bigger. I wander around different buildings, looking for anything that might help. Finally I see some students dressed in what look like doctors' white coats, and follow them to a hospital. I explore its corridors, but nothing feels familiar, and nowhere do I see Mum or her name.

I leave the hospital and go to buildings nearby, one after another, but nothing.

What am I going to do if I can't find her?

One more building. Then one more again. This one has a cafeteria downstairs, next to an office for Bacterial Cell Biology—that doesn't sound right. I'm about to leave when I see another office on the other side: the Institute of Health and Society.

I pause. I don't even know what that is, but there is something about the words that clicks.

I check the rest of the building. There are offices upstairs, names on doors. I go past one, then another, and another.

When I finally see the words, I almost can't take them in: Dr. S. Tanzer.

Is this her office? Is she here?

The door is shut, but there is a small gap underneath it. I'm afraid. What if she's not here?

I make myself thin and flow under the door.

Mummy? I whisper. She's sitting at a desk. Dark hair swept back in a ponytail. Small lines around her eyes, but she's beautiful. So beautiful. I drink her in, hungry for every detail I can fill in now to replace what I've forgotten.

There is a photo on the side of her desk. Me and her, and my brother. Kai, he likes to be called; his middle name is Kai. The details are coming faster now.

Mum sighs. She's typing on a laptop. She sips at something in a cup, then makes a face and puts it down again and types some more. I look at what she is writing for a while, but it's boring medical stuff.

Instead, I just stare at her face.

My mummy.

CHAPTER 9

SHAY

IONA COMES BACK on the bus to Killin with me after school. She grumbles about being doubled on my bike up the endless hill out of town until I offer to swap and let her do the pedaling. She screeches and clings to me when I let the wheels spin down the lane from the main road to our house, then brake at the last minute.

"You must have a death wish," she says.

I lean the bike against the house, some part of me still weirded out by not having to chain-lock it ten times to stop it from disappearing, like I always had to in London. Of course this house is truly in the middle of nowhere.

Mum's car isn't here: we've got the place to ourselves. Good.

I open the door and rub the Buddha's tummy in the hall on the way past, Iona impatient behind me.

"So we're alone now, tell me! What's going on?"

"Yes, yes, I said I would and I will. But I need to find my phone first so I can give you your phone back."

"Where did you last have it?"

"Um . . ."

"When did you last use it?"

I shrug.

She calls it as we wander around the house: no ring. The battery must be dead.

We spend ages hunting for it: on counters and tables, under books and sofa cushions, behind furniture. My desk, under my bed, in coat pockets. Until finally Iona finds it in the pocket of yesterday's jeans in the laundry bin.

"Right. I'm taking care of this," Iona says, brandishing my phone. "Going through your dirty socks is too much punishment."

"What do you mean?"

"Lost phone app. I'm linking your phone to mine so I can use my phone to find yours. If—I mean, when—you lose it again, it'll show where it is on a map on my phone. Give me your charger and password."

"Okay, fine." I find the charger and tell her the password, and she plugs it in, then downloads and sets up the app.

Then I text Kai. Hi, found my phone!

Moments later, my phone beeps: he's answered. Keep it close, Shay. You never know when you might need it. Tomorrow is arranged. What time and where do you finish school? I'll meet you there. K xx

Two kisses. Maybe he always ends texts like that. Maybe he doesn't. He didn't when he texted me from Newcastle the other night.

"You're grinning at your phone like a goofy," Iona says.

"Hmmm?"

She grabs it away. "Ah, I see: *K xx*. And he'll be meeting you after school, will he? Who is K? And are they proper kisses for you then, or just the casual signing-off sort of kisses? I see that you are hoping for the real thing. Tell me *everything*."

"Just let me answer him back." I text McLaren High, Callander, think on the time, factoring in long enough to change out of my school uniform, and name a street corner near the school. I hesitate, then end it with S xx. Hit "send."

Iona peers over my shoulder and howls with laughter.

113

"What?"

"That's a wee bit forward, Shay."

"What are you talking about?"

"Autocorrect. It autocorrected." She's laughing so hard she can hardly talk, and my stomach sinks.

I look at the phone. My text ends with see you then Sexy.

"Oh. My. God." I look at her, horrified.

"I'm sorry for laughing. It's just . . . it's so . . ." And she's shaking with suppressed mirth.

"Should I text back and say it autocorrected?"

She shrugs. "That'll draw attention; maybe it didn't register."

"I can't leave it, I can't." I think for a moment, then text back: *ahem* that should have been "S xx"

It vibrates seconds later: damn.

Iona looks over my shoulder. "He's flirting with you."

"Nah. He's making fun."

"He so *is* flirting," Iona says. "All right. Whole story now, please."

"You have to promise not to put this in the school paper, or your blog, or anywhere." Iona blogs anonymously as Jitterbug: Journalist-in-training (JIT)—she's forever looking for scoops to go on it.

She sighs and crosses her heart with her finger. "I *promise*. Now go."

So I tell her: starting with kneeing Duncan in the Co-op—Iona finds this immensely satisfying and makes me describe over and over the way he hit the floor—to finding the flyer, calling Kai, and the rest. But I end the story where Kai hugged me goodbye at the café. I leave out Duncan grabbing me, Kai beating him up, then coming home with me after and holding my hand. Some things I want—*need*—to keep to myself.

"So, this face in the paper is the man you saw with Kai's sister?"

"Yes."

"And your hot date involves going to talk to the police? Not exactly the right ambience to hook up."

I roll my eyes. "Exactly."

"Have you got the photo from the paper still?"

I pull out the bit of paper from my pocket and hold it out to Iona. She studies it.

"Shame he's dead: dead men don't answer many questions."

That night, after Iona's brother collects her and Mum gets home, the two of us settle in front of the news channel with our dinner. A new habit since the Shetland disaster.

There is the continuing speculation about what caused the explosions. There was seismic activity recorded in the area just before the oil reservoir exploded. But reports from some witnesses suggest the explosions started somewhere else, not at the depot, and experts argue about whether an earthquake of that nature could cause the destruction it did. There are tragic tales of those lost too, and the miraculous escapes and heroic rescues that reporters hunt for.

Then news from Aberdeen:

"Just in. Cases of a particularly virulent new strain of flu are being reported around Aberdeen. Schools in the area will be closed from tomorrow as a precaution. People are advised to avoid nonessential travel to the area."

Mum shakes her head. "I wonder if that's why I haven't heard again from Davy? Perhaps they all have the flu." Her face is worried.

"Well, even if they do. How many times have I had the flu?" I'm the one every germ in the area seems to navigate toward. Swine flu was the *worst*. "I'm sure they'll be fine."

Mum's still uneasy. "I'm dosing up your immune system with a special mixture right now."

"No . . . not a special mixture!" Mum's not into conventional medicine, and her "special mixtures" taste *horrendous*. "I'd rather have the flu."

"You *will* drink it, and so will I."

She returns from the kitchen minutes later, two small glasses of murky green sludge in her hand.

I know a losing fight when I see one, and clink my glass against hers. "Bottoms up!" I say, and swallow it fast so I taste it less; then mime choking and fall on the floor, twitching.

115

"You crazy girl." She holds out a hand. I put mine in hers and she helps me up to sit next to her on the sofa. The news is running still—now back to Shetland. Fires are still burning, on land and at sea, on oil rigs. There is talk of an environmental disaster, and other islands in the area are being evacuated as a precaution.

Mum sighs. "First Shetland, now some new flu in Aberdeen. Bad luck comes in threes. What will be next for poor Scotland?"

CHAPTER 10

CALLIE

IT'S OUR HOUSE: *MY HOME.* But nothing on the outside of it is familiar, nothing at all.

Mum had biked home from work. She turned by a sign that said Jesmond, then went down leafy streets and stopped in front of this house in the middle of a row of terraced houses. She locked her bicycle to a rack in the front yard.

Mum opens the front door and takes off her helmet.

"Hello?" she calls out.

I don't wait to see if anyone answers—I speed into the house, as anxious to see my adored older brother as I was my mum.

But when I go into the front room, only one person is there, and I don't know him. Could I have gotten what Kai looks like so wrong? But no—the photo on Mum's desk jived with what I remember. This isn't my brother.

Mum walks into the room now. "Hello, Martin," she says. "Good day?"

He looks up from a computer and makes a face. "It's slow going."

"Ah, hang in there; it'll come together. Where is Kai? Have you seen him?" she says, a quirk of concern between her eyes.

"He tore off on his bike this morning. Not back yet."

She sits and they talk about some science thing Martin is writing. He seems to be a student staying here—some sort who is already a doctor himself—and what they are talking about is soon boring.

Instead I explore.

The house has four bedrooms. The one that must be Mum's is on the top floor. Next to it is a smaller one. It's done in red and white. There are kids' books on shelves, girls' clothes in the wardrobe. My room? It must be.

The floor below has two more bedrooms. One is full of books and must belong to the student downstairs. The other must be Kai's. There are posters of motorcycles on the walls; models of bikes hang from the ceiling. Soccer gear thrown in a corner. It's a mess, like he doesn't care.

Downstairs now, Mum is in the kitchen, clattering about. I go back into the front room, where the student has given up on his laptop; the TV is on. I sit next to him. He's watching some quiz show with questions no sane person would know the answers to, and yet he is shouting them out.

There are photos on the walls—Mum, Kai, me. I drift over to them, study them, and drink them in.

Kai with a dirty face and soccer trophy—he must be about ten. Mum young and in funny black robes and hat. There are old people next to her, beaming: my grandparents? Baby photos of me. Me and Kai together at all ages.

I try to fill the corners inside me, tucking each of these old memories away like a new one: *This* is who I am.

No, that's not quite right. I sigh, gripped by sadness. Martin is eating his dinner in front of the TV, and there are empty places at the table where Mum sits, eating alone. Kai may come home and take one of them, but one chair will always be empty to them. Even if I sit down in it, next to them, they'll never know I'm there.

This is who I was.

CHAPTER 11

SHAY

IONA INSISTS ON COMING WITH ME to check out Kai. She's still in uniform, waiting while I do a quick change into jeans, a T-shirt. Despite Iona's teasing, I know this is serious. This is about Calista, Kai's sister. Nothing else could be more important to him right now, and that's the way it should be. But I still brush my hair and fuss with it in the mirror in the school bathroom. As usual the curls have a mind of their own, and today they've decided to twist and tangle into a mess.

"You'll be late," Iona says, and pulls me away from the mirror. "Come on!"

Iona marches me out of the school grounds and gate, down the road to the corner where I told Kai we'd meet. There were showers earlier, but the sun is out now, glinting on the wet trees and grass. He rounds the corner just as we reach it. The sun is behind him when he pulls in and takes off his helmet. He shakes it and water droplets fly.

"Hi," he says.

"Hi," I answer. His eyes move to Iona, next to me. "This is my friend, Iona; it was her phone I was using yesterday."

"And you must be Sexy," she says, and he laughs. When laughter finds him, it softens his eyes; the intensity in them eases.

Iona is smiling back at him, tilting her head to one side. I push her shoulder.

"Right. I'm off," she says.

He shakes his head, watching her go. Her skirt is too short; I've never noticed this before. I bet *he's* noticing, and I swivel to stare at his eyes, to watch them, but now he's wiping rainwater off the back of his bike seat with his arm. He gets the red helmet out for me, hands it over. I just stand there and look at him.

"Is something wrong?" he says.

"Nothing. Just nothing." I put the helmet on, and off we go to the police office in Callander.

I've never been in one before, and it's not much like the movies. We say who we are, and moments later Dougal comes out. He shakes Kai's hand, says hello to me, ushers us around to a desk.

He has a copy of the newspaper in front of him with Brian Daugherty's photo circled.

"So, Shay. You're sure this is the man you saw with Calista Tanzer on the twenty-ninth of June last year?"

"Yes. It's him. It's the little scar here, by his eye." I point. "The way his hair is. It's definitely him."

"I've done some checking. Mr. Daugherty's body was found by search and rescue teams on a footpath. They're not sure yet why he died; it wasn't from the fires. Also, we're not sure why he was on Shetland in the first place. He doesn't work there, own or rent property, or report income. If he was on vacation, he wasn't registered as staying anywhere—as much as we can check, with the mess on Shetland at the moment. He didn't fly in or take the ferry."

"Well, if he wasn't from Shetland, can't you find out where he did live and check there, see if anyone knows anything about him?" Kai says.

"No. He's an enigma. In fact, there've been no records of him being *anywhere* for over five years. He hasn't paid taxes or had a speeding fine or claimed benefits: nothing."

"Then how did they work out who he was, if he wasn't supposed to be there and no one knows anything about him?" I ask.

Dougal hesitates. "Fingerprints," he finally says.

"Doesn't that mean he's got a record or something, or why would you have his fingerprints?" Kai asks.

"I'm not at liberty to answer that just now," Dougal answers.

Kai frowns. "Is that it? He might be the man who took my sister, but you can't find out anything about his recent movements and won't tell us everything you can about his past?"

"Kai, calm down. We'll continue to look into him, I promise you. I'll call if anything turns up. But at the end of the day, dead men don't answer many questions." Iona's words, almost exactly the same.

Kai argues with Dougal a while longer until finally we leave.

He radiates tension as we walk to his bike. "This can't be a dead end. There has to be *something* they can find out about that man that will lead to Calista." He shakes his head, looks at me. "I need to ride. Fast. I can take you home first, if you want. Or do you want to come along?" There is challenge in his eyes, and my pulse quickens.

"I'll come. Just don't kill us." I'm half kidding, half not. His eyes are wild. Maybe he'll drive safer with me along? Maybe he won't.

"I know just the place to go," he says.

We get on the bike. He drives close enough to the speed limit to not get in trouble. We head out of Callander, farther into the Trossachs National Park. All the way, I think the bike is straining to run, to be set free. Finally he takes a turn that I know: Three Lochs Drive. A scenic drive past lochs, down twisty single-lane roads that are all one-way: no one will be coming from the other direction.

He pulls in, stops at the turn, and twists around to look at me. "Are you sure you're up for this?"

My adrenaline is already pumping from the drive to this place. "Hell, yeah!"

He grins. "Hold on here," he says, and pulls my hands farther around him, lower, near his hips. "Lean with me, the way I do; don't fight the bike. Pinch me if you want me to slow down or stop for any reason."

I glance up as we start off. The sun is still out—just. Clouds are pulling in and the wind is picking up as we take off.

He gears up; fast, then faster again. There is an edge of control still, and I can almost feel him longing to lose it and let go completely. It's like flying!

The darkening sky, the increasing wind almost don't register. When the rain starts, I'm startled.

Kai slows.

The rain intensifies, and he pulls in under some trees.

"Let's wait a moment," he says. "See if it passes."

He obviously doesn't live in Scotland: this could go on all day.

We get off the bike, and he takes off his helmet. I take mine off also, shake out my hair. The wind whips it around my face. The rain is thundering down in sheets but hasn't made it under the canopy of this heavy tree. Yet.

The wild weather seems to suit Kai's mood. He turns to me, jaw set. "I've made a decision."

"What's that?"

"I'm going to go see my ex-stepfather with this Brian's photo. I still think he's involved. I want to see if his reaction gives anything away. It's obvious that *Dougie* isn't going to do much, so it's up to me."

I gaze steadily back at him, then nod. "Okay, then. I'm coming with you."

His eyebrows go up; he's surprised. "No, you've done enough, and thank you for all you have done. You don't need to come."

"Yes. I do. I'm the one who saw Brian Daugherty, aren't I?" That's what I say, but what I'm thinking is this: I know the anger inside Kai, and what he thinks of his ex-stepfather. He can't go alone. He might do *anything*.

"Really, you don't need—"

"I'm stubborn; I don't take no for an answer. I'm afraid you're stuck with me." I stare back at him, a hand on each hip.

He half frowns, then half smiles. "I can see that. If you insist, you can come. But I don't want to leave it for the weekend. Anyhow, he's easier to find at work on weekdays."

I shrug. "I'll cut school. Exams are over, so no drama. Mum doesn't mind if I have a good reason." There is a voice inside that says going to speak to someone that Kai thinks is a potential abductor of children wouldn't fit into Mum's "good reason" category. "Where is he?"

"Edinburgh. He works at the university. Can you make it there tomorrow?"

"Yes. Tomorrow; no problem. I'll get the bus from school to Stirling and then get the train to Edinburgh, and meet you at the station there. Deal?" I hold out my hand.

He hesitates, then takes mine in his. Shakes it. "Okay, deal," he says, and keeps hold of my hand longer than needed for a handshake. His fingers curl around mine, light warm pressure, then finally let go.

The rain starts to drip through the leaf canopy over us, but Kai doesn't seem to care. He steps out into the rain, looks up, and lets it pour down on his face while he laughs.

The sun struggles through; the rain breaks with tradition and stops moments later. And likewise with Kai: now that he has decided to *do* something, his tension is gone.

We continue, more circumspect than before, on roads now running with water.

CHAPTER 12

CALLIE

THE FRONT DOOR SLAMS.

"Hello?" is called out. It's my brother, it's Kai!

He walks into the front room, and I drink him in. Tall; he's so tall. Has he grown since I've seen him? The blond streaks in his hair catch the light as he turns, takes off his bike jacket, and puts it on a chair.

"Hey," he says to Martin, who is still on the sofa, answering all the quiz questions between mouthfuls of dinner.

"Where've you been, Kai?" Mum says, and Kai walks toward her, to the table.

"Nowhere." He smiles.

"I don't like that look. Tell me you're not getting into any trouble."

"If you must know, I went for a long ride. With a girl. Are you happy?"

She's surprised: very. So am I. Has Kai got a girlfriend?

"Can I meet this girl?" Mum asks.

He shrugs. "Maybe one day. I'll be out with her tomorrow too." He peers at Mum's plate with a hungry look. "That looks good."

She raises an eyebrow at the change of subject but lets it go. "I kept some warm."

He goes into the kitchen, and I follow while he scoops dinner onto a plate, takes it into the front room, sits on a chair near the TV. I lean against the chair by his feet. If he's got a date tomorrow, then so do I.

The news is on now and something Mum hears makes her get up from the table and go around to stand next to Kai's chair, listening.

"... and doctors are warning at-risk groups to have their flu shots, but will the standard vaccine protect against this new strain of flu? We have this report from Aberdeen."

The screen changes to another reporter, standing in front of a hospital.

"Schools are closed again today in Aberdeen, as medical officials continue to be concerned about the new flu that has swept through the city."

Kai looks up from his dinner. "I can't remember them ever closing schools for the flu before."

Mum shushes him, but the report is already over.

"That report was very short. And thin on detail," she says.

Martin puts down his fork. "I've heard that it is much worse than they're letting on."

"You've heard—how?"

"I have a friend who's a post-doc at the University of Aberdeen. They've called in the army to quarantine whole neighborhoods, but it's being kept out of the news. They're afraid of panic, of people leaving and spreading it further."

Mum's face is grave. She gets up, goes to the phone in the hall, and quickly dials a number.

"This is Dr. Sonja Tanzer. I need to speak to Dr. Lawson."

She waits a moment. "Hello, Craig? Yes, it's Sonja. Tell me: what's really happening in Aberdeen?"

She's quiet for a while. Interjects with questions a few times. Finally says goodbye and hangs up.

Her eyes are open wide, her head shaking side to side.

"Mum?" Kai says. "What is it?"

"That is just the right question: what is it? They don't know. My friend Craig is with Public Health England; he liaises with Health Protection Scotland. He wouldn't tell me much, but from what he did, I'm very worried. Many have died, and far faster than with any *flu*." She shakes her head. "The flu story is covering something, but what?"

Kai and Martin are looking at her.

"He told me to stay available, that I might be needed. They're setting up a consultation group, something like that. To decide what category to escalate the situation, and cooperate between England and Scotland." She shrugs, impatient. "Politics! What they need is science, and they need it now. They have to work out what they are dealing with and how to contain it, before it spreads. Simple as that." She snaps her fingers.

If only I could speak in a way she could hear, I'd tell her.

It got out, didn't it? It must have. It got out from underground in Shetland, and it must have spread to Aberdeen with all the injured and dying they rescued from the island and took there.

Many people will die, and there is nothing they can do.

CHAPTER 13

SHAY

IF I COULD EVER PICK one thing from all the many things there are to study, how I'd love to come to Edinburgh for university. But how can I decide? I want to really understand the quantum paradox that is Schrödinger's cat—how can it be both alive and dead at the same time until you open the box? I want to know how everything in my body works, from blood to heart to brain cells; the way genes interact with environment to make everyone the separate unique person that they are. I want to know *everything*. How can I narrow that down to study one thing?

At school I'm always getting in trouble for lack of focus—they say if I'm always distracted by something else, I'll never be really good at anything. And what's the point of university if you don't know what to take?

But if I ever do decide, Edinburgh has something about it that I like, particularly as it zooms past from the back of Kai's motorcycle. And, as Mum keeps pointing out, if we live here long enough to convince them I'm Scottish, university will be free. Though I'm sunk if they check my accent.

Kai seems to know where he's going.

He pulls in to a campus of the university that is high above the city, and parks his bike. We walk to an old building. It almost looks like a block of council flats.

He pauses away from the door and turns to me. "Having you along might be useful after all."

"Might be? Gee, thanks."

"I've been told to never come here again, and there's someone by the door who might recognize me and call security. But if I hang back and you distract them with a question or something, perhaps no one will notice I'm there."

"Why were you banned?"

"I might have gotten angry the last time I was here."

"Ah, I see."

"They might have called the police too."

"Were you charged?"

He looks sheepish. "No. Not *that* time."

"I see." I shake my head. "And not today either, right? Losing it isn't going to help."

"Of course. Today we're going for the calm and rational approach."

"What approach were you going to use to get in if I hadn't come with you?"

"Well, I was thinking of climbing in through a back window."

I roll my eyes.

We wait until some students head for the main doors, and go in behind them. I distract the receptionist, saying I'm visiting a grad student whose name Kai had told me, and ask for directions while Kai slips down the hallway.

As easy as that.

I follow behind Kai, up the stairs at the end of the hall. "He's on the fourth floor," Kai says.

We climb the three flights of stairs and then go down a hall.

"His office." Kai gestures; a plaque with Dr. A. Cross, Professor of Theoretical Physics hangs on the door.

He knocks on the door; no answer. He turns the knob; it's locked.

Kai lurks around the corner while I wait. The hallway is bright; there is artwork on the walls, all blotches of crazy color that somehow says *I am very expensive*. Is this usual in a university science building?

It's class change time now. There are voices, footsteps. Another professor-looking type passes, goes into an office. Students in lab coats go past.

Finally Dr. Cross comes around the corner. I recognize him from Kai's photo, but somehow it's more than that—have I met him before? He's tall, with silver hair. Piercing blue eyes. He puts the key into his office door, and I step forward.

"Hello, Dr. Cross?"

He turns and smiles as he opens the door. "Yes?"

"I was hoping I could speak to you for a moment. Well, we were."

"We?"

Kai steps out from around the corner.

Dr. Cross's smile doesn't falter. "Hello, Kai."

"Hello, Alex," Kai says, with no trace of one of his own.

"It's good to see you, if a little surprising. Are you and your mother well? And who is this?" Dr. Cross gestures toward me. His accent is American, though the edges are softened as if he hasn't been there for a long time. He turns to smile at me again, and I'm struck by *something* he has. Some charm—but that isn't the right word. He's, like, ancient, but so appealing at the same time, and something about him makes me smile back. I can't stop myself.

"Come in, both of you. I'm sure you will retain civility, Kai, in the presence of a young lady." His voice is gently chiding. "I'll make us some tea, and we can catch up."

He steps into his office and we both follow. He fills a kettle and I look around us.

His office is huge, well furnished. He must be *somebody* to have an office like this.

There's a photo on his desk. Him with his arms around Calista, taken perhaps three or four years ago. He walks across and sees where my eyes are looking.

"My beautiful daughter. Kai's sister, Callie."

"*Your* daughter?"

"Did you assume that as I was Kai's stepfather I was also Callie's? No. She was my daughter," he says. Of course: his blue eyes are so like hers.

She *was* my daughter: he used the past tense, and Kai is bristling. "She *is* your daughter, though I try to forget that," Kai says.

Dr. Cross's face saddens. "You must accept that which you cannot change, as I have begun to do. As hard as it is. After all this time, we're not likely to find her."

"How could you know that, unless you know what has happened to her?" Kai's voice is discordant, harsh, next to the melody of his stepfather's—gentle and reasonable.

"Kai, as I have told you over and over again, I don't know where Callie is. I wish I did." His voice is so sad, wistful. "But this can't be why you've come today, to go over the same ground again. And who is your lovely friend?"

His eyes are back on mine. "I'm Shay," I say. "Well, Sharona, really." *Why* did I tell him that? I never volunteer my name.

"Ah, a beautiful name—from a classic song!"

His eyes, on mine, still say *why are you here?* I glance at Kai. He nods slightly. "I saw Calista after she went missing."

He turns toward me now, all eager attention. "You did? Where?"

And I tell the whole story, including the man I saw, the car he came in that Calista got into.

"Have you been to the police?"

"Yes. They didn't seem that hopeful."

"It has been almost a year. How hard must it be to trace this man and car from so long ago?"

"But now I know who he is."

"You do? How?" His eyes are on mine: warm, intense. "Tell me."

I take the page from the paper out of my pocket. Brian Daugherty is circled. I hold the paper out to him, and he takes it.

He studies the photograph. "This is him? Why is he in the paper?" He unfolds the page and sees the headline. "Ah, I see. He has died in the Shetland disaster."

"Yes. And it's hard to question a dead man," I say, parroting Iona, the police. I'm watching him, as is Kai.

"Surely they will pursue this? I'll hire a private detective again, get them back on the case." He makes a note on his tablet as he says it.

"Friend of yours, is he?" Kai says, unable to stay silent any longer.

"The detective? More an acquaintance, though highly recommended." A wry, slightly raised eyebrow.

Kai takes the paper and points at Brian's ugly face. "You know what I mean."

"Ah, unfortunately, perhaps I do. But I assure you, this man was no friend of mine." He speaks truth; I feel it in every fiber inside me. Kai is wrong about him; he must be.

I glance at Kai. His fists are clenched by his sides, his eyes cold and fixed on his stepfather.

"I think we should leave," I say.

Dr. Cross inclines his head. "That's probably a good idea."

I give Kai a little push, and he starts to walk to the door, me behind him. By the door is a model on a table I didn't notice on the way in. Despite the need to get Kai out of here, there is something about it, and I pause.

Dr. Cross sees where I'm looking. "A curious mind is a wonderful thing. Do you know what this is?"

And somehow I do, though it is miles in complexity beyond what we've studied in school physics. "It's a model of an atom. Isn't it? But there are more particles than what we've been taught. More than Higgs Boson, even."

"How do you know about this?"

"My science class went on a trip to CERN last year—to see the particle accelerator." That's not the whole answer, though, is it? I'd been fascinated by this massive accelerator they'd built under the earth in Switzerland—amazed that the snorefest that was physics at school could lead to this: giant experiments to discover the very smallest things in existence. After that came a phase when I was convinced I wanted to be a physicist, and learned all I could about particles and quantum physics—before I got distracted by the curly hair gene.

131

He raises an eyebrow like he knows there is more I'm not saying. "More than a curious mind; an observant, questioning mind. This model represents what we are theorizing now. You won't find it in a classroom, even an undergraduate university classroom."

Kai had been waiting for me by the door, but now he stomps off down the hall, heading for the stairs. I know I should follow him, but I stay, staring at the model, trying to remember: there is something about it, something it reminds me of . . . and then I have it.

"You're wrong. I *have* seen it before. Or something very like it."

"Oh?"

"Calista's necklace. She had a gold necklace with a pendant like this. Didn't she?"

There is real surprise in his widened eyes. "I gave it to her as a gift the last time I saw her. You saw it?"

"She was wearing it." I picture it inside: look at the model, and compare what my eyes can see with my memory. "But it wasn't exactly the same as this. It was more complex."

He comes closer, looking at me searchingly. "You have a remarkable eye. A remarkable memory."

And there is something about *his* eyes. Something . . . not quite right. They're a brilliant blue, like Calista's, unusual in itself, but that isn't it. It isn't how he looks at me, either; it's something about his actual eyes. He blinks and turns away.

I'm intrigued and uneasy at the same time, but unease wins. I walk out the door.

What did I see? It was as if his eyes for that moment changed. Something dark swirled in the blue iris of each of them. I shake my head: that just isn't possible. I *must* be imagining things.

I hurry down the stairs to the ground floor, but there's no sign of Kai.

He wouldn't have left without me, would he?

I go out the front door of the building: he's not there.

I rush to where he parked his bike. It's gone.

No way. He wouldn't, would he?

He has.

132

CHAPTER 14

CALLIE

SOMETHING MADE ME WAIT OUTSIDE, not go in and see this step-father. Kai hates him, I can hear it in his voice, and that's good enough for me to want to keep away from him.

Besides, the whole day has me confused, and I want some time to think. First, Kai said to Mum that he was going out with this girl, but then he rides all the way to Edinburgh and picks her up at a station? She's not very local, then.

And Shay isn't what I expect. I don't know *what* I expected, exactly, but she isn't it. She's got loads of dark curly hair, an intelligent glint to her gaze. I'm guessing she's a little younger than he is. Attractive enough with those big blue eyes, but slight, slender, not the type something tells me he'd usually go for. And she says what she thinks, seems to unbalance him.

And this isn't a date either, that is clear. From the things they said when they got here, they're on some kind of mission.

But when Kai bolts back out front without Shay, I'm surprised. He's angry. The muscles are set in his arms, his jaw. He throws on his helmet and starts the bike.

Where is Shay? I shrug. Maybe they had a fight. I don't like her wearing my helmet and hanging on to him the way she did from the station on his bike.

Good riddance.

But when we get to the main road, he slows, and finally stops. He turns the bike, and we go back.

Shay is standing where the bike had been parked. She watches us approach, her arms crossed in front of her.

"For a minute there, I thought you'd left without me," she says.

"I almost did."

"Why?"

"You were giving him that starstruck look, like his students do. Like Mum used to before she figured him out. Like Calista did." He says the last sentence so quietly I'm not sure if I heard or imagined it.

"You *idiot*. If you'd waited a moment, you'd have heard what I found out."

"What?"

"That model of the atom by the door was similar to the necklace that Calista was wearing."

"And?"

"He was surprised I recognized it. He said something I don't think he meant to say."

"Which was?"

"That he gave it to her the last time he saw her. And I'm sure he was telling the truth. Did you ever see it?"

"No. I don't think so, anyhow. Though she'd hardly make a point of showing me something he gave her."

"How about your mum? Surely if he gave Calista a gold necklace with a model of an atom, your mother would know about it."

"You're right. I'll ask her."

"You know, it is easier to find out stuff from somebody if you're nice to them. That's all I was doing."

"Okay. You're right, again."

"And? Is there anything else you want to say?"

He looks sheepish. "I'm sorry."

"Thank you. And why didn't you tell me he's Calista's dad?"

I turn in shock. Kai's stepfather . . . is my father? How can I not remember this? I look back at the building they came out of. Is it too late? Could I go back in and find him?

But I don't even know what he looks like. Shouldn't I know this? I stamp my foot. I want to *scream* at all the things I've forgotten, but no one would hear me if I did.

"I try to blot who her father is out of my mind," Kai says. "Does it make any difference?"

"I just didn't like looking surprised in front of him, that's all."

"I'm sorry. Again. But none of this changes the fact that I'm sure that, somehow, he was involved in Calista's disappearance; I just need to find a way to prove it. Then I can find her and bring her home."

What? My own father?

"I know," Shay says, and puts her hand on his arm, her posture softening. "I know that you think he is responsible. But until you have proof, maybe you should try to accept you might be wrong. Having an open mind might help you find what you're looking for."

Kai stares back at her, then finally nods. "I'll try," he says. "And I know he seems so reasonable and nice when you meet him. I used to think that too. But you don't know him like I do. He's got a way of manipulating people. . . . Well. It's hard to explain, but he used to play around with all of us, like we were pieces on a chessboard that had to stand where he wanted."

Shay listens, nods. "Just because he wasn't a good husband or stepfather doesn't mean he took your sister, though."

"Maybe not," Kai says, but I can tell he doesn't mean it. "Now, can I give you a lift home?"

She shakes her head. "I got a return train ticket, might as well use it."

"Are you sure? I don't mind."

"It's fine."

Kai takes her to the station. When she says goodbye, there is a struggle, a hesitation, on his face. One hand half raised that falls back. Does he want to reach out, to hold her? Even though he doesn't do so, jealousy wriggles inside me.

All the way to Newcastle, I ride on the back of his bike, just the two of us. The way it should be. I imagine things I cannot feel: the red helmet on my head, the breeze in my face, my hair streaming out behind me. The sway of corners and bumps of the road. The force of speed.

And I think about the man they went to see: my father. It seems weird now that before I found them in Newcastle, all I could think of was finding my mother and brother; *father* never came into it, and I didn't even wonder why.

Maybe I didn't like him either.

Kai thinks he had something to do with what happened to me; Shay seems to think Kai is wrong. I missed the chance to look my father in the eye and see what, if anything, I remember.

Another time, Daddy dearest, I promise myself. *Another time.*

CHAPTER 15

SHAY

FIRST ON THE TRAIN AND THEN THE BUS, I stare out the window without seeing what rushes past.

I'm feeling uneasy inside about what I said to Kai and about how I made him apologize. I was annoyed that he almost left me stranded there, fair enough. But there was something about his stepfather that had me in thrall. I can see why his students would idolize him.

Why women would too.

But what was it about his eyes that half freaked me out? It was almost like he knew I saw something in them—he blinked and looked away. When he looked back again, whatever it was—it was gone.

And why did my memory tickle inside when I saw his face, just like it did when Kai showed me his photograph? What was it about him? Dr. Alex Cross. Not a name I remember hearing before, yet something inside says I've seen him, or I've met him—but that doesn't feel quite right. Something else, then?

If I'm patient, the memory will come.

It always does.

It happens when I don't expect it. Mum is making dinner—I'm help-ing—and the radio is on. She's dancing to some old song while she peels vegetables.

Mum . . . dancing.

And it *clicks* into place, inside.

I close my eyes and go *back* . . .

I'm in Mum's bedroom when she isn't home, looking for—looking for presents? It's near my birthday. My tenth birthday. I shouldn't be snooping around like this, but I am.

In her top drawer, under knickers and socks, one questing finger feels the edge of something. I catch it with a fingernail, lift it up, and take it out.

It's a photograph.

I hold it in my hand. It's Mummy, but not like I've ever seen her before. She's much younger, and her hair is up. She's got lipstick on, and she's wearing some long, swishy dress. It's green. And she's dancing with a man.

I don't know him, I'm sure of that. But there is something about him that makes me look, and look again.

He's older than Mum, and in some sort of fancy suit like you see in the movies, with a bow tie. He's tall and has dark hair, a bit long. His eyes are blue. A deep, piercing blue.

I go back to look at the photo now and then, somehow knowing that when something is hidden away like that, it isn't for asking about.

And then, one day, it's gone.

Mum snaps her fingers.

"Earth to Shay. Are you going to elope with that lettuce, or make it into a salad? Because dinner is nearly ready."

I shake my head, coming back to here, to now. I put the lettuce I'd absentmindedly held up against me down on the cutting board and turn to Mum.

"I have to ask you about something."

"Go on."

"Years ago, you had a photo hidden away, of you all dressed up. Dancing with a man." I describe it: her dress, his suit. The way he held her close. "Who was he?"

She shrugs, turns to get plates out of the cupboard. "I don't really remember. Somebody I dated years ago, maybe. Why?"

"He just looks like somebody else, that's all."

She turns to me now. "Who? Who does he look like?"

I shrug, somehow not wanting to answer, and not knowing why—beyond not wanting to admit that I skipped school. "Somebody I saw, that's all."

"Where?"

"For someone you can't really remember, you seem very curious. Who was he?"

"Nobody, Shay. Nobody at all."

She's lying. I'm both convinced of it and shocked. Mum doesn't *lie* to me.

Who was Dr. Cross to her?

That night we're watching the late news. The Aberdeen flu, they're calling it now, and there are mixed reports about what is happening there. And rumors that it's spreading south. A doctor comes on and describes the early symptoms: a slightly raised temperature and a headache that begins like a tension headache, one that quickly becomes more severe, with a high temperature. Within hours, aches and pains intensify, leading to severe internal pain and organ failure. They don't fill in *and death*, but that's what organ failure means, isn't it?

Now there are scenes of tented hospitals set up in fields. Doctors and nurses in full protective gear, like giant plastic suits, head to toe.

This is happening *here*, in Scotland? Mum and I look at each other, and back to the screen, unable to take it in.

There are concerns about how it is spreading so quickly, what causes it.

Undisclosed numbers of casualties.

Schools are to be closed across all of Scotland from tomorrow; there is a ban on travel. Door-to-door temperature checks will begin.

Mum gets up, says she is going to call a friend in Aberdeen.

I take out my phone: no message from Kai. Should I send him one? I bite my lip for a while, unsure, but at the end of whatever internal debate I'm having on texting dos and don'ts, I'm just worried about him.

Hi Kai, schools are closed across Scotland tomorrow, hurrah! Hope all is OK S xx.

I check it carefully for any unintended autocorrects, then hit "send," whispering, "Please answer, Kai," as I do. If there is no answer, I won't know if that means he's annoyed I'm pestering him, or if he isn't okay. I shake my head. Why am I being like this? It's not like he's in Aberdeen, but I'm worried just the same.

Mum comes back a moment later, her face pale.

"They're taking people away. They're going to their houses in those funny suits and putting them in bubbles. And taking them away in big ambulances. No one ever comes back. Is that what's happened to Davy?"

A number flashes on the screen, and a voiceover says, "Anyone having these symptoms is to stay at home and call this number."

CHAPTER 16

CALLIE

KAI SLIPS INTO what must have been my room. He shuts the door behind him and stands there, hesitant, like he's in a church and should pray but doesn't quite know how.

His phone beeps in his pocket, and he jumps, takes it out. Smiles a proper smile, one that makes his eyes crinkle and light up. I look over his shoulder: there's a text from Shay.

He starts touching the screen to text back. Enjoy your holiday! I'm fine(ish), better now I've heard from you. Take care, K xx.

He hits "send," then takes a deep breath and starts going through a small wooden jewelry box on my dresser. Fascinated, I watch: will I recognize anything? His hands are tentative at first, then more certain, as he goes through each little drawer. I didn't have much, and what is there is mostly kid stuff. Though there is one pretty thing I like: a fine silver chain with a dolphin hanging from it. Kai touches it in a way that says it means something to him.

What is he looking for? Is it the necklace Shay said was like the model of an atom?

But Shay said I was wearing it when I disappeared.

How would Shay know what I was wearing?

It is *so* frustrating! Not being able to ask questions, to talk to people. All I can do is watch and listen.

Kai reaches for another small box on my dresser, and his hand knocks something to the floor; there is a small tinkly noise as it breaks. Kai makes more noise when he sees it on the floor. He starts picking up bits of glass and curses when he cuts his finger.

There are faint footsteps on the stairs.

Mum opens the door, and Kai spins around.

"Hi. I thought I heard you up here." She looks at the pieces of glass in his hand. Her face saddens. "Ah, Teddy Bear. Have you jumped off the dresser?"

"I'm sorry. It was my fault; I knocked it."

"It's all right."

"No, it isn't. It was her favorite." His face is anguished.

"Let me see that hand."

She draws him into the bathroom, washes it. "Antiseptic, bandage. Sometimes being a doctor feels useful. If only all your hurts were so easy to fix. Were you looking for something in Callie's room?"

Kai shrugs. "I don't know. There was a necklace, kind of like a model of an atom. I think *he* gave it to her." *He* is said in a way that needs no explanation: the one he hates. My father.

"Why were you looking for it?" She looks at him closely and sighs. "You've been to see him again, haven't you." She says it as a statement, not a question. Maybe mothers can read guilty minds.

He shrugs. "Yes, but I didn't take a swing at him, or even raise my voice." She raises an eyebrow. "I may have wanted to, but I didn't. And yes, before you ask, there was a good reason to go there."

"Come on. Tell me."

They go downstairs, and Mum makes tea. Kai tells her that he was with Shay, the girl who said she saw me. That the man she'd seen with me was in the paper and died in Shetland. He draws out a page from the newspaper, shows it to her. I peer over their shoulders, curious if I will recognize him.

142

And I know that face! But not from what they are talking about. He was the man who was dying on the footpath on Shetland; the one they'd sent to look for Dr. 1. If I'd known he was the one who kidnapped me, I wouldn't have been so nice to him.

Mum shakes her head. "But I still don't understand why you went to see Alex because of this."

"The police weren't that interested. And I thought if I showed the photo to him, if he reacted or anything—"

Mum shakes her head. "I know you never liked Alex, and I understand some of your reasons. But you have to get this out of your head. He didn't have anything to do with Callie's disappearance."

"How can you be so sure?"

"I asked him, and I believed him when he said he didn't. She was his daughter too, you know. He loved her."

Did my father really love me? Then why can't I remember him?

Kai shakes his head. "She was more like a pet he fed more and more facts and figures, and then when he realized she wasn't any smarter than me, he dropped her. He dropped you."

I cross my arms. I'm not clever; I'm a disappointment. *That* I remember.

Mum's face is set, her lips in a thin line. "I've heard your theory before. That he married me for my high IQ and expected children with high IQ, and was disappointed when Callie was just a little over average. Such an imagination you have, Kai. Anyway, what has this got to do with a necklace?"

Kai relays what Shay told him.

"But if Shay said she was wearing it, then why . . . ?"

"Well, Shay said I should keep an open mind and accept I might be wrong. I just thought I'd look at every possibility. If there was that one necklace, could there be something else in her room that could lead to an answer?"

"This young lady sounds very sensible to me."

"She also said I should ask you about the necklace."

"Which makes more sense than ransacking Callie's room." Kai winces. "I'm sorry, I take that back. It's fine for you to go in there;

143

I thought you didn't like to, so I was surprised. That's all." Mum shrugs her shoulders. "I don't remember seeing anything like that. The last time Alex saw Callie was the same day we went to stay by the loch. We went to Edinburgh on the way, as you know. The two of them had lunch while I did some shopping."

"If he'd given it to her then, you'd have seen it, wouldn't you?"

She frowns. "I'm sure she'd have shown it to me."

"So if she was wearing it when Shay saw her, where did she get it?"

"I don't know. Look, maybe she was wearing it and I didn't notice, or I forgot. What does it matter?"

"Don't you see? He slipped up. He said he gave it to her the last time he saw her."

"That isn't any kind of proof of anything. There was a lot going on just then; I probably forgot about it. Let it go, Kai! *Please*."

Kai breaks his gaze with Mum and sighs in exasperation.

So, there was a necklace: a gold necklace, like a model of an atom. But what does an atom look like? I frown, concentrating—it is almost there, like something I've seen, but I don't remember when or where.

Kai sits down, pushing Martin's laptop out of the way as he does so. He frowns. "Why can't he put his stuff away?"

Mum glances at the laptop. "That's odd. It's where he left it last night. Usually he's almost attached to it. Did you see him this morning?"

Kai shrugs. "No, I don't think so. See if there is any food left; then you'll know if he's been here."

She looks in the fridge and then appears really worried. "He hasn't eaten. Check his room."

"What, really?"

"I'm not going to do it. What if he's got a girl in there?" Kai raises a skeptical eyebrow. "It's not impossible. Just do it."

"Fine." Kai gets up and goes up the stairs. He knocks loudly on a door and calls out, "Hey, Martin, are you still in bed?"

There's no answer.

He knocks again.

I hear the door open.

There are footsteps above us. Mum is rinsing teacups.

"Mum? You better get up here. Now." There is a note in Kai's voice that makes her put the cups down and rush up the stairs.

I fly ahead of her and get there first.

The room is a mess of books on every surface, like it was when I looked yesterday. And inside it, in bed, is Martin. Eyes open and bloody. Dried blood on his face trailing down like tears.

It has got him; that's how they look when they die.

Kai is standing next to the bed when Mum rushes in.

"I think he's . . . Is he . . . ?"

Mum kneels by his side, feels for a pulse. She looks up at Kai, eyes wide with shock. "Dead. Yes. For some hours, I should think. Get me the phone."

Kai turns to grab it from the hall, but before he can pick it up, it starts ringing.

CHAPTER 17

SHAY

"BUT *WHY* CAN'T I GO TO IONA'S?"

"You heard what they said on the radio. People are advised to stay at home until the area is given the all clear. What's the point of closing school if you all get together and swap germs anyhow? If you're bored, you can help me do some things around the house."

I groan, but the hours are ticking slowly past. Mum is afraid of heights, and in this house of high ceilings, everything involving a ladder is mine. Soon I'm lugging it around and cleaning cobwebs from corners. When I'm finished with that, she finds a bucket and sponge for me to clean the windows.

I *hate* the smell of window cleaner. I swipe viciously at the glass, not worrying too much about being neat.

I've nearly done the front of the house when I see a car through the window I'm cleaning. A police car?

"Mum! Have you broken any laws lately?" I call, and she comes out of the kitchen. She looks through the window and frowns. "What are they doing here?"

The front car doors open; two policemen get out. Then the back door opens, and out steps Mum's friend Shelley, in her nurse's uniform. What is she doing with them?

"Should I make tea?" I ask.

"Finish that window," she says. Groaning some more, I continue.

Shelley sees me in the window and waves, calls out a hello. She walks to the door, the two policemen coming along behind her.

Mum opens the door. "Good afternoon," she says.

One of the policemen has a clipboard. "We're doing door-to-door checks of all houses in the area, ma'am."

"I see."

"And Nurse Allardyce is checking residents' temperatures."

"Oh, is she?"

"Sorry, it must be done," Shelley says, and looks unhappy—she knows Mum's views on conventional medicine. They've argued about all matter of things, from vaccines to antibiotics. "It's just a thermometer, Moyra. I promise."

Mum sighs. "Okay, fine."

One policeman asks the full names of all those in residence.

"I already told you!" Shelley says, clearly exasperated. The other one says he has to check the house to make sure no one else is here.

Shelley has some weird thing that she puts in Mum's ear. "98.7," she says loudly, and a policeman writes it down.

"Sharona?" he says.

I roll my eyes, get off the ladder, and proffer my ear. "99.9," Shelley says, and checks it again. "99.8. Probably you're a little warm from running up and down ladders. We'll come back and check you again tomorrow morning. In the meantime, stay at home. If you have any signs of headache or internal pain, call this number." She hands me a paper.

As soon as they're gone, Mum chucks it in the recycle bin.

Mum asks me to wash her car next. I start to protest that you don't need a ladder for that, but one look at her face and I go. When I finally come back in, her face has a set look, one I know. Trouble is on the way.

"What is it?"

"The army. I've been phoning a friend up the top road. There is an army jeep at the end of our lane, blocking it so we can't get out. It's not right, Shay. Marching into our house without a warrant, demanding to know who lives here, and checking to see if we lied. This is a free country."

I shrug. "No big deal having a temperature check, is it? They're just making sure we haven't got this flu." That's what I say, but why are they blocking our lane? Unease grows inside. What if my temperature is higher tomorrow? What happens then?

"I've a good mind to see them off with a shotgun."

"If you had one."

She grins. "If I had one." There are few thoughts more incongruous than Mum with a shotgun: she's campaigned for increased gun control, against hunting, against war.

That evening we watch TV for a while. It's early, but I'm dead tired after all the chores, and looking for an excuse to head up. A text from Iona pings, asking me to call. I take the excuse to go to my room, and shut the door. Being off school sounds great, but when you're under house arrest, it's kind of boring.

I flop on my bed and hit Iona's speed dial. It rings once, then she picks up. "You won't believe what I've found out," she says, her voice fast and eager.

"Hello to you too. What is it this time?"

"Log on to JIT," she says. "You talking about Kai's sister got me thinking. There's been a lot of traffic about missing people lately, mostly not the sort that hits the news: like the homeless and runaways."

I pull out my laptop and log on to Jitterbug while she talks. Once logged in, I can see the unpublished blogs that she's writing. She gets me to check her stuff, to make sure she hasn't jumped to too many outrageous conclusions and to keep the slander down to a reasonable level—that and to correct her spelling.

There are a few new drafts since the last time I logged on. She's started one on Multiverse, that weird truth commune she was talking about, but it looks like she's abandoned it for something new.

I click on the one at the top, titled *The Untold Missing*.

"All right, go," I say as my eyes scan what she has written.

"There has been a huge increase in internet traffic searching for missing people of a certain type. Running over three years now. Most are from particular areas of Scotland and northern England—it's hard to know where the boundaries lie, exactly."

She's listed page after page—links, names, many with photographs.

"How much of an increase?"

"Big, really big."

"Have you got any numbers on that?"

"Well, no, but—"

"And if that were true, wouldn't the authorities have picked up on this?" I say, playing my role as official skeptic.

"Look, really look, Shay. Most of these people are on the fringes of society, the sort that no one would miss other than their few friends, who no one would believe. But the story is there."

"Do you think Kai's sister Calista could be part of this?"

"I don't know. She doesn't fit the profile. Can you read it and tell me what you think?"

"Can I do it tomorrow? Mum's had me doing chores all day; I'm exhausted."

"Tomorrow, you promise?"

"Yes. Now let me go to sleep."

Iona laughs. "She must really have worked you to the bone. You'll be glad when school is back on."

We say goodbye, and I am tired, but I can't stop myself from scanning through her draft blog again. So many people—literally *hundreds* of them—many, as Iona said, from particular areas of Scotland and northern England.

Where did they all go? What could have happened to them?

Should I tell Kai, or Dougal the policeman, in case it has anything to do with Calista? I bite my lip and think. It's just conjecture that there is any sort of connection between all these missing people. Is it really a big increase on normal numbers, or is Iona seeing what she wants to see in her excitement at finding a story no one else has spotted?

Anyhow, as Iona said, even if there is something happening here that she has stumbled across, it can't have anything to do with Calista: she doesn't fit in this group at all.

I'll stay quiet for now and see what else Iona comes up with.

I take out my phone and read Kai's message again: better now he's heard from me.

I smile, and text back: You call this a holiday? I wasn't allowed out of the house except to wash the car. Hope you're having more fun than me. S xx

There's a dull ache behind my eyes; I take some pain medicine and head for bed.

CHAPTER 18

CALLIE

WHEN MUM GETS OFF THE PHONE, her face is white.

She swears in German.

"What is it?" Kai asks.

"That was Craig—Dr. Lawson—who I spoke to last night. The one who is with Public Health England. He called to ask for my help. As I'd guessed, the so-called Aberdeen flu is no ordinary flu. Cases have been reported from Aberdeen to Edinburgh. And now in Newcastle." Her eyes move to the room behind Kai, and his follow.

"Is that what . . ."

"Perhaps, perhaps not." She shakes her head and sighs. "Poor Martin. What am I going to tell his parents?"

Kai's eyes move from Martin's body to Mum, and he steps closer to her and farther from him. "Does that mean that we'll get it too?"

"I don't think so. I think we'd have symptoms by now if we were infected. But I don't have enough facts about how it is spread, or how he caught it. Assuming that is even what caused his death. It could be something unrelated." But she doesn't think so. It's all over her face.

"Should we call that ambulance now?"

She shakes her head. "Craig is taking care of that."

Very soon, sirens ring loud in our ears. I rush to the window to watch. There's not just one ambulance coming to this house—there are two, and a truck also.

And they're not the only sirens we can hear; there are more in the distance.

When Kai answers the door, his eyes open wide. He's surprised to see men in plastic suits standing there.

I'm not surprised; I'm horrified. They look very like the suits everyone wore underground in Shetland. Everyone except subjects, like me. It's like what happened underground is happening here, now. Will Mum and Kai get *it* too?

And it's even worse: inside the suits you can see enough of them to work it out. They're *uniforms*—army, I think, but army or police or whatever are all the same to me. They mean *trouble*.

Some of them bag up Martin and his bedding and so on from his room and take it all away. They ask Mum and Kai for a list of everywhere he has been in the last few days.

"Nowhere. He's been nowhere," Kai answers.

"It's true," Mum concurs. "He's writing up his PhD. He hasn't left the house. At least, not while either of us have been around to see him go. I can't imagine how he's come into contact with anything."

"Ma'am, I have orders from Dr. Lawson to bring you with us. You'll need to put on a biohazard suit."

"What about my son?"

"He can stay here. Under house quarantine."

"What is your name?"

"Bryson, ma'am."

"Well, Bryson, I'm not going anywhere without my son."

"But—"

"Unless you want to drag me kicking and screaming away from him, he is coming with us."

She has a staring contest with Bryson, and he finally sighs. "Sure, why not?"

They help Kai and Mum get into biohazard suits and usher them into the other ambulance. Behind us, wide tape is being put across the door. Like police tape, but this is red, with funny symbols on it, and QUARANTINE in black letters. Neighbors are watching through windows, but their doors stay shut. As if that could save them, when all the precautions and suits and sealed doors underground couldn't: once *it* gets out, it's unstoppable.

"Where are we going?" Mum asks Bryson.

"To a temporary army operations base. We're assisting setting up a group to analyze the spread of the disease. We'll have to put both of you into quarantine for a day. If you make it through that without signs of illness, we're hoping you'll be able to help us."

"I'm rather hoping for both of those things," Mum says.

"Yeah."

I'm scared. When we get to the base where they are putting Mum and Kai in quarantine, it is too much like being a prisoner underground on Shetland. I want to go with them, but I just can't handle being locked up again. Their temperatures are checked, and they're told if they don't have any symptoms and they pass another temperature check in twenty-four hours, they can come out. Mum demands access to all they know so far on the situation.

What if they have it? Will they die? I didn't die when I caught it. There was so much pain that I was sure I was going to, but then I got better. But if Mum and Kai die, will they be ghosts, like I am? Will we all be together, and will they be able to hear me and talk to me?

And what I want and don't want are all twisted around in a confusing knot. I want them to know I am here; I want them to talk to me. But I don't want them to scream in pain. I don't want them to die.

I watch them for a while. Kai keeps looking at his phone like he wants to use it, then putting it back in his pocket. Mum is pacing, waiting for them to send a computer through with the data they have on the Aberdeen flu so far.

Watching them through the transparent wall just makes me think the worst. And now, not only can they not hear me, I can't hear them either.

Instead I wander around the army base. It's set in fields on hills above Newcastle; the city skyline is in the distance, green all around. Bryson said the base was temporary, and while it is tents, not buildings, and everything looks new, the grass freshly trampled, it is somehow serious and solid at the same time. There are high fences all around, barbed wire on top. The gate we came in seems to be the only way in or out, and it has guards in biohazard suits, guns in their hands. Other guards patrol the fence.

I don't think they built this in a day. They were ready.

I wander around the base and listen, in the cafeteria, in meetings. Some sneak away and use their phones when they think no one is watching, and warn people to get away, to hide.

One thing is clear: things are bad, very bad. Everyone is scared.

It has escaped from Shetland, and nothing will ever be the same again.

CHAPTER 19

SHAY

I'M ASLEEP BUT NOT ASLEEP, both at the same time. My head *hurts*, and I can hear a voice calling out, "Mum, Mum." Is it my voice? It must be, but it is distant, like it belongs to someone else.

The door opens. Light from the hall spills in, a blunt ax that splits my skull and makes me cry out.

Mum's voice is soothing; her hand is on my forehead.

There is pain deep inside me, and I'm crying. I try not to, but I can't stop.

Mum says something like "No one is taking you away, not while I'm here to stop them."

She's bustling around. She puts something cool on my head, has one of her concoctions for me to drink. I can't lift my head and she helps me, holds the cup to my lips. It tastes all right. I must really be sick.

She helps me sit up. The movement reverberates in pain in my head, as if I'm the clapper in a bell, hitting the sides over and over, and I'm crying again.

"Be brave, love," she says, and I try to stop, but my eyes are still leaking tears.

"Have I got it? That Aberdeen flu? Am I going to die?" I can only whisper the words.

"No way. You probably just ate something funny," she says. "You'll be all right."

She's easing me into clothes, and I make myself pick up my phone and put it in my pocket. I promised Kai, didn't I?

We're outside now, and the cool air on my skin is good. I breathe a little better.

"Where are we going?" I say.

"Away. I think we need a little vacation." And she's drawing me down the path to the loch. I'm leaning on her, trying to help, not to stumble, but I have no strength. My arms and legs feel wooden and disconnected, like they belong to somebody else.

We finally reach the shore, and she helps me onto the bench by the small pier where our boat is tied. The water is lapping softly, but it sounds like a tsunami in my pounding head.

"Wait here just a minute, Shay. Don't move."

I whisper a promise not to move. Not that I could if I wanted to.

She's gone for more than a minute. I look up at the night sky. The pain hasn't lessened, but I'm getting used to it. I can almost bear it without crying, so long as I don't move. But the sky looks . . . wrong. The moon and stars are so bright I can barely stand to look at them, with colored halos all around.

Mum comes back. She carries loads of stuff. She helps me into the boat, tells me to lie down if I want to—puts something soft under my head when I do.

She's rowing. I'm not sure if I'm awake or asleep. The cool air and the swaying on the water are soothing, but there is still pain inside me: my head, my chest.

Everywhere.

I can close my eyes and breathe. And try to compartmentalize the pain. Put it away in a drawer, and shut it. Don't open it. It's still there, I know it's there, but I can pretend it isn't.

Time passes. I might sleep, I don't know. The boat bumps into something and jars my head. I cry out.

"Sorry, Shay. We're there now. You're going to have to help me a little."

I open my eyes. It's night still. The stars are even brighter now, unnaturally so—they shine like our sun, and light up the sky. I try to sit up, but I can't. Mum eases me up.

"Where . . ." I whisper, then swallow. The words won't come.

"Where are we? We're going to the bird hide on that proposed development site. A good place to hide away. No one has found it yet, and believe me, they've tried."

A good place to hide away? Her words float around inside my head, but the meaning is lost.

She helps me walk. She takes most of my weight; I can't move otherwise. I try to say I'm sorry, but speaking jars my head and it hurts so much I start to cry again.

"Shhhh. Shhhh, Shay. We'll be there soon." She starts humming a lullaby, and I focus on that, and on stuffing the pain away in a drawer. A drawer isn't big enough now; it's a cupboard, then a wardrobe. Then a whole room in a house.

We're there. It's a sort of tent shelter, made of mottled canvas that blends into the trees and bushes that surround it. She leans me up against a tree. She's got one of those air mattresses where you push a button and it somehow inflates itself. She puts it inside the shelter, puts a blanket on it. Helps me lie down.

"Shhhh, baby girl. Go to sleep. Shhhh . . ."

I'm not sure if I sleep, but later I open my eyes, and she's gone. The pain is in a soccer stadium now. I haven't got a ticket, so I can't get in; it's safe.

She comes back, lugging stuff from our boat, kisses me, and goes back for more.

I close my eyes, and everything goes black.

CHAPTER 20

CALLIE

I GO BACK TO WATCH Mum and Kai sleeping. It's late at night and dark behind the glass in their enclosure, but outside is a watcher. He has a screen where he can see them through an infrared camera, and the temperature of the air where they sleep is monitored for change.

It stays safely in the green.

I'm counting down the minutes until they can let them out tomorrow. An hour passes; another, and another. There is the slow tick of a clock on the wall. The breathing of the watcher.

The phone buzzes next to him, and he picks it up.

"Sir! But how— Yes, sir!"

He puts the phone down and runs—for a large cupboard in the corner of the room. He opens it and takes out a biohazard suit, and puts it on faster than I'd have thought possible. Somewhere nearby an alarm starts to ring.

Curious about what is going on, I drift outside.

Everywhere I look, lights are on or switching on, bathing the tent city in a strange orangeade glow under a weak new moon. People emerge wearing biohazard suits, and they seem agitated and afraid. Inside what was the dining tent, there are now people lying on camp beds. Some are sweating and silent; some are screaming out in pain.

Mum's friend Dr. Lawson is in there, but he's not in a suit. He's on a camp bed.

There is fight in his face and pain in his eyes. He has a notebook and scribbles something on the page.

The newly suited watcher from Mum and Kai's quarantine tent arrives and is waved over by Dr. Lawson. He helps him get up.

Slowly they walk outside, Dr. Lawson refusing the offer of an arm. They head toward the quarantine tent.

Inside of it the lights are on now, and Mum and Kai are awake, up and dressed. When Dr. Lawson walks in, the relief on Mum's face soon turns to horror as she gets a better look at him. His gray face, the way his body shakes and shudders.

He gestures to the watcher to unlock their door.

"But that's against—"

"There doesn't seem to be much point in that now, with half the camp laid out sick in the dining tent, does there? Just do it, and then leave us. Go back to help."

Controls are manipulated, and the door swings open. Mum rushes out to Dr. Lawson, Kai following more slowly behind. The watcher salutes and leaves.

Dr. Lawson clutches her arm. In his other hand there is the notebook, and he holds it up. "From the beginning . . ." He breathes heavily, eyes clenched tight, then opens them again with a grimace. "I've written down my symptoms. Everything, with the time. I can't hold a pen anymore; I need you to do it for me now. And I need you to take over the task force meeting tomorrow. We're one of five centers linking to discuss . . ." He stops again, his body shuddering. "To discuss what we've found out so far. To find a way forward."

"What, me?" Mum says. "But I don't know—"

"You are the only doctor left here who is not infected, and not likely to be: this doesn't skip victims. You are still alive so you *must* be immune." His shoulders are rigid with effort. "Take it."

She takes the notebook. "Kai, help me," she says. Together they help Dr. Lawson up and onto a bed in the surgery that adjoins the quarantine tent.

"Kai, note the time. Write down everything he says." She's rushing about, checking equipment, and soon has Dr. Lawson hooked up to some weird medical thing with little electrodes here and there on him. A thing on his fingertip measures something else.

"The lights are strange," Dr. Lawson says. "Broken into components, as if my eyes are a prism. When we were outside, the stars even more so." His whole body shudders and twists, and he groans. His face is slick with sweat.

"Isn't there anything you can do for him?" Kai asks.

"There is no known treatment, no cure. Craig, are there any supplies of morphine, or other painkillers?" she asks him.

He shakes his head. "Yes, but not for me. Record. The stars were wondrous! I could see the plasma, magnetic fields; the elements are a rainbow, each its own color." He gasps. "Each moment, the pain in my head, in my chest, intensifies. Waves against the shore, drowning." He grimaces.

He continues to describe what he can see, what he feels, and it is so like what happened to me when I was infected that I can almost feel it again. I wrap my arms around myself, wanting to leave but afraid to lose sight of Mum and Kai. In case they get it too.

I focus on Mum. She's taking readings off equipment and tells Kai to write numbers and stuff down. Her face is still but pained; a different sort of pain than Dr. Lawson's—one that comes from seeing her friend like this.

She holds his hand.

"But even as it intensifies, until there could be no worse pain, then, it eases." You see it instantly on his face. A calm. Wonder in his eyes.

"Who's your friend?" Dr. Lawson says.

"What friend?" Mum and Kai exchange glances; Dr. Lawson is looking straight at me.

He can see me? "Tell them I'm here!" I say, frantic to give him a message for them before he dies.

"But who are you?"

"She's my mother. I'm Callie! Callie's ghost."

"Ah, I see. I'm not sure she'd want to know this."

"Craig? Craig?" Mum says. "What is happening?" She strokes his hand. "Who are you talking to?"

"There is peace inside me. I see things I shouldn't see; the dead. I'll be one of them soon."

Tears glisten on Mum's face.

"Tell her! Tell her I'm here!" I'm screaming at him now. He looks at me and shakes his head sadly. His eyes close, and his head slumps back. Blood leaks out from his ears, his mouth. The eyes that just seconds ago could see me.

And then *bzzzzzzzzz*. Flat line on a machine. Even I've watched enough TV to know that means he's dead.

Kai's hand is on Mum's shoulder. She has tears in her eyes and she stands there, still holding Dr. Lawson's hand. But I'm *angry*. Why wouldn't he tell her I'm here?

If the illness has spread, there will be more people who are dying. Maybe more of them who will be able to see me and pass on messages.

She shakes herself a little, lets his hand fall away. "Kai, I must go help. Others are ill."

"But what can you do? There is no cure, no treatment. You said so."

"Then we can just hold their hands. Sometimes that is all that can be done. Stay here. You don't have to come with me."

Kai's scared. I can see it in his eyes, in the way he stands, leaning forward, like he's about to fight. But he shakes his head. "No. I'll go with you. We stay together."

They go to the dining tent, and I follow, but at a distance, staying away.

She wants to hold their hands, to ease their suffering. She doesn't want them to see me, to hear that her dead daughter stands at her shoulder. I can't do it, I just can't.

I watch from above.

Some of those who were in suits are becoming ill, taking their suits off. Like the watcher. He's lying on a camp bed with the rest. Some people have already died. Kai helps carry bodies away to another tent, now a morgue—a blank, set look on his face, his body so rigid it must be hard to move.

There is a nurse in a suit who seems clear of the illness, at least so far. She's found morphine, but it soon runs out. And Mum soothes those in pain as best she can. She tells them it will ease, and when it does, she holds their hands. She watches them die.

It's dawn; pink streaks cross the sky. One of the nurses who is ill and past the pain now murmurs about the coronas around the sun. The colors.

And then, like all the others, she dies.

CHAPTER 21

SHAY

MUM KISSES ME. She puts a cool cloth on my head and lies down beside me.

Through the slit windows in the green canvas walls of the hideout, I can see that the sun is coming up. The light—a rainbow of colors—hurts my eyes, but I can't stop looking. It isn't right; that isn't how the sun looks.

Then I'm drifting, not sure if I'm awake or in a dream.

There's an echo inside my head, a ringing sound.

It's a dream. I think it is.

Mum is there. She's holding me, saying she's sorry. That she failed.

Am I dying? I ask her.

No. I am. She smiles. She's talking to me, but our words aren't out loud. They're inside me.

She's in pain too, and I try to show her how to put it inside a soccer stadium, but she can't.

She's braver than me. She doesn't cry.

CHAPTER 22

CALLIE

THE MOST SENIOR SURVIVING OFFICER isn't very senior, and he's scared; he wants to wait until a more senior officer arrives.

But Mum bosses him around. From all the reading she did in the night, and what Dr. Lawson told her before and after becoming ill, she says she knows what to do. She tells him that Dr. Lawson said to do this and that, and he believes her.

Except for Mum and Kai, the only ones on the base who escaped infection were those who were suited when it broke out. They begin to carry the bodies from the morgue tent to a field behind the base. Soon smoke rises into the sky.

And then Mum has lots and lots of coffee, and she finds the only tech still alive who knows how to use all the computers and stuff to set up our end of the virtual task force meeting. He explains as he does so. The monitors are linked between Aberdeen, Edinburgh, London, here in Newcastle, and something called the WHO. Which, the tech explains to Kai, isn't a rock band—it's the World Health Organization.

Just in time they're ready: one by one the monitors become live, and each screen shows a group of people from all the different places.

"Hello, I see we're all here now." A voice from the London monitor. "I represent Public Health England in London and will be chairing today. Let's start with some introductions."

He introduces himself and then names those in his group in turn, and with each name someone nods. There are doctors and some politicians that even I recognize.

"Newcastle next." He frowns when he sees Mum, and the most-senior-not-very-senior surviving officer. "Where are Dr. Lawson and the rest of your group?"

Mum answers. "Hello; I'm Dr. Sonja Tanzer, an epidemiologist from the University of Newcastle. Dr. Lawson called me in to help. I'm afraid we had an outbreak last night at this so-called secure facility. Apart from me and two nurses, there is no medical contingent left here of the Newcastle team. In fact, the only survivors were the suited guards on the perimeter, and those not present when the outbreak began who were suited on their return."

There are shocked sounds from all the monitors.

"Are there any thoughts on how the breach occurred?" asks the chair.

"None. My son and I were brought here in contained quarantine after our tenant died. Dr. Lawson let us out when it became clear what was happening, and that we weren't infected. He bravely recorded his symptoms—and I carried on when he couldn't—until he died. This illness is like nothing I've seen before."

"With all due respect—I know Dr. Lawson wanted to include you, Dr. Tanzer, but you are a researcher, not a clinician." This from one of the white coats on the London screen.

I bristle at his tone. He might as well have said, "Sit down and be quiet, little girl," something I've heard often enough.

Mum raises an eyebrow. "Doctor—sorry, I don't remember your name?"

The chair points out that the white coat spoke out of turn, and he scowls and is introduced again.

"The standard medical approach doesn't appear to be working, from everything I've heard and seen," Mum says. "Perhaps the eye of an epidemiological researcher will yield useful information."

"Edinburgh here. We concur with Dr. Tanzer, who is an expert in her field. And frankly, we need all the help we can get."

The chair continues introducing everyone from the monitors, then asks a doctor in Aberdeen to begin with a summary for those less versed in the facts.

He clears his throat and begins. "The so-called Aberdeen flu does not behave like any previous flu epidemic, or indeed, like any previous epidemic or pandemic, period. Original thoughts were of an environmental contaminant—some sort of poisoning. Suggestions of terrorists poisoning the water and all sorts of things have been investigated and ruled out. No toxins have been found. While the quick course of the illness seemed to back up some kind of mass poisoning, it soon became apparent that it is communicable. It *is* infectious."

London: "Which doesn't rule out bioterrorism."

Aberdeen: "No. There appear to be two forms of the illness. One type spreads from contact with infected individuals, and initial symptoms appear about twenty-four hours after contact. But in some places, particularly Aberdeen, Edinburgh, and Newcastle, the spread has been much faster than this model would predict: huge numbers of people have been infected simultaneously, and often points of contact with infected individuals can't be traced.

"Both appear to run the same course and time frame, once symptoms present. Patients come down with light fever and headache. This progresses within a few hours to severe fever, headache, and internal pain, and death follows within hours. Autopsies show cause of death as widespread organ failure. Many patients are hallucinatory with pain, though just before they die they often become lucid and calm for a short time."

London: "What is the fatality rate of those infected?"

Aberdeen: "It appears to be virtually one hundred percent."

There are gasps of shock from WHO, from London, but not the other places. They all know.

London, a politician this time: "So everyone who catches it dies?"

Aberdeen: "There have been a very few unconfirmed reports of survivors. A few in Aberdeen, one in Newcastle. We need to look into the claims. It is possible the individuals in question were actually sick with something else and didn't survive *this* illness. Also, some people who are exposed don't catch the disease—like Dr. Tanzer and her son. Perhaps about five percent are resistant to infection, but we're still gathering figures. This resistance appears to be genetic, as it tends to be particular families and related individuals that don't come down with the illness, even if everyone around them does. We also need to look into that to see if it is something we can exploit more widely."

WHO: "What is the infectious agent?"

Edinburgh: "We haven't isolated it as yet. It's not bacterial, we're sure of that. No traces of influenza virus or any other type of known virus or agent have been found so far. It may be something completely new."

WHO: "How can we fight something when we don't know what it is?"

London: "Exactly. Containment has been the implemented approach so far, but it's not working, at least not well. Schools are closed throughout the UK as of today. Travel, both domestic and international, is banned without a permit or immune pass. Airports and ports are closed. The coast guard and navy, both ours and international, are watching our coast in case anyone makes a run for it. The army is being deployed along with police to place roadblocks around all affected towns and cities as we speak."

Edinburgh: "Because of your immunity, Dr. Tanzer, you can travel. And that may be very helpful indeed."

Mum inclines her head. "If I am indeed immune and not just lucky so far."

The not-so-senior officer next to Mum stirs. "Excuse me for interjecting. Dr. Tanzer, I was out with my containment team when the outbreak here began. Central Newcastle, the university area where you worked, and Jesmond, where you lived, are all quarantined. There are reports that over ninety percent of residents in those areas have died so far. You *must* be immune."

Kai, offscreen, gasps. Mum sits up straighter, but her face doesn't register the shock.

Mum: "If we don't know the causative agent, how do we stop the spread, or treat it?"

London: "Exactly. These studies must receive priority."

WHO: "So, basically we're looking at an epidemic that we don't know how to treat or prevent that has the potential to kill ninety-five percent of the population of the world."

London: "Yes."

Mum: "In the meantime, we need to examine the patterns. Map all the cases. See what connections we can find. This may help contain it and identify the cause."

Edinburgh: "Data from some places is sketchy, but we'll do what we can."

London: "Dr. Tanzer, could you visit this patient in Newcastle who was infected and appears to have survived? We'll get you issued with an immune pass so you can travel."

Mum: "And one for my son. He's eighteen. He's been up all night helping with the sick and the dead, as have I. I want him to come with me."

London: "We'll send an escort for you once we replace biohazard suit supplies."

Mum: "I want him to come with me so I can do this now, and get back to analyzing everything we know."

London: "One moment." There is a pause; his eyes focus off camera. Then he turns back. "Very well. Two passes will be with you along with reinforcements by airdrop this afternoon."

Edinburgh: "In the meantime, Dr. Tanzer, I suggest you get some sleep."

The groups say goodbye one by one, and the screens go dark.

Kai goes to Mum and holds her. They can't see me or feel me, but I go to them too and hold them both.

They're sad about all the people they know that have died. I'm glad Mum and Kai haven't gotten sick, haven't had to go through all that pain; that they're immune, so they won't.

But I'm sad too. If they got sick, they might have become like me. Even if they didn't, then right at the end they would have seen me, heard me. Now that I know they're immune, I also know that they'll never see or hear me ever again.

CHAPTER 23

SHAY

THE SUN HAS GONE DOWN AGAIN NOW.

Mum shows me things, from her memories, her past.

Including a man who could dance—the one from the photo she had hidden away, the one I recognized. Dr. Alex Cross.

He swept her off her feet—both literally and in the other, more figurative, way. There was something about him; she couldn't help herself.

His eyes, a blue so pure, mists and magic inside them. I'm her, he's holding me, and we're dancing. And she's falling, spinning, on fire . . .

I pull away from her memory. There are some things you *don't* want to share with your mother.

Then, when she found she was pregnant with me, she ran away—she left Scotland to get away from him. She was starting to see that he wasn't right. Not just for her, but in a more general way: there was a wrongness inside him.

Yes. Kai's stepfather—the one he hates—is my father.

Aunt Addy helped her. Wonderful Aunt Addy, who left us her house when she died. She who wrote poetry about the lochs and sang to the birds.

We didn't come back to Scotland until Mum knew for sure that Alex didn't own his house by the loch anymore: his ex-wife got it in their divorce settlement. That's why she was there with her daughter, Calista.

I'm shocked when I realize—when I put it all together: Calista and I have the same father. She's my half sister.

No. My father doesn't know about me.

The random rock fan at a Knack concert was her cover story.

Couldn't she have come up with something better?

What could be better than being made at a rock concert?

We'll have to agree to disagree on that one.

We drift in and out of each other's memories and dreams.

CHAPTER 24

CALLIE

THERE IS A GIANT MAP ON THE WALL, with colored pins. Blue for isolated cases. Red for ten or more. Black for a hundred or more. Newcastle, Aberdeen, and Edinburgh are so black with pins they cannot be seen.

"It just doesn't make sense," Mum mutters to herself, and then says something in German. I don't know the words, but I can tell she is swearing by the way she says them.

Kai is there, half-asleep in a chair. "Maybe it'll make more sense if you get some sleep?"

"How many more people will die while I sleep? How can I sleep?"

Kai sits up properly. "Tell me. What doesn't make sense?" he says, and she gives him an impatient look. "Maybe if you state the problem out loud, you will see it more clearly."

She nods. "Well, it seems to skip entire places or just affect them lightly, like Dunbar, Alnmouth." She points at them on the map. "Others—well, Newcastle is now worse than Aberdeen, where it started. Why does it spread so quickly in some places, and slowly in others?"

Kai gets up and stares at the map.

"Could it be something to do with the train?"

"What do you mean?"

He points. "Travel by train from Aberdeen to Newcastle, and you stop in Edinburgh. Aberdeen, Edinburgh, and Newcastle are the worst affected." He studies the map. "And many of the places where there were small outbreaks are near the east coast train line."

The tiredness leaves Mum's eyes. Her face is animated as she traces the train line among the pins. "So could there be a number of people who have traveled this route who are contagious? But why wouldn't they move on to other train lines? Why wouldn't it spread further? Unless . . ." She grabs Kai and gives him a hug. "You're a genius, as I've always said."

"Well, of course! But you've lost me."

"This only makes sense if there is a person or persons who are carriers who have traveled this path. They were in Aberdeen for a while: the first outbreak. Also in Edinburgh: second outbreak, but they can't have been there as long since so far it is more limited, to around the university and the train station. Then Newcastle, and the outbreak is now the worst here, because here they have stayed. Thus the outbreak hasn't spread farther south, other than in sporadic small numbers of cases. What if there is a Typhoid Mary? Someone who carries the disease but isn't infected by it themselves? Places where they've stayed, it spreads rapidly, directly from them; other places where it is spread by other infected individuals, it spreads differently, more slowly. As those who are infected die quickly, these cases can be contained by quarantine more easily."

She stares intently at the map.

"But if there were some Typhoid Marys, as you call them, why wouldn't they die themselves?" Kai asks. "Are they immune? We're immune, and we don't seem to give it to anyone else."

"Those who are immune, like us, are not carriers. This has been established, as they've been around others who hadn't otherwise been exposed without incident—many of whom died later in outbreaks, so they can't have been immune themselves. This person—or persons—

we are talking about here must be something very different. Now, what we need to do is find out where the very first cases took place; find out who was there and was also in Edinburgh and is still in Newcastle now."

"Do you think if you can find this person, you can stop the spread?"

"Perhaps; perhaps not. We must try. The most important thing we need to know now is this: where and when did it start? Was it in Aberdeen, or somewhere else? We need to know the precise time zero of the outbreak. From there, pray that the rest may follow."

Mum bustles off to talk to the not-very-senior officer, to call the centers in Aberdeen and Edinburgh. She promises to have a nap once she has done so.

I sigh. If only she could hear me, I would tell her it started underground in Shetland; it wasn't in Aberdeen at all.

Kai takes out his phone. He texts Shay: Hello, still enjoying your vacation from school? If you've heard things are bad in Newcastle, don't worry. Mum and I are fine. K xx.

Kai gets back into the armchair and is almost instantly asleep.

CHAPTER 25

SHAY

I'M FOLDED UP IN A DRAWER NOW. I've pulled it closed. The pain fills the rest of the world.

Hang on. You can do it, baby. Mum's thoughts are inside me.

I open my eyes.

I love you, my Sharona, she says, and for once I don't say "Shay" back at her.

I love you too, Mum. I think rather than say the words, like she did, but we can still hear them. They're inside us.

The sun is up again as she kisses me goodbye. She sighs, her hand on my cheek. Then she drifts away.

I'm utterly alone.

I can't keep the drawer shut any longer. Pain and tears are all I have left.

CHAPTER 26

CALLIE

THE HELICOPTER LANDS IN THE FIELD behind the army base, not far enough away from where they're burning the bodies. Smoke swirls in the air. I hear someone say it smells like a barbecue. Even though I can't smell anything anymore, I stay away from the smoke: what if their ghosts are flying away inside it?

Mum and Kai haven't slept long enough. I didn't even have time to get bored before someone came to rouse her. They told her that the immune passes would be here in a moment and that the trip had been arranged. It was time to go and find the survivor.

"Are you sure you want to come, Kai?" Mum says. "I know I said I wanted you to, but you don't have to. They've found a driver with a suit who can be spared."

He yawns and rubs his eyes. "I'm coming. Don't argue."

"I don't know what we might see."

"Could it be worse than what we have already?"

"Yes."

He stares at her, slowly nods. "Then you shouldn't face it alone."

I'm proud of my brother: he's brave, isn't he? I'm not. I'd stay here if I wasn't afraid something would happen to them if I didn't keep them in sight.

They are led out to the truck by a suited guard. Kai takes his phone out of his pocket as they walk, frowns, and puts it back.

"Is something wrong?" Mum asks.

He shrugs. "I've texted Shay. She hasn't answered."

"She lives near Loch Tay, doesn't she?" He nods. "There are no cases reported west of Perth. Maybe she's just busy, or misplaced her phone."

"Yeah. That's probably it." He still looks worried, though.

"I'll check that the area is still clear."

"Thanks, Mum."

They get in the truck.

The driver is Bryson, the same one who collected them from the house when Martin died. That isn't so long ago, but he's changed: he seems to have lost his army starch.

He grins inside his suit. "Are you ready for the magical mystery tour?" he says, and drives toward the gate.

Kai's hand grips the grab bar over the door; his knuckles are white. For all he said, he's scared of what we might see.

Mum is on her phone as we drive out the gate. "Sorry to trouble you, could I get an update on Perthshire and Stirlingshire? Yes. Uh-huh. And where is that? Thank you." She hangs up and turns to Kai. "Killin and area are clear. The closest now is Stirling, and that is a small outbreak."

"Thanks for checking."

"Do you really like this girl?"

"Mum. Another time."

Bryson whistles. "Have you got a girlfriend? If I've learned any-thing lately, it's this: enjoy life while you can."

Before long there is a roadblock ahead. Bryson stops, rolls the window down, shows his ID and our papers, and we're waved through.

He's on the radio and suddenly halts, reverses, and takes another turn. "There's trouble that way. We've been told to divert."

"What sort of trouble?" Mum asks.

"Attempted roadblock breach. I'm sorry; this way is safer but it isn't very scenic. It's been quarantined; cleared but not collected."

He doesn't explain, and they don't ask.

He rounds a corner, and at the end of every second or third driveway, there are bodies. Piled up, haphazard. Arms and legs spill out. Bloody eyes stare at the sky. Old people, middle-aged, young. And this isn't like the ones who deserved it underground, or even the still forms at the army camp. I want to look away, but I can't. Babies or teenagers or grandparents, everyone is dead.

Mum crosses herself, wordlessly praying. Kai's eyes are fixed and staring straight ahead, as though if he stares at the road hard enough they'll leave this place sooner, but my eyes can't stop looking at the horror around us.

We drive on, and Bryson starts whistling. Maybe he's pretending he's somewhere else. Mum jumps when he begins, but says nothing.

Bryson finds the right house. We're in an area where the original residents have died and been cleared. Bryson tells us that the immune have been brought together here to keep them safe.

"Safe from what?" Kai asks.

He doesn't answer at first, then says, "Sick people can be pretty desperate."

We knock on the door. An old man answers. "Yes? What do you want?"

Bryson answers. "We heard that you know a survivor. We'd like to meet him."

"Right, I do know one. Invited him to come and stay, but he wouldn't. Stayed out there, in his own house."

"What is the address?"

"I don't know."

"What was his name?"

"Fred something."

Bryson and Mum exchange a glance. "How are we supposed to find him, then?" Bryson says.

"Well, I don't know the address, but I know where it is. I can show you. Are you sure you want to find him? He's pretty odd. Says he can talk to dead people."

"Yes. We still want to find him."

He gets in the truck with us and directs us down one turn after another. Finally we stop at a small house. There's a C on the door.

"Means this area has been cleared," Bryson says, and knocks. There's no answer. He knocks again, then tries the door. The handle turns; he opens it.

We step inside.

"Not cleared very well," Bryson says, looking up. A man hangs from the ceiling, a rope around his neck. "Is that him?" Bryson asks.

The old guy looks up, his face ashen. "Yes. That's Fred," he says, and then backs out the door.

"We need the body for postmortem," Mum says.

"Right," Bryson says.

Kai steps back outside too, breathing deeply. Bryson follows him, finds a ladder in a garden shed.

"Do you need help?" Kai asks.

Bryson grips his shoulder. "No. I'm as strong as an ox."

He cuts the body down. There seems to be a supply of body bags in the back of the truck, and Fred joins us for the drive back.

"It's so sad that he survived this infection and then hanged himself," Kai says. "Why would he do that?"

"Maybe he lost everyone he loved. Maybe he couldn't handle it," Bryson says.

"We don't know for sure he had it; he might have been immune," Mum says.

"He had it all right," the old man says. "I saw him when he was sick. But it wasn't that sort of sadness that did it. It was the dead people, all talking to him nonstop inside his head. It was driving him crazy—he told me so. Guess he couldn't take it anymore."

Mum asks him more questions.

I can tell she thinks it isn't possible—talking to the dead—that Fred must have been not right in the head to think that he could. But I wish Fred were here without the body bag: maybe he could have talked to me.

We drop the old man off and start to head back to the army base.

Bryson's radio beeps. "Yes? Okay." He swears.

"What's wrong?" Mum asks.

"Nothing, don't worry. We're being diverted. Again. This area hasn't been cleared, but it should be okay."

He's hypervigilant, looking every way at once as we drive. But it's just a street, an ordinary road. No bodies are piled up; in fact, there are no people, period. A tumbleweed could rustle down the street and be right at home.

But then we round a corner, and there's a car crashed into a tree, smoke coming from the engine. A man inside it is hunched over the steering wheel.

"Wait. He may be hurt," Mum says.

"I can't stop; it's too dangerous," Bryson answers.

"But I'm a doctor. I may be able to help him. Stop now or I'll open the door and jump out!"

He hits the brakes. "Fine. Sure. Why not?" He turns and looks at Kai. "You, stay and watch the truck. I'll cover her." He's got a gun in his hand.

Mum is out of the truck and rushes to the crashed car. The car doors won't open at the front, so she tries a back door. It opens. She climbs into the car and checks the driver.

She backs out again, shaking her head.

"Help me!" A girl is banging on the back door of our truck.

Bryson looks between the truck and Mum, like he doesn't know whether to run to Kai or stay with Mum. The girl goes around to Mum's door on the other side; she didn't lock it. The girl opens the door. That's when I see she has a knife in her hand.

I throw myself between her and Kai. *Leave my brother alone!*

She screams. She can see me? That's when I see the blood in her eyes. She's dying.

She strikes out with her knife—at me. There's a weird feeling, like pressure—her knife goes through me and sticks into the car seat. She pulls it out of the seat and stares at me, at her knife. Kai has climbed out the door on his side; he's gotten away.

Bryson is here now and pulls the girl out of the truck. She struggles and strikes out at him.

"Calm down, no one wants to hurt you," Mum says, reaching them both, but the girl did want to hurt somebody and she has—the knife in her hand has stabbed through Bryson's suit and into his arm. There's blood.

He lets her go. She staggers, falls. Her body arches in pain one last time, then lies still. She's died of *it*, and now he will too.

"I'm sorry, Bryson," Mum says. "Let me see."

"It's just a nick. It's nothing." But he knows what it means. He shrugs, and takes off his suit.

Mum ties his arm to stop the blood, while he looks at the girl's body and shakes his head.

"She looks a little like my girlfriend," Bryson says. "Dark hair, brown eyes. She's dead. My girlfriend, I mean. My mother, father, sister, too. Everyone. Maybe I'll get to be with them now. But what really bothers me is I never told my girl that I love her, and it's too late." He grabs Kai's arm. "Don't leave it too late."

They get in the truck.

"It's my fault," Mum whispers. "My fault. I'm so sorry."

"No, it isn't. It's whoever or whatever caused this plague. Isn't it? Now lock the doors," Bryson says. He starts the truck, and we pull away.

Kai takes out his phone, looks at the screen. No text. He hesitates, presses "call."

"Shay? What's wrong? Where are you? Tell me!" Kai curses. He calls again. Waits and waits. He says nothing more: is there no answer?

"Kai?" Mum says. "What is it?"

"It's Shay. She answered the first time, but she sounded all wrong. She wasn't speaking properly, and then the phone went dead. Now she's not answering."

She frowns. "There aren't any cases in that part of Scotland. It must be something else."

He shakes his head, horror on his face. "She's ill. She said something about the lights on the sun, like Craig did before he died. I have to go there."

"Kai, you can't."

"I have to. I'm immune; nothing is going to happen to me."

"But how?"

"I've got an immune pass to get me through roadblocks. I'll go on my bike."

"But what can you do?"

"I can hold her hand."

Mum stares back at him, then slowly nods.

Shay . . . ill? With *it*? So many people have died already. Now she is ill too?

Kai's face—his pain—makes me go to him and put my hand over his. Even though she was annoying, she was so alive—the way her eyes said things as much as her words. I somehow can't believe it any more than he can.

"Where's your bike, lad? At your house? Your neighborhood's been cleared." Bryson reverses around a corner. "Let's go and get it. I'm ignoring all sorts of orders, but what are they going to do: court-martial me?" He laughs.

On the way he gives Kai hints for the trip: ways to go, ways to avoid. What to do and say at roadblocks. When we get home, Bryson gives Kai another immune pass.

Mum's face is white. She hugs him. "*Ich hab dich lieb*."

"Love you too," he says.

"Promise me you'll be careful," she whispers. "I can't lose you too."

My name hangs between them without being said: I'm the lost one. I want to scream, "I'm right here! I'm not lost!" But what is the point when they can't hear me?

When he gets on his bike, it's like I'm torn in two. Do I stay with Mum? Do I go with Kai? There's this fear inside me that whichever way I choose, I'll never see the other one of them ever again.

I stand there, undecided, as his bike goes down the road one way and the truck goes the other. Soon both will be out of sight. What do I do?

Kai is the one who is going off alone. I fly after him and settle against him on the bike.

He turns and waves as Mum and Bryson disappear in the other direction, in the truck with Fred's body in the back.

Bye, Mum, I whisper.

CHAPTER 27

SHAY

I'M THIRSTY, COLD. What life is left will soon be gone. I slip in and out of dreams. Whether they are waking dreams or sleeping ones, I can't tell. They are just the same.

In one of them, my phone rings. It's in my pocket, where it's been all along. It's Kai. I try to answer, to talk to him. His voice is insistent, he wants to know where I am, what's happening.

But there are other things I want to tell him. That I love him. That's crazy, isn't it? I barely know him. But somehow, now, all I can see is truth, and it is there.

But before I can say the words, the phone falls away, out of my hand.

CHAPTER 28

CALLIE

THE FIRST ROADBLOCKS are within Newcastle and are much like the ones we went through earlier with Bryson. Kai takes his helmet off like Bryson said to, and waits his turn. Armed guards in biohazard suits peer at his pass and wave him through.

But the closer we get to leaving the city, the longer it takes—the more guards, the more guns.

When we're finally about to leave Newcastle, it all looks very serious. Guns are in hands, ready, and everyone looks nervous, jumpy. There are heavy barricades on both sides, and the opening between is narrow. Only one vehicle can go through in either direction at a time.

Apart from a few army vehicles and supply trucks, no one is trying to get into Newcastle. The other way, though, is different: there are lines, long lines, of cars. One by one, they are turned back. Some of the people argue, yell. Cry. They're not sick yet and want to leave before they are. But if they don't have the right pass, they go nowhere.

Kai's jaw is tight; he keeps clenching and unclenching the muscles in his arms and fists. We're near the front now, just two cars ahead of us, and the jumpy armed guards are starting to watch him. It's good that Bryson told him what this would be like, or Kai might have exploded by now. He still might, but—

Kai's head turns; movement has caught his eye. The woman in the car in front of us is sliding across the front seat to the passenger side. She opens the door slowly and slips out of her car. The driver of the car in front of her has been arguing with the guards and refusing to turn back; now he's being arrested, and the guards are intent on him as he is cuffed, dragged off. There's a police van to the side there; he's thrown inside it.

The woman runs for the gap in the barricades. One step, two, three, and then—

"Stop or I'll shoot!" a guard yells.

She doesn't stop.

The guard holds up his gun, and—*BANG!* The woman drops to the ground.

Red is spreading on her back. She was only a few short steps away from the way out. Kai draws in his breath sharply; he's breathing in and out, shallow now. His eyes are wide.

Some of the others waiting behind us choose now as a good time to back up, to leave.

"Anyone else?" the guard who shot her yells. He doesn't look *right*. Some of his fellows check the woman lying on the ground, then unceremoniously pull her by her feet, drag her out of the way.

Now it is Kai's turn. He holds out his pass. The guard who just killed a woman walks over, takes Kai's pass, studies it. His hand is shaking.

"You can go," he says, and gestures toward the exit. Kai gets on his bike. He goes through but doesn't go straight; he swerves to avoid the patch of blood on the ground.

From then on, Kai very carefully does all the things Bryson said to do. He takes the controlled route and keeps well away from Edinburgh and other affected areas. He slows right down whenever he approaches a roadblock, gets off his bike before reaching them and takes off his helmet, holds out his immune pass. He stands back and does his best to look calm when I can tell he wants to *go, go, go*, like the wind.

When we were still close to Newcastle, the roads were almost empty, and everyone was jumpy, like that trigger-happy guard. But the farther we go, the more traffic there is and the more relaxed they are. You can tell they don't know what *cleared* means, or *collected*. There are no fires rising in the sky. Yet.

I lose track of time—has it been hours? We must be getting close by now. There are mountains. We cross over a bridge by waterfalls in a village, and a sign says this is Killin. Kai heads up a hill out of town; there is water sparkling below us. He slows down, watching the right side of the road, and turns in at a sign that says *Addy's Folly*.

We drop down a lane; there's a house below, with a car in front. Kai parks next to it, then almost falls in his hurry to get off the bike.

He races to the front door. It looks like the lock is broken.

He knocks and rings the bell but doesn't wait long before rushing in. "Shay? Shay?" he calls out. He runs through the house, top to bottom.

No one is home. But either they're very messy or they left in a hurry, packing things so fast that drawers and cupboards have been left open.

Kai sinks, defeated, onto the sofa, his eyes moving to that broken lock on the door. "Shay, where are you?" he whispers. There's a big plush polar bear next to him on the sofa, and his arm reaches out around it. "If only you could talk."

Moments later Kai gets back on his bike. There's a house up on the main road just along from the lane, and he pulls in there.

He takes off his helmet and knocks on the door.

"Hello?" A nervous voice above. He steps back. An old woman looks down at him from an upper-floor window.

"Hello. I'm a friend of Shay McAllister's. Do you know where she is?"

She shakes her head and leans forward. "Well, I heard that Shay and Moyra have disappeared!"

"Have they?"

"Oh yes. It was the talk of the town."

"Their front door lock is broken. Has someone . . . ?" And he can't finish the sentence.

"No, dear. That was the army!"

"What?"

"Well, Shay had a temperature, and they were told to stay at home. There was even an army car at the end of their lane so they couldn't leave! But when they went back to check her temperature the next day, no one answered the door, so they broke in. And they weren't there!"

She looks a little too happy to be relaying such an interesting story.

"Do you know where they might have gone?"

"No, no idea, as I told that nice young army man. What was his name?" She looks confused, then smiles again. "That Moyra had *friends* all over; they could have gone anywhere." She says "friends" like it means something else. "She didn't believe in medicine, you know. She was a very odd woman."

But Kai's already putting his helmet back on; he's stopped listening. He heads into Killin. He goes to the pub where Shay's mum worked, to the café they'd been to. He asks everyone he sees, but they all say they don't know where they are.

"What do I do now?" he says to no one. "I don't know any of their friends, or where they might—"

He stops in midsentence, starts going through his pockets and takes out his phone. Goes into call history. There's a number there from days ago, one without a name.

He hits "call."

"Hello, is that Iona? Hi, this is Shay's friend Kai. We met when— yes. That's right. Do you know where Shay is?"

I slip myself against Kai's ear so I can listen.

It's a girl's voice: "I've been trying to call her; she hasn't answered, but she's always losing her phone. I didn't think much of it."

"Listen, I'm in Killin. I came to find her. I called Shay from Newcastle hours ago, and she answered. She didn't make sense; I think she's ill. They're not at home, and neighbors say they disappeared. No one in town seems to know where they've gone. I have to find her."

"Oh no." Iona's voice is panicked. "I don't know, but—wait a minute. I put an app on our phones to find hers when she's lost it. I could try to trace her with that."

"Where are you? I'll come and get it."

"I'm at home, but it's miles away. Plus, well, my brothers have blocked the lane. They won't let anyone near the farm. They're convinced everyone has that Aberdeen flu. Oh—Shay; no. Do you think she . . . ?"

"I don't know. Maybe."

"Wait a sec. I'll activate the app and direct you."

Soon Kai is back on his bike, going another way out of Killin. Around the other side of the loch. He stops a few times, speaks to Iona again, and keeps going.

She directs him to go down what is more of a track than a road, past piles of logs, felled trees. Eventually he has to get off the bike, leave it, and follow a path on foot.

He calls Iona again. "Are you sure this is right? I'm in the middle of the woods. There's nothing here. Hello, hello?"

He curses. His phone is dead.

"Shay! Shay!" He calls out her name and punches a tree in frustration. "Shay, where are you?"

Kai's anger is something he hides behind. He needs to find her; if he fails, he won't be able to bear it.

Maybe it's because he never found me.

I have to help him.

CHAPTER 29

SHAY

LIGHT AND COLOR DANCE in beams of sunlight. There is music too: the rustling of leaves on the breeze. The beating of my heart. The movements of insects on the floor of the forest, and the beat of birds' wings. Their songs.

I'm dying.

I know I am.

It doesn't seem so scary, not anymore. If Mum can do it, so can I. She'll be waiting for me, won't she?

Somewhere near me, I hear or imagine I hear a voice. Kai is calling out to me—calling my name.

Am I a foolish sixteen-year-old for thinking that I love him?

No. It might have been just a start, but there was a beginning there. Beyond just how he looks, how I respond to that. It was the way he struggled not to cry. How he couldn't control his anger too. His good and bad, all wrapped up together, that somehow I knew needed me as much as I needed him. It was all a start that could have grown into more. Maybe it would have, if I wasn't dying.

Kai's voice calls my name again. And then there is another voice: a young girl's.

She's in here with me now. Her form is darkness. It cools my eyes to look at her.

Shay, you have to fight, she says, and she says it fiercely. *Don't give up. He can't lose you too.*

"Who are you?" I whisper.

She is still now. Staring. *You can hear me?*

"Yes. And see you." Cooling darkness; shadows in sunlight. "Who are you?"

I'm Callie, Kai's sister.

"He's been looking for you."

And now he's looking for you. But you have to help him. He can't find you; you have to call out. Say his name.

Dimly I hear "Shay" again and again.

"I can't. I'm too busy dying."

Call his name.

She's insistent, and I try. My words to Callie have been quiet, barest whispers. My voice is harsh, rusty with disuse. My mouth too dry.

Do it!

"Kai," I say. Still a whisper, one even I can barely hear.

Louder.

"Kai!" A little louder. And again: "Kai!" This time my voice is a little stronger.

Keep doing it. Scream! Remember the pain and scream it out.

"Kai!" I put all I have into the volume.

"Shay? Is that you? Where are you?"

He answered me. Is he really out there?

And again. Do it again.

"Kai!" This must be a dream, a cruel dream. He can't really be coming to find me.

But I say his name, again and again: "Kai, Kai!"

"Shay?" He's closer.

"Kai!"

And then he's there.

191

He's leaning over me. His hand is on my forehead, then stroking my hair.

"Shay?"

He's crying, and so am I.

CHAPTER 30

CALLIE

SHAY'S EYES FLUTTER AND CLOSE. Is she dying?

Kai's hand is on her throat, light, checking for a pulse. He leans over her, to feel her breath on his cheek. She is unconscious now, or she sleeps. Does that mean she will live? With others, when they could see me they died very soon after. They didn't take a nap.

She's in a weird tent shelter, and she's not alone. On her other side lies a body: a woman's body. Is this Shay's mother? Kai gently smooths the hair from the woman's face. Her eyes are open, staring and bloody, yet not with the mask of horror that some have had.

Kai picks her up and carries her away.

I stay with Shay, watching her breathe, counting her breaths, somehow knowing that the more of them there are, the more chance she has to live. And yet, apart from for Kai, I also wonder why I even want her to. She was annoying that day in Edinburgh with Kai, like he had an extra appendage that got in my way.

But she could hear me; she could see me.

Live, Shay; fight to live.

Maybe I need you too.

CHAPTER 31

SHAY

WHEN I WAKE UP, Kai is still there. It wasn't a dream.

I beg him to leave. "Please go. You'll catch it, and you'll die. Like me."

But he won't leave. He tells me some nonsense that he's immune, that his mother is too. That he came to find me.

And that I'm a survivor. That some people get this thing, and they don't die. And I'm one of them.

There is another voice; a dark figure. It says it is Callie, Kai's sister. My half sister?

But no—she must be the Angel of Death. She's come to take me away.

To join Mum.

Mum's gone. I know it, even though Kai hasn't been able to bring himself to tell me yet. Her body isn't next to me anymore; he must have moved her while I slept. But I can taste the pain of it in Kai's thoughts. And she said goodbye to me, didn't she? She caught this thing from me, and now she's gone.

The Angel of Death whispers that I've gotten through the worst; that the good and bad are finding a new balance inside me. That all I have to do now is decide to stay, and I will. But how can I, without Mum? And what if I make Kai ill?

"You have to leave me," I beg Kai. "Before it's too late."

"No. Never."

He holds me as I cry, and something has changed inside him. Some realization is there, one that mirrors mine.

He kisses me, so gently his lips are the barest brush on my skin. "Never leave me, Shay. Stay with me, forever."

And I anchor myself to this feeling inside him. Something new, and fragile, but strong enough to make me want to *live*.

CHAPTER 32

CALLIE

"KAI, WHERE'S MY MUM?" Shay's eyes are on Kai's, and he stares back at her, and the conflict is there. He needs to tell her but is afraid to, afraid she is so fragile she'll shatter like a flower caught in frost. Her skin is pale, almost translucent, her face thinner than it was, all making the pale blue of her eyes seem to take over.

"Shay, I don't know how to tell you." He shrugs helplessly.

"It's true—she's died, hasn't she?" she whispers. Her eyes shimmer and blur, with tears and more. "I hoped it was just a dream, the worst dream I've ever had. But it wasn't."

He shakes his head.

She blinks, and the tears spill down her cheeks. "She caught it from me, and she died. Where could I have gotten it?"

"I don't know," Kai says. "It isn't in Killin or this area; it's all still clear. It might have been when we went to Edinburgh—there's been an outbreak there." As the realization hits Kai fully, he's horrified. "I'm so sorry. You were only there because of me."

"Don't. We don't know where it came from," Shay says. "But tell me what I've missed. Don't sugarcoat it; tell me."

And Kai, haltingly, tells her about Newcastle and the other places. He doesn't go into the horrible details, just gives the facts, like a reporter would—about Newcastle, the army base. The city.

Shay's eyes seem to grow even bigger as she takes in what he's said. "So, this kills ninety-five percent of people. Five percent, like you, are immune. There are a few unconfirmed survivors, like Fred. But he hanged himself."

"And there's you."

"Maybe I'm still dying. Maybe I'm just slow about it."

"No. They die much faster. I've seen it; I know. I should call my mother, tell her about you—that you are a survivor. And that I'm all right. But my phone died."

Shay wriggles around, finds her phone under the pillow, and hands it to Kai. He dials.

"Mum? Yes, it's me. I'm fine. I found Shay, and that's not all—"

"Hello, hello?" He shakes his head and looks at the phone. "The battery is dead."

"At least now she knows you're all right. How did you find me out here?"

"I remembered you called me from your friend Iona's phone. I rang her to see if she knew where you were. She didn't, but she had this lost phone app on hers for your phone; she gave me directions all the way."

"It led you to me here, in the woods?"

"Well, not exactly to *here*. It landed me in the middle of the woods, and then my phone died. I was convinced she'd gotten it wrong. I just started calling your name."

"I heard you. I thought it was a dream."

"But you called back."

"Yes." Shay's eyes are searching the shelter, looking for me. I've been lying on the floor, but now I sit up. *I helped you*, I say. But she doesn't answer, and her eyes slide away from mine.

Shay, I'm Callie, Kai's sister. Her eyes snap back to mine, wondering, then she shakes her head slightly, side to side.

Please, Shay! Tell Kai that I'm here! I yell it this time, and she jumps.

197

"Shay? One more thing. There's something we need to do." Kai snugs his arm around her. He hesitates, as if there is something else he must say, but he isn't sure how to say it.

"Where is my Mum now?" Shay says in a small voice. She radiates so much pain that I flinch away from her. "Where is her body?"

CHAPTER 33

SHAY

KAI MAKES A PYRE IN THE FOREST, then gathers wildflowers when I ask him to. I know this is how Mum would have wanted it.

My legs are weak; he has to help hold me up as I dress her in spring: yellow, pink, and white tiny blossoms. I wind bluebells, her favorites, in her hair.

I hold her hands in mine and say goodbye. Hers are stiff and cold now, but they are still hers. The hands and arms and heart and soul that always loved me, no matter what.

I close my eyes and *reach out* to her—like I'm pouring part of myself into her. I don't know what I'm doing, or how, but her last thoughts are waves I can catch, imprinted from her to me. They're not full of fear for herself; they're all of me. I let Kai pull me away, and I'm washed in her love as her body is in flames.

Callie, as she calls herself, stays away, at the edges, silent. I think she is crying too.

CHAPTER 34

CALLIE

NOW THAT I'M CERTAIN SHAY WILL LIVE, I'm back to not being sure I want her around. She can hear and see me, I know she can—in so many little ways she reacts when I speak to her.

But she refuses to answer. She pretends I'm not here.

I finally found someone who can hear me, and she does her best to ignore me. It's making me crazy!

And unlike everyone else I've come across since I was cured, she isn't a blank. With other people, like Kai, I have to guess what they are thinking or feeling from their faces, what they say. With Shay, her emotions pour out of her: melted sugar when Kai kisses her; pain like burning acid when she thinks of her mother dying. So much so that when her Mum was placed on the pyre Kai made, it felt like it was my Mum—her pain tore into me so intensely, I could hardly stand it.

And she can read me too. She reacts to things I say, both out loud and in my mind.

She must be like I was, when I survived the illness. Before they *cured* me with fire. Different; changed.

I have to make her see what has happened to her. Maybe then she'll understand that she can talk to me.

CHAPTER 35

SHAY

YOU HAVE CHANGED, Callie says. *Your eyes have changed.*

I ignore her, or I try to. It's hard when she is there as clear as the trees straining for light beside me, the pulsing earth under my feet.

Go to the loch. Go and see your reflection, she says.

I resist for a while. She doesn't exist, unless I'm completely crazy. If I don't answer her, she'll disappear like the figment of my imagination that she is. A hallucination left behind from the fever—probably because of that dream I had, of Mum saying Calista is my half sister. Another load of crazy imaginings from my fevered brain.

I ask Kai, "Do I look different since I've been ill?"

He strokes my cheek lightly with his fingertips, and I shiver, almost vibrate, with the touch of his warm skin on mine. "Let's see. You're a little thinner. Try to eat more."

"You need to be a better chef. What about my eyes?"

He looks into them carefully. A sense of confused wonder crosses his face and mind, then is gone. "Beautiful blue, as always," he says, and kisses me, carefully, gently, like I could shatter with too much pressure. Or too much pleasure.

I'm unsteady on my feet. I can only stand on my own for a moment. But I tell Kai I need to wash—I do, for sure—and that I want to be alone. He helps me to the loch's edge and finally goes when I insist.

My legs are shaking. I sit by the surface of the water. The trees both stand by the water and are laid out in it, perfect replicas of vibrant wood and chlorophyll green. Leaves move in a slight breeze on the shore, or in the whisper of a wave on the water. Which are more real?

Kai's worrying continues beyond in the trees.

I'm fine, I reassure him with my thoughts, and send him away.

You're different, Callie says, and I jump. She's in front of me. *When could you speak to people inside their heads before without them even knowing?*

I frown, not answering. Is that what I did?

Look, she says, insistent. *Look at your eyes.*

I lean over the water.

Like the trees, there are two of me—one leaning over from the land, and a water girl.

What a sight. My hair is the worst mess in history. At least with being curly it doesn't sit lank on my head like it otherwise would.

But my skin is clear. Cheeks nicely rosy, as if I'd never been ill.

And . . . ? Callie says.

My eyes? I look, and look again. They're perfectly normal. My sight drifts, from water girl to what lies beneath her, the sounds and movements of fish in the loch, insects on its surface, those on the tree behind me, ducks quacking and swimming by the far shore, and then—

Not normal, not at all. When I was listening and reaching and feeling the life all around me, it's almost like a cloud passed through my eyes. Swirling weirdness, like the weirdness in my head, and then I couldn't see what was before me anymore—just what I reached to, *beyond*.

I shake my head. What madness. I take off my clothes and brace myself for the cold water. Splash it on myself, and wash as best I can while sitting on a rock just under the surface. I dip my head under cold water, wash my hair, chilled to the bone.

I stand, carefully, and just manage to walk out of the water. I dry myself with the towel I brought, wrap myself up in it and lean on a tree. What little energy I had is gone. The sun is warm today and my skin is greedy for it, but inside I'm still so cold.

You're different, Callie says again. *That's why you can hear me!*

I frown with the effort of ignoring her.

I'm shivering, but thinking about being cold isn't going to help. Instead I imagine waves of heat reaching out to me from the sun, my skin getting warmer and warmer, and waves reaching from inside me too . . .

A warm flush spreads from inside to my skin.

I'm so shocked, I let go of the tree and stand straighter. I try to take a step without holding the tree, but my legs are still weak and I almost fall.

"Shay? Are you okay?" Kai's voice calls out to me from above.

"Fine, but I'm naked," I answer.

"Don't tempt me. I'll keep my eyes shut; let me know when you're dressed, and I'll help you back up."

I so wish I could just go to him. I imagine strength flowing through my body, into my arms and legs . . . I imagine walking normally.

I step forward, and my legs are steady, my steps even and natural. Even though I'm not cold anymore, goose bumps rise on my arms.

See how different you are? Callie says. *When could you think yourself well before?*

I turn to her, almost answer, then shake my head. Maybe it was just time for me to start feeling better. It's crazy to think I *made* it happen.

I get dressed, then walk silently to where Kai stands, his eyes shut, as he promised. I slip my hands around his waist. He turns, kisses me, and I kiss him back properly for the first time. Rising on my toes to reach him better, my hand on his neck, in his hair, pulling him closer.

He forgets I'm fragile, that he must be gentle. He kisses me again and again.

CHAPTER 36

CALLIE

KAI IS CHECKING THEIR FOOD AND WATER SUPPLIES—all stuff that Shay says her Mum brought when they came here in the middle of the night.

"We've only got enough stuff for another day or so," he says.

"I want to stay here."

"Forever?"

"Yes, forever. Just the two of us."

Bleugh. More melted sugar pours out of Shay as Kai kisses her.

You're not alone, remember? I'm still here! I picture pulling Shay's hair in my mind, and she flinches away from Kai.

"We can't live on kisses," he says.

"We could catch fish! And find berries. I know the ones we can eat, how to find edible plants. Like nettles. You can make soup out of nettles. And there are wild oats and all sorts of things we can eat."

"Sounds tasty. How do you know that stuff?"

A shadow crosses her face. "Mum was really into camping, and living off the land. I used to like it when I was little; not so much lately." She's sad, thinking of times she insisted no more camping, that she didn't want to go anywhere there wasn't any Wi-Fi.

Kai hugs her, strokes her hair.

"Well, you might be a genius at all that, but I'm craving pizza. Can you rustle up one of them out here?"

She looks around at the trees for inspiration. "Probably not."

"So?"

"One more day. Let's have one more day alone. Please?"

"All right. Tomorrow, then."

CHAPTER 37

SHAY

I KNOW WE CAN'T REALLY HIDE OUT here forever. I know we're running out of supplies; that with both our phone batteries dead, people, like Iona, must be mad with worry with no word from us.

But I want to stay alone in the woods with Kai.

We have this one last night. Alone, if only Callie would go away.

When he kisses me, in that perfect moment, all the pain of losing Mum, and all the fear of returning to the real world, is held away. When he stops, it rushes back so fast it is like a sledgehammer to my gut. And what will happen when we get back to Killin? I don't want to think about that either.

I don't want to think or feel pain: I only want Kai.

But that night, when I hold him and kiss him, and kiss him again, when I want to be close and then closer, he hesitates. He says he wants me, but it isn't the right time. That I need to get stronger, to recover, and be whole again.

The pain rushes back, and he holds me while I cry.

Our last morning. We debate whether we should take the boat and go across the loch to my house, or take Kai's bike. In the end, the bike wins. He says we'll come back for the boat when I'm stronger, when I can row and he can ride and we can meet across. For now we're walking through the woods to the forest road to his bike.

I'm scared. There is the gaping loss of Mum, and I don't want to go back to town without her. What will happen to us? And what will they think of us burning her body in the woods like that? I know Kai said that is what had to be done, that she had the Aberdeen flu and this will prevent spread of the disease—but didn't we break about a hundred laws doing it on our own? And I'm underage. Will they take me away from Kai, make me live in some awful foster home or something?

We find his bike. We get on and head for Killin.

The closer we get, the more I know: the things I was worrying about should have been the last to make the list.

PART 3

THE BITE

Seek knowledge, but be wary of facts.
*They are always subject to the vagaries
of human observation.*

—**Xander,** *Multiverse Manifesto*

CHAPTER 1

CALLIE

I DON'T LIKE BEING ON KAI'S MOTORCYCLE when Shay is on it too. She's wearing my helmet; she's behind him, her hands reaching around him to hold on. I go to the front instead and sit on the handlebars.

At first we bump along slowly on a rough track, back the way Kai and I had come when we were rushing to find Shay. Kai tells Shay this must be a logging road, that this is the way that Shay's friend—Iona—had directed him to find her. Not that he would have managed it without my help. When Kai says "Iona," there is eagerness and longing in Shay. She cares for Iona, wants to see her; feelings she doesn't have for me. It hurts that the only person who can see and hear me wishes I would go away.

We leave the track for a lane that is more like a road, and now go a little faster through the trees. We climb higher and then can see the loch, stretching out below us.

We go around a bend; Kai curses under his breath and slows down. Up ahead, something moves in the road—there are two guards and a roadblock.

"It's the army," Kai says.

Shay gasps when she sees what they're wearing: they're covered head to toe in suits—biohazard suits. She hasn't seen them before? Her hands grip tighter to Kai.

Kai stops, and they get off the bike. Kai takes off his helmet and nudges Shay to do the same. She clings to his hand. One of the guards walks over to us.

"You don't want to go this way, son. The village is under quarantine."

"How . . . how bad is it?" Shay asks.

"Very bad. It's swept through the whole village." Shay's face pales. "Sorry," he says. "And if you want to go back the way you came, you'll have to hurry, or you'll be trapped. The quarantine loop is being extended."

"Let's turn around," Kai says to Shay. "Come to Newcastle with me."

Yes! Let's go to Newcastle!

But Shay shakes her head. "I can't. This is my home; I have to see what is happening."

Kai argues with her—as do I—but she shakes her head at him and ignores me.

She's stubborn but scared. She's afraid if she insists, Kai will leave her here, alone; that she won't see him again. But he can't hear what I want, and anyway he'd never do that.

"I have to see for myself," Shay says again.

"It's a death sentence," the guard says.

Shay winces, shakes her head. "Not for us. We're immune."

"Have you got passes?"

Shay shakes her head no; Kai gets out his immune pass. The guard takes it, reads it, and notes Kai's name down, then hands it back and turns to Shay.

"I haven't got the paperwork, but I'm immune too." She puts slight stress on the word *immune*, and Kai's eyebrow goes up. Why doesn't she tell him she's a survivor?

"What's your name, and where are you from?"

"Shay McAllister. I live nearby, on the other side of Killin. Across the loch."

"That's within the quarantine zone." He notes down her name. "Your say-so that you're immune will get you in, but it won't get you out. You'll have to apply for a pass if you want to leave."

He opens the barricade, and Kai pushes his bike through. Shay hesitates behind him.

Don't do it! What if you get in, but you can't get out again? You'll be stuck with people who are sick and dying, until everyone is dead. Like me.

Shay trembles and steps through.

CHAPTER 2

SHAY

I CAN'T TAKE THIS IN.

Killin—quarantined?

Kai goes slowly into town. There's no one on the street or sidewalk; no cars move on the road. The sun shines on the snow on the mountain above. We head over the bridge, and there is music in the falls like always. Apart from that there is silence. On a sunny spring day like today the village is its usual postcard-perfect self, but there are no tourists on the bridge with their cameras getting in the way of traffic.

It's a ghost town, and the farther we go, the more an overwhelming sense of dread twists around my gut.

Smoke hangs in the sky ahead as we start down the main street. In one house I think I glimpse a frightened face in an upstairs window, but when I look back again no one is there.

The smoke is coming from the park. I tug on Kai's shoulder to slow down as we near it; there are tents there too. "Pull in," I say, even though I want to ride and ride *fast*, leave this place and never come back. I'm afraid of what we will find.

He slows and stops, and I get off the bike, start taking off my helmet.

"What now?" Kai says.

"I need to go over there. See what's what." There are waves of dread, fear, and pain washing against me, like a relentless sea on an eroded coast—plucking at me, pulling at my resolve.

"Are you sure, Shay? If it's anything like Newcastle, well . . . Are you strong enough, so soon after being ill? And losing your mum. You don't have to do this."

"Yes. I do. I have to see if there is anything I can do to help," I say. Even though I struggle to say the words, I am sure that I *must* do this, that I need to know what has been happening here while I've been gone.

The whole time I've lived here, I've wanted to be back in London, but now, suddenly, I feel the shift of allegiance that has happened inside without me even being aware of it. This is my *home*. I turn to Kai. "You don't have to come with me. Wait here if you want."

He shakes his head and holds my hand firmly. "I go where you go."

We walk toward the gate of the park, not that it is really there anymore. The pillars are gone, and we soon see why as an army truck comes up behind us. We get out of the way, and it drives through a space that would have been too narrow if they were still there. There is a soldier in a biohazard suit just inside the park who speaks briefly to the driver of the truck—he's in a suit too. The truck carries on, and the soldier by the park entrance turns to us.

"What is your business?"

"We're immune. We want to help," I say, and my voice only wavers a little.

"We can use all the help we can get. Check in over there." He waves us through, points to where the truck has pulled in ahead of us.

There are tents arranged around this end of the park; smoke rises from the other end, by the tennis court. The truck has pulled in at one of the largest tents.

As we walk over to the truck, there is a sound. It is both ahead of us and in the truck, louder now that the back of the truck is being opened, and it is something I've heard before. It is the sound I made

214

when I was ill—crying, moaning, even screaming when I really couldn't take it. The sound is *pain*.

But it's not just what I can hear. The closer we get, each step I take forward, I'm assaulted by *agony*. I *feel* what they feel. It started when we drove into town, and got stronger and stronger. Now it is all I can do to stay standing upright, to not curl into a ball on the ground and scream.

Callie is next to me, staying close, and for once I don't mind. *You have to shield yourself, or you'll lose it*, she says.

I answer her inside my head. *Shield myself? How?*

Imagine there is a wall between you and the rest of the world, and they can't get through it.

Kai is speaking to the suited man who was driving the truck. He nods; I think Kai is introducing me, but I can't hear what he is saying. All I can hear are the cries of pain, reverberating inside my head. I can't think or move or breathe with the effort not to scream. Build a wall? How?

Let me help, Callie says, and then she is there: waves of cool, soothing darkness I can plunge into to avoid the fire. The flames still lick the shore, but I'm safe.

See? she says, and I do. If I visualize a barrier of cool darkness, I can still hear and feel the distress, but it's held away.

Thank you.

Do what you have to do, but I won't stay here. Callie blurs into the distance so fast she vanishes in seconds.

Kai is getting into the truck. He and the driver start helping people down and into the tent.

He passes me a little girl, maybe three years old, screaming for her mummy. There's a boy several years older climbing out of the truck himself, but each step is strange and jerky, as if he's concentrating hard to move at all.

"Is this your sister?" I ask him.

"Yes."

"Is your mummy here too?"

"She's in the other truck."

215

Another truck is driving in now, but it doesn't stop where this one did. It goes past us, continues across the park on a rutted track worn by wheels in the grass. The boy starts to chase it. The driver who came on this truck turns, catches him, brings him back; he tells me to hold the boy's hand tight and take him into the tent. Now the boy is crying too, like his sister.

The driver turns to go, but I call him back. "Why weren't they in the same truck as their mother?"

"Because they're still alive."

His words struggle for the meaning I know they have, but don't want to believe. I look across the field; the other truck is being unloaded. The boy pulls to get free of my hand, howling.

"I'm sorry," I say. "My mum died too."

He stops struggling, looks up at me with wide brown eyes.

"Come on," I say, and tug on his hand. He lets me lead him and his sister into the tent.

Along with the others from the truck of the living, places are found for them in a sea of camp beds. There are a few army nurses in biohazard suits, and several people without suits or army uniforms who are helping. One I recognize. It's the red-haired waitress—the one who was reading *Fifty Shades*. It's not that many days ago, but it seems like a lifetime. She's pale and looks like she hasn't slept in ages, but when we walk over, her face creases into a smile. She hugs both me and Kai, hard.

"Are you both immune too?" she asks.

"Yes," Kai answers.

"That's two more of us that beat this, then. I'm Lizzie," she says, "and that one over there"—she points at a man who is carrying something toward the back of the tent—"is my brother, Jamie."

We introduce ourselves, but my eyes can't stop looking at what lies around us.

Camp beds. A hundred or more, in a large open space. Most are full.

Some of the occupants are lying still, unmoving. Some are crying, screaming for help. Lizzie asks me to help remake beds now and I do, trying not to think why they are being changed. Kai is enlisted to help Jamie carry still forms away, and I avert my eyes.

My barriers are still in place and with them comes a degree of calm. Yet I feel like I'm moving underwater, like the concentrated pain and misery in this place is thicker than air.

A hand grabs my leg as I walk past to get more sheets.

It's Amy from school. Her skin is pale, her usually perfect blond hair lank.

"Shay?" she whispers.

I kneel next to her, hold her hand.

"It hurts so much." But she's not in pain, not now; she's past the pain.

Her eyes are full of tears, but then it's not tears; they're red. It's blood. Her hand slackens. Her head lolls to one side, her bloody eyes still open. They're staring straight ahead. Not seeing anything, not anymore.

But I am seeing. Amy's mother dying. Her two little brothers. Her father. She watched them all die and then was brought to this place. My barrier has slipped, and I see the pain and fear in a kaleidoscope that is spinning inside me, twisting and pulling me apart. I'm battered by Amy's pain and the pain all around us. I let go of her hand and stand up. Stagger for the square of daylight where we came in, and leave the tent. Outside I breathe in again and again, wanting to clear my lungs of the air in that place.

But then it's worse. Out here, out of the tent, smoke is still rising from the other side of the park. The place the other truck went to—the one not for the living. The wind must have shifted, and the smoke drifts this way. I didn't smell it before, and now I'm sick with it, with knowing what it must be.

The stench makes my stomach twist, and as I breathe—which I only do as much as I must—I can taste who they are burning. The sweat and cigarettes of the grumpy guy from the Co-op; a boozy overlay from Mum's jolly friends from the pub. The painful twist of sunshine and smiles of children from the playground. Soon there will be a whiff of Amy's sarcasm and perfume to add to it.

And they're all mixed up. They shouldn't be; each soul should have its own send-off to wherever they're going now. Each mother

217

should have a grieving daughter like mine did; every child, a family standing together to withstand the shock. It shouldn't be like this.

But when a whole family dies, like Amy's, who can grieve for them? Maybe it's better this way. No one is left behind to suffer.

I want to scream, to throw myself on that fire. The urge to walk toward it is so strong that I'm shaking with the effort to stay still.

Someone comes up behind me, and then there is a hand on my shoulder. It's Lizzie. She passes me a cup of tea. She stands next to me for a while. Somehow her hand on my shoulder helps my heart stop racing enough that I can concentrate and shore up my barriers.

"Do you know who else is immune?" I ask her when I'm able to speak again.

She starts listing names; some I know, some I don't. Some whole families spared. But not that many; not many at all from the whole village—how many lived here? Eight hundred, something like that?

"Does that mean . . . is everyone else . . . gone?"

"They haven't finished checking all the streets. From what I've heard, everyone they've found lately is either sick or has already died."

"What about other places near here? Like Crianlarich, Monachyle, places around them?" *Iona.*

"I don't know. There's a map on the BBC website that shows which areas are quarantined. You could try there, or one of the news channels. But I'm not sure how up-to-date it's kept."

Iona's family lives on an isolated farm miles from here. It's so remote one of her brothers had to drive her to catch the school bus.

Maybe it has missed them.

CHAPTER 3

CALLIE

I WAIT ON KAI'S BIKE FOR A WHILE, but I'm soon bored. I wish I could go to sleep. Maybe I can, if I try really hard?

I curl up on the grass by his bike and close my eyes. I try to empty my thoughts, think of nothing, but that doesn't work. Then I count sheep, but whoever came up with that was stupid. Anyway, why'd I think it'd work now, when it never did when I was alive? That's just plain crazy.

I could follow Kai or Shay around, but when I peek back at what they are doing, I soon give up on that. Shay is in the main tent, doing her best to help with the sick; she's not coping well. Kai is carrying bodies to the pyre on the tennis court, his face grim and set, like it was in Newcastle.

I explore Killin. It doesn't take long; it's small, and besides—I've been here before with Kai, when we were looking for Shay. There's a main street with shops and stuff, streets that lead off it with houses. All is quiet. Dead quiet.

Then a few uniforms walk up the road toward the park. Minutes later, another group of them comes back this way. Shift change time? I follow the ones walking away from the park.

They walk down the main street, then stop at a large tent. One of them says something to a guard outside and then they go in. There's a decontamination setup, sheets of plastic, hoses. One at a time they go through, taking off their biohazard suits and chucking them in a huge biohazard bin. None of this is as high-tech as it was underground on the island where I followed the nurses. Finally they each shower and change, and go through a door at the end of the tent.

It leads into a building. There are other army types there, looking at a big map on the wall with pins on it and red and green circles. An older guy barks at the others—he must be in charge.

There's some sort of meeting in progress between those here and other uniforms on screens.

Behind them, someone else is drawing another red circle on the map, outside the ones already there, like rings on a tree stump. But within the red rings are a few small places circled in green.

"How do you expect us to contain this increased area with the personnel we have?"

"We're all stretched to the limit. We'll try to get more to you, but in the meantime you have no choice."

"We'll have to cut back to single guards on all the roadblocks, not just the minor ones."

"Or withdraw from lost causes like Killin."

"We can't do that!"

"How many immune are in this village? They can continue what you've started."

A list is consulted. "Thirty-eight, but some of them are only children."

"There are two more to add—they came through a roadblock earlier today, though I gather they may not be staying."

"Names?"

"Kai Tanzer and Shay McAllister."

"We'll leave a command presence to enforce all containment measures. Everyone else is to pull back beyond the inner quarantine zones."

"But, sir—"

"Do it."

CHAPTER 4

SHAY

EXHAUSTED BY THE END OF THE DAY, we finally leave the village behind and head up the hill. Away from the hospital tent, away from the burning, everything looks so ordinary. The mountain stands above and the loch glistens below like they have done since long before people ever came here. And will do so long after we're dust.

Kai turns down our lane and stops in front of our house. And it looks as it always does. The sun glints on the windows I washed at the front of our house; I can see the streaks where I didn't bother doing a good job. Mum was bossing me around, and I was bored and annoyed. And that was the last normal day we had together.

We get off the bike, and then I see something that doesn't look as it should at all. "What happened to our front door?"

"The old lady at the end of your lane said the army happened. When you didn't answer when they came back to recheck your temperature, they broke in to find you."

"But all they found was an empty house."

"Yeah."

I step through the door. Mum's Buddha is there, his belly shiny from us rubbing it for luck every time we come in the house. Can't say we've been that lucky.

Callie appears at my side just when I thought we'd finally lost her. *You* are *lucky. You're still alive.*

Exactly. I answer her in my thoughts before I remember I'm ignoring her, and she smiles.

I roll my eyes. *That just proves you are a figment of my imagination,* I think at her. *If you were real, you wouldn't know what I just thought: that proves I've made you up. You're an imaginary friend, like lonely little kids have sometimes. Must be all the trauma and stuff.*

You're different now, Shay. We can share our thoughts, sense each other's feelings.

I frown. *She's not real, she's not real, she's not real . . .* I chant it to myself silently, over and over again. If I do it often enough, maybe she'll go away.

No chance.

I sigh.

"Shay?" Kai says, and it's like an echo—has he said my name over and over, without it really registering?

"Hmmmm?" I look up, realize I've followed him into the front room and sat next to Ramsay my bear on the sofa without noticing what I was doing.

His eyes are concerned, and worry rolls off him in waves. "You seemed, I don't know, to zone out, same as you did when we first got to the park this afternoon. I said something to you, and you didn't answer."

I stare back at him, afraid. I can't let him know I'm losing it; I can't scare him away.

"Just thinking about Mum," I say. And guilt slams into me that I lied and that it was Mum I lied about. He sits next to me, slips an arm over my shoulders, and pulls me close. I lean my head against his chest.

Sharing thoughts: what rubbish.

Or is it? I thought I shared Amy's last thoughts. And Mum's too—and not just as she died. Afterward too, when I was putting flowers in her hair.

222

Can I share thoughts with Kai? I *felt* his worry. But I also knew he was worried; I saw that on his face. I didn't need to read his mind to know it.

No. No way. I sigh and wish Kai would kiss me to stop me from thinking about everything.

He leans down and his lips are on mine before I even notice that was what I was thinking. But that doesn't mean anything. When doesn't he kiss me when the opportunity is there?

I kiss him back.

But didn't he want to call his mum as soon as we got here?

He abruptly stops. "I forgot. I should call my mother and let her know we're okay."

I point out where the phone is to him, and he gets up and starts to walk toward it, but then stops, a puzzled look on his face. "My head feels all wrong," he says. He frowns and picks up the phone.

I don't answer him; I don't say or think anything else. I very carefully think nothing at him at all. Did that really happen? Did me thinking about something make him think of it too?

Stricken, I look at the back of Kai's head as he dials the phone. Maybe him kissing me and all this weight of feeling between us has only happened because I wanted it to. Maybe that is all there is to us.

I shake my head; this is madness. He meant to call his mum when we got here, and he got up just then because that was when he remembered. That's all.

It can't be true. It can't.

CHAPTER 5

CALLIE

WAVES OF SHOCK AND FEAR are rolling through Shay. I remember when I first found I could control people: I told them to do stuff, and they did it. I wasn't scared of it—I loved it. I nearly got a nurse to let me out before someone stopped her.

Then they had me fitted with that mask so I couldn't talk anymore. Could I have just *thought* things at people rather than said them, like Shay did to Kai? If only I'd realized, I might have gotten away before the cure.

But once I was cured, it all ended. Now I can't make anyone do what I say; I can't even make them *hear* me.

But I put all that aside for now; Kai has just said, "Hello" on the phone. I press myself against the earpiece so I can hear Mum's voice.

"Kai! You're all right?"

"Of course. Sorry to worry you; there was nowhere to charge phones. We've just come back to Killin."

"We?"

"Shay and me."

"She's all right? You shouldn't have taken her to Killin; it's—"

"Quarantined. Yes, we know. Shay was sick, but she survived. Very sadly, her mother died."

"Are you sure that it was Aberdeen flu that Shay had? And she survived?"

"Yes, completely sure. I saw her mother's body too—there's no doubting what killed her."

"Does Shay have any other family?"

"Not any that can be reached. Her uncle was on Shetland and was taken to Aberdeen with his family; they lost contact with them."

"You must take her to whoever is in charge of the army there and explain: tell them she's survived, and that they need to get her to me as soon as possible. But listen to me, Kai: this is very important. Don't let anybody else know she's a survivor."

"Why? What's going on?"

"The only other confirmed survivors disappeared or killed themselves before we could get to them. The army can protect her and bring her to me. Keep her safe, Kai. She could be very important to solving all of this."

"She's very important to *me*."

"I'm sorry; of course she is. But in this instance, all of the human race have more of a claim to her than you do."

"Ouch."

"*Ich hab dich lieb.* Take care."

"Love you too."

"*Tschüss.*"

Kai hangs up the phone, stands there for a moment. His eyes are on Shay. She looks small, fragile. Her arms are wrapped around that big, soft toy polar bear, and she is miles away. Her eyes change; they go that weirded-out way they do when you're *reaching* around you—the blue spins and swirls. Mine used to do that; I remember the doctors and nurses saying so.

Can Kai see, or is he too far away?

He walks over to her, sits down, and takes her hand. Her eyes turn to his and are normal again.

225

"Shay, my mother says we shouldn't let anyone know that you're a survivor; that we should go to the army here and tell only them. Then they will take us to her. You might be able to help them work out how to beat this illness."

"You mean leave here? And go to Newcastle?"

"That's what she said."

"But this is my home."

CHAPTER 6

SHAY

THE NEXT MORNING, I tell Kai that I will do what his mum said we should. But not yet. There are two things I have to do before I can leave: find out if Iona and her family are okay and then do everything I can to help in Killin.

According to BBC maps on the news we watched late last night, the whole of the Trossachs is quarantined now—this includes Iona's family farm. Despite the hour, I almost called her there and then, but I was afraid.

You won't know unless you call her, Callie says. *I told you last night: there were places on that army map I saw that were green inside the red quarantine zone.*

But what if no one answers? What if . . . I swallow. *What if it's the worst: do I want to know?*

"Call Iona," Kai says, almost as if he is listening in to Callie and me. "If she's all right, she'll be worried sick about you."

He's right, and that is the thing that finally makes me do it. Kai and I charged our phones overnight, and I take mine upstairs now, to my room, and shut the door.

Callie, my shadow, has beaten me up the stairs. She's sprawled on my bed.

I sit next to her. "Can you go? Please. Let me do this alone."

She sits up and tilts her head to one side. She's darkness in light, coolness to eyes that see too much heat and color everywhere. She smiles.

Yes. Of course I'll go. And you want to know why? Because you asked me to. She gets up, walks to the door. *That is how to get along, you know. If you treat me normally, I can help you.* Her dark eyes—are they eyes, or just darker places in darkness?—fix on mine. *We can help each other.* She turns, and changes—flows under the door—and is gone.

I shake my head. I'm bonkers, completely nutzoid. There's no doubt that on the nut meter, I'm well past peanuts, walnuts, and brazil nuts—I'm right at the top of the nut chain. Coconuts: that's what I am.

But at least I'm alone.

I stare at the phone for a long time before I dial.

It rings once . . . twice . . . three times . . .

"Hello?"

"Iona?"

"Oh my God. Is that you, Shay?"

"I was scared to call. I didn't know if you'd answer, and . . ."

"Did Kai find you? Why didn't he tell me?"

"His phone charge didn't last; neither did mine. We only just got back to Killin yesterday, and home last night."

"Were you ill? I don't understand. I thought everyone who got it . . . well, that they . . ."

"Died. That's the way it usually goes. And . . . and . . . Mum died, Iona." Now I'm crying, and I *so* want Iona in this room, not down the phone line. I want someone with me now who knows me, who knew Mum, who knew us together; who knows what I've lost.

Iona is crying too. "I'm so, so sorry. I loved your Mum," she manages to get out.

"I know," I finally say, between the tears, and it takes both of us a while to get enough of a grip to carry on talking.

"Iona, you can't tell anyone what I'm about to tell you." I know I wasn't supposed to tell anybody myself, but this is Iona. Besides,

228

she knows stuff. If her networks are still up and running, if there is anything out there about this, she'll know.

"Of course. I promise."

"I had it, but I didn't die."

"Oh my God. You're a survivor?"

"Kai's mum is a doctor and an epidemiologist, part of the task force studying the disease in Newcastle. She says we should go to the army and tell them about me, and then they'll take me to her. That I might hold some key to help other people survive."

"Don't. Don't tell *anyone*." Iona's voice is sharp.

"Why?"

"There are all kinds of rumors flying around about survivors. That they're like witches or something."

"Nice."

"And that they're really dangerous: they can do things like talk to the dead and make people do stuff they don't want to."

"*Where* have you heard this stuff?" I say, automatically switching into my role of skeptic for her blog, JIT, and trying not to think about what Iona actually said. Talk to the dead? Control people?

My stomach twists. Isn't that just what I've been doing?

"Nowhere official, but people are scared of survivors. It could be dangerous to be one."

"Isn't that all the more reason to go to the army and let them look after things?"

"I don't know. Sources tell me that survivors have been taken by the army, but they're never seen again. Is that good or bad?"

"Wait a minute. Kai's mum says the army hasn't managed to find any survivors. They either disappear or kill themselves."

"So which is true? I don't like the sound of this, not one bit."

"No."

"You need to take off, Shay; hide away."

Iona's paranoia is legendary. If there's a conspiracy theory around, she's all over it. But I'm uneasy too.

"Be careful," she says. "If you need help, use JIT; you can message me there."

We talk for a while longer. Iona's family farm is in a cluster that has stayed free of the Aberdeen flu by cutting itself off. They've blocked off their private roads; one of her brothers and a neighbor guard it with shotguns. They've got generators for power and can live off the land as long as they need to.

It's ages before we can say goodbye. Every time we try, there is one more thing one of us wants to say, and another, then another.

When we finally do, when I hear the click that says Iona has hung up and then silence, I stare at the phone in my hand. Finally I put it down, grab my laptop, and enter *Aberdeen flu survivors* into the search engine.

I soon wish I hadn't.

CHAPTER 7

CALLIE

SHAY COULDN'T *STILL* **BE ON THE PHONE,** could she? Finally I give up waiting and slip under her door. She's slumped over her laptop.

Shay?

No reaction.

Almost like he's followed me, Kai walks in behind.

Shay looks up, tears wet on her cheeks. "She's all right. Iona and her family—they're all right."

He gathers Shay into his arms and holds her.

CHAPTER 8

SHAY

WHEN WE GET TO THE PARK, the army trucks are pulling out. Lizzie stands watching them, arms crossed.

"What's happening?" Kai asks her.

"They're leaving. They're just leaving us to cope on our own."

"*What?*" I say.

"It's true. They've given us a list, so we can continue checking the streets that haven't been done yet, but they won't help us anymore. They're pulling out beyond the quarantine zone."

Kai takes my hand, pulls me away from Lizzie, toward the road. "We have to tell them about you *now*. Get you taken away from here before they're all gone."

"No. Can't you see Lizzie and the others need our help even more now? We can't leave them."

"Believe me, I understand how you feel. But what if you hold an answer to all of this? What if you can stop what is happening in Killin from happening in other places?"

The last truck pulls out of the park. Kai moves to walk to the road to flag it down, and I'm furious. This is *my* life; he can't decide for me.

I won't let him.

"Stay where you are!"

He stops abruptly, caught in midstep, but he's fighting to go on to the road; I can see it in the *struggle* on his face, his rigid muscles.

The truck disappears up the road. Suddenly released, he almost falls forward.

Now Kai's fury matches my own. "What did you just do to me? You told me to stay where I was, and I couldn't move. *How* did you do that?"

"How could you go to tell them about me when I've told you not to? It's my life—my choice."

"Not when you're not making sense! There is nothing you can do here that will help. Nothing. And there may be everything you can do to help if you leave."

"You can't make decisions for me!"

"But you can make them for *me*? *How* did you even do that?"

How can I answer when I don't know? I turn and walk away.

CHAPTER 9

CALLIE

I'VE NEVER SEEN KAI SO ANGRY. Shay meddled in his head and didn't hide it, almost like she wanted him to know what she did. And he does. He doesn't understand it, but somehow he does.

Lizzie and Jamie come over with a clipboard; Lizzie brandishes it. "This is the list of streets that haven't been checked. One of us needs to go with Jamie in the truck; the rest need to get on with things here."

"I'll go," Kai and Shay say simultaneously.

Lizzie looks between their set faces. "One of you stay, one of you go."

Without discussion Shay stalks off toward the truck; Jamie follows.

"Are you two okay?" Lizzie asks Kai.

"I don't know."

"There are enough things to worry about without quarrelling among ourselves."

"Are you all right?"

She shrugs. "I'm alive. Which is more than I'll be able to say by the end of today about those who are left." She gestures at the tent.

"Some may survive."

"I haven't seen it happen, and I'm glad."

He turns to her, eyebrows up. "Why?"

"Haven't you heard? Survivors are changed. I don't think they're even human anymore."

"What do you mean?"

She shrugs. "They can talk to the dead, and it makes them crazy." She taps on her head. "They're suicidal and worse: they can make other people kill themselves too. Just by telling them to do it. Better to burn in the fire."

I stare at Lizzie. I was a survivor, but they still sent me to the fire. Did they think like she does? Is that why they did it?

Her words felt like she slapped me in the face. I slap her in the face back. She doesn't feel it, but it makes me feel better just the same.

CHAPTER 10

SHAY

JAMIE PULLS THE TRUCK IN BY THE FIRST HOUSE.

He doesn't knock, just opens the door—it's unlocked. That most people don't lock their doors in Killin makes this job easier.

He looks at me sideways and sighs. "Guess I'll be doing all the carrying today. This is what we do: check every room. Go upstairs, I'll do downstairs. Call out if you find anyone."

I start up the stairs, nervous about what I might see and feel. Even my imaginary friend isn't here; Callie stayed with Kai. I'm surprised to find I wish she were with me. Lately there has been something comforting about having her there.

Kai was so angry. He'll leave me after today, won't he? And Callie will go with him; she's his sister. There is still a core of anger inside and I hold on to it, nurse it, afraid that if I let it go the pain and fear of losing him will take over.

I head up the stairs. The first door is a bedroom. It looks unlived in, like a guest room, and it's empty.

Another door: bathroom. Empty.

I breathe a little easier. There is one more door. I walk toward it, but before I open it, I know. They're in there—two of them. There are tendrils reaching out, waves of entwined thoughts.

"Jamie?" I call out. "Up here."

A man and woman lie still and silent on their bed. Bloody eyes stare blankly ahead. White-haired; they look like someone's grandparents. And their hands between them . . . they're clasped together. Fingers interlaced.

We carry on from house to house. Bodies are piled in the back of the truck without ceremony. Jamie has a set look on his face that says he isn't here; he isn't throwing a ten-year-old girl on a pile of bodies with her mother. He's away somewhere else: at a farm, maybe, with sacks of potatoes.

It's easy to find the dead, now that I've worked out how. The tendrils I felt with the first ones are like footprints, traces of their thoughts left behind as they died—a trail I can follow. Jamie starts giving me odd looks as I unerringly lead him to one body, then another.

I can't have my barriers all the way up to find them, though—I'm battered by the fear and pain of their final thoughts. If it's true, I'm starting to understand why so many survivors kill themselves.

But then there's something new.

It's urgent; it's now.

Someone is still alive.

CHAPTER 11

CALLIE

TWO ARMY JEEPS ARE APPROACHING.

Lizzie comes out of the tent when she hears them, Kai close behind her.

"Did they change their minds?" she says. "Are they coming back to help us after all?"

The jeeps pull in, a group of biohazard-suited army types inside. One of them is the soldier who was in charge here before, but he's deferring to someone else now.

They get out of the jeep, and the someone else smiles inside his suit. It isn't the sort of smile I like.

"Good afternoon. Lieutenant Kirkland-Smith, at your service. Where is Shay McAllister?"

CHAPTER 12

SHAY

I TELL JAMIE THAT WE HAVE TO GO BACK, down the hill and around a corner. Not the street we're meant to be doing, he says; that one has already been cleared. But I insist, and he drives there.

The trail of pain is getting stronger as we go.

"Stop here," I say in front of a run-down cottage, on its own at the end of the street. There is long grass and rubbish all over the yard.

We get out and walk to the house. I hesitate, and instead of barging in, knock on the door. Then open it and step inside.

"Hello?" I call out.

Jamie looks at me oddly, but then there's a sound above us—movement. We head for the stairs.

The place is a mess and smells as though the food on the dirty dishes piled up everywhere has gone bad. There are clothes on the stairs that we have to step over to climb up.

Once upstairs we pass one open door, then another, but it's through the closed door at the end of the hall that I sense someone. I keep walking, and Jamie, used to me now, skips the other rooms as well.

I knock on the door. "Hello? Can we help?" I say, then open the door.

In the corner of the room is a boy. He's crouched down, his arms wrapped around his head, moaning.

"Hi. I'm Shay." I kneel down next to the boy, and he moves his arms away from his face.

"Well, if it isn't *my Sharona*." He hums a little, then groans again. It's Duncan.

CHAPTER 13

CALLIE

SOMETHING ISN'T RIGHT.

I'd thought Shay was wrong to not do what Mum and Kai wanted, that she should have told the army she's a survivor and gone back to Newcastle with Kai. But now I'm not so sure.

There's something about these men.

When Lizzie tells them what street Shay and Jamie are checking, they don't wait. They go to find her. The one in charge, and two with him. The other—the one who was here before—stays to help Lizzie and Kai.

They drive to the street where Jamie and Shay are supposed to be, and I go with them. But the truck isn't there.

"Has she been tipped off somehow? We can't let her get away. We should have brought more men."

They have guns inside the jeep—serious-looking guns.

"She's just one girl. She has nowhere to go. She can't get past the roadblocks, can she? They're already under instructions to hold her if she shows up at one."

"Don't forget, she's not just a girl. If she's worked things out, she could be dangerous."

"We'll get her, one way or the other."

"Let's head back to the park for now. Maybe we missed them and they've gone back there."

I sweep up into the air, looking for Shay, and the truck she and Jamie left in.

No sign.

CHAPTER 14

SHAY

WE PULL UP IN FRONT of Lizzie's tent. Because I think I should, I try to help Duncan out of the truck. He shrugs me off. He can walk, he says, and follows behind me.

Jamie drives the truck and the rest of its contents to the tennis court and the waiting fire.

A soldier approaches—the one we spoke to when we arrived yesterday—Kai next to him. But they all left, didn't they? I look quickly between the two of them.

"Did you come back to help us?" I ask the soldier.

There is guilt, quickly suppressed. He sighs. "I'm sorry, but no. I came to guide a contingent from SAR. They came to find you. They're out looking for you now but should be back soon."

I glare at Kai, but he holds out his hands—a gesture of surrender. "Mum must have told the army."

"What is SAR?"

"Special Alternatives Regiment," the soldier says, and shrugs. "The name is all I know about them."

There is a dark blur in the air, and Callie suddenly appears next to Kai. *Shay, you have to hide!* She's radiating alarm.

Why?

The others that came aren't like normal soldiers. There's something wrong about them. They've got guns, and they said you could be dangerous. And something about getting you one way or the other.

What?

"Excuse me for interrupting, but remember me—the guy who's dying?"

Kai turns and really looks at who stands next to me this time, then recoils. "Duncan? You're helping *Duncan*?"

"Of course." I help Duncan walk into the tent—this time, he lets me and leans on my arm. A wave of pain is washing through him, but somehow he manages to keep going.

"Who's your friend?" Duncan gasps out between clenched teeth.

"Kai. You met him before."

"The meathead who beat me up I remember. I mean her."

He gestures at Callie, and I'm shocked. He can see her too?

But Callie ignores him. *Shay, listen to me! You have to hide before the others get back. They'll hurt you; I could feel it.*

There are the sounds of a vehicle approaching, and Duncan and I both look out the door: it's an army jeep.

Duncan swears and spits at the ground. "I've been hiding from these camouflage creeps all week, but what would they want with you?"

I shrug, uneasy. "So why did you come here with us now? We wouldn't have made you."

"Because it was you."

I take that in, saying nothing.

"In case you have to take off, *Shay*," he says, laying stress on my name, "I have something to say. I'm sorry I've been such a jerk."

I'm surprised, and forgetting Callie and the army, turn to him. Duncan, apologizing? Another wave of pain nearly takes him over; he buckles, then stands upright again, looking at me like that is the greater pain.

"In the circumstances, don't worry about it," I say.

"Yeah, I'll carry on with dying. Can I have a last request?"

"What?"

"A kiss. Just to piss off that Neanderthal you hang out with."

"He's not that bad."

"Oh?"

Shay, you have to run; do it now. They're coming. Callie is frightened for me, I can feel it coming off her in waves, but she must be wrong. They're the army, aren't they? They won't hurt me—this is the UK, they don't do that sort of thing here. They're meant to be the good guys.

I walk to the door. The jeep has pulled in; three biohazard-suited soldiers get out. Kai speaks to one of them, then gestures at me.

They start to walk toward me, and now I can feel it—growing stronger as they move closer. The *menace.*

One of them smiles inside his suit, but it is all lips, not eyes. "Are you Shay McAllister, reported to be a survivor of Aberdeen flu?"

"Yes. That's me." I hide my reaction. "And you are?"

"Lieutenant Kirkland-Smith. Delighted to meet you."

Lizzie steps back. "You're a survivor? You said you were immune." She's scared, repelled.

"I am. Survivors *are* immune."

Duncan is somehow still propped up next to us by the door, despite the waves of pain he's emanating. He slips away from the tent while everyone's eyes are on me.

"Well, you are a tricky girl to find," the lieutenant says. "Now that we have, we'd like to take you to some doctors who are studying the flu to see if you can help."

He's lying; I can feel it. What do they want with me? "Of course," I say, a fixed smile on my face, somehow sure I shouldn't aggravate them.

Kai is at his shoulder. "I'm coming with her."

"I'm sorry, son, you can't do that."

"Nothing was said about that. Where are you going—aren't you taking her to the research team at Newcastle?"

"It's classified. I can't tell you. Now say goodbye, we've got to get on our way shortly."

Kai turns to me, appalled. "I'm sorry about earlier. I'm sorry I can't come with you."

"But this is what you wanted, isn't it? For the army to take me away."

He shakes his head. "Don't be an idiot. I want to be with you."

"Me too," I whisper, my anger at him dissolving. I fight not to cry. He gives me a hug and murmurs in my ear that he'll go home and find out from his mum where they're taking me, that he'll find a way to get to me there.

When he starts to move away, it is all I can do to not cling to him, but I have to let him go, to get him away from the menace. So he won't get caught up in what might happen next.

He gets on his bike and disappears up the road.

I walk toward the door, forcing my steps to be even, calm, measured. Two wait there with the lieutenant; another one comes up behind me, then stands next to the others.

Look away, look away, look away, look away . . . I hold images of the sunset in my mind, and they all pause and look to the west.

I take one step back, another. It's actually working!

Look away, you can't see me; look away, you can't see me; look away, you can't see me; look away . . .

Then I run for the back of the park.

I get ten paces, twenty, before they realize I'm gone. I think misdirection at them all—imagining myself running out of the front of the park. They start to run the way I sent them, but then one of them—that lieutenant—turns himself around and looks back this way. I stay close to the ground, willing myself invisible. I can't get across the park without being seen while he's there. Instead I slip into the back of the hospital tent and onto a bed.

I pull a sheet over my head, play dead.

I'm assaulted by the last painful memories of the occupants of this bed. Not one or two, but more and more.

I throw up my barriers, try not to feel or think.

Seconds tick slowly past. There are no voices, no running footsteps: they're searching elsewhere.

For now.

Shay? Callie whispers in my thoughts, and I jump again. She didn't leave with Kai? *They're checking the edges of the park and the main street, and Lizzie has gone to make tea. Slip out the front way now and they might not see you.*

I peek out from under the edge of the sheet.

The light is nearly gone. There are few, so few, in this hospital tent who are still alive. None of them are in a condition to raise the alarm, even if they wanted to.

I creep out the front of the tent and slip into shadows, heading for the front of the park.

Wait! Callie says. *One of them is coming back.*

I crouch against a low wall by the café grounds at the park entrance. Can I go past it without him seeing me?

Not likely.

I imagine a noise, back the other way, near the bridge—and send the thought toward him.

He turns to look, and I slip over the café wall.

But I'm not alone. Another's ragged breaths say someone else is hiding here too.

"Duncan?" I whisper.

"Yeah."

"Why did you leave?" His breathing is fast, but the pain is gone. He won't last much longer.

"I can die anywhere; why do it where I'm told?"

Shhh, Callie says. *He's coming back.*

I stay still. There are footsteps that get closer, then continue on past us.

"I'm sorry, I've got to go," I say.

"No problem. I'm good."

I hesitate, then crawl closer to him—give him a swift kiss on the cheek. When my lips touch his skin, I feel it all: he knows he's about to die, but he's happy—happy I did this small thing for him.

Go, go! Callie says.

I slip out the front of the café but then trip over something in the dark; there's a loud crash. I freeze.

247

Footsteps. Running footsteps, coming this way.

Now I run. No point in being quiet anymore. I take off full tilt down the street.

Duck! Callie screams, and I do. There's a loud bang, and something whizzes past my head. My ear is hot, then wet.

Are they shooting at me?

Yes.

Now there's a soldier coming the other way. I double back, staying low, but then the other one appears in front of me holding a gun. He points it at me, and all I can see is light reflecting off the cold metal, the rainbows inside it—circles of heat, and explosive force—that say it has been fired a moment ago at me. Blood drips down my neck from my ear. I'm frozen, a statue, too scared to think anything useful at him.

All I can do is give up. I stay where I am, and slowly stand up straight and raise my hands.

But he still holds the gun, trained on me. It's held steady, and he's taking sight. This is the UK; this is the *army*. He couldn't . . . he's not . . . *NO*—

Noise—fear—a blur of motion. I'm pushed roughly to the side. It's *Duncan*? There's a *bang* and his body contorts, red spreads across it. He crumples to the ground, a moment that seems to take forever.

Shock—mine and Duncan's—and pain, waves of pain, that are all his. His death was close from the illness, but this pain is all to do with a bullet ripping through his gut.

I reach for him, but now the pain has gone. Instead there is peace. His body is still warm, but he's gone.

But his last moments, his last thoughts, batter against me: *Run, Shay, run!* And he didn't think, he just reacted—he threw himself at me. He saved me.

He died.

There's a scream rising in my throat; fear and anger swell hot inside me and fling outward at the one who did this.

Run, Shay, run! still lingers in Duncan's thoughts.

I get up and run.

CHAPTER 15

CALLIE

SHAY RUNS FAST, but she's too noisy. She runs blindly, not watching where her feet go. She trips again and sprawls to the ground, breathing hard.

Stop, I say. *Wait here, behind this car. I'll check where they are. Shay? Are you listening?*

Her eyes turn to mine. She nods. "Wait. Here. Okay." She pants more than says the words, but that is still too loud.

Sorry, she thinks, catching my thought.

Just stay out of sight and be quiet.

I go back to the entrance of the park. Duncan's body lies on the road. The one who shot him lies there too—still, unmoving. What happened to him? He was about to shoot Shay, but then his body jerked like he'd been shot himself—but no one was shooting at him.

The lieutenant and the other two that came with him are there, and then Lizzie runs up.

"What happened?" Lizzie says.

"Shay attacked one of my soldiers and stole his gun. That boy tried to stop her. She shot him."

"*What?*" Lizzie says.

"We've got to find her. Where would she go?"

"Her house is off the A road above the loch."

"She's not likely to go home, not after that."

Lizzie kneels on the road next to Duncan, her hand on his wrist. She shakes her head and lets go, fury in her eyes. "Where is Kai, Shay's boyfriend? She'll go to him," Lizzie says, and now I want to slap her again.

"He was leaving Killin, going back to Newcastle, wasn't he? Alert the roadblocks on the way. If he appears, detain him and have him brought back here."

Ride fast, Kai: don't let them get you.

CHAPTER 16

SHAY

I CRADLE MY HEAD against my knees. It didn't hurt when it happened—it was just an impact and heat—but now the pain is growing. The side of my head is wet with blood.

Callie saved me. She told me to duck; if I hadn't, that bullet wouldn't have just caught my ear, giving this trickle of blood. I'd be dead.

Like Duncan is dead.

I've seen so many die in the last few days, yet his death still shocks me. He had Aberdeen flu, he was on his way for sure, but he had reached the point where the pain from the illness was over. Throwing himself at me—pushing me out of the way and getting shot in my place—brought all kinds of pain to his last moments. That bullet hastened his death in the most violent way.

He did that for me?

I don't understand. He has been beyond awful to me since I moved here; he attacked me on the footpath. Then, today, he apologizes. And he takes a bullet with my name on it?

I'm glad I kissed his cheek. Something Kai maybe wouldn't understand, but I'm glad.

Did Kai get away? Is he safe?

The night is quiet, cold. I listen carefully, but beyond bugs chirping and birds singing and the thudding of my heart, I can hear nothing. I'm dizzy, disconnecting from my body, like I'm floating away from myself.

I *reach out*. Above, to the sky; below it, to the trees, the earth, and the things that grow and burrow underneath its surface. I think I see through a cat's eyes as it prowls through gardens, and then the eyes of birds in trees, and insects that fly, crawl, or spin—thousands of pairs of eyes. Multifaceted eyes see Killin from every angle. *Where are you, Kai?*

A moth on the motion detector light watches as Kai leaves my house.

My throat catches; he has his bike gear on. He walks to his bike by the side of the house, slowly, like he's weighed down, doesn't know whether to stay or go.

Stay, Kai. Please.

The motion light goes out, and the moth flutters away. I find a spider on a web in the eaves instead. Kai—splintered by spider eyes—starts his bike, and I panic: he's leaving.

He heads up our lane as I watch from one set of eyes, then another. He hesitates at the end.

Don't turn right, Kai; don't ride away faster than I can follow. Turn left instead. Come and find me. I plead with him inside but am powerless to reach him from this far away.

He turns right.

CHAPTER 17

CALLIE

SHAY?

She's still, slumped on the ground where I left her. There is more blood on the side of her head, some dark and clotted, some fresh. Red swirls on her skin with the raindrops that have started to fall, and I panic. She can't die. She's the only one who can talk to me.

Shay! I say it loud, inside her head.

She moans, stirs.

Get up.

Why? Kai's gone. Mum's gone. Her thoughts are murky and sad, running into each other: Abandoned. Lost. Alone.

I'm still here. Get up!

I nag her over and over inside her head until finally she struggles to her feet, using the car she was hiding behind to pull herself up. She winces as she moves.

Okay, I'm up. Now what?

Get out of the rain.

Her house—*home, but how can it be home without anyone there?*—flashes through her thoughts.

No. We can't go to your house; one of the soldiers was heading there. He's probably there by now. The others are searching for you. You need to get out of sight before any of them come back this way.

Okay. Shay staggers to the corner and down a side street. She tries doors until one opens, and we go in. She locks the deadbolt behind her and leans against the door for a moment, then walks slowly down the hall, one hand on the wall, until she finds the bathroom.

She switches on the light and looks in the mirror. Her hair is wet and tangled, mud on one side of her white face and blood on the other.

I look like shit.

Pretty much.

Gee, thanks.

She takes a hand towel, holds it under the tap, and dabs at the blood around her ear, wincing as she does so. She rinses the towel under the tap, and there is a swirl of old and new blood in the water. She does it again and again, tears rising in her eyes, until it is clean. There is more fresh blood dripping down her neck now, and her ear is half hanging off.

That needs stitches, I say.

I've never been good with a needle and thread. But maybe . . .

What?

I made myself better by the loch, when I was all weak from being sick. Maybe there is something I can do now.

Her eyes go weird, black swirling into the blue. I've never seen this happen so close up before, and I stare, curious. She's looking straight at me, but can she even still see me?

Her face that was so pale goes pink, warmer—and her ear goes red and blurs, and then, where it was hanging off, it is whole. Healed and together. She blinks, and her eyes are normal again.

She looks in the mirror. *Wow.* She holds out a hand, shaking a little, and touches her ear. "How the hell did I do that?" she says, out loud this time.

I don't know. I didn't know you could do anything like that.

She walks down the hall, still holding one hand to the wall, like she'll fall over if she doesn't.

"Kai left," she says, and sighs. "Did you know?"

Yes. I followed the soldiers around and then zoomed up to your house. I saw his bike take off up the road from there.

"And you didn't go with him? Why?"

You need me more right now.

Shay is blinking back tears. "But he's your brother."

And you're my friend.

"Thank you, Callie. For helping me. For everything," Shay says, and she means it—she does; I can feel the truth in her thoughts—but I need *more*. I need her to say the words.

Am I your friend too?

"Of course. I owe you one, more than one; big time."

You won't ignore me anymore? Do you promise?

"No. Never. I thought I was going crazy, that I'd made you up, and you weren't real. But now I know: it isn't me or you going crazy: it's the whole damn world. It's gone from peanuts to macadamias and all the way up the nut chain to coconuts. The world is an insane asylum, and we're just two of the inmates, trying to work it all out."

Ha! I like that. But how about, instead, the rest of the world is crazy and we're the sane ones. And we're in this together. Right?

"Okay. Deal." She holds out her hand, and I hesitate, then put mine in hers. She shakes it as if she is holding it, and something catches inside.

Shay is my *friend*. I have a friend. Friends are there for each other, aren't they?

Then she yawns and rubs her ear. "It sort of tingles," she says, and yawns again.

You need to sleep. I'll keep watch.

"Okay. Thanks." She wanders into the front room and settles on the sofa, not wanting to climb the stairs and look for a bedroom. *Maybe the people who lived in this house died in their beds*—a nervous thought leaks out of her. *Maybe they're still there.*

I'll check, I say, and quickly search the house and report back: *No one at home, dead or alive. Go to sleep; I'll wake you up if anything happens.*

But once Shay is asleep, I rush up the road the way Kai had gone.

I reach the first roadblock without seeing him; he must have gotten through this one. I'm about to continue up the road, past the roadblock, when something catches my eye.

There, pulled in off the side of the road.

It's Kai's bike.

CHAPTER 18

SHAY

KAI LIES NEXT TO ME, his hand stroking my hair. His eyes are on me in that special way only his eyes have ever looked into mine; that warm way that tingles through my whole body and in my mouth and throat until all I can do is kiss him.

But then he's gone. My arms are cold.

He's in trouble.

I reach to find him: out and out, but there is silence, absence.

He's not here, but even worse: he's not anywhere.

A scream rises in my throat, and my arms and legs flail out. I fall off the sofa onto hardwood floor with a thump.

My heart still beats fast from my dream—but that's all it was. A dream.

I sit up. Light is leaking through under unfamiliar curtains in an unknown house—one I paid so little attention to as an uninvited guest last night that now it feels as though my eyes are seeing the neat room for the first time.

"Callie?" I say, out loud, then try again with my mind—*Callie?*

No answer, so this is a good time to think things through and know she's not listening in on my thoughts.

If she's really real—after last night, I think I have to accept this now—then I haven't been going crazy. Does that mean that all I remembered of those dreams with Mum before she died is true too?

Then Callie is my half sister, and my father is the man Kai hates more than anybody.

At least Kai isn't my half brother: now *that* would be beyond weird.

My stomach growls. *How* can I possibly be hungry with everything that has happened?

I wander into the kitchen, open the fridge, and close it again in a hurry. Something in there has gone bad.

But in the cupboard is peanut butter and in the freezer is bread. Into the toaster it goes. I'm on slice four when Callie appears, a blur that rushes down the hall and stops in front of me abruptly. She's radiating alarm.

"What's wrong?"

I followed the road Kai would take, and—

"What's happened? Is he all right?"

I don't know! His bike was behind the roadblock, but he wasn't there.

Panic rushes through me, like I'm back in my dream. They shot at me; they killed Duncan. That soldier was still going to shoot me, even when I was surrendering. What will they do to Kai? But I don't understand. They let him go, so why . . . ?

Callie is hiding something, shielding her thoughts. "What is it? Tell me!"

I couldn't tell you last night. You were too upset and needed to sleep.

"Tell me what?"

They said they'd try to catch him at the roadblock.

"But why would they do that, when they let him leave before?"

They said they had to find you, and Lizzie said you'd go to Kai.

"What?"

I was hoping he got away, that they were too slow and he was

258

through the roadblock already. *But when I went to check, his bike was there. They must have him.*

"Where is he?"

I don't know. Just now I swept through the whole village but couldn't find him. What are we going to do?

I'm shaking inside. It's me they want. Isn't it? Not Kai.

She reads my thoughts. *No! If you give yourself up, they'll have both of you. What good is that?*

"Look. The first thing we have to do is find him."

I told you, I couldn't. He's not at the park or with the soldiers that you ran away from or at the army base.

"Try again. Go!"

Callie hesitates, and then there is a dark blur where she stood. She's gone.

I sit down and *reach*. Like I did last night, I stretch out to find all the eyes in the village. Two-legged, four-legged, six or eight; I'm not fussy.

But I can't *feel* Kai anywhere. I can't see him either. And it's so like my dream that I'm afraid.

CHAPTER 19

CALLIE

I'VE BEEN THROUGH THE WHOLE VILLAGE again at blur-speed and am about to give up, to go back to Shay and tell her I failed.

But something makes me return to Shay's house one last time.

In the garden behind her house there is a bench, one that over-looks the loch.

It was empty the last time I came here, but now Kai lies on the bench. He's still. His eyes are closed. His hands are tied together behind him and to the bench.

I'm scared to see him like this, not moving. Is he all right? I can't even tell.

He has to be all right.

I kiss his cheek.

Don't worry, Kai; we'll save you. Me and my friend.

CHAPTER 20

SHAY

WE GO ALONG THE SIDES OF THE LOCH, keeping away from the roads. I'm careful to be quiet even though I'm sure the thump of my heart is loud enough to broadcast where we are. When Callie came streaming back, I'd already found Kai: I saw him through the eyes of a butterfly balanced on the edge of the bench.

He was still, so still it wasn't natural—he wasn't just asleep. His face was pale except where the skin was purpling, swelling, down one side of it. Rope tied his hands behind him and to the bench.

I longed to reach him, to touch him, so much: did it broadcast to the butterfly? She flapped her wings, circled, landed lightly on his cheek.

Still he didn't move.

I'm coming, Kai. I'd sent the thought then, and over and over again now, and with each step closer.

Callie returns. *All clear*, she says, and then goes off again—scanning side to side of the path ahead, making sure no one lies in wait.

They must have him tied up like that to draw me there. I know going to him must be a trap, that walking into it won't help either of us.

But even as fear makes me tremble and want to run fast the other way, there is nothing else I can do.

We're in the trees between our house and the loch. I can just see Kai's still form with my eyes.

Callie is back.

There's no one there! Go and untie him.

You must be wrong. Why would they just leave him like this?

I'm not wrong! Help him. She's angry. *You're afraid.*

Yes. I am. I sigh. *Callie, he's the bait in a trap. Let me try to see.*

I sit on the grass. I'd tried and failed at various points on the way to reach Kai, but had to stop walking when I did: I couldn't see or feel where my body was anymore when I reached out.

I *reach*—not to Kai this time, though I long to; not yet. Instead I *reach out* all around us. Close by to begin with, then farther away and a little more, and again. And a little farther, and . . . *there*. There is a soldier, hidden, a gun trained on Kai. It's got a scope thing on it. I scan again and again and find another hidden soldier, another gun. I open my eyes.

Callie, there are two of them. Both with guns trained on Kai. If I go there, they'll open fire. I tell her where they are as best I can; she rushes off to see for herself.

And now I reach again: to Kai.

He stirs. I'm relieved the terrible stillness he had before is gone, but it is replaced by *pain*. His head aches, his body too—there are bruises I couldn't see. He tries to move his arms but can't, and that hurts too.

Can I reach him, can I soothe him? I'm closer than I was when I tried before.

I pour love from myself into Kai, like I'm giving him an inside-out hug.

He's startled.

Kai? It's Shay. Can you hear me?

He tries to move his lips to answer.

No, don't speak. Think instead.

Shay? I don't understand. Where are you? Are you all right?

I'm close, but I can't come to you right now.

How are we talking? His thoughts are muddled; he thinks he's dreaming.

A nice dream. I caress him inside and try to take his pain away like I took my own away when my ear was hurt. I give him waves of my energy, and he wakes up more.

It really is you?

Yes. We're going to get you out of this. Just stay put.

Like I can do anything else. Who is we?

Another time for that one.

Don't do anything stupid. Leave me here—save yourself.

Can't do that. Sorry.

You didn't want to go with them. I should have listened to you.

Shay? Shay! Callie is back.

I have to go now. I imagine a kiss and feel it on my lips and his, then do the only thing I can think to do that will help him right now. *Sleep, Kai, sleep.* I send him into a deep, healing sleep.

CHAPTER 21

CALLIE

WE WAIT UNTIL DUSK.

Shay is creeping up on the first soldier. He's sitting on a log, his eyes and gun trained on Kai. Then he sneezes and turns his head, and I tell Shay to freeze until he moves his head back again.

Can she really do this?

I'm frustrated by what I am, like I never have been before. When Shay helped me find where the soldiers were hiding, I'd tried to burn both of them: fling myself through them, hot, like I did with that boy by the river in Aberdeen. But it didn't work. I can only guess it's because they're wearing biohazard suits—something in the suits must block me, just like it stops them from catching it.

If only I had a body, I could flatten him.

Could you? Shay says in my head, reading my last thought.

Oh yes. But can you do it?

Shay doesn't answer. I'd told her the soldier who shot Duncan was lying still on the ground when I'd gone back, and she said she thought she'd done something to him. She's been trying to work out what it was, not trusting that she can hit this one hard enough with the rock in her hands.

I could. I imagine his head splattered with blood, and Shay's stomach recoils from the image in my mind.

Remember who they are, and what they're doing. They'd shoot you and Kai if they got the chance. Now concentrate.

Shay is moving as quietly as she can, the whole while projecting calming thoughts at the soldier: *It's quiet, you're alone, the night is still.* I see better in the dark than she does, and I'm telling her where to put her feet, watching him, trying to get her in as close as possible.

Wait, I say, and Shay freezes. He's turned his head and is saying something on the radio in his suit, voice too low for us to hear.

He stops and trains his eyes and gun back on Kai.

We creep closer.

It's time, Shay. Do it for Kai. Do it because you have to.

CHAPTER 22

SHAY

HOW CAN HE NOT HEAR MY HEART BEAT?

Callie had pictured what to do inside me so clearly. Swing the rock as hard as I can at his head. Kick away his gun.

Me, a sixteen-year-old weakling, against a trained army killer. Yeah, that'll work for sure.

Do it!

Do it because I must.

I breathe in, focus. He obligingly moves his head back a little farther. *Now.*

I swing the rock toward his head with both hands as hard as I can, my stomach sick with dread and fear.

Just as the rock is about to connect with his skull, he twists to the side.

The rock only gets him with a glancing blow. He gets up, half staggering, but doesn't drop his gun. But I'm too close for him to aim and shoot, and instead he swings it at my head. Somehow I pull away enough that it only hits my shoulder, but pain vibrates through my body.

I fall to my knees.

He steps away, raises the gun, and smiles.

Fear, pain, and now, most of all, *anger* surge inside me. How can he do this? What gives him the right? A wave of heat and fury rises inside me and swells, then flings itself out in a rush.

He convulses and falls to the ground.

See, easy, Callie says.

I'm stunned, and acid rises in my stomach. Did I just do that? Can my anger hurt people, make someone like this tall soldier lie still on the ground?

Callie reads my thoughts. *Good thing, as you're terrible at hitting people with rocks. One more to go, and—*

"Shay McAllister!" A voice booms out into the still night. "Enough of this. Turn yourself in, and we'll let him go."

We turn toward the house. And there is the other soldier, holding a gun to Kai's head.

CHAPTER 23

CALLIE

HIT HIM WITH YOUR ANGER, like you did to this one—do it again!

But Shay is radiating fear for Kai, and that is all that is in her thoughts.

Gather your anger together again!

She tries, but it doesn't work. Is he too far away?

"Shay, your lover boy here may look dead at the moment, but I promise you, I checked—his heart is beating." The voice again. "He still lives. You have ten seconds to come here with your hands raised. Then I will start shooting. I'll start with his feet and work my way up every ten seconds."

"One!"

Shay gets to her feet.

"Two!"

Don't do it. He'll hurt you!

"Three!"

I have no choice.

Shay runs out from the cover of the trees to a clearing, and I'm scared—for her, for Kai—and there is nothing I can do.

"Four!"

She waves her hands. "Here! I'm over here," she shouts.

"Come here. Five!"

His gun is still trained on Kai, not on Shay. He wants her to go closer to him.

"Six!"

She walks toward them, stumbling on the ground.

"Seven!"

CHAPTER 24

SHAY

I QUICKLY MEMORIZE THE PATH I must take.

And *reach* to Kai. I can't see my feet or the ground anymore and stumble, but I keep walking. Not straight to them, but a bit to the side so the soldier will have to shift his position a little to shoot me.

Because that's what he is going to do, isn't it?

"Eight!"

Kai? Seemingly random images drift through his thoughts: is he dreaming? *Wake up, Kai, but don't move.*

Hmmmm. He begins to be aware, of himself, of me, here in his mind. His thoughts are sleepy at first, but then he's awake in a hurry as he remembers. I urge him to stay still when his muscles are screaming to move after too long in one position. *What's happening?*

I show him a picture of his body on the bench, the soldier, the gun. Me walking down the hill.

"Nine!"

I leave Kai and open my eyes just as I step clear of the trees.

The soldier moves his gun away from Kai and points it at me. "Just in time!" he says.

I stand there, hands over my head. Dying isn't so difficult; I've seen many people do it. But every cell, tissue, organ inside me screams to move, to fight—to *live*.

But there is nothing I can do to stop this now.

Kai opens his eyes. The soldier isn't looking at him. He stands alongside the bench and is enjoying this moment, taking his time to aim his gun at me.

Kai's feet swing out and kick the soldier hard in the gut. The gun goes off but the shot is wild, over my head. I run toward them.

The momentum from Kai swinging his body to kick is so great that the bench his hands are tied to topples over. He and the bench knock the soldier from his feet, half land on top of him.

The soldier is struggling, tangled up with Kai under the bench. There is another shot, and my heart almost stops, but it's wild again and pings into a tree.

Callie is screaming. *Hurry!*

The soldier is half sitting up and pushing the bench away when I reach them. I yank the bench back hard to slam it into his head. I kick his gun away. He falls back and lies still.

"Kai! Are you all right?"

"Shay!"

I move the bench up on its side and wrap myself around Kai. He's shaking and kissing me, even with his hands tied behind him. "I've never been so scared," he says, and I know he doesn't mean for himself.

Shay! Behind you! Callie screams.

I whip around, and the soldier is half up, his hand behind him, and then he has another gun, a pistol, in his hand.

This time the wave and the anger rise inside me in an instant: they slam into the soldier, hard and fast. He convulses and falls to the ground.

"Shay? Did you do that?" Kai asks. His eyes are wide and full of alarm and fear, but not fear of the soldier. He's looking at me.

CHAPTER 25

CALLIE

"WHAT'S THAT NOISE?" Shay tilts her head to one side, listening. *Callie, can you check?*

I rush past the house and to the road, then stream back even faster.

There's an army truck heading this way, going fast, I call down, staying up above them so I can see over the trees and the house.

Shay rushes to undo the rope that ties Kai's hands to the bench. She curses. "I can't get the knot."

It's on the lane now. Hurry!

Shay runs for the house and seconds later comes back with a knife. She hacks at the rope until finally Kai's hands are free. He struggles to his feet, looking at the body on the ground.

"Is he all right?"

Shay turns to face him. "I don't know. But he was going to kill me."

They're just standing there, looking at each other, when they should be running.

The truck squeals to a stop in front of the house, and they both turn to the sound.

Run!

They dash down the hill, into the trees, crashing into the under-growth.

Then Shay takes Kai's hand and pulls him toward some bushes. They crouch down behind them.

"Shhh," she whispers.

Callie, what's happening?

There are two of them; one of them is that lieutenant. They've just found their friend in the yard. I think he's dead. They look unhappy; the lieutenant kicked the bench. The other one has funny binocular things and is using them to look all around.

Are they saying anything?

I go to listen. The one with the binoculars is still sweeping the woods below and to the sides.

Finally he stops and curses. "There's no sign."

"They couldn't have gotten far. Larson only radioed the sighting minutes ago."

"Reinforcements will be here soon with the dogs. We'll find them."

CHAPTER 26

SHAY

WE WALK IN DARKNESS, in silence, down to the water, as fast as we can without making too much noise. I whisper to Kai that there are reinforcements coming, and dogs—that we need to get to the pier and out on the water as fast as we can.

Kai must wonder how I know these things, but he doesn't ask. I shy away from his thoughts. They are disturbed and want to be left to themselves. I don't want to think about *why*, or the way he looked at me when he knew that somehow I'd done something to that soldier. But I block that out: I can't think about what I did and keep putting one foot in front of the other at the same time.

I'm dizzy. All I've eaten today is toast and peanut butter, in a morning that seems long ago. Kai must be hungry—and thirsty—too.

The stars aren't out tonight; they're hidden behind clouds. Let's hope it stays that way when we're on the water. But for now it makes finding our footing difficult.

We've just reached the shore of the loch when Callie reappears in a blur. *Hurry! Another truck has arrived, and—*

She doesn't finish the sentence before the baying of dogs fills the quiet night.

"Run!" Kai says. "In the water."

Will that stop the dogs from being able to follow us? I gasp at the icy coldness as we splash along up to our ankles. I hope the dogs are making enough noise to cover ours. Finally we see the dim shape in the dark that is the pier. Our boat is still across the loch. If our neighbor's rowboat isn't here, I don't know what we're going to do. Swim?

There is crashing through the trees above us; barking, shouts. A light flickers and bobs in the night.

They're getting closer.

We scramble down the pier. I almost cry with relief when I see the rowboat. "Get in!" I say to Kai, and fumble to undo the rope. I follow him into the boat and push against the pier with an oar as hard as I can.

"Let me," Kai says of the one set of oars. He takes them and starts rowing hard.

There's splashing as the dogs find our scent at the water's edge, more splashing as they follow it along the shore. So much for that putting them off—it doesn't work as well as it does in the movies. I'm sure they can't follow our scent as we move away from the shore, but they're so close now that they're lit up by the flashlights of those following. They'll follow the dogs to the pier, shine their flashlights out on the loch, and have us in the sights of their guns, won't they?

We're pulling away, stroke by stroke. Kai's arms are straining with effort.

The dogs are getting closer. The pier is in the light now; the dogs are on the pier. They run to the end, barking.

Light shines out on the water, to one side, then the other, but it doesn't quite reach us.

You can't see us, you can't see us, you can't see us . . .

I'm chanting the words in my head, willing it to be true.

Then shots sound around us in the water, and I almost scream. We both drop down in the boat.

But the shots are wild, all around. They *can't* see us; they're just taking potshots in the dark. And they soon stop.

I touch Kai's hands, motion that I'll take the oars now. I row slowly, slipping them in and out of the water as quietly as I can.

You can't see us, you can't see us, you can't see us . . .

"How did you know they were bringing dogs?" Kai whispers, so quiet it's a barest breath.

Callie is next to him, arms crossed. *I told you about the dogs. Tell him I'm here!*

"We'll talk later," I whisper back to Kai.

But how can I tell him about Callie, after everything he's been through? All the stuff I have to tell him about me is hard enough. How can I tell him his adored sister has died, that her ghost has been with us all this time and I've said nothing about it until now?

I can't.

CHAPTER 27

CALLIE

I GLARE AT SHAY, but she's ignoring me again, something she said she wouldn't do anymore.

"We're nearly across to the other side of the loch now," Shay says softly.

"Where should we go?"

"They might take the dogs around the shore to try to find us. I wonder if we can put them off?"

"How?"

"We left our boat not far from here. How about we go there, pull up the rowboat. Run up to the road, then back again the same way. Get into our boat."

"So if the dogs find the rowboat and follow our trail up to the road and then our trail ends, they'll think we've somehow driven off? Good thinking."

Shay is warm at Kai's praise.

You said you'll talk later, I remind her. *What will you say?*

Her warmth falls away.

Shay maneuvers the rowboat to the shore. Kai stands in the water to pull it up, into the trees, by Shay's boat.

"Fancy a jog?" she says.

"Not really. But I don't think we should take our time."

They run, not worrying about being quiet now, crashing through the trees, up the slope to the mining road. They pause there, gasping.

"Easier back down," Kai says.

"Yeah, right."

They run back down to the boat and pull it into the water. They get in.

Shay is still gasping, holding the side of the boat, as Kai pulls away from the shore.

"Now I know you like to bike up steep hills, so I'm guessing that run isn't the problem," he says. "Are you seasick?"

"No. Hungry sick, I think. And thirsty."

"So am I. Do you think it'd be safe to drink from the loch?"

"I don't know. But if we don't have some water soon, we're going to be sick anyway. I think we should risk it." She dips a hand into the cool water and drinks, again and again. Kai watches, then he does too.

"Time will tell, but it's made me feel better for now," he says. "You're the local: where to next?"

"Maybe we need to rest before we can work that out. There's a place we can try. Stay near this shore and keep heading away from Killin."

Shay gets her breath back and takes the oars when they are near where she wants to go: a sort of house on the loch. She maneuvers the boat up to a ladder that reaches down.

"What is this place?" Kai asks her.

"A crannog—a house on stilts in the water. Used centuries ago by Scots as homes. They're meant to be good for defense."

I don't think much of it.

The sun is just starting to lighten the sky enough to see a sort of wooden structure. Calling it a house is too much; it's more like a floating round shack on stilts. It's big enough, but looks like a good push would knock the whole thing over.

It's sturdier than it looks, Shay thinks at me.

Kai ties the boat on a long rope. Then Shay goes up the ladder to the top while Kai perches on the lower rungs and pushes the boat with an oar until it is out of sight under the crannog.

Kai climbs up. Shay gestures, and he follows her inside. She takes out her phone, puts on the light, and shielding it a little with her hand, shines it around. There's a circular seating area in the center with low benches, and they sink down on one—next to each other, but not touching.

"How'd you know about this place?" Kai asks.

"We had to come here with our history class. It's like a museum. But I knew you could get into it from the loch because I heard some teenagers meet up here to, you know . . ." Even in the dim morning light her face visibly reddens.

Shay is shivering. Kai sighs, shuffles closer, and wraps an arm around her shoulders. She droops against him.

"Time to talk?" he says.

"Yes," she whispers.

"So. What the hell is going on?"

"You think I know? The army seems to want to kill me."

He shakes his head. "None of this makes any sense."

"Tell me what happened to you."

"I got to the roadblock and was stopped. Told to wait. Then two soldiers in a truck—not ones I'd seen in Killin before, though they came from that way—told me to get in their truck. They said you'd shot and killed Duncan."

"That's not true! They shot at me when I ran away. Duncan pushed me out of the way, and they shot him instead."

He touches a hand to her cheek. "I never believed it could be true; I thought it must be some terrible mistake. Then they took me to your house. By this time I'd worked out they weren't the good guys, and tried to get away—not very successfully. They beat me up pretty good. When I came to, I was tied to your bench."

"I'm so sorry." Shay's eyes have tears in them. "It's all my fault."

"You're not the one who beat me." His hand absently strokes the side of his head. "But the pain is gone now. What's going on, Shay?

279

I thought that I felt you in my mind, like I did on the street in Killin. That time it was like you stopped me from doing what I wanted to. Today, it was like you . . . made me feel better, sent me to sleep. Later you woke me up, showed me what was happening in time for me to kick that soldier who was going to shoot you. Am I imagining these things? And . . . and what you did to that soldier? You just looked at him, and he fell over. Did you do something to him?"

"I don't know how or what, but I think I must have."

"Lizzie said survivors can control people, and a load of other crazy stuff."

"Something in me *has* changed since I was sick. There are ways in which I'm different—both the way I think and things that I can do. Like talking in your mind. I can reach out to the world around me; I see things differently."

"Can you read my mind?"

"No. Well, sort of—more your feelings, and your thoughts when you project them at me."

"Don't." Kai's voice is sharp.

"Okay. I won't, I promise." *I'll try not to* leaks into Shay's thoughts.

"And don't *ever* tell me to do stuff I don't want to do."

"I won't."

"Though if you want to help me get rid of a headache again, I guess that's okay."

"Sure. But I'll ask first?"

"Yeah. That's it. Unless I'm unconscious and tied to a bench. Then you can use your judgment." Kai half smiles; Shay tentatively smiles back.

"What happened to that soldier . . . I don't understand," she says. "I thought he was about to kill me, and something in me just kind of snapped and lashed out."

"That is on the side of freaky."

"Yeah. I'm pretty freaked out by it myself." Shay slips her hand into his. "But I'm still me."

Kai hesitates, kisses her forehead lightly, then her lips. "You kiss the same. At least I think you do; I might have to check some more to be sure. But is that everything? Is there anything else I should know?"

Tell him about me!

Callie, I can't.

You said you're my friend.

I am, but—

But what? I'm furious. *How can you be my friend and not tell my brother that I'm here?*

Think what it would do to him; really think. Then if you still want me to, I will.

No amount of thinking will change my mind. Tell him!

CHAPTER 28

SHAY

"THERE IS SOMETHING ELSE I haven't told you. This is really hard to talk about and will be even harder for you to hear." I swallow. "We're not alone right now."

Kai looks quickly around us, as if someone has crept in without him noticing.

"No, not like that. You can't see them."

"But you can?" Kai has a look on his face like he's trying to listen to what I have to say, but he thinks I've gone coconuts.

"Yes. See and hear too. You remember you asked me how I knew the army was bringing dogs? She went and listened to them and told me what they said."

"She?"

"She. Without her, I'd be dead. She saved my life; she got me to duck when they were shooting at me. It's—I'm so sorry to tell you this, Kai. It's your sister."

He recoils. *"What?"*

"She's here, right now. Sitting next to you on the bench."

He turns and looks at Callie, but what does he see?

Nothing.

"This isn't funny."

"No. But it's true."

"Lizzie said survivors can talk to dead people. Are you saying Calista's *ghost*"—he shudders—"is here, right now?"

"Yes."

"No. You've gone too far. What is with you?" He's angry. He stands up, walks away toward the door, as if he can't stand being so close to me a second longer.

"But Kai—"

"No! I don't want to hear it. You must have some sick need for attention or something. All this stuff is made up. It has to be."

"It isn't, I promise!" *Callie, help me.*

How?

Tell me something I shouldn't know.

He's at the door now.

I had a glass teddy bear—it was my favorite.

"She says she had a glass teddy bear—that it was her favorite."

He stops walking, turns, face stricken. "It broke. It fell off the dresser and broke."

It doesn't matter.

"She says it doesn't matter."

"Calista? Are you really here?" He's looking around the room, as if by looking hard enough he'll be able to see her.

I'm really here.

"She is."

He shakes his head. "No, no; this is too much. It can't be true."

He's distressed, and without thinking I *reach out* to him, to comfort him—

"No! Keep out of my mind, Shay. I warned you." His speech is more clipped, the German accent I normally can't really hear coming through.

"I'm sorry," I whisper.

Tell him! How I used to go to his soccer games with a book on my knees. Tell him! And how he has models hanging from his ceiling of bikes. That he made them.

And I repeat everything Callie said.

"I told you all that!" he says, anger in his words. "When you asked about my sister, were you just storing up details to parrot back?"

I step back as if I'd been slapped. I shake my head. "No, of course not! And you never told me anything about stuff in your room."

"Let me ask her something, then." He turns, arms crossed. "What did I give her for her last birthday? I was late with my present; I gave it to her just before she went on that last trip with Mum, before she disappeared. No one saw it; she left it in her room when she and Mum went away. To keep it safe, she said."

"Callie? What was it?"

I don't remember!

What?

Stuff that happened to me has mucked up my memory.

Try, Callie!

I don't know.

"She says she doesn't remember—her memory has been mucked up."

"Yeah. Sure."

He starts walking out the door. There is fury on his face, tears on mine.

How can he not believe me?

Because he doesn't want to. He doesn't want to think his sister has died.

Wait! I think I know. Was it a silver dolphin? A necklace?

"Callie says a silver dolphin! On a necklace."

He turns around, tears on his face now too that he doesn't try to hide.

"Calista?" Kai whispers, and she goes to him—she wraps her dark arms around him.

"She's here; she's with you right now," I say, and take his hands and put them around her even as it tears into me inside, knowing how much this truth is hurting him now. Will it help him heal in the long run? I hope so.

I shield my thoughts from Callie. Are there more things I should tell Kai, so there are no more secrets between us? That Callie is my half sister. That she and I share a father—a man he despises.

No—Kai doesn't need to know this. My mother fled before I was born to keep me away from my father; she said there was a wrongness inside him. Kai's opinion of him backs her up, and I trust both their judgments. He's not really my father, not in any way that counts.

Though there was something about him that day we met . . .

In Edinburgh. We met in Edinburgh at the university. I'm careful to keep the shock from my face when the realization slams home: the Aberdeen flu is all over that part of Edinburgh.

My father is almost certainly dead. He most likely died before I even knew who he was.

Thinking this gives me a weird, uneasy feeling. Despite my conclusions about him, despite everything, the thought that he is probably gone sits strangely in my gut. I don't know how I feel about it.

And what about Kai? Maybe he wouldn't look at all this in quite the same way. Maybe he'd want to know who my father is.

But he's had too much—*way* too much—to deal with today.

I bury these truths down deep where Callie won't spot them. I go to Kai and hold him.

CHAPTER 29

CALLIE

THEY SLEEP THROUGH THE DAY while I keep watch, their arms around each other. There is mist in the morning that creeps from the loch to surround us, so that the land—the world—is no longer there. But the sun burns it away in the afternoon, and all is revealed. A thin bridge to the shore. A building and fence above, and a road. I watch it, but no one comes.

I slip out now and then to see what the army is up to. No more uniforms have come to the area since the ones with the dogs last night; altogether, there are six of them and three dogs. They're taking the dogs around the shore of the loch, barking and snuffling and running back and forth. They find the rowboat Shay and Kai left behind and the path they took up to the road. From then on they concentrate on the road and the places it leads. Shay's trick seems to have worked.

And the whole time I'm waiting and watching, I'm thinking.

I should be happy that Kai knows I'm here, but I'm not. He was so upset. I didn't think of that. I thought he'd be happy to know I am with him, but he wasn't. And he wanted to know how I was taken away, but I couldn't tell him. I don't remember. And then I didn't want to tell him anything else that happened to me, the stuff I do remember. It would just upset him more.

Shay knew how he'd react, didn't she? She tried to tell me, but I wouldn't listen.

But I know where I was. I know it was Dr. 1 who did this to me. And I know he got away. Just thinking about him makes me start to burn inside, so much so that I'm afraid I'll burn down the crannog by accident, and I go sit on the shore instead.

If I tell Kai and Shay about him, they'll want what I want, won't they? Especially if they think it is their idea.

The sun is low in the sky again when they finally stir.

Kai sits up and droops, head in hands. "I feel like I'm hungover, and I haven't had a drop," he says. "My head—ouch."

"Can I try to make you feel better?" Shay asks shyly.

He's uneasy, but she pulls him to his feet, pushes him down to sit on the bench. She slips behind him and rubs his shoulders, neck, temples. He sighs, leans back into her, and her arms go around him. He twists his head around, and she leans down and he kisses her.

Bleugh! I say.

Shay pulls away from Kai and rolls her eyes.

"What?" he says.

"Callie said '*Bleugh.*' I don't think she's into watching us kiss."

He shakes his head. "I can't get my head around this. That Calista is here."

Callie, not Calista.

"She likes to be called Callie," Shay says.

"I know. Sorry, Callie. Her father called her that, so I didn't." A shadow crosses his face when he says *her father*, and something flits

287

through Shay's mind, but the thought is gone before I see what it is. "But if that is what she wants to be called, Callie it is." He shrugs. "Anyhow, I need to know when she is watching. Seeing us kissing isn't something my little sister should be around for."

Give me a three-second warning, and I'll go away!

Shay smiles.

"What?"

"She says she'll go away if we warn her first."

He half smiles. "That requires advance planning."

"Speaking of planning, what do we do next?"

"Okay, let's analyze this situation."

"Sure."

"So, Mum says we should go to the army. She tells them you are in Killin. They then try to kill you, knock me out, tie me up, and use me as bait to try to kill you again. This is not normal army behavior."

"No."

"And I'm pretty sure Mum wasn't expecting it either."

"I hope not. That'd be a bit of an extreme reaction to your son getting a girlfriend, wouldn't it?"

"Huh."

"Iona said not to tell the army I was a survivor, that survivors go missing."

"Mum said they disappear before they can be brought to her, so they're not making it there. She wanted you to be taken to the research center in Newcastle. How about we go there on our own?"

"But how do we know the same thing wouldn't happen again with the army once we get there? And this time your mum might get in the way."

"What else can we do? What she wants—what everyone *should* want—is to find out what causes this illness before it spreads any further. She says she needs you for that."

I know where it came from.

"What?" Shay focuses on me, and Kai looks between her and the space where I am.

I know where the illness came from.

Shay repeats what I said. They look at each other, and Shay turns to me. "Okay, tell us, then."

It came from where I was. The islands where the huge explosions and fires were.

"Shetland?"

Yes.

"Explain."

So I do, with Shay repeating what I say to Kai. That we were in a research institute underground; that they made people ill on purpose and then watched as they sickened and died.

But I didn't die; I survived. Like Shay. That's how I know what it is like to be as she is now.

And then they cured me.

When I tell them what that means—the sealed room, the fire—Kai is furious. Shay's eyes fill with tears.

And then the sickness spread in the medical staff. There were accidents—explosions underground that became explosions above ground too. It escaped.

"In the news, they said the Shetland disaster started with an earthquake—that it damaged the oil reservoir, made it go up in flames," Shay says. "Maybe the same earthquake destroyed the underground research institute as well."

"That could be," Kai says.

"I don't get it," Shay says, frowning. "Why would anybody deliberately make people sick in some sort of big experiment?"

I heard a nurse say they were looking for a cure for cancer.

Shay relays what I said.

"But they can't experiment on people, even to find a cure for cancer—not like that," Kai says.

"Not legally, no. That must be why it was hidden away. Callie, how many people were there who were made ill?"

I don't know. When I got there we were all in a big group, all ages, maybe thirty of us. I saw another group being infected after I was cured. Oh, wait: there were these numbered bags of ashes of people. There were over four hundred of them.

"So many." Shay is horrified. "When I told Iona about Callie, she said there's been a surge in missing persons in northern England and Scotland the last few years. How long has this been going on?"

I don't know.

"If this is all true, then the Aberdeen flu didn't actually start in Aberdeen," Kai says.

It's true! Sick people from the islands took it to Aberdeen.

"Callie says it came with sick people from Shetland to Aberdeen."

"Mum has to know this. She said identifying the starting point and path of the illness was really important in working out how to stop it. We have to tell her."

"But none of this explains *why* they were trying to kill me. Was it just because I'm a survivor of this illness they created?"

"I don't know."

There is someone who may know. The doctor who was in charge.

"Who was he?" Shay says, and Kai looks at her, raises an eyebrow.

I don't know his real name. They all called him Dr. 1. He had a house on the island; I went there looking for him after I got out. There was a desk full of his stuff. Maybe if we go there, we could figure out where to find him.

Shay relays what I said. "If he was involved from the beginning, he may know how to stop it," she adds.

"Well, it's not like we've got anything better to do," Kai says.

"Yeah. Hiding out in a crannog could get boring."

"Plus, I'm starving. The catering here is shit."

"Nonexistent, you mean. But you *can't* tell your mum where we're going."

"I have to!"

"Think about it. She told the army to come and get me, and how did that turn out?"

"She didn't know what would happen. She couldn't have."

"I believe you, Kai. But if she doesn't believe us about what the army has done, she might tell them where we are going and think she's doing the right thing. Even if she doesn't, they might be listening in, or they could try to make her tell them what we're up to. You can't tell her."

Kai stares back at Shay and eventually nods. He sighs. "You're right, but she'll be so worried. And what if the army catches us before we get there, and nobody knows what we know?"

Shay tilts her head to one side, thinking, then nods. "You're right. We need to get word to Iona."

"You can't call her either—doesn't the same reasoning apply? She's a known friend of yours. They could be watching her, or listening."

Shay shakes her head. "She has a blog under another name—no one knows it is hers. I can log in and put up stuff only she'll see; it won't be on the internet. We *have* to tell somebody what we know."

"What if they're monitoring her internet usage too?"

"She's got it all teched up in a major way; some friend of hers who is a total computer geek set it up to be untraceable. She said it bounces around the world. They can't trace it, I promise you."

"How do we leave Loch Tay without getting caught?" Kai says. "There are roadblocks, so we can't go by road. There are dogs that can follow us if we go on foot."

"We could bike, off road? Could dogs follow us if we were on bicycles?"

"I don't know. Maybe they could: they seemed to follow us okay when we were wading in water."

Shay nods. "Okay, let's think about this. What if we drive out of range of where the dogs will be looking for us, but go off road before we hit the roadblocks? We could get another car once we're out of the quarantine zone, or maybe bicycles would be better. We could stay off road, use the bike route to the coast, and worry about how to get to Shetland once we're there."

"All right. So, first up we need to get our hands on a car to get us away from the dogs."

"Yes. We'll have to scope out the best place to try that we can easily reach from the shores of Loch Tay. Callie can help us work out where is safest."

They continue to talk about what to do, and how, and when, but I leave. I tell them I'll watch the road to see if the army is moving

291

about again, but really I just want to get away from Shay so I can think without risking her listening in.

Can we really find Dr. 1?

I want to find him, wrap myself around him, and make him burn.

I want to watch him die, screaming in pain like so many others have done—and then, just before he dies, he'll be able to see me, hear me. And I'll tell him who I am, what I've done to him, and why.

I

WANT

REVENGE.

PART 4

THE FALL

Once all possible solutions have
been eliminated, the impossible
becomes not only possible,
but probable.

—Xander, *Multiverse Manifesto*

CHAPTER 1

SHAY

WE SLIP OUTSIDE AT DUSK. Kai climbs down the ladder and pulls the rope to haul our boat out from under the crannog. He steps into the boat, and it rocks wildly in the water. Once it settles I follow him down the ladder and get into the boat with not much more grace. No food for a day and a half and my hands and feet are wobbly and uncoordinated.

"Ready?" Kai whispers.

I nod, and he starts rowing—pulling us away from our hiding place and out into deeper water. His strokes are calm, sure, quiet. He hasn't eaten for longer than me, and has coped with being bashed on the head and tied to a bench for a day, but still keeps going.

I watch him as he rows. The stars are out tonight; the colors around them are bright to my eyes and reflect on the water, on Kai. His muscles flex in his arms as he pulls the oars through the water; his hair curls at his neck, and my fingers ache to reach out and touch him.

"Stop it," he whispers.

"What?"

"Looking at me like that. I'm trying to concentrate."

Callie reappears from checking on the soldiers. *Three of them are still in the area. One is at your house with the dogs; they seem to be asleep. Two are on the move: one going between the roadblocks above the loch and the other below the loch. Kenmore is clear.*

"Callie says we're good to go," I say, and give Kai the thumbs-up. He turns the boat to the right, toward Kenmore.

It's a small village, about the farthest point from Killin on the loch. It wasn't within the quarantine zone when we first arrived in Killin, but it is now. It hasn't been cleared, and Callie told us earlier that there are bodies there, and sick people, and now that the army has pulled out—apart from those who seem to be here to find me—no one is helping them.

Kai pauses in his rowing.

"Do you want me to take a turn?" I ask.

"No. I'm fine. I was just thinking: we should throw our phones in the loch. They'll be traceable. We can't use them."

"Oh. Okay." I sigh and take it out and run my fingers over the cover, then struggle to take it off. Mum gave it to me. It's a polar bear design, like Ramsay, and I can't let it go. Something catches inside at all the things I'm leaving behind for the unknown. But with Mum gone, does any of it really matter?

The case goes in my pocket, and our phones slip into the cold waters of the loch.

Soon we're nearing the pier at Kenmore. I feel it before I see the village: the pain, the dead. I have to block it out. Callie says she'll keep watch on us from above, and zooms up into the sky.

Kai maneuvers the boat near the pier, and I step out, slip the rope around a post. He follows.

It's time to steal what we need.

We walk down one street, then another, looking for likely houses to try. Some are empty, or only occupied by the dead; others have the sick and dying inside them. I keep my barriers up most of the way, just loose enough that I can still sense which is which, so we can avoid the latter.

We try front doors, back doors, sometimes windows, and let ourselves in to one house after another, trying not to think what has happened to those who lived here. It's hard, when what is left of them is often still there.

We find and wolf down cereal bars and fruit, anything we can eat quickly, and stuff small backpacks with more food and bottles of water. We hunt for clothes that almost fit and change into them. There is a shelf of maps in one house, and I quickly memorize relevant ones and then leave them behind.

I've always had this photographic memory, but since I was sick it seems to be even more precise. I can glance at a map and see it in my mind, and more: I can integrate it with other maps and information and manipulate it all. It's like everything I ever knew is there, accessible, just when I want it; there is none of this having to hunt around in my memories to try to find what I need.

I scavenge through handbags and drawers, then even the pockets of the dead, for smartphones—ones with a decent charge and no security code. I find five, and then I've had enough of this grim task. That will have to do. Kai leaves me where I found the last one while he goes to look for a car. I turn off all but one of the phones, then wrap them over and over in plastic in preparation for the river crossing. The one I left on I use to log in to Iona's blog, JIT.

In the draft blogs section is one headed: Are you all right?

I hit "edit."

Shay: We're fine. We found out that the Aberdeen flu didn't start in Aberdeen; we're going to Shetland. There was an underground lab there, doing questionable research into finding a cure for cancer—the flu started there. We're going to try to trace the doctor who was responsible.

I hit "save," trying to work out what else to say, but then another edit drops in while I'm thinking. Iona must be online.

Iona: Wow. What a scoop!

I snort.

Shay: Gee, thanks!

I save it and wait a moment, then hit "refresh." A new edit appears.

Iona: Sorry, so glad you're both okay. They said you are a murderer—what a pile of shit. Are they after you because of what you know? Soldiers came here, all suited up, and had a big standoff at the blocked road before my brother and our neighbor decided best let them in. They spoke to all of us—demanded to know where you were—and searched the house, the barns. We pointed out we had barricaded the road before the area was even quarantined and that no one had gotten in or out since then. Until they turned up, that is.

I bite my lip as I read what she's sent.

Shay: Oh my God, Iona; I'm so sorry that happened.

And I'm also appalled, chilled to my gut. If they hadn't let them in, what would the soldiers have done?

Iona: Don't be, I'd die for this scoop. Tell me all you can as you go. I'll spread it around my sources to make sure it is known through networks, so if anything happens to you or me they can spread it around.

Shay: Iona! DON'T SAY YOU'D DIE FOR IT!

I internet-shout at her, all in capital letters.

Iona: Sorry. Figure of speech, yada yada. Have you worked out how to get over the sea to Shetland?

Shay: Nope.

Iona: This you may not know yet; it's just been in the news: the whole of the UK is quarantined now. Our coastline is being patrolled by our coast guard and navy, and beyond that by an international UN containment force.

Shay: What?? How are we going to get there now?

Iona: There's always a way; there've been reports of boats slipping through and making it to other parts of Europe. I'll see if I can come up with something. Check in when you can. I'll delete this thread when we're done.

Shay: Isn't this secure?

Iona: Yes. But I'll delete it anyhow. Take care of yourself and that hunky man. (((hugs)))

Shay: (((hugs)))

I stare at the screen a moment longer, then hit "refresh"; the post is gone. I'm shaken, and I'm scared for Iona, her family. For Iona to delete *anything* to do with a story shows that she's scared too, and she is the one person I know who is never, ever, scared of anything.

Kai is back.

"I found a good car by an empty house but couldn't find the keys. We're going to have to widen our search."

"Okay. Let's make it fast."

We take the stolen packs and supplies and head for other streets, ones we've avoided so far because they have too much pain—from the still living.

"That one?" Kai gestures at a dark-colored four-wheel drive. We peer through the car window, just in case we're having a lucky moment, but no—there are no keys in the ignition.

I walk up to the door, look at him, shrug and knock.

No answer, but there is *pain* inside the house—even through my barriers I can feel it, rippling out all around.

The front door is locked. We go through a gate; the back door opens. We go in.

The downstairs is messed up, like someone has had a temper tantrum and thrown everything they could. Quietly we hunt around on surfaces, coat pockets, drawers for keys, but no luck. I gesture toward the stairs; Kai reaches out a hand to my shoulder, motions that he'll go first.

Up the stairs in a bedroom, lying next to a dead woman, cradling her in his arms, is a man who is the source of the pain. His eyes are wild.

"Who are you?" he gasps. His death is near, so near that drops of blood shine red in his eyes.

I step around Kai. "Hi. I'm Shay, this is Kai. We're hoping it'd be okay if we borrow your car, but we can't find the keys."

He laughs. Which is quite a feat for someone who is dying and in pain. "Why should I tell you where they are?"

"Does it matter anymore?"

"No. But that's not the point."

I glance at Kai, not sure what to say.

"It's like this," Kai says. "We've found out where the epidemic started and that someone did it on purpose. We're going to find the guy who was in charge. We need a car for that."

The man tilts his head to one side. His face, which was contorted before, suddenly relaxes: the pain has gone. He breathes easier, and so do I.

"Why didn't you say so?" He gestures at a bedside table. "In there, second drawer. But there is one condition."

"What's that?"

"If you find him, kill the bastard."

"It's a promise," Kai says, and he says the words with so much truth in his voice, so much hate, that it makes me take a step back. He opens the drawer and grabs the keys.

By the time we leave the house and start the car, I feel its owner let go upstairs—he's dead.

When we head up the road, Callie rejoins us.

"Where are the soldiers now?" I ask her.

The one above the loch is heading away from us, toward Killin. You should have enough time to get to your turnoff before he comes back again.

Kai drives out of Kenmore slowly, lights off. Callie scouts the road up ahead again, and I know all the soldiers in the area are accounted for and none of them are near us, but I still hold my breath, convinced an army vehicle will loom up in the dark. But the road stays clear.

We reach our turn—a winding, narrow road, barely used at the best of times, let alone now. It goes up, to quiet places in the mountains, higher and higher above Loch Tay.

CHAPTER 2

CALLIE

KAI DRIVES SLOWER THAN ANYONE has ever driven in the history of cars. He's making sure he doesn't have to brake, so the brake lights don't come on. We creep up, past a huge dam that gleams in the night, and keep going higher. The road is even narrower now, and finally he stops altogether and puts on the hand brake.

"It's too dangerous. Without the lights on, I can't see the road at all."

"Really?" Shay is surprised. "I can—the stars are so bright."

They are to us, maybe not to him?

"I can't drive, but I'll steer," Shay says.

"That sounds dangerous too."

Shay punches Kai in the arm.

"Ouch! Callie, is the soldier below us still on the same road?" Kai says, speaking to me directly, and I smile.

I'll go and check!

I find the solider on the road by the loch, heading toward Kenmore now as part of his endless circuit back and forth.

I return. *He's still by the loch*, I say, and Shay relays what I said.

"How far are we from the roadblock at the bridge now—about three miles?" Shay says. "Maybe we should start looking for a place off road we can leave the car out of sight. Can you check the roadblock above again too, Callie?"

I zoom up the road, higher and higher, and reach the point where this narrow road meets another. There is a bridge over a river, and the roadblock is there. There's a little hut and one suited-up guard in it, and I swoop down to check on him.

That's odd. He's out of his hut and talking to someone: there are two of them. There's always been just one every other time I've checked.

They seem to be saying goodbye, and—oh. Is it shift change time? The other one is staying, and the one that has been there all day is getting on a motorcycle, and . . .

Taking the road down to Killin.

I blur past him, back to Kai and Shay, and stop with an abrupt bump.

A soldier from the roadblock is coming down the road this way on a motorcycle.

"What?" Shay says.

He'll be here really soon!

"Callie says a soldier is coming this way on a motorcycle."

"We need to get off the road and hide."

"Do we have time to double back to the dam, park down there, and hope we're not spotted?"

A light appears in the distance, then disappears again as the road dips down.

No.

They scramble out of the car and grab their packs.

"Follow me," Shay says. "I know the paths. Callie, tell us what is happening!"

They run down the road a little way until they reach a path, and they only just clear a rise and dip down behind it when the light of the motorcycle reappears in the distance. He gets closer and then must see the car. He stops and gets a radio out.

I rush to listen.

". . . stopped on the road, above the dam. Now checking."

301

He comes forward slowly, lights on, then gets off his bike and checks inside the car and around it with a flashlight. He holds it up to shine all around.

Then the radio comes out again.

"There's no one here. Suspect someone has gone on by foot in attempt to avoid the roadblock and breach the quarantine zone. Call in reinforcements to monitor river-crossing points. I'll come back up to assist."

CHAPTER 3

SHAY

THE WAY IS HARD TO SEE, even for me; harder for Kai. I slow so he can keep up without wiping out on the rocky path, even as everything inside screams *go, go, go!*

Callie returns with a blur. *He stopped and called for help, and went back to the roadblock.*

"What did he say, exactly?"

That they'll monitor river-crossing points.

I repeat what Callie said to Kai.

"What now?" he says.

"We could lie low for a while down here. But what if they bring the dogs?"

Shhh, Callie says, and I hold up a hand to Kai. She disappears, comes back a moment later. *There's someone with funny binoculars up the hill.*

"Funny binoculars? Can they see in the dark—like infrared or something?"

I don't know. Maybe. Wouldn't be much point in using them if they couldn't see.

We shrink down.

"I think we should head back down toward Killin and do a wide loop before we go back up and cross the river," I whisper.

"The dogs are in Killin. We'll be getting closer to them if we do that."

"Got a better idea?"

"No."

We change direction, head downhill, away from where we want to go. We reach the woods above Loch Tay and disappear in the trees while Callie goes to check what's happening again.

She's back moments later. *There are five of them up above now. Two watching the higher paths with binoculars, two along the river, and one at the roadblock.*

"And the dogs?"

Still asleep at your house.

"That's weird. I'd have thought getting the dogs up to the car to follow our trail from there would have been the first thing they'd do."

None of the soldiers from Killin have come up. It's just the two from the roadblock, and three more that came from that direction.

So maybe they didn't tell the ones down below with the dogs? I frown. I can't think what this means.

CHAPTER 4

CALLIE

SHAY AND KAI DECIDE TO STAY HIDDEN in the trees through the day and sleep. I keep watch. There are still five uniforms above. Now one is at the roadblock, three are stationed near the easiest places to cross, and the last one is walking back and forth between them, sweeping around him with binoculars. No one from below comes to join them, and the dogs are still in Killin.

When dusk falls, Kai and Shay hike back up, up, until finally they are near the river. They decide to leave their packs behind, tucked under some bushes. The water is high and noisy, rushing and tumbling against rocks in the river, and trees on flooded banks—it'll be hard enough to cross without them. But first Shay gets out the plastic-wrapped phones they'd found and zips them into her jacket pocket.

They creep closer to the river.

He's on his return walk now. Be quiet.

Thanks, Callie, Shay thinks, and gestures to Kai to stay silent.

Footsteps approach, and light sweeps across the water down below. Footsteps recede.

Okay: go now.

Shay nods, and they creep out and hurry down the slope toward the riverbank. Kai slips, and rocks clatter down the slope.

He's coming back!

Shay grabs Kai's hand, pulls him down against a dip in the ground, and they shrink down in the darkness.

A beam of light sweeps over their heads, then back to the water.

The soldier stands there for a moment but doesn't radio for help. Finally he turns around and goes back the way he came.

Okay, he's gone: go!

They stand again and reach the riverbank.

Kai swears softly when he sees the river, dimly lit by the stars: the swirls, the eddies, the rocks. "Sure this is the best place to cross?"

"Callie says it is—that all the easier places are watched. Nothing else to do, right?" But I can hear the fear in Shay's voice.

They clamber down the bank, slipping and sliding on wet stones into the water. Both gasp when they go in. Kai pulls out to the center with a few swift strokes, Shay slower behind him, both of them being swept far downstream by the current at the same time.

But Shay's not in control in the swirling water, not at all. Her head dips under the water, then she comes up, coughing.

The rapids are getting closer.

Swim to the bank!

Her thoughts are muddy and panicked. She's not trying to swim; her arms are flailing. She swirls around again.

Her head disappears under the water.

CHAPTER 5

SHAY

MY LUNGS ARE BURNING, and I'm so, so cold. There are funny spots in my vision—round, like little bubbles that form and vanish and re-form again. Callie's panicked thoughts prickle at the edges of my awareness, then fade away.

The surface of the water rushes above. I'm pinned down by the current. There are rocks just under the water, forming a channel it rushes through, and this current is pulling me down; I'm almost wedged between the rocks. Straining against them and clawing up with my arms, I manage to break the surface of the water and gasp in a gulp of air, but then the water closes over my head once again.

Why is this happening? I'm bemused and annoyed. The fear is gone. My consciousness is slipping away. The strength of will to not breathe in is almost broken, and all there is to breathe in is water.

Water, full of fury and life. I *reach out*, all around me.

The cold and crush of the current on my body recede. I dance with tiny amoebas spinning in the current; flash silver with fish that flit below and look up at my feet.

They know the way. From one set of eyes, then another, I focus on the rocks and the water itself, the patterns and swirls and eddies.

The current that holds me under the surface of the water rushes downriver to rapids and waterfalls: there's a shortcut channel below me that goes underground through rocks. That's why the water pushes relentlessly down, down: both current and gravity draw it this way to plummet to the falls.

I need to move downriver just a bit more, past this rush of water plunging down through the channel, and then the river should let me come up again.

I return to my body, and the oxygen deficit slams into me once again. *Do it, Shay,* I say to myself. I feebly maneuver my body sideways to move along the channel—and I'm pushed both downriver and farther under the water's surface. Fear makes me want to claw upward, but I make myself head down and forward instead—until I reach a point where the water pushing down and water rushing forward are equal, and I'm held still.

Go forward a bit more, Shay. You can do it.

One final pull against the rocks, and I'm past the battling currents. The water rushing forward has me now, and I kick up to break the surface. I gasp air into greedy lungs again and again.

But I'm being dragged to the falls, closer and closer—no strength left to fight it.

None.

I'm sorry, Kai.

I spin toward rocks near the top of the falls.

An arm reaches out, grabs my shoulder. Kai pulls me against him, nestled against rocks in the middle of the river.

I'm coughing.

"It's okay, I've got you. I've got you." He says it again and again as if he needs to hear the words as much as I do.

The soldier is coming back! Callie says.

I cough, try to tell Kai. Then give up and point at the bank we came from.

"He's coming?"

I nod.

"We haven't got time to get the rest of the way across without being seen. We'll have to go around the side of these rocks and hold on to them tight, hide behind them so he can't see us. Got it?"

I nod, terrified at the thought of going into the current again.

"Callie, tell us at the last moment when we have to go. It'll be hard to hold on there for too long. Shay, you can just hold on to me, okay?"

Panic is swirling inside me faster than the river.

Shay, you'll be all right; Kai's got you, Callie says. *He won't let go.*

Seconds pass that seem long.

Now!

I signal to Kai, and he pushes us around the other side of the rocks, back into the current. It pulls and plucks at us, but my arms are around him, and he's holding on to the rocks so I'm pressed between him and them.

A beam of light sweeps over the rocks where we're hidden; it seems to hold there forever. Finally it moves on.

Kai pulls us back into the shelter of the rocks, the current holding us there again. He's breathing hard.

You have to cross the rest of the way before he comes back. Go!

"We can do this, Shay," Kai says. "We're close, so close. All we have to do is get across this little stretch of water fast and get up the bank before he comes back."

Shay?

I don't answer either of them. I can't think and breathe and move at the same time.

"Ready?" Kai says.

I nod.

"Hold on to me."

He turns, and I put my hands around his shoulders so I'm holding myself against his back now; he pushes off with his feet, hard, against the rocks. We swirl into the current and I fight to not panic, to not scream and make things worse than they are.

Not that they can get much worse. The roar of the falls is loud in the night: they're so close. The River Lyon wants us for dinner.

Kai struggles to pull us across the water to the shore before the falls, and I have no physical strength left, no way to help, but—

I close my eyes and *reach*—pour waves of energy into Kai. All that I can.

We jerk in the water; I open my eyes. Kai is holding on to a tree branch, pulling us out of the water and onto the riverbank, inch by inch.

We lie there, gasping. I'm unable to move at all, half in and half out of the water.

Get down!

A beam of light sweeps over the river, closer and closer to us. Does it shine on our legs in the water?

If it does, the soldier doesn't see. The light carries on, past where we lie.

With Callie urging me on and Kai's help, we somehow manage to pull ourselves to our knees. We scrabble up the riverbank and far enough away that the soldier's flashlight won't find us when he returns.

We're soaking wet, covered in mud, cut from the rocks, scratched from thorns on the bank. Frozen, shaking, and exhausted.

But we made it: we're out of the quarantine zone.

CHAPTER 6

CALLIE

I FIND THEM AN EMPTY HOUSE. It isn't hard; I'd have thought since we're not in the quarantine zone anymore, since people won't be dead or sick, that they'd all be at home and tucked up in bed. Not so. It looks like they've run. A whole village near the river is a ghost town.

Kai breaks a back window and climbs in, then opens the door for Shay. The hot water had been turned off, so they have to switch it on and wait for baths, then scavenge clothes.

Kai is recovering quickly, but Shay is limp and shaking; she can hardly move. She's not talking to Kai or to me.

Kai holds her, helps her eat a few bites of canned fruit and cookies raided from the kitchen, but she holds up a hand and wants no more.

"What happened?" he asks her. "You disappeared under the water for so long. I was sure . . ." And he can't finish his sentence. He's shaking now too.

"Sorry," she whispers. "The current held me down, until I found a way around it."

He wraps himself around her, and I don't wait for Shay to tell me to go, to leave them alone.

I go.

CHAPTER 7

SHAY

THE SUN FEELS GOOD ON MY SKIN. It's cold, but I'm warm from my legs going around and around on the pedals. I can't believe how fast I recovered from the river crossing: a good sleep and eating everything we could find, and I was fine. But I know how close I was to dying, and not just from drowning. If I'd given Kai any more of my energy, there would have been nothing left to keep my heart beating.

Yet somehow nearly dying makes the sun and the bike ride even better.

Kai bikes alongside me. He glances over and grins. "It's good to see you smile."

"It's crazy, but I feel like I'm on vacation. I've always wanted to take the bike route up to Inverness. Mum wasn't into biking and wouldn't let me go on my own." My smile falls away.

He reaches a hand across, lightly touches my arm. "Well, we're here, now; might as well make the most of it. Callie, is there anything to worry us up ahead?"

Callie disappears.

"She's much happier when you ask her to do stuff than when I do."

"I keep thinking there'll be roadblocks, or army."

"Me too. Though this area is free of the epidemic, and we're miles and miles from the quarantine zone now." We've gone over sixty miles from the zone, past Loch Rannoch and on into the Cairngorms National Park, from Dalwhinnie to Aviemore, and every little place on the bike route along the way. And there's been no army and no roadblocks. The odd person we've seen hasn't seemed to be worried that we were there, at least not beyond the weird looks they'd give to anyone they didn't recognize. It all feels so *normal*.

Callie is back. *No army, no roadblocks. A village a few miles ahead with shops and pubs and stuff.*

My stomach is growling. "Maybe we could get something to eat? Something hot. What do you think—good idea, bad idea?"

"Hmmm. Well, no one seems to care when we pass by, so why would they if we stop for a while?" Kai says. "Let's do it!"

When we reach the village, we find a small pub with a bike rack outside. We go in and sit by an open fireplace.

I pull out the next phone to check in with Iona, and log on to JIT. There's a new post: Traveling in Scotland and need a quiet place near the sea? Try Elgin. I recommend Café Marbles. Ask waiter Lochy for recommendations.

So Iona's friend works at a café in Elgin, near the sea that we need to cross. He must know the way.

I delete her post and add one of my own: Iona is Awesome.

I turn the phone off. We'll find a place to dump it later. I try not to think about where we have to go and why, and pretend: we're on vacation, aren't we? We didn't escape the quarantine zone and break into a house, half dead. We didn't steal clothes and food and bicycles, and set out for Inverness a day later on an impossible mission. Instead, we planned this ages ago and got everything together carefully. We even researched places to eat along the way, and thought we'd try this one today.

We order. Kai holds my hand, and it feels like we're any boy and girl on a date, and all the things that have happened lately fade away.

Sleepy and warm, I close my eyes, lean on his shoulder, and he slips an arm around me. Without even meaning to, my mind drifts; it *reaches*.

It's so hard not to reach to Kai inside. He never said anything about what happened on the river, when I gave him my strength: maybe he didn't know? Maybe he also doesn't know how close I came to going too far, to giving him all I had.

Anyway, that was an emergency: he doesn't want me to touch his mind, he's made that plain enough. But it's like the one place I most want to go is off-limits.

I send myself out, around us, instead—to the trees in the yard, the insects, the birds. A robin is hopping along the window ledge, looking in, and I watch from his eyes—see Kai and me sitting warm inside from his perspective. The robin abruptly turns the other way—ah, a car is coming. A police car.

I stir, open my own eyes. "Don't turn around, but a police car has just pulled in outside the window," I whisper.

"Probably a coincidence," Kai says.

The waitress brings our lunch. "Here you go. Enjoy!"

Callie? What's the policeman doing?

Chatting to someone across the road. He looks relaxed.

I start to relax a little and dig into my pie and fries: my first hot food in how long? And it's good.

He's crossing the road again; I think he's coming to the pub now.

He walks through the door, and I can see him for myself. He looks around, says hello to a man sitting at the bar. He talks to the waitress, then sits at a table on the other side of the fireplace.

I glance at Kai and he nods, ever so slightly. He gives me a reassuring look—one that says it's all right.

He's just here for lunch, Callie says. *Policemen have to eat too. They need energy to chase all the criminals.*

Like us.

The waitress brings him a sandwich. She's walking back across the pub when the old guy at the bar says, "It's time for the news: put it on. There's meant to be a press conference today."

315

She hits a switch on the bottom of an ancient screen that is hung over the bar.

"Just in. The quarantined areas are increasing in Scotland and northern England. This from our reporter at the quarantine zone perimeter."

A reporter in a biohazard suit looks at the camera and describes the new boundaries. A map goes up, and the waitress gasps: "That is so close to us."

It switches back to the studio. "Now to Norway. A ship with over a hundred refugees from Scotland has evaded the coast guard and containment cordons, adding to the numbers that have already landed. Coastal quarantine camps are being stretched to the limit." Her eyes focus away from the camera a moment.

"We'll return to that report soon; the prime minister's press conference in London is about to begin."

The prime minister's face fills the screen. She's smiling, like she always does, but doesn't look like she's slept much lately.

She starts reading from a prepared statement about the challenges facing us all, about how they're doing all they can to find a cure for this terrible disease. Then she looks directly at the camera.

"Stay calm, stay where you are. The best thing we can do to stop the spread of this epidemic is for people to avoid travel."

The waitress looks over at us. "Where did you two come from today?"

Everyone in the pub is looking at us now.

"Not far. We've biked up from Aviemore," Kai says, which is true, but it wasn't our starting point.

Everyone visibly relaxes. There is no quarantine anywhere near there. I find Kai's hand under the table and give it a squeeze.

"Heading back there, are you?" the policeman asks.

"Yes, sir," Kai says.

He's looking at me, the policeman. I half smile, try to look ordinary, not to look scared.

"Are you from around here?" he asks. "You look familiar."

"Me? No, Aviemore," I lie. "London originally."

He nods and goes back to his lunch.

I want to get out of here. I look at Kai, move my eyes toward the door. He gives a slight shake of his head. Would it look odd if we bolted?

I try to finish my pie, but it's like dust now.

The policeman's phone rings. He picks up the half of his sandwich he hasn't eaten yet, waves at the waitress, and heads for the door.

I breathe easier again. The news is still on and has moved to local stuff now. I stop paying attention until a new report makes me take notice with a rush of fear.

"The hunt continues for a Perthshire girl wanted for questioning in connection with the shooting death of seventeen-year-old Duncan MacFaddon in Killin last week."

My ears hear the words, and my eyes are drawn to the TV screen. It's me. A school photo, one I hated from last year, is plastered across the screen. I sit forward so my hair falls over my face and glance around us. The waitress is wiping a table; the old guy is taking a swig of beer. Neither is looking at the TV.

The waitress turns back to the bar just as my face disappears from the screen. She goes behind the bar and into the kitchen.

Kai is standing, putting money on our table. My hand in his is clammy as we walk to the door.

We step outside.

"Move normally," Kai hisses, pulling back on my hand when my feet want to *run*.

We walk across the front of the pub. The police car is still there; the policeman has his phone in his hand and is tapping at the screen. We start to walk around him toward our bikes.

"Wait!" a voice calls out, and I jump. Kai turns; it's the waitress. "You forgot your change," she says.

"Keep it," Kai says—smiles and waves.

The policeman is putting his phone in his pocket. His face has changed; it is cold, serious. Eyes intent on me. He steps forward.

"Shay McAllister?"

317

CHAPTER 8

CALLIE

THEY RUN: KAI AND SHAY, full tilt back to the path in the woods they'd biked up earlier. The policeman is on a radio now, even as he runs after them, panting. He's had too many pub lunches, though; they'll get away. They are pulling away a little already, off the bike path now and dodging between trees. Shay glances back and then—

Crack.

She's run into the low branch of a tree. She crumples, slowly, to the ground.

In the time it takes her to fall, Kai has almost left her behind, but then he realizes she isn't following. He turns back—just as the policeman reaches Shay.

Run, Kai! But he can't hear me and rushes to her.

"Shay? Shay?" Her face is white, and blood trickles down her forehead. She doesn't answer.

"What did you do to her?" Kai demands, with rage in his words.

"Nothing—she ran into an overhanging branch. Don't try to move her. And you're under arrest, and so is she. Give me a sec." He's calling an ambulance, and for backup, breathing heavily all the while.

Run, Kai, before it's too late!

But Kai just holds Shay's hand.

CHAPTER 9

SHAY

I'M DRIFTING. I can hear voices that fade in and out, like someone is turning the volume up and down. Someone holds up my eyelids, one after the other, and there is a bright light shining at my eyes that I can feel more than see. Then my body is moving, even though it's not me doing it. There are hands; my head is strapped to something. I'm lifted up.

Kai is angry about something. I try to focus on what he is saying: he wants to come with me? But then his words fade away.

Later I hear voices again. Someone calls my name, and my eyes flutter open. I'm in a bed with high metal sides. A room with light walls. There's a woman in front of me wearing a white jacket. Am I in the hospital? I try to move, to raise my head, but there is pain like a drum beating inside my skull.

"Stay still, Shay. You've had quite a knock to your head—best not to move around too much. I just need to ask you a few questions."

I can't think of any I want to answer just now.

"What day of the week is it today?"

I'm confused; why are they asking me that? "What?"

"What year is it?"

I close my eyes, pretend to lose consciousness again, and soon the voices go away.

My head throbs with pain, but it's still nothing like as bad as when I was ill.

I can get through this. Can I fix myself like I did after I was shot in the ear? I let my mind drift, and try to *reach*, inside, but it hurts too much. I can't do it. I'm tired; I need to sleep.

When I wake up again and risk peeking under my eyelashes, it must be night: the place is relatively quiet, the lights dimmed. I'm alone.

Through the window in the door, someone stands in an alert kind of way. Am I under guard?

Where's Kai? I need to get out of here and find him.

But the pain still beats a drum inside my head. My thoughts are heavy, confused; I can't do anything when I'm like this.

When I healed myself before, I just kind of *reached* and did it instinctively, but now the feeling for what to do is gone. How do I fix what is wrong when I can't focus?

I have to try.

My pain ebbs and flows with each heartbeat, with the surge of my blood. Eyes closed, I *reach* for that, inside.

My heart contracts, pushes blood through my body. Red blood cells travel to every tissue, swapping oxygen for carbon dioxide in a merry, chaotic dance that is as it should be.

Focus in: where is the pain? There are white blood cells too, and sticky platelets, called to heal the wound on my forehead. But the bruising and swelling behind the injury is the cause of the confusion and pain that intensifies with every heartbeat.

Look closer: every constituent of my body is made up of molecules, then atoms; particles within atoms. Particles dance and spin, all in their own perfect trajectories. I'm lost from my purpose, and spinning with them . . . for how long, I don't know. There is something *else*, some other flickering weirdness I can almost sense, and I want to go deeper and deeper . . .

But then I remember: waves. It was waves of heat inside me by the loch that warmed me; waves of healing for my ear; waves of energy I gave to Kai.

Waves I can shape and send to heal the injury on my forehead.

They hurry along the healing process, yes, but also channel the swelling away, soothe the inflammation, reduce the pressure I feel with each heartbeat.

It works: the headache eases.

I open my eyes, caught in wonder. I did *that*? Used the smallest particles inside me as healing waves? It's like how light can be waves but can also act as particles: this is the reverse—particles inside me acting as waves. Now, there's a use for quantum physics that my physics teacher would never have dreamed up.

Is that how the other freaky things I can do work too?

But there's no time for this now; I've got to get out of here.

Through the window in my door, the guard still stands in the hall. He's facing the other way.

There's a blanket over me, and I stir a little, afraid of the worst. Yep, great: I'm in a hospital gown, and there is no sign of my clothes.

Is Callie here? *Callie? Callie?* I cast out with my mind, but there is no answer, and no sense of her being nearby. She must have stayed with Kai.

I've gotten so used to her being able to check our surroundings that I almost forgot that I can do it myself. Eyes closed, I *reach*: not inside this time, but out, and all around.

There are people asleep in other hospital rooms around me, and the guard outside my door. A nurse at a nurses' station down the hall. A phone rings; she answers it.

Elevator doors open, and a man steps out. He speaks to the nurse; the guard outside my door walks down the hall toward the other man. I'm tempted to bolt out the door while he's distracted, but there are two of them here now, and even though I might have fixed my concussion, I wouldn't bank on being able to outrun anybody just now. The last time I healed myself, I could barely walk straight afterward.

I listen.

"I don't know why you're guarding that girl," the nurse says. "She's had such a knock to her head—severe concussion. She'll not be going anywhere."

"Orders." The one who was outside my door yawns. He nods at the newcomer. "Happy to leave you to it now."

He gets in the elevator and is gone.

The new one borrows a chair from the nurse, settles it outside my door. She goes back to her station.

I *reach out* to him gently, not wanting him to be aware I'm there. His mind is full of what he meant to be doing tonight instead, involving his girlfriend, and it's enough to make me blush and want to retreat.

Instead I send thoughts of sleep, of being tired, so tired. He yawns.

The nurse walks past. She laughs softly. "I won't tell anyone if you want a few zzz's. I'll wake you if anything happens."

A bell rings and she walks quickly down the hall to another patient's room.

Yes: sleep, sleep, sleep . . . I'm doing such a good job I almost send myself to la-la land.

The nurse walks past again. She chuckles to herself but says nothing. He's not asleep properly, just in the drifting place before sleep, but I get out of bed cautiously, wanting to try my feet. I hold on to the bed for a moment, then walk across the room and look through the window in the door.

Now he's actually snoring.

I can just see the back of the nurse's head down the hall. If I can get out the door, I could go down the hall the other way to avoid her.

I prop pillows under my blankets, hoping that to a casual glance through the door it'll look like I'm still in bed asleep. I ease the door open, but Sleeping Beauty is half leaning on it, and I have to prop him up a little against the door and then the wall, afraid he'll wake up. He keeps snoring.

The nurse is on her phone now, her low voice echoing around the hall.

I tiptoe down the hall the other way, past one room, another, and another.

323

A bell rings.

I duck into a room, hoping it isn't this one that has called the nurse, but there is a sleeping shape on a bed, breathing noisily.

Footsteps go down the hall, past the room I'm in now: either the nurse didn't look through my door or she was fooled by the pillows.

I'm cold in this hospital gown. There's a cupboard in this room. I open it, keeping an eye on the occupant of the bed. Inside hangs a purple cardigan and purple stretchy trousers.

I sigh. Any port in a storm?

I take the gown off, slip on the trousers—too wide around the middle and way too short—then pull the cardigan on and start buttoning it up.

"Not sure purple is your color, dear."

I jump violently. Sitting up in the bed is an old woman, probably in her eighties.

"Sorry. I—um—"

"Are you escaping?"

"Sort of."

She claps her hands. "How exciting! I wish I could too. Have a good time, dear." She lies back down in bed and is asleep again almost instantly.

The nurse walks back down the hall to her station. I wait a few moments, then peek out into the hall.

The guard is still asleep.

I tiptoe, feet bare, and realize I didn't think to look for shoes. But I'm not going back.

There's a stairwell at the end, and down I go.

Hospitals are one of those places where people wander around at all hours of the day and night, in all manner of attire, and no one takes any notice. Or so I tell myself. I head through the emergency room. It's full of people with fun things like broken arms and knife wounds and appendicitis—not that fun to them, maybe, but so much better than what the sick people I've been around lately have had. There are so many patients and too few harried staff; it seems like the best place to not be noticed.

There is a TV up in the corner of the waiting room, and the news is on. I walk faster, scared my picture will flood the screen. But instead it is an update on quarantine zones.

The patients and the medical staff all seem to pause in whatever they are doing, to look up at the screen, to see if it is coming their way.

I can't stop myself from pausing and looking too.

No way—it's all the way to Aviemore? The river we crossed after we left Killin is nowhere near the edge of the quarantine zone now. That zone, that is: there are zones spreading out from Aberdeen and Edinburgh too; in England and beyond.

And there are small numbers of cases scattered around Europe, North and South America, Asia, and Africa. Australia and New Zealand alone are still completely free of it.

Only when people around me start talking about the zones in hushed voices do I come back to myself and remember what I'm supposed to be doing.

I slip out the door and into the night.

CHAPTER 10

CALLIE

KAI PACES IN HIS CELL.

The muscles are standing out on his jaw, his arms; his fists are clenched. And there is nothing I can do to help him.

Everything is so messed up. I didn't know whether to go with Shay or go with Kai, and I couldn't ask them because Shay was knocked out and Kai can't hear me.

There are footsteps in the hall, and Kai goes to the door again. "Please, somebody tell me if Shay is all right!" he shouts.

No one answers.

He punches the wall and then stands there, holding his hand. He shakes his head and sits down.

"Callie, are you there?" he whispers.

I'm here, Kai.

"Leave me. Find Shay; help her get away. And tell her to keep going; keep herself safe, do what must be done. I'll be all right."

We can't leave you, Kai! Even if I could, Shay wouldn't.

"No backtalk, just do it."

I'm startled. Can he hear me? No. He's just guessing what I'd say.

He's pacing again later when there are more footsteps, but this time they stop at his door. A window opens in it.

It's the policeman who brought him in, who called the ambulance for Shay.

"She's got a pretty bad concussion but should be just fine. They said they'll have to keep her in the hospital at least another day, perhaps longer, okay? So get some sleep. More than I can do."

"Thanks for letting me know."

"I understand how you feel, even if I question your taste in girls."

Kai bristles.

"Well, she is a murderer, or so they say, and you've been aiding and abetting."

"It's not true. She's innocent!"

"Now, I've never heard that one before," he says, but he doesn't walk away from the door. Why not?

Kai is wondering too. "What's going on?"

"Damned if I know. Army said to keep you company, hence I'm pulling a double shift. They're coming to get the two of you."

"Isn't this a police matter? Don't let them take us."

"It should be a police matter. I've been told to do as they say." He's not happy about it.

"Look. If you hand us over, they'll kill Shay. They've tried to several times already; they're the ones who shot that boy. He got in the way when they tried to shoot her."

"And why would they be doing that?"

Kai hesitates. "It's a mystery to us. But she is an Aberdeen flu survivor; it must have something to do with that."

The policeman's eyes widen. "I've heard rumors about survivors, but . . ." He shrugs.

"Like what?"

"Just idle gossip I'll not repeat."

"Can I talk to a lawyer?"

"Sorry. We're violating rights now too, apparently."

327

His tone is disgusted. He closes the window in the door and starts to walk away. "Try to get some sleep, son," he says again.

I hesitate. *Find Shay*, that's what Kai said to do. I slip under the door and follow the policeman.

He goes to the end of the hall, unlocks a door, and steps into an office. He chucks his keys on top of the desk, then opens the bottom drawer and takes out a bottle of whiskey—stares at it in his hand, then unscrews the cap and has a swallow.

He makes a face and puts the bottle back in the bottom drawer.

The phone rings, and he jumps and glances at the clock. It's almost midnight.

He answers.

"What? Now, hold on a minute here—

"But—

"I see."

He hangs up, rubs his eyes. His hand reaches out, hovers over the phone, then pulls back. Finally he reaches out again, and this time he picks it up and dials.

He waits and waits, then finally hangs up and dials another number.

"Hello? Please put me through to the editor . . . Yes, I know what time it is; I also know he's there, as I just tried him at home. Tell him it's his nephew, Euan. And it's urgent."

He waits a few moments, drumming his fingers on the desk. They hover near the phone like he's thinking of disconnecting.

When it picks up, the answer is barked so loudly that I hear it across the room.

"What the hell is going on? It's late."

"Yeah, sorry about that. Just listen, will you? Did you hear I arrested that Killin girl and her boyfriend today? . . . Don't congratulate me; listen. I've been told to do whatever some idiot in the army tells me to do. The station has been cleared; I'm on my own. They say they're taking the girl out of the hospital—she's underage and has a severe concussion. And then there's something her boyfriend told me: she's an Aberdeen flu survivor. The whole thing, well. It's just fishy. No social services involved, no phone calls allowed, no family contacted, and no lawyers . . . The guy's name? Kirkland-Smith. I don't know rank . . . Uh-huh. Yeah. Well, you do that, but don't leave me waiting long. They said they'll be here in an hour, and I've got a decision to make."

He hangs up and reaches to open the drawer with the whiskey in it. He hesitates, then slams it shut.

The army and their guns will be here soon. Kai is locked up; the keys are on this desk.

There's nothing I can do by myself.

I have to find Shay.

CHAPTER 11

SHAY

IT'S COLD AND STARTS TO RAIN. My bare feet seem to pick out every sharp pebble on the footpath, and I wince. My forehead itches, and I reach up to scratch—there's a bandage there. I tease up a corner of it and yank it off.

It's covered in blood, but when I reach up again to touch where it was, my forehead is whole, healed.

That *is* pretty cool. If only I could conjure up some shoes and an umbrella, and a change of clothes.

Now, where will Kai be?

My thoughts are vague and disjointed, and it's hard to focus on how I ended up in the hospital. I hit my head on something—what was it?

We'd had lunch. I frown, concentrating. And there was that policeman. He recognized me, and we were running away from him, weren't we? We ran up the bike path, and then—I don't know what.

And I was taken to a hospital. Did Kai get away? If he didn't, what happened to him? Was he arrested? Maybe he's at a police station.

A man and woman walk past under an umbrella.

"Excuse me, where's the police station?"

They ignore me and walk faster.

I'm shivering and shaky, and I lean against a tree off the road, feet on cool grass instead of stones. Forehead against the bark.

Callie, where are you?

I call again and again, but she doesn't answer. Not here, that's where she is.

What now? I have no answers. I'm cold, wet, hungry; my head is spinning. A wave of shivering shakes through me from inside out, and tears are pricking at the back of my eyes.

Something is coming down the road fast, very fast, and a man walking a dog runs out of the way, cursing and shaking a fist at whoever it is. They're past me before my eyes process what they see: two army jeeps—rushing down the road toward the hospital.

CHAPTER 12

CALLIE

I STREAM UP INTO THE SKY to try to work out where we are. Lights are spread out below me in all directions; we're in a city, by the look of things. How am I ever going to find Shay?

Hospital: she's in a hospital.

I rush back down to street level and search up and down main roads until finally I spot what I'm looking for: an H on a sign. I follow the turning it points out and find another one. An ambulance rushes past me: I must be heading in the right direction. I speed up to follow it, and it takes me straight to where I want to go: a sign at the front says Raigmore Hospital.

And parked next to the sign?

Two army jeeps.

Shay, where are you? I cast out, but there is no answer.

I go into the hospital and zip around, looking for Shay, looking for the uniforms.

I find the latter. They're at a nurses' station; a scared-looking nurse and a policeman are facing them.

"I don't care whose authority this is on; my sergeant called and said you're not to take her, and that's it until he tells me otherwise." The policeman is standing upright and staring the leader of three army guys in the eye.

The nurse straightens her shoulders. "She has to be discharged by a doctor before she can go anywhere," she says.

Shay, are you here? She doesn't answer.

The soldier looks impatient. He finally snaps. He gestures at the other two with him, and they push past the nurse and policeman and start down the hallway, looking in each room.

The policeman sputters and objects. They ignore him.

They've reached a room with a chair next to the door.

"I really must insist—" The policeman pushes between them and the door, but they manhandle him out of the way and throw the door open.

One of the soldiers goes in but comes back out seconds later. "Empty," he says to the other ones. "Pillows under the bedding."

"What?" The policeman goes into the room. His jaw drops. "But she was right here—"

"She seems to have gotten away from you," the soldier answers, with a scathing look. One of the others is on a phone, asking for help to search the hospital and area, but before he's finished his sentence, I'm down the hall and out the front of the hospital.

I have to find her first.

I rush down one road from the hospital, then back again and down another, calling *Shay, Shay, where are you?* the whole time.

Is that a faint answer back? *Shay?*

Callie?

I home in on the direction of her voice. It takes me to a house about a mile from the hospital; no, behind a house. In a garden—some sort of wooden building in a garden.

She's sitting on the floor, knees up and arms around herself, soaked and shivering. She lifts her head. Her face is covered with tears, but she smiles. "Am I ever glad to see you."

CHAPTER 13

SHAY

"**SO BASICALLY,** what you're saying is that I ran into a tree."

Yes.

"I just hit my head on a tree and knocked myself out."

That's pretty much it.

I thunk my head on the steering wheel and try to put the car in reverse again. It makes a horrible grinding noise, and I struggle with the gear stick.

Bingo! I find reverse.

I peer over my shoulder through the rain and nudge the car backward onto the road, going up the sidewalk on one side as I do. Good thing it is the middle of the night.

I wrestle with the gear stick some more, and the car shudders up the road.

Can you go any faster?

"I'm trying," I say, teeth gritted.

I'm going back to check on the soldiers. Keep going straight; I'll find you.

And she's gone.

I ease up the road. Couldn't Callie have found an empty house with an automatic parked out front for us to break into?

She's soon back.

They have reinforcements. They're on foot around the hospital and spreading out. They've got dogs.

"If they find the house we got this car from, they might work out that we took it. We'd better hurry."

On to the police station.

"Seems a strange place to take a stolen car, but hey."

Callie directs me on back streets, disappearing now and then to orient herself. Finally she tells me to pull into a quiet road and wait while she checks on Kai.

She's gone longer than I expect.

Then she zooms back in a hurry.

There's an army jeep outside the police station. They're trying to break in, but I went in and they're not there.

"What?"

Kai and the policeman: they're not there!

"Where are they?"

How should I know?

"This doesn't make sense. The police aren't going to move a prisoner in the middle of the night. The army obviously doesn't have him. What's going on?"

Maybe the policeman took him somewhere else, sort of unofficially.

"Why would he do that?"

He called somebody and told them about Kai and you, and about you being a flu survivor, and that the army was demanding your release. He was angry about it.

"Who did he call?"

His uncle—he's an editor. And his uncle was going to check something and get back to him.

"An editor—like a newspaper editor?"

I guess.

"Wow. Maybe the policeman took Kai there. Where are we? Is this Inverness? What newspapers do they have here?"

I don't know!

"Let's find a shop that sells papers, and find out."

Wait; I'll tell you which way to go so we don't run into the army.

Callie disappears for a moment, then directs me.

We find a service station that is still open. I wander in, glad the house we'd stolen the car from had some clothes I could wear without looking like a complete freak. They're boys' clothes, but the jeans fit okay with a belt. The shoes are too big, but not clown big with the double-thick socks I found.

I check out the newspapers and confirm what I'd suspected: they've brought us to the closest city from where we were picked up—Inverness. And as far as papers go, there seem to be two main candidates.

I smile at the guy behind the till. "Have you got a phone book I can borrow?"

"Business directory any good?"

"Yes, please—can I have a look?"

He rummages around under a desk and passes it over. I find the addresses of the two newspapers and commit them to memory.

"Do you stock maps of Inverness?"

He finds one. I memorize it, then fold it up and hand it back.

"You buying that?"

"No. But thanks for your help."

I head up the road to where I left the car and Callie and get in.

"Okay, I've got the addresses for two newspaper offices, and I know the way. Let's try them."

The car grinds and jerks up the road. "I think I'm getting the hang of this."

Yeah. I can see that.

The first office we try is dark and empty.

We find the second one and park down the road a little. It must be 2:00 a.m. by now, but there are lights on behind the blinds.

I walk up the road with Callie, hugging the shadows. We walk around the building, and there, parked in shadows behind it, is a police car.

Bingo.

I'll go and see if he's there, Callie says. A moment later she's back.

336

She's smiling. Kai is half-asleep on a chair. The policeman is there, arguing with someone who must be his uncle, the editor.

"I'm going to try to reach Kai, so he knows we're here," I say.

I close my eyes. I know Kai said not to do this, but isn't this an emergency?

I *reach out*, all around me.

And into the offices up above.

Kai's mind is like a familiar footprint, one that fits mine. I hover outside him at first. There's a spider in a web in the corner, and I use its eyes to check out the room.

Kai is near the door, in what looks like a waiting area. His feet are up on a chair. The other two are deep in discussion.

Kai? I say his name inside like a caress. *It's me, Shay.*

He's startled. His first reaction is to push me away, but then, like he realizes what this is and what it means, he makes himself relax and lets me stay.

Shay? he thinks, hesitant. *You're okay?*

Yeah. I got away from the hospital. You okay too?

Yes. What are you doing here?

Rescuing you, of course.

I told Callie to tell you to go. Didn't she tell you?

No, but it wouldn't have made any difference. Now listen. Callie and I are parked around the corner. I picture the car we came in. *And I'm just outside the back of the building now.*

You drove that? His thoughts chuckle.

Yes! Now, how do we get you out? Any suggestions?

These people aren't the bad guys. But I'm not sure they'd let you leave if they saw you. Give me a moment; I'll see what I can do.

He stretches, stands up.

"Where's the bathroom?" he asks.

"Down the stairs. Left door. You need a key." The editor throws a set of keys at Kai; he catches them and walks down the stairs.

He tries the back door; it's locked. The ring of keys has several on it. He tries them all, but the door won't open.

Wait.

I leave Kai's mind, open my eyes, and move to the back door of the building. I can see Kai through the glass window in the door, and I hold my hand up against his on the pane.

"You all right down there?" a voice calls from above. Kai looks behind him.

"Yeah," Kai answers out loud. *I'll see if there are windows in the bathroom,* his thoughts say.

He tries a few keys in the door to the left until one opens it; he goes through and returns a moment later, shaking his head.

He tries a door to the right; it's locked. He tries one key in it, another.

There are footsteps above. Someone is coming this way.

The lock clicks open. Kai goes through the door. Seconds later he's pulling a window open and climbing out. There are footsteps coming down the stairs as he jumps to the ground.

I take Kai's hand and we run.

CHAPTER 14

CALLIE

THIS IS MUCH MORE RELAXING.

"Callie prefers your driving to mine."

Yes!

"Turn left," Shay says, thankful she'd memorized enough of the map to know the way out of Inverness.

He turns the corner and sighs. "I feel really bad about running out on Euan like that. I hope he doesn't get into too much trouble."

"Euan? Isn't this the guy who arrested us?"

"Well, yeah. He also put you in an ambulance. And when he worked out that the army was up to things they shouldn't be, he called the officer guarding you and told him to stop them from taking you."

"I was probably gone by then."

"But Euan didn't know that. And when his uncle called back, he got me out of the cell, out of the station."

"Before the army got there."

"Exactly."

"Why would a policeman do that?"

"Told you: he isn't one of the bad guys."

"Roundabout, take the second exit. I mean, what did his uncle say that made Euan get you out of there?"

"He looked into Kirkland-Smith. You remember him, from Killin?"

"The lieutenant in charge of the soldiers who killed Duncan, tied you to a bench, and shot at me? Hard to forget."

"Yes. He was the one demanding that both of us be released into his custody. Anyhow, apparently that army regiment he's in charge of—SAR—is some kind of shadowy secret. No one quite knows what they do or under what authority. Which way now?"

"Left at the lights. We should dump this car somewhere it won't be seen. They have dogs. If they trace me to the house I got it from and work out a car is missing, they could report it stolen and driven by a famed murderess."

"Good point. Should we try to get another car?"

"It's harder to steal stuff around here; we could get caught. Everyone is at home this time of night, or if they aren't, their neighbors are. It's not empty like in or near a quarantine zone."

"How far are we from Elgin?"

"I don't know; I didn't look at maps that far. Wait a sec."

She opens the glove box and roots around; nothing. She feels behind the driver's seat and reaches into the pocket. And presto! A map of Scotland. She opens it up.

"It's about—oh. Forty miles to Elgin."

"We can't walk that far."

"Not in a hurry. But I'm nervous staying in this car. What do we do?"

"Let's drive a while longer and hope it'll take some time for them to work all that out. Callie can keep an eye on the road ahead."

Shay stifles a yawn. "Now that we're on the main road along the coast, you just keep going straight on for ages." She folds the map back up and yawns properly this time.

"Get some sleep while you can," Kai says.

Shay closes her eyes, and soon her breathing is even, her body relaxed into the seat.

"Callie?" Kai's voice is low. "Listen to me. I'm not very happy with you. I asked you to tell Shay to get away and not risk getting caught coming back for me. You should have told her what I said, but you didn't. And you should at least have tried to convince her to go."

I stare at Kai. He's sitting there, calmly driving and telling me off at the same time. After all I did! Rescuing his stupid walks-into-trees girlfriend, telling her about the editor so we could find him.

I scowl, arms crossed. *Thanks a lot for nothing!* But he can't see me or hear me, can he? He can say whatever he wants, and I can't tell him he's an idiot.

"Anyway, can you watch the road ahead and behind? Check there aren't any soldiers, or police, or roadblocks—swing back and forth between the two? And wake Shay if there's anything we need to know about."

And now he's asking for favors?

He can shove it.

"Thank you, Callie."

I glare at him, but he doesn't know it. I'm so sick of this, of not being heard—of *do this, Callie; do that, Callie.*

I could fly out of this car and go anywhere I want, just let them fumble along running into trees and roadblocks on their own.

But I can't. I need them. I need them to find Dr. 1.

And *then* they can shove it.

For now, I do the next best thing and leave the car. I fly through the night air free and alone. I stay on this road and know where the car is behind me but pretend it isn't there.

CHAPTER 15

SHAY

SHAY, SHAY, WAKE UP.

Callie's voice is insistent, and I give up trying to ignore it.

"Mmmm. What's up?"

There are police and army up ahead! Tell Kai.

Fully awake in a hurry, I pluck at Kai's sleeve. "Police and army ahead. Get off this road."

He brakes dramatically to make the first turn to the left.

"What are they doing?" Kai says. "Are they looking for us?"

How should I know? Callie says. She's sitting behind me on the back seat, arms crossed, and holding herself as far away from us as she can.

"Where are they?" I say, and add, inside: *Are you okay, Callie?*

I'm just fine. They're pulled over on the shoulder; you'd have gone right past them if you kept going that way.

I turn around and look at Callie. *"Just fine" doesn't sound fine. Are you really all right?*

She shrugs. *Sorry, I'm in a mood.*

I smile at her, nod. *Rough few days for all of us.*

Yeah, Callie says, and gives me half a smile back.

"How far do we still have to go to Elgin—where are we now?" Kai says, and I pull out the map, study it, and find the turn we just took.

"It looks to be less than ten miles now." I commit the map to memory, then stash it away.

"Time to dump this car, I think," Kai says. "Do we walk?"

"It'd be risky to try to steal another one. There's a bike trail down this coast. We can join it not far from here and walk, if we can find it in the dark. Do you need a rest?"

"No. I'm good. Let's find a place to stash this one out of sight."

Kai drives down a narrow lane; there are farms all around, fields, buildings. There's a gate to a field. He jumps out to open the gate and maneuvers the car behind a ruined barn, watched by some bemused, sleepy sheep.

"Hopefully it won't be noticed anytime soon," Kai says. "Let's go."

We step out of the car, go through the muddy field, and close the gate. We head down the single-track road.

"I think it's straight this way, back to the other road we were on," I say. "Then let's find some street signs if we can, and I should be able to work out the way from the maps I looked at before."

We pass under some lights.

"What *are* you wearing anyway?" Kai asks.

"The height of stolen fashion." I pirouette in my boys' jeans, rolled up at the bottom, too-big hoodie, and too-big shoes that are already rubbing, even with double-thick socks.

He wolf-whistles, takes my hand, and we walk.

And walk.

And walk . . .

The sky is starting to lighten when we finally stop for a rest, above the coast. The sun rises: beautiful pinks and reds streak through clouds over the sea.

"Red sky in morning, sailors take warning," Kai says.

"I thought it was shepherds?"

"Them too, but we're the ones who hope to get on a boat soon."

I lean against Kai, and his arm wraps around me. I'm hungry and thirsty, and there are blisters on my ankles that I could probably heal if I could summon the energy, but I'm too tired even for that. Kai leans down and kisses my forehead, and his arm tightens around me.

I push everything else away, to be in this one perfect moment—Kai warm against me; the sunrise; the sea and the early-morning birds twittering; the spring countryside at our feet.

Past him, down the path, Callie sits on a rock. The sunlight doesn't touch her; she is darkness in light, a shadow cast by nothing—absence in presence.

As if she feels my scrutiny, she turns. Her eyes—darker patches of darkness in her face—meet mine, and I shiver.

CHAPTER 16

CALLIE

IT'S LUNCHTIME when we finally find Café Marbles in Elgin. It's busy and trendy, with people dressed in the kind of clothes that cost a lot but are made to look like they don't.

I can feel Shay's hunger when she and Kai go through the door and see food on tables around them.

A harassed-looking waitress walks over to where they stand. "A table for two?" she asks, with a raised eyebrow and a dismissive glance. The last days have them looking scruffy.

"Can we speak to Lochy?" Shay asks.

"He *should* be here, but he's late. Do you want a table?"

They exchange a glance. They don't have any money.

"Yes," Kai says.

They are shown to a table by the kitchen door and bathrooms at the back.

"How are we going to pay?" Shay says, voice low, after the waitress rushes away.

"At this point I'm too hungry to care. Hope Lochy turns up and wants to buy us lunch? Wash dishes?"

They study the menu. "One of everything?" Shay says, and Kai laughs. When the waitress comes back with a jug of water and a basket of bread, the bread vanishes so fast she looks puzzled when she walks by again.

"Could we have more bread, please?" Shay asks.

"Are you planning to order as well?" she asks, eyebrow up again.

"Of course."

She brings another basket, which is soon empty as well.

Maybe that is Lochy, by the door? I say. A twenty-something guy in dark-framed glasses and a T-shirt that says "time is relative" is getting an earful from the waitress at the front. She must then say something about us, as he glances over to our table and nods his head.

He comes over. "Hi, I'm Lochy, Iona's friend. Shay and Kai, right?"

"Yes." Shay smiles, so pleased to have found him, and he smiles back.

"Jess thinks you're going to eat all the bread and run out." He laughs. "Are you hungry?"

"Just a little. But broke."

"Lunch is on me; I recommend the pasta special. Then you can go back to my house." He tells them the address, how to find it, then pretends to lean down to point at something on the menu and slips a key into Shay's hand. "Have a sleep or a shower, or both. I'll be back tonight."

CHAPTER 17

SHAY

THE FRONT ROOM OF LOCHY'S FLAT is like Iona's bedroom tech multiplied by a factor of a thousand, with computers, screens, and wires everywhere—all in organized, neat chaos. There is also a minimal kitchen at one end and a futon against the wall. There is one bathroom and one bedroom, door open. The bedroom is the opposite of the organization elsewhere—it's a disaster.

"Shower?" Kai asks, rubbing his eyes.

I shake my head. "Should. But tummy full, time to sleep," I say, and take his hand. We somehow work out how to fold down the futon, and sleep has us in seconds.

"Helloooo . . . ?"

I open one eye. Lochy stands there. Kai stirs as I sit up. It's dark through the blinds now: it's night.

I yawn. "Did we really sleep all day?"

"You must have needed it," Lochy says. "Feel better now?"

"I think so, once I wake up."

"We've got some things to talk about, but no hurry. First up, I've got to get over the horrors of catering and capitalism with level sixteen of *Martian Massacre*."

I get up, and Lochy takes my hand, leads me to a cupboard. "Just a suggestion. Towels are in here, shower is there. I've got some clothes somewhere"—he starts going through a wardrobe—"from an old girlfriend. She left in a hurry." He hands me an armload of stuff. "Here. See if any of that fits."

He looks over at Kai. "You're bigger than me, but I might have something . . . yes, here. Try this. From an old boyfriend."

"Did he leave in a hurry too?" I ask.

"Don't they always?" He grins.

I shower, then Kai goes in. I rifle through Lochy's ex-girlfriend's clothes. There must have been more than one ex-girlfriend; there's stuff in different sizes, and some of it is a reasonable fit for me. I wander out into the main room: Lochy is shooting at space aliens with grim determination.

There is a TV screen up on the wall; the news is on. They show a quarantine zone map of Scotland, and I gasp to see how the red areas have grown. They stretch beyond the Cairngorms now and enclose Inverness.

When Kai emerges from his shower as well, in borrowed clothes that are a little tight, Lochy whistles and shuts his game down.

Time to talk.

"How much do you know?" I ask Lochy.

"The theory of relativity. How to make a mean soufflé. Too many things about computers to add to this list, unless you have a few days to listen." I raise an eyebrow, and he grins. "Oh, do you mean more specifically? Iona has told me you need to get to Shetland and a little of why. That it may hold a key to unmasking the fact that this disease rampaging through the UK is manmade and what can be done about it."

"Iona also told me the coast is being guarded. Can we get there?"

"You can. It's not legal, or comfortable. There are boats taking paying passengers who want to escape the epidemic and go to other parts of Europe. I've found one that will stop in Shetland on the way to Norway. But it'll cost, and not just a little. And you're broke, right?"

I exchange a dismayed glance with Kai. "Yeah, totally."

"I've got some friends with deep pockets. I'd have to tell them about you, but if I do, I think they'll help."

"Who are they?"

"Part of an online group Iona is in too—that's how we know each other. She trusts them, as do I."

Kai and I look at each other. "I'd rather as few know as little as possible," Kai says. "For their sakes as well as our own."

"Understood."

"Can I ask Iona?" I say.

"Of course. I know you've been in touch via her blog, but you can use our group system if you want. Which means you'll look like me. But it's encrypted and bounced. Even if someone finds and decodes it, they can't trace the source."

"Okay, sounds good."

"Here, let me start it up."

His fingers move quickly to type a complicated login sequence, but not so fast that my eyes can't take it in, that my memory can't store it away.

An avatar of a heart appears on the screen.

LOL: Calling JIT.

There's a ping noise.

JIT: Hey LOL, break any hearts lately?

LOL: Alas no. But I have a few houseguests. Over to . . .

He looks at me.

LOL: Curly.

JIT: Curly? That fits!

LOL: JIT? Is that you?

JIT: Hurray, you made it! Is LOL taking care of you?

LOL: Yep, think so. He wants to finance us via some group
       you're both in. Is that okay?

JIT: That's cool, they're safe.

LOL: Wish we could talk properly.

JIT: Me too. Best not. (((HUGS)))

LOL: (((HUGS)))

I turn back to Lochy and Kai. Kai, who'd been reading over my shoulder, nods.

"Yep, okay, let's do it," I say.

"Can you tell us more about what is involved?" Kai asks.

"It won't be pleasant. Crowded boats run by the sort that will do anything for enough money."

"Where do these boats go?"

"Wherever they can. They were slipping through to various points in Europe with good success for a while; it's gotten harder now as the cordons have gotten tighter. Some countries won't let them land. Others are putting refugees into quarantine camps. A few camps have had outbreaks and were sealed off without medical aid or assistance of any kind. And the crossing is not without risk: you could get arrested by the coast guard, and some boats haven't made it in rough seas."

"Oh my God," I say. "I didn't know it was that bad. Why do people still try to leave if it's that dangerous?"

"Easy: they're more scared to stay." He grabs a remote, finds a twenty-four-hour channel with quarantine zone updates. A map fills the screen.

"What? It's in Inverness now too?" Kai says.

"Yes, and with that, Elgin is surrounded. It stretches from Inverness above to Aberdeen below. It's changed in a rush this week."

"And that's why people will risk anything to leave," I say. "They're trapped."

"Exactly."

"What about you, Lochy? Do you want to leave?" I ask.

"Me? No way! I must be bug proof, or I'd have caught something shocking by now for sure," he says. He winks, but there is fear behind his bravado.

"Come with us," I say.

He shakes his head. "I can't run away. Too many people who can't leave mean too much to me here," he says, looking uncomfortable admitting it, then shrugs. "Anyhow, I've been checking into Shetland as much as I can, to see if there is any information that can help you. But it's weird: it's almost like an information vacuum. I had to hack to even get these."

Lochy opens another screen and shows us recent satellite images of the islands, with the Shetland Mainland in the center, then zooms in. "As you can see, there are vast blackened areas where everything was completely destroyed by the explosions and fires. But even though not everywhere was affected, they're not letting anyone return. There were people still on the other islands, but they've since been evacuated—supposedly due to environmental concerns."

"Supposedly? Do you think there's another reason?" Kai asks.

"There's got to be something else going on for them to limit access like this. I mean, all that is there is a temporary air force post that's been set up to monitor the seas and keep an eye on the international cordon." He adjusts the map and points out the base. "And there are various officials and cleaners-up and so on at the Sullom Voe site, doing what they do. But not as many as you'd expect, and little is said about it. Anywhere—officially or unofficially."

"Maybe with everything that is happening in Scotland and England right now, it isn't making the news," Kai says.

"That could be part of it, but not all. It's just so intriguing. Something high on the weird scale is definitely happening or has happened over there. I hope you find out what it is."

"Can I look at the images of the Shetland Mainland again?" I say.

"Of course." Lochy shows me how to zoom in and out on the giant screen, and I take over the controls.

Callie, do you recognize where we need to go?

She studies the screen.

Where is the oil place?

"Where is Sullom Voe?" I ask Lochy, and he points out the spot.

Zoom in there and then to the left. Yes. It's on this part of the island. She moves closer to the screen. *It's somewhere around here that I got out of the research institute. And then, up top, there, is about where Dr. 1's house is.*

Lochy has some maps of the Shetland Islands as well, and I study them in detail, committing them all to memory.

Callie looks from the satellite images to the maps and back again.

Yes. This is definitely the place. She gestures to a point that reaches out into the sea, near the top of the main island.

I zoom in. Even though close to Sullom Voe, this part of the island was less affected than most. It is almost surrounded by water, with only a narrow finger of land attaching it to the rest of the island. It is wild, barren, steep. The whole landscape is eerie, oddly red in color.

And we're going there.

CHAPTER 18

CALLIE

IT'S ALMOST TIME TO GO. Lochy has set up what he says is an untraceable line so Kai can call Mum. After much debate, they decided the need to find out what she knows outweighed the risk. But I can tell Kai just wants to hear her voice, like I do.

I get closer to Kai than I have in a while, close enough to listen in. "Hello, Mum?"

"Kai! Where are you? Are you all right? Is Shay?"

"Can't say, and yes, and yes."

"What have you gotten mixed up in?"

"We're doing what is right, I promise you that."

A slight pause. "I believe you, but—"

"I can't talk for long, and I have a question for you."

"What is it?"

"Has any progress been made on the origin or source of the Aberdeen flu?"

"No. The biological agent still eludes us. We need survivors—send Shay to me."

Lochy gestures—the safe time for the call is up in a few seconds.
"I have to go."

"*Ich hab dich lieb.*"

"Love you too, Mum. Never forget that." The line cuts off.

I love her too.

Kai stands there, pain in his eyes, and the anger I felt toward him before relents. Shay slips her hand into his.

"Ready to go?" Lochy says.

We follow him out the back door and down a lane and wait a few moments. A van pulls up. Lochy passes Kai a pack full of bottled water and food and gives Shay and Kai a quick hug. He thumps on the van door. It opens.

There are many eyes inside. People move a little to make room for Kai and Shay, though it isn't easy. It's a standard-sized van, and there are already two men, three women, a crying baby, and so many children squirming about that they're hard to count.

I back away and tell Shay, *I'll ride up top.*

CHAPTER 19

SHAY

THE VAN JOLTS and lurches down the road. The baby is still crying, and one of the children is sick. The smell is making me feel sick too, and I wish I could join Callie outside.

Kai's body shelters mine against the side of the van. Even though it is Kai so close against me, the lack of air and space makes me want to scream.

When we finally stop and the door opens, the fresh air is a relief I breathe in deep—sea air, and I can hear the sea nearby too. We're behind trees, by a small lane. I get a better look at the others. Scared and some a little vomit-spattered, they are otherwise completely ordinary—they could be any of the families in Killin.

Before the flu came, that is.

We're told to be quiet, to walk quickly.

There is a path through trees, down to a narrow rocky beach. It's windy and the sea is rough. There is what looks like a fishing boat anchored near the shore, a decent size, and I'm relieved we won't be as crammed in as we were in the van.

We're told to clamber into a rowboat, four at a time, and we get half-soaked in the process. The water is freezing. We're rowed out, bouncing on the waves, to the fishing boat, and then must climb out one at a time up a ladder that lurches sickeningly with the movement of the sea. Arms from above help pull us on board, and then I see our group isn't the only one. There are so many people crammed in the darkness already that even though we're in the open, it is, once again, hard to breathe.

"Well, this is an adventure," I whisper to Kai.

"Lucky I like standing close to you, though not so sure about all the rest," he whispers back.

Callie makes a face. *Are you sure this is safe, with so many people on it?*

I'm sure it is, I say to her, but more to convince myself than for any other reason. Callie leaves the deck behind, sits on the top of the cabin above us, and once again I find myself wishing I could join her.

Me too, she says. *Climb on up!*

I have a feeling they'd rather I didn't.

At least we must be the last to board. The anchor is pulled up, and soon we're heading out to sea. We're warned again to keep quiet, that sound carries on the water and there may be patrols nearby.

This far north it isn't properly dark in July, even though it's late. Stars are hiding behind clouds and there are no lights on the boat, but white faces reflect what light there is. The sway on the sea increases as the dark shadow that is Scotland disappears behind us. A woman is crying soundlessly, a man rocking her back and forth. Children are shushed.

A baby cries, and her mother cradles her. The baby cries louder, and the mother holds her, jiggles her, but she still cries. "I'm sorry," she breathes in the barest whisper. "She's not well, she won't stop, and—" Her words cut off like she realizes what she said. "No, no; it's not *that*!"

Everyone on the crowded deck shrinks away from the woman and baby. An angry muttering starts up as the baby cries again.

The feeling all around us is ugly, full of fear: that the baby will bring the epidemic to us all—that we'll all die.

"Shhh!" one of those running the boat says.

Someone says something to him about the baby, and he pulls away in fear too.

The woman is sheltering her baby between her and the railing. The baby's cries are muffled and getting weaker.

Callie has come down off her perch to investigate, then radiates alarm.

Shay, she's holding her baby too tight!

What?

It can't breathe—do something!

I push through the people and touch the mother's shoulder. She flinches.

"Let me," I say. "I'll get her to stop crying; I've got the knack." I smile reassuringly, but she's as terrified as if I'd said I'd throw the baby overboard. That's what she thinks someone will do, isn't it? She's holding her child even tighter.

I *reach* . . . and soothe the mother's fear and distrust. She loosens her grasp enough: the baby is weak but gasps in air to fill her lungs and cries.

The mother lets me take the baby from her arms. I know nothing about babies—totally zilch. But I rock her, thinking soothing, gentle, happy, sleepy thoughts, and she settles—it's working.

But when I look up, the other passengers around us are still staring at the baby, their faces fearful, angry, and my concentration is broken. Like she feels the threat from them through me, the baby draws in air to cry again, but her breathing is ragged, her lungs congested. She coughs instead.

"She hasn't got the Aberdeen flu; she's got a cold. Back off!" I say to the passengers around us. The baby coughs again and falls asleep.

People shuffle awkwardly—with shame, embarrassment. I ease her back to her mother.

But soon they forget all about the baby, the patrols, the epidemic they are hoping to escape and where we are going. The sea swell increases. The boat lurches from side to side; it rises up with each wave and crashes down hard in the trough between them, and then does it again.

Now we are all more scared of the sea than of anything else.

CHAPTER 20

CALLIE

SOMETIMES I'M GLAD TO BE AS I AM. So many people are sick: some manage to do it over the railing, but many don't. Even as far from them as I can be, I'm glad I can't smell anything anymore.

The sea is calm in the early morning, but it is still a boat full of misery that sneaks toward the Shetland Islands in mist. It hugs the coast and slips into a cave.

"You two." One of the sailors points at Kai and Shay. "You leave the boat here?"

"Yes," Kai answers.

"We stay here in sea cave until dusk. We row you out soon."

They are busy with the anchor and then start to swing the rowboat down to the water.

"Wait." There's a hand on Shay's arm; it's the mother of the baby. "Thank you. For last night."

Shay shrugs, uncomfortable. "No worries. I hope you are happy where you go—Norway, is that it?"

"Yes. Well, it depends on the sea where we land, I think, but that is the plan. But you're leaving us now? Why?"

"There's something we have to do."

"Best of luck."

"You go now," the sailor says.

Kai and Shay climb down the ladder and get into the rowboat. The others wave, wish them luck, and they wave back. The water is like glass now; after last night it's hard to believe it is the same sea.

They're rowed out of the cave and along the shore. The sailor steers the rowboat toward a cove.

"When you're ready to leave, go back to the cave. There are a few of our boats that stop there; I can't say what day, depends on many things." He shrugs.

"How do we get to the cave without a rowboat?" Kai asks.

The sailor shrugs again. Kai and Shay exchange a glance.

Chuck him overboard and keep the rowboat.

Callie! Shay is shocked.

Let him *swim for it.*

We can't! They might need it.

You need it. Kai might make the swim, but judging by how you were in the river, you won't.

We'll find another boat somewhere. It'll be all right.

The sailor maneuvers the rowboat into the cove, near the shore. There are high cliffs above.

"Can we climb up here?" Shay asks.

"Your problem. Now get out."

CHAPTER 21

SHAY

WE STAND ON THE ROCKY BEACH. The sea laps gently behind us; cliffs tower above. To the left, a waterfall tumbles down. There is a cut in the rock to the right, a place we should be able to clamber up to a grassy slope above. The only sounds are the sea and the cries of seabirds. It is desolate, lonely—beautiful.

Kai points to the cut where I was looking. "That way up?"

"Yes, but not yet."

"What do you have in mind?"

"A wash, there." I point at the waterfall. "A picnic, here." I gesture around us, at the beach. "Then climb to the grass above and take a nap in the sun."

Kai smiles. "I like the way you think."

Callie scowls and crosses her arms. *Shouldn't we get a move on?*

"Callie thinks we should get going."

"We need a rest, Callie, and some sleep, or we'll be useless," Kai says.

Fine. I'm going to check things out.

She disappears in a dark blur straight up the cliff.

"Race you!" Kai says, and runs for the waterfall, chucking his shirt off as he goes.

Later we lie on the grassy slope above, breathing hard. It was a challenging climb. We're nearly out of food and water and can only hope that we will find some where we are going.

When I have my breath back, I go on my side, up on my elbow, lean down, and kiss Kai. He kisses me back, once, twice, and then, like he always does, pauses—stops, pulls away a little, looks at me. His pupils are dilated, his heart beats fast, but he keeps me at arm's length like he is afraid of what will happen with just one more kiss.

Warm and sleepy now in the sunshine, our eyes soon close. My head rests on Kai's chest, his arm around me, the *th-thump*, *th-thump* of his heart against my cheek. His hand strokes my hair.

My thoughts wander and I'm drifting, half-awake, half-asleep— needing to rest but not wanting to let go quite yet, wanting to stay here, with Kai, with the sun warm on my skin and his heart beating and the music of the sea murmuring below us.

Without even meaning to, I *reach out*, all around us—to the grass pulsing with life, the insects and spiders and burrowing things; to the fish in the sea and the birds in the air.

And to the island itself.

The island is alive: the earth and the rocks all have memory and purpose. It has been hurt but will heal and live again.

And here, so close to me, is another life that is separate but linked and wound together with mine, like his hand is in my hair.

My mind touches Kai's. He's almost asleep too, but he startles awake. He shakes his head, both inside and out, and I know he doesn't want me there, not inside him like this.

"Sorry," I whisper, and back away.

His heart still beats close and his arm is still around me, but I feel shut out and alone.

CHAPTER 22

CALLIE

I HAVEN'T BEEN TO THIS PART of the Shetland Mainland before, and it takes me a while to work out where we need to go. It turns out to be a good thing Kai and Shay stayed where they did for so long. The air force base Lochy told us about is in a high place not far away, and they might have been spotted if they'd set out across the island in daylight.

And I know they need to sleep—that they were awake all night on that awful boat.

But everything inside me is *screaming* to get going. We're so close to Dr. 1's house! I can get there in minutes—how long will it take them to walk? Once we get there, and find out where he is, then we can leave.

Then I can burn him and watch him die.

But I *hate* being here. It makes me remember what they did to me, and so many others.

Much of the island was destroyed, burned and blackened, but now there are signs that it wants to return to how it was. There are green patches in the black, reaching for the sun; birds and insects and scurrying things. Parts of the island, like where Dr. 1's house is, weren't even touched, and live and breathe and grow as they were before. There are people too, in that air force base, and others near the oil place that blew up.

It's wrong that it should change; it's wrong that people should be here. The island should be dead and dark, like all those burned or buried alive underground.

So many died. Where are others like me? Why aren't there more ghosts? I'm both scared to think I might find someone like me and scared that I never will. If I'm the only one, I'll be unheard and alone forever.

Apart from Shay. She can never leave me.

CHAPTER 23

SHAY

I LIE BACK IN THE GRASS, my head on her lap. Mum winds wild-flowers into my hair. She's humming a song, one I know, but I can't remember the words.

It goes la-de-dah, and de-de-dah; slower, then faster and repeat—something like that. La-de-dah, de-de-dah . . .

"I've missed you," she says between verses.

"So stay."

She shakes her head and starts to sing the words that go with the tune this time. They're nonsense words, ones she sang to me long ago, a child rocked in her arms.

"Why did Callie stay, and you couldn't?"

She smiles. "Why do you think?" she says, and goes back to her song, humming again.

The question niggles. Mum would never have left me if she could have stayed, so it's not that.

La-de-dah, de-de-dah . . .

Shay, it's time to wake up.

Mum didn't say it; she's still singing. I frown and sit up.

Callie is there: cool darkness in the light, where Mum *is warmth and light in the darkness. Not the same thing, not at all.*

Why do I think . . . ?

Wake up, Shay, Callie says again. *It's time to get going.*

I sit up, awake in a rush. Kai is stretching, yawning. Callie is next to him, impatience all over her stance and face. Everything I am lurches with loss, aching to reach back to my dream, to Mum—to be in her arms, to listen to her sing.

Kai reaches his hand to mine. "What is it, Shay? Is something wrong?"

I can only nod my head wordlessly. The tears start to come, and he gathers me into his arms.

CHAPTER 24

CALLIE

"WHAT TIME IS IT?" Kai says, looking at his watch. "After midnight, and it's not really dark at all."

"No, and it won't get any darker than this now: we're too far north," Shay says. "It's the summer dim. This time of year it never gets truly dark; for a time in the winter, it never gets truly light."

"You've been here before?"

"Yes. My uncle and his family lived here." Shay is struggling not to cry again and turns her face from Kai so he won't see. "We visited a few times, but not in the winter dark. My cousins told me about it, though."

"Now the dim makes it easier to see the way, but also easier to be seen."

"True enough. But only if they're watching, and why would they, when they think they've got the island to themselves?"

No one is near, I say.

"Callie says no one is near."

I stay just ahead of them on the path I'd found, one that loops away from the air force base and then heads in the other direction, away from the ruins of the oil depot and toward Dr. 1's house.

They're so slow.

Shay is lost in her own thoughts, her boundaries up. But she's been upset since she woke up, like this place unsettles her as much as it does me.

I drop back to walk next to her.

Shay?

What?

Are you okay?

She's silent for a while. She sighs. *More or less. You?*

Much the same. Why were you crying when you woke up?

I was dreaming about my mum.

Oh.

When I woke up, I felt like I lost her all over again and that I was completely alone.

You can never be alone, Shay. I'll always be with you.

CHAPTER 25

SHAY

THE SUN IS RISING OUT OF THE SEA when we finally reach the white house. We had to cross a burned-out wasteland, and then a spit of sand that links to this almost island. The fire didn't reach here. It's lush, green; wildflowers grow everywhere. The house is in a beautiful place with views over cliffs and the sea, but the smell and taste of ash and death are so near that the sea breeze can't take them away.

Kai tries the front door. "Locked," he says.

We walk around the house, trying every door and window: no luck.

"We'll have to break in," he says. "Though the windows look like special reinforced glass, probably because of high winds here from the sea. Could be hard work."

"There's a keypad by the door," I say, and flick the small box open. "Maybe there is something I can do to work out the code."

It's a standard digital-type keypad with numbered buttons. How many numbers would the code be? Three? Four? To my eyes and my fingertips, the buttons are the same, but are there any traces left behind? I close my eyes and *reach*.

There are circular marks on five of the numbers—slight pressure patterns, oil from skin—on 1, 2, 3, 5, 7. So the code has at least five numbers, and maybe more if some are used more than once.

That is way, way too many combinations to try them all. I open my eyes again, stand back, and stare at the house. The numbers could be random, or they could mean something. Even if they mean something, if they are personal, like a birthday, I'd never work them out.

I spin the numbers around in my mind, faster and faster—running combinations over and over, looking for any sort of logic or pattern—but this is pointless, isn't it?

The wind has picked up, and now that we're not walking, I shiver. Beautiful, maybe, but a cold place for a house—on a high, isolated point, surrounded on three sides by the sea.

Kai has found a rock and holds it up. "The panes in the door might be easier to break; maybe we could reach through one and open the door. Should I smash it?"

There are three small glass squares in a row in the door, decorative and not reinforced like all the bigger windows. They look like those antique squares you get with hand-blown glass, with a round bull's-eye pattern. It seems a shame to break one.

I run my fingers across the middle one. Is there a faint letter K etched in the middle of the circle? Maybe it's a manufacturer's mark.

Cold through and through now and wanting to get inside, I'm about to nod yes to Kai when something clicks into place:

A circle—or a zero—with a K: 0 K. Zero degrees Kelvin is the coldest temperature—absolute zero. We did this in chemistry last year. And in Celsius it is . . .

273.15.

Could it be? That Dr. 1 stood here and saw the K in the 0 in the glass and made this his code? They're the numbers that have been pressed.

It seems pretty thin. I shrug, reach up, and enter 2 7 3 1 5—just in case.

The lock springs open. I turn the handle and open the door.

"You're one freaky girl," Kai says, his voice uneasy. He puts the rock down and follows me inside.

I'm a freak. That's it, isn't it? That's why he always pushes me away.

But I can't let any of this get to me right now. There are things we have to do.

Kai points at the electric clock on the microwave. "The power is still on."

I think there's a generator, Callie says.

"Callie says there may be a generator. But we shouldn't use lights in case the air force flies over or anyone goes past on the water and wonders," I say. "It'll be light enough to see without them soon."

Kai and I explore. Downstairs is a kitchen, open-plan lounge with fireplace, a bathroom. The lounge has a desk, laptop, and bookshelves and leads to a shuttered conservatory. There, under a cover, is what looks like a fancy telescope. Upstairs are two bedrooms and another bathroom. Kai checks the water, and it comes out hot.

"Ladies first?" he says.

"No, you go. I want to get started."

He's soon in the shower, and I wander back downstairs. The sun has come up a little more; there's enough light through the windows to begin.

I sit in the desk chair: it's massive, comfortable. Callie is on the kitchen counter, her feet swinging over the side, watching me. What kind of man sat in this chair, looked at the stars through that telescope, and killed people like Callie?

It's time to find out.

CHAPTER 26

CALLIE

FOLDERS AND PAPERS ARE NEATLY STACKED around the kitchen, all the things Shay has already gone through—and found precisely nothing that says who Dr. 1 is or where he's from.

Kai, frowning, is going through each pile again in case she missed anything, and getting more and more frustrated.

Imagine how I feel.

Shay comes back downstairs, clean and wearing a robe that must have belonged to *him*.

"Any luck?" she says to Kai.

"No. But I'll keep going. Did you try his laptop?"

"Yes. It's password protected."

"You couldn't magic up a code like you did for the door?"

Shay raises an eyebrow and sighs. "No. There are no obvious clues on a keyboard where every key is used."

"If he lived here and there is nothing that says who he is or where he came from, that must be on purpose. Maybe there is nothing to find," Kai says.

"There *must* be some trace of him, something left behind." Shay goes to the bookshelves. "I'll check he hasn't used anything personal as a bookmark, or written his name inside any of them," she says. She does that to start with, picking each book up one at a time, looking inside and flipping through upside down to see if anything falls out. Then she starts looking at them more closely.

"Callie, was Dr. 1 a medical doctor?" Shay asks after a while. "I assumed he was, if he was trying to find a cure for cancer."

I'm pretty sure the other doctors were all medical doctors. I thought Dr. 1 was too, but he never did any medical sort of stuff that I saw. Maybe because he was in charge.

"Callie thought he was, but doesn't know for sure."

"Does it matter?" Kai asks.

"I'm just trying to work him out. Okay, here's a guy with money, obviously, by the look of this place. He has a telescope—he likes looking at the stars. There are masses of books here, and they all look like they've been read, so he likes to read. But his book collection is—well—*weird*. There are books and papers on really strange, random subjects. From philosophy to stargazing to specific areas of quantum physics, and even alternative stuff, like reading auras. And his fiction? Not much of it, and what there is doesn't seem to go together: *The Hunchback of Notre-Dame, The Curious Incident of the Dog in the Night-Time, Dr. Jekyll and Mr. Hyde,* and a load of obscure things I've never heard of. But there is nothing here that even vaguely has to do with medicine or biology, other than a few papers on experimenting on tissue culture. Though maybe this is like his holiday reading, not work stuff?"

Kai has finished going through Dr. 1's papers and starts looking in the kitchen cupboards, and then the fridge and freezer. "There's loads of long-life food in the cupboards; a well-stocked freezer; nothing much in the fridge, and nothing that could go bad. All vegetarian, by the way—no meat or fish."

Shay nods. "So perhaps he wasn't living here regularly, and by the looks of the place, all neat and tidy and no milk left to spoil, he didn't leave abruptly. So he likely wasn't here when the disaster happened."

"Maybe he has a complete life somewhere else. Like you said about his reading, maybe this place is like a holiday home."

Shay sits down on a chair with an armload of books and starts reading one of them.

What good will that do?

She pauses, looks over the page. "I'm trying to think like he thinks. The books a person likes can tell you a lot about the person, can't they?"

"True. The things Callie used to read!" Kai says.

"Callie, what sort of books did you like?"

I stare back at Shay. Books? I used to read books, at soccer. When Kai was playing. But what did I read? I don't remember, and it scares me—I should know. What did I like? But the only books I can remember were ones they made me read in school.

And then I'm angry. If my memory is a mess, I know who to blame, and talking about my books or his books isn't going to do anything to find him.

I don't see what this has to do with anything! I scream, really scream, the words.

Shay jumps. Her eyebrows are raised; she's surprised, but I'm way beyond angry and have to get away from them *now*.

I punch the wall and disappear up the chimney.

CHAPTER 27

SHAY

THE SUN WILL SET AGAIN SOON AND STILL I READ, lost in Dr. 1's books.

Kai yawns. "Time to sleep?" he says.

I shake my head. "I want to read some more while we still have enough light."

Kai kisses me and then wanders up the stairs, and I pick up the next book. Callie still hasn't come back, and I didn't tell him how angry she was. I have to keep reading.

The pages turn so fast. I've always read quickly, but now this is something else. Everything I pick up I'm hungry for; everything I read stays with me, not just memorized but understood in a way I haven't before—integrated into a larger whole.

Whatever happened to me when I survived the flu, it's really like it booted up my brain into some sort of supercomputer—like earlier today when I could spin numbers in my head, looking for significant combinations. And days ago in the hospital, when I worked out how to focus inside and fix my concussion—not just by instinct that time, but by working out what needed to be done and then doing it.

Freaky girl I am indeed.

And the more I read, the more I feel like I am getting closer to this mystery, this Dr. 1.

He doesn't somehow equate with what I think a psychopathic mass murderer should be like. His books are all logic and philosophy, some science and religion. No politics or propaganda, no medicine or biology in his science titles—mostly physics and astronomy.

Though there is this interest in auras. Weird hippie stuff, and I'm about to dismiss it, to pick up something else, but . . . it sounds like something Mum was into. I scan the shelves. His collection includes books on sensing auras, healing, decoding colors.

I get up, gather them together, and spread them out on his desk. There's a color chart tucked in the back of one of the books.

I unfold it, and a piece of paper flutters down. It's a hand drawing of the outline of a man with an aura sketched in all around him in colored pencil. It almost looks religious—a halo drawn around the head and body. Did Dr. 1 draw this?

A single word is written above the drawing: *Vox*. What does that mean? There is something familiar about the word, and I frown, thinking. Doesn't it mean something like *voice*?

I start to read and get goose bumps on my arms. Since I was ill, I have begun to sense the feelings of those around me all the time. The descriptions of the waves of auras and what I sense sound so similar . . . could it be the same thing?

It says that to those sensitive to auras, they can be seen or heard as much as felt. To sense auras like this, the eyes and ears need to adjust, to defocus; to leave solid matter behind—to focus on the space *inside* matter. Matter is made up of atoms, which are made up of particles— particles that spin through space.

Particles that can also behave like waves.

My stomach does a weird flip.

That is just like when I healed myself; with waves, from inside me. Was I using my aura without knowing that was what I was doing?

And it's not just living things that have auras. Since we arrived, I've felt the island was alive, that the history of the place was imprinted

375

in the rock and earth, like a memory. The book says it is easier for beginners to see auras at a distance, and where have I seen colors around objects? The sun, the moon, and the stars—they all have radiating color and energy patterns around them. This was one of the first changes I noticed when I was ill.

I put the book down, wander upstairs, and stare at Kai as he sleeps. And I can feel him—without touching him or *reaching* to his mind. There is a pattern of energy to him that I recognize as unique to Kai. I'm sure I could find him in a crowded room with my eyes shut by following this. Even while he sleeps, everything that makes him Kai is still there: his energy, passion, protectiveness and care—and anger too, directed at himself as much as at anyone or anything else.

I touch his hand, and he stirs in his sleep. He's warm, solid, real. Yet all matter is ultimately made up of atoms, and atoms—with tiny particles spinning in orbit around a tiny nucleus—are mostly empty space, aren't they? Our eyes are used to focusing on the dense level of energy, and so we see objects and ourselves as solid and still, but neither of these things are really true.

I *reach*, but not to Kai inside: to Kai *outside*, past the physical and into the space around him.

Colors shimmer and vibrate, and I gasp: it's there. His aura is there, where it must always have been; colors that reach out from his skin and surround him. Until I looked as I am doing now—or maybe *unlooked* is more apt—I couldn't see it. The red and pink of passion, the blue of caring, the edges of black anger. And other, more subtle touches too, that I haven't felt in as much detail before seeing them as I do now: flashes of silver—of intuition; another shade of soft blue—of truthfulness. So much of what he has been, is now, and will be is here, in these waves of color, in the variations of hue and vibration—sort of like, but not the same thing as, color and sound.

It's like his fingerprint, the pattern of energy that is his individual voice.

His . . . Vox? Is that what that word written on that drawing really means?

And what of myself?

I hold out my hand and *unlook* in the same way. I move my hand around in wonder and watch the colors ripple. It's a rainbow—it's around both hands, intensifying up my arms. It is *so* like the drawing I found in Dr. 1's book. There are other colors and subtleties, but the rainbow is the overall effect.

Downstairs again, I delve further into the books and charts: what does my aura mean? There are several references, and the answer isn't exactly the same in every book. But overriding it all is that those with rainbow auras may be skilled at energy work: they are healers. And they may also be *star people*—first incarnations on the earth. Whoa, what the hell does that even *mean*?

The more I read—the books, the charts, about the colors—the more my mind spins. Somehow it feels like Dr. 1's books were left here for me to discover; they relate to me and what I am.

And I can kid myself that all I'm doing here is trying to figure him out, to help find him, but there is a hunger inside me to know, and know more—to figure out *my new self.*

Healers can adjust auras to make people well. Is that what I did when I fixed my ear, and helped Kai after he'd been beaten up and tied to that bench—and at the hospital when I had a concussion too?

I didn't know how I did it the first times; I *reached out* and then *into* the hurt. But when I was in the hospital with my thoughts muddy and confused from the concussion, I had to work it out, and . . . yes. I think that is what I did. Maybe if I examined the aura first, I could use it to target things more specifically, and not do it all by feeling my way.

My intake of breath is sharp when the implications fall into place. If adjusting an aura can heal, can it also hurt? Those soldiers; I struck them with my anger, and they fell to the ground. I shudder: a way to heal, twisted around to cause pain.

Page after page, I read until the light is so dim that my eyes hurt. Finally I have to stop. I stand and stretch, then wander to the door.

The stars are out tonight.

I read all about how to use telescopes in one of Dr. 1's books earlier, and now I'm ready to give it a try.

The shutters and roof of the conservatory are in the way, but there are switches by the wall. I try them, and the shutters slide away, the roof and the doors slide open. I uncover the telescope and switch it on.

Despite the colors I can see around them, the stars above me are still cold and distant, as they always have been. I'm somehow nervous—of what I will see, or what I won't see—through the lenses of this telescope.

I'm thinking about what I'll try to find in the sky when the screen and controls come to life. The whole telescope moves, adjusts, without me touching it.

This model is far more advanced than the ones in Dr. 1's books. It looks like it isn't off an assembly line either. Was it made to order? I study the screen and controls, trying to work it out.

Interesting. It looks as though the telescope has been programmed to track particular coordinates through the sky, adjusting for the movement of our planet and the stars. As soon as I turned it on, it oriented itself. What did Dr. 1 find so fascinating that he wanted it always in view when he turned on his telescope?

Hesitant, I line my eyes up with the eyepieces. There is a blurry splash of radiant light and color on a background of inky darkness, so beautiful that I gasp. I adjust the focus for my eyes, and a binary star system jumps into stark relief, centered and bright. The star pair is so beautiful, it almost hurts to see it with such clarity—a luminous golden star, and a smaller blue one that shadows it. Streaks of multicolored aura surround them both, fine trails of color I can feel and trace in ways I couldn't with my naked eyes.

The maps of the sky, of the constellations, are in my mind from one of Dr. 1's astronomy books. This binary is the bottom star of the Northern Cross, the head of the Cygnus swan. It's called Albireo.

The beauty, clarity, and remoteness of the stars captivate me, and with them, their auras—the record of all they have been and the traces of all they will be. And as I stare at the night sky again and again, and think about that instead of everything else I should be thinking about, a realization settles in. Dr. 1 isn't the only one who isn't quite what I thought. Neither am I, and neither is the illness that made me this way.

CHAPTER 28

CALLIE

I STARE AT SHAY. Can her blue eyes see things my dark ones can't? I want to believe her. I'm so desperate to find Dr. 1, I'd do anything.

What can I do to help?

Shay covers the telescope and flicks switches that make the shutters and glass roof and doors slide closed. She faces me.

"You haven't told us very much about that research place underground. I need you to tell me everything you can remember."

I don't want to; I hated it there! There is panic leaking into my voice and thoughts.

"I know. I'm sorry. But I really think it could help. You see, I think maybe we're on the wrong track about the epidemic, but I can't quite figure out exactly how or why. There might be something you know that will make all the pieces fit together."

Would I really do *anything* to find Dr. 1? I'm not sure I even can remember what she wants to know, but the thought of trying to makes me want to run away, far and fast.

I'm scared.

There is something about all of this—Dr. 1, the epidemic, how I am now, the auras, his drawing, particles being waves, waves affecting particles—that all fits together. But I can't quite see *how*, not yet. Something is missing.

I feel more than see when Callie comes back. She stands behind me and watches.

"Hi," I say, and stand upright. I turn to face her and *reach* around her for her aura at the same time. But Callie has no color, at least none I can see, just darkness.

Hi.

"Sorry I upset you before. I didn't mean to."

I know. Callie sighs, leans against the wall. *It's being here, on this island. Just being here makes me angry, and we don't seem to be any closer to finding Dr. 1.*

"Maybe, just maybe, we are. I've been thinking. I've got some ideas about this Dr. 1 and what he did. I need your help to work it out."

Shay sits on the sofa and holds out a hand. I put my dark one in hers and sit next to her.

Can you feel my hand is there? I ask her, wistful.

"Sort of; there's like a tingling or something. Can you feel mine?"

I shake my head. *Not the way you mean. There is a resistance when my hands or feet or any part of me is pushed against something—I can't go through things. But I can't tell the difference between your hand and a wall. I can't taste or smell anything either. I can only see and hear.*

"But you can see that I'm holding your hand. And you know that I'm your friend and I care about you, don't you?"

I believe her. But is that only because I want to?

No. Shay *is* my friend.

I nod.

"And I wouldn't ask if I didn't think it was important."

I stare back at Shay, at her steady eyes locked on mine—the only ones that don't look straight through me. I finally sigh. *All right. What do you want to know?*

"Everything you can remember about being underground, right from when you first got there."

I lean back on the sofa, and after a while I begin. I tell her everything I can, though much of it—especially early on—is hazy, mixed up.

We arrived in groups. I had a friend—one I met in my group. We used to talk all night sometimes to keep from being scared. I frown. *I can't remember her clearly apart from that, not even her name.*

After lots of blood tests and scans and stuff, one day they took some of us and put us in these little rooms, one to a room. I was injected with something through a wall—there was a window, and a nurse who had her hands in heavy gloves that came through the wall.

It hurt. I got very sick, like you were—everything hurt so much, I screamed. It seemed to go on forever. I thought I'd die, but I didn't.

Then I was better. They seemed very excited about that at first. I remember Dr. 1 coming to see me. I frown again, struggling to remember. *That was the first time I saw him, I think. It was obvious he was the boss; they all did what he said.*

They did lots of tests; some of them hurt. I don't want to think about that.

"It's okay, Callie. I'm here, and they can't hurt you anymore."

I worked out I could tell people what to do and make them do stuff—like you can now. Once I almost got a nurse to let me out before someone stopped her.

And then they didn't want me to talk. They made me wear a mask so I couldn't.

Then, one day, they said I needed to be cured. Even though I wasn't sick anymore.

I stop talking for a moment, and Shay doesn't press. She waits, but does it in a way that I know she wants me to tell her. I take a deep breath—my version of it, anyway—and go on. I'd told Kai and Shay a little about this before, but now I tell her all of it—how it hurt, and then it didn't; that I was out of my body and watched it burn to ash. Then it got vacuumed up, taken away, and put with all the other bags of ash.

How I followed a scientist down below to some big control room. Then followed some techs down a hatch to a huge round thing that hummed—a giant worm in an even bigger tunnel.

Shay's eyes light up when I mention the worm. "Tell me more about that; everything you can."

I try to describe it, but my words don't seem to be enough for her.

"I wonder if . . . Callie, would it be all right if you remember it and I see if I can see what you remember? Like how sometimes we can see each other's thoughts?"

Okay. You can try. Shay's thoughts link with mine, and I go back . . .

I'm flying, faster and faster along the giant worm. It calls to me inside. Something inside it is part of me.

I stop; there are doctors next to a section of the worm, doing something with equipment attached it.

Then they go to their next victims; sedate and inject them. I hide my head under my arms and cover my ears so I can't hear or see what they are doing anymore.

Then Shay wants to know all about the night I escaped. I show her people getting sick; the guns and the blood. The explosion underneath us; smoke and fire. No, no earthquake or anything before that. And the explosions above ground, away from us, that come later—I didn't know then, but that must have been the oil place.

And we sit there as the sky begins to lighten, me wanting to forget, and Shay slowly sifting through my memories.

CHAPTER 29

SHAY

THERE ARE FOOTSTEPS ON THE STAIRS and then into the room. "Have you been up all night?" Kai asks.

I stir and look up. "Yes. And with Callie's help"—I smile at her—"I think I've worked a few things out."

He comes in, sits on the chair across from us. "Such as?"

"What Dr. 1 was doing on this island; why his research was being done here, in such an isolated place. They built a particle accelerator underground. You know, like at CERN in Switzerland—a massive structure that spins particles around faster and faster, and then has them collide."

"A particle accelerator? Are you sure?"

"Yes. Callie saw it. She didn't know what it was, but when she described it and showed it to me in her memory, I was sure. We went to CERN on a science trip last year. It was basically the same equipment."

"But what does this have to do with the epidemic?"

"There are some papers here that I read yesterday, but I didn't realize how important they were until I saw the particle accelerator in Callie's memory. At CERN, one of the experiments they were doing was creating antimatter, and experimenting with using it to kill cultured tumor cells—with the goal of one day being able to inject a tumor with antimatter to kill it. What I think they've done here is just another step: using more antimatter to kill more cells."

"Antimatter?" Kai's eyes widen. "That sounds way too Doctor Who."

"It does, doesn't it? But that's not the worst of it. They weren't trying to cure cancer, not the way they were going about it; that must have been some sort of cover story, or a way of getting doctors and nurses to work for them. They weren't targeting antimatter at cancer cells to save someone's life; they were targeting it at whole human beings."

Kai frowns. "But if they weren't looking for a cure for cancer, then *why* were they doing this?"

"I'm guessing here, but could they have been developing a new type of something like a biological weapon? It's not biological in this case, but it could be used in a similar way to target and kill enemies. That could be why the army—that Special Alternatives Regiment—are involved, and also why they seem to act on their own. I bet it isn't the sort of thing everyone would know about, in the forces or in the government."

"My God. That's a hell of an alternative." Kai crosses his arms like he wants to keep out what I've said.

"And then their weapon got out and gave us the Aberdeen flu. Though it's misnamed: not only is it not from Aberdeen, it's also not a flu, or any sort of disease—not in the sense we think of diseases. It's not anything biological at all. They had a particle accelerator, not bacteria or viruses. Callie's memories of the accelerator—of it being run, followed by extraction of something from the accelerator, and then injection into subjects—yes. It all confirms that that is what they were doing."

Kai's frown deepens. "But if the illness is caused by antimatter, isn't that like a poison? How could a poison be contagious and spread the way it has?"

"From quantum physics we know that light can act as both waves and particles, right? And that matter can do that too. It makes sense that antimatter can as well: that antimatter particles can be *things*—like a poison—but can also be waves. Waves that can spread out and cause contagion. It may be they didn't even know it would spread like it did until it happened. In fact, I'm guessing they didn't know—a weapon is only useful if you can aim it where you want."

Kai shakes his head. "I can't take this in. Quantum physics? Particles and waves? You're starting to sound like Alex."

When Kai mentions his stepfather—my father, not that Kai knows—I flinch inside, but keep it from my face. I tell myself there are more important things to deal with now . . . or maybe I'm just avoiding it.

"We still need to find out more," I say. "But there is one thing I'm sure of: the epidemic began with something that came out of a particle accelerator, here on this island."

That night, we all head out to the remains of the barn, the one that hid the elevator shaft—where Callie escaped from underground. I can't let her go alone, and Kai won't let us go without him.

He's having trouble believing; he thinks it sounds too sci-fi, too far-fetched. But if you went back in time and showed cavemen that you can shoot a mammoth with a gun, they'd think it was magic, wouldn't they? Even just go back a hundred years, and our ancestors would have trouble believing our computers and all the things they can do.

To get to what is left of the barn, we have to walk through dead, black places. Walking through cold ashes feels like disturbing the graves of the dead. A hundred Callies could rest here; more.

"Okay, Callie?"

Yes.

She's been subdued; the anger dulled down since she told me everything and showed me her memories. But her resolve inside is strong. Even if it means going back to the one place she never wanted to go again—she wants to get Dr. 1 more than anything.

Yes. I do.

We link our thoughts again when we reach the burned-out barn. Callie searches for a way in and finds a crack that leads into the elevator shaft. She heads down below, and I feel her terror of this place—of being locked up underground, of not being able to find her way out again.

The fires are long gone; it's cold and dead. She goes up and down corridors, finding ways to travel down and down again. The place is so destroyed that none of the locked doors are intact enough to stop her. Skeletons huddle in corners, behind locked exits; flesh burned away and eye sockets empty.

Callie hopes to find an office or some trace of Dr. 1, some clue to his identity, but nothing has escaped the fire.

The further down she goes, the more complete the destruction. When she finally reaches the tunnels below, the worm is dead. The place where it was encased is completely obliterated.

This is where everything started, isn't it? There was some sort of accident down here, and the accelerator was blown to smithereens. This either caused the earthquake or was the earthquake; in turn, this caused the destruction of one of the largest oil reservoirs in Europe. With both the oil reservoir and the accelerator up in flames, much of the island was destroyed.

Some people must have escaped from underground and with them, the epidemic—brought to mainland Scotland with the evacuated islanders.

And the proof lies here, buried with the dead underground.

CHAPTER 30

CALLIE

"YOU'RE REALLY SURE?" Kai asks. "That the Aberdeen flu actually started here, from injecting people with some sort of antimatter out of a particle accelerator?"

"Yes. Absolutely sure," Shay says.

"Will knowing this help stop the epidemic?"

"I don't know. But knowing the cause has got to take us further along toward doing something about it, doesn't it?"

"Yes."

"How do we get word out? We *can't* screw this up. It has to get out."

"Right. My mother?"

"And JIT. Yes and yes. But that's not enough. I think we should go to the air force, here on the island."

"Isn't the air force like the army and likely to shoot first, ask questions later, as far as you're concerned?"

"I don't think so. Listen, that Lieutenant Kirkland-Smith wasn't in with the rest of the army. He wasn't informed when a car was found near Killin—if he had been and he'd brought the dogs, they'd have had us. And that policeman in Inverness didn't believe the lieutenant was doing the right thing either, did he? When he looked into him, he whisked you away."

"What, are you saying that the lieutenant has gone rogue or something?"

"Maybe his *special alternatives* were so secret that no one else knew what they were up to, and now that things have gone wrong, they want to keep it that way."

"When you put it all together like that, it makes sense," Kai says, and straightens his shoulders. "All right, then. Tomorrow I'll go to the air force and tell them what we've learned."

"No. I have to go."

"Listen, it's you the army was after, not me. In case you've gotten things wrong and the air force agrees with Kirkland-Smith, it makes sense if I go."

"But I'm the one who worked out what they were doing with the particle accelerator; I'm the one who saw Callie's memories. I can explain it better."

Kai and Shay are staring at each other in a way that says neither will give an inch.

Will they both end up going?

I'm scared. What if Shay is wrong, and the air force won't listen? What if the whole government is in on the cover-up, and the first thing they do is kill both of them to keep it quiet?

Kai and Shay seem to think that can't be the case. They can't believe the government would take people like me and experiment on them—that if the authorities knew what was really happening, they'd have put a stop to it.

They also seem to think it is somehow worse if the point of it was to make weapons instead of trying to cure cancer. Dr. 1 may have used the cancer story to trick people like Nurse 11, but what difference does *why* really make to what they did?

They injected me and made me sick. When I survived, I was burned alive, leaving me as I am now. I don't care *why*.

Even though I'm scared Kai and Shay are wrong about going to the air force, I don't say anything. We have to—we have to tell them what we know, and hope they'll find Dr. 1.

Dr. 1 must pay for what he's done.

CHAPTER 31

SHAY

I HAVE TO GO, DON'T I? Kai is doing the man thing: that the man must be the one who puts himself at risk. Even when it's not logical. We can't both go, in case we get disappeared and there is no one left to tell the story, and I'm the obvious one to go: I'm the one best able to explain it all.

I sigh and put off the argument. "Look, let's leave deciding who does what for now," I say. "First up, we need to work out how to contact Iona, Lochy, your Mum, anyone else we can think of, and tell them everything that we know. I think we should try Dr. 1's laptop again. Maybe we can work out the password."

We try everything we can think of: the name of each of the islands, this peninsula, *Dr1*, *Drone*, *DrOne*; the door code again; author names and titles from his most thumbed books. After every three attempts we're blocked and have to restart the laptop to try again, but nothing works.

I sit back and rub my eyes. It could be any random string of numbers and letters that we have no chance of finding.

But Dr. 1 isn't a random sort of guy. Who has absolute zero as his door code, just because there is a manufacturer's mark on the window? There *must* be some way to work this out.

What else could it be . . . ?

My eyes trail around the room to his telescope. This whole house—its position, the design, the retractable shutters and roof—was designed to accommodate that telescope: a telescope that was programmed to track beautiful Albireo. Could that be it?

I enter *Albireo*—no. I try it in all uppercase, then all lowercase—no.

Frustrated, I flick the switch on the laptop again and rotate my stiff shoulders while I wait for it to restart.

"Take a break," Kai says. "Tea?"

I shake my head, unwilling to stop trying. Somehow I felt sure that would be it, but—

Wait. I read in one of those astronomy books that Albireo is also known by another name: Beta Cygni, the swan.

The laptop is ready again. I enter *Betacygni*—no. *betacygni*—no. One last chance before I have to restart again. I bite my lip and enter *BetaCygni*.

Hand already on the way to hit the switch to restart, I stare at the screen, then blink and look again—*yes!* It actually worked!

"I've got it! It's the alternative name of the binary star system the telescope was tracking!"

"Of course, how obvious," Kai says, one eyebrow raised. He shakes his head. "However you worked it out, good going. And now?"

"I'll try Lochy's web group login first—that'd be a way to get in touch with both Lochy and Iona," I say, and go to the web address and follow the steps.

It doesn't work. I try again in case I miss-hit a key; no.

"Damn. Maybe it only works on Lochy's computer? I'll go to JIT and Iona instead. It's evening, a good time to hope that Iona might be on her computer."

I start a new post.

Shay: Are you there?

Pause. Hit "refresh."

Iona: Oh thank God, it's you! Are you both okay?

Shay: Yes. We got to Shetland, solved all the mysteries, and now need to tell everybody what we know.

Iona: Go.

And I tell Iona as much as I can as fast as I can type.

Iona: Wow. I can't begin to understand how you worked all that out. Are you sure about the particle accelerator and everything?

Without telling Iona about Callie—something I can't do without risking she'd then discount everything else I said as craziness—it's hard to explain how the pieces came together. Yet it feels wrong to not tell her everything. I bite my lip and go on.

Shay: Yes, I'm sure; not enough time to get into the reasons just now. Can you spread the word? We're going to tell the authorities on the island tomorrow—there is an air force base. But just in case—well, you know—they aren't very friendly, can you tell Lochy and friends, and Kai's mum, and everyone else you can think of?

Kai gives me his mother's details, and I post them up next.

I hit "refresh" again and again, but there's nothing there. Just when I'm starting to panic that something has happened to Iona, a new paragraph appears.

Iona: Sorry, sorry. I had trouble answering. Lochy died. Of the flu. It's spread so much.

I stare at her words on the screen, unable to take this in. Lochy is . . . dead? I finally type back.

Shay: No. It can't be.

Iona: It is. I'll do what I can to spread this around, Shay. I never told you: I loved Lochy. I know he was a hopeless case, but I really did. I need to go now.

So Iona has secrets too. I want to reach down the internet all the way to her bedroom and hold her.

Shay: I'm so sorry.

Kai, reading over my shoulder, slips an arm around me. I hit "refresh" again and again, but Iona must be gone.

I look up at Kai. "We knew him for such a short time, but Lochy was amazing," I say. "And all that stuff he did for us; we never could have gotten here without him. And now he's gone? How can this be?"

"I can't believe it either," Kai says.

I stand up, and Kai's arms are around me, holding me. I hear his heart beating *th-thump, th-thump* in his chest in a way that Lochy's never will again.

We have to stop this epidemic from spreading any more. Stop it from taking more lives.

You need to find Dr. 1—maybe he knows how to stop it, Callie says. *Can you find out where he is from his computer?*

Good question. I tell Kai what she said and sit down again, turn back to the computer, but there is nothing personal I can find on it. No email or social logged in. There's not even any browsing history beyond what we've done.

"I bet if Lochy were here . . . " I start to say, then stop.

"Yeah," Kai says. "He'd be able to figure it out, wouldn't he?"

Kai and I go up to sleep. I'm exhausted like I never have been before. All those books I've taken in, all the delight of working things out and thinking about them and coming up with answers—and then Lochy.

I'm saddened by the news of his death more than I even understand. Beginning with Mum, so many people have died. But it is like he is one too many—the one that makes me feel the other losses all over again.

And I'm troubled in a way I can't put together. Not yet.

I wake up a few hours later, places in my dreams spinning in my mind on an endless loop: Aviemore . . . Inverness . . . Elgin . . .

There is a knot in my stomach like I'm going to be sick. My head is hot with fever. There is fear inside, and horror. I can't face any more; *I can't.*

I can't stay still in bed either. I slip downstairs and turn the computer back on.

Callie appears and looks over my shoulder. *What are you doing?*

"There's just something I have to check."

I do a search and find the government website with the quarantine zones. They're marked in red. I draw in my breath when I see how much they've grown.

There's a date function. I can see how they were yesterday, the day before, and so on. I put it back to the day we left Killin.

And then forward, a day at a time.

I trace the zones on the screen with my finger, hand shaking, stomach rising. I swallow, trying not to be sick. I put the dates back and forth again to be sure, watching how the red shrinks and grows on the map.

What's wrong?

"Look, Callie: look at the path we took to get here. From Killin, to Aviemore, and Inverness. Then Elgin. The quarantine zones grow to cover all the places we've been, a day or so after we were there. It's us: the epidemic is following us."

What? What do you mean?

Tears spill down my face. I flick them away.

"It's me, isn't it? I'm a carrier. I must be."

CHAPTER 32

CALLIE

SHAY, A CARRIER? Could it be true?

I study the maps and get her to take them back further in time.

There are lots of places people got sick that you haven't been, I point out.

"But there have been other survivors. Don't you see? It must be survivors who go on to carry the disease."

Shay does another search: *Scottish refugee fishing boat.*

She gasps. "There's a photo of the boat we took to get here: it's the same one, I'm sure of it. And the headline: 'Plague Ship Turned Away From Norway.'"

She touches the screen. "That was posted a few days ago. All those people; that mother and baby too. They'll be dead by now . . . because of me?"

She's crying silently, tears running down her face.

But I'm still staring at the quarantine zones, the maps, and remembering when and where it all began.

The explosions on the island; I escaped.

I went to Aberdeen.

Then Edinburgh.

Then Newcastle.

Back to Edinburgh; then to Killin with Kai; then from Killin to Aviemore, to Inverness, to Elgin.

All the centers of the epidemic: I've been to every single one of them, and it appeared the next day. Every single place I went; every single time.

Ages ago in Newcastle, Kai and Mum were talking about the spread of the disease. They'd wondered then if there could be someone Mum called a Typhoid Mary, someone who carried the disease wherever they went—someone who spread it quickly, while sick people only spread it slowly.

If there is a Typhoid Mary . . . maybe it's me.

But that's crazy. I'm a ghost.

Even if it is crazy, it's the only answer that fits.

It's not Shay who is the carrier at all. It's me.

It *must* be me: everyone I go near gets sick and dies, unless they're immune like Kai—or a survivor, like Shay.

It was me who made Shay sick, wasn't it? And then her mum must have caught it from Shay before Shay got better, since I never saw her mum until after she died.

I'm stricken. It's still *my* fault her mum died, isn't it? I gave it to Shay; she gave it to her mum.

But I didn't know! I didn't know that just by going near someone, I could make them sick.

It was bad enough under the island, even though all those doctors and nurses deserved what they got.

But everyone else?

Not all people are good, I know this, but it was whole families—not just mums and dads, but little children too. The pain—the pyres. The smoke rising into the sky.

I have to go and be somewhere alone where no one can get near me; no one can get sick and die ever again . . .

But then what about Dr. 1?

Dr. 1 made me like this.

If we find him, I can infect him: making him burn is too easy. I can infect him and watch him die—slowly, in pain.

Dr. 1 *must* die: this is the most important thing, more important than anything or anybody.

Once he's dead, *then* I'll go away, stay away from people so they won't get sick and die anymore.

I study Shay: has she been listening to what I'm thinking? No, she's still wrapped in on herself, crying, in shock.

I shield my thoughts. Shay is so close to the truth. I have to make sure that she doesn't find it. She doesn't want people to get sick; if she knows I'm the carrier, she won't help me anymore. But she's so clever, how do I stop her from working it out?

She can't think straight if she's upset.

Yes, it must be you! That's why SAR was trying to kill you. They must have known survivors are carriers.

Shay flinches. "But I didn't know," she whispers.

It's your fault that Lochy died.

Shay gets up from the computer. She paces the room, arms crossed tightly like she's trying to hold herself in.

And my mum. She thinks the words she can't say out loud.

What are you going to do?

"I don't know," she says. She's shaking, her arms wrapped around herself, but then, moments later, she stands straighter. "I do know. I have to turn myself in."

CHAPTER 33

SHAY

THE SUN IS WARM, but the waves are lively today. I'm sitting on a rock above the cliff, watching them roll in and out again far below.

The sea has an aura too, an emerald green that chases the waves. It calms the tumult inside me—a spinning that echoes the white froth as the waves break on the cliff below.

A door opens. There are footsteps behind me.

"There you are." Kai's voice. He lowers himself to sit on the rock next to mine, reaches a hand to my chin. I turn, kiss him. Eyes closed, I feel his aura; eyes open, now I can see what I always felt. It's as though opening my mind to what was there has made it plain.

He starts to move away, but I slip a hand around his neck, pull him closer and kiss him again, and his heart beats faster, like mine; his aura deepens to clear red. I stop and look at my hand: mine too.

He takes my hand and holds it.

"Shay, stop distracting me and listen up."

"Okay. I'm listening."

"You have to let me go to the air force on my own. We can't both go."

He starts detailing a list of reasons, but all that is behind them is that he doesn't want anything to happen to me. Blue protectiveness shines bright around him, an integral part of who and what he is.

This is the moment. This is when I should tell him that it's too late; it already has happened to me, and to everyone around me. I'm a carrier, and I must be the one to go.

But I can't tell him what I must do. I know who he is—I can see it shining clear in his aura. It would destroy him to let me go alone, like it destroyed him that he wasn't there to save his sister. I have to take the decision away from him.

"Things are changing, aren't they?" I say. "I agree that only one of us can go. If whoever goes . . . doesn't come back again, then the other must carry on, get the word out and do what they can. So whether you go, or I go, we might not see each other again."

"Don't think that." His hand tightens on mine.

"So, here's the deal. You can go." There is yellowy-green deception in my aura now, but he can't see auras, can he? I lower my eyes, look away. "But first, we have tonight. Together, alone." I look up again, and my eyes meet his.

"Alone?"

"Callie's promised to stay away."

His hand lets go and traces a path up my bare arm. I shiver. I long so much to *reach*, to touch him inside like his hand touches my skin outside. I sigh.

"What's wrong?"

His eyes are warm hazel, almost green in the late-afternoon sun. Do they see more than I think they do?

"It's hard to explain."

"Try."

"You touch me, like you just did, but I can't touch you. I don't mean like this"—I raise my hand to his cheek—"but inside. It's like I have an extra sense I can't use. As if you'd said to me, *Close your eyes and never look at me. Keep your hands away and never touch me.* It feels like that."

"Having you—having *anyone*—in my mind scares me," Kai says.

"It could be amazing. To touch, like this." I hold out my hand, and he holds out his, and I link our fingers together again. "And this," I say, and kiss him, then pull back and smile. "And inside our minds too, at the same time. To touch all ways, at once."

All ways for always. But that can never be.

"It makes me feel like I'll lose control."

"It's not a loss; it's to share, even more. You have to trust me." I study his aura and see something else. "You don't like to lose control, do you, Kai? Is that why you always stop? Why we never go too far?" I can feel the color rise in my cheeks, even as the way he looks at me makes everything spin with *want* and confusion, at the same time. Why are we talking about this when we should be saying goodbye?

"It hasn't been easy—when you kiss me like that, when we're alone like we are now. But you're only sixteen, Shay. And you've been through a lot."

"We both have." *And there is more to come.* "You don't have to protect me, not anymore." You can't.

Kai stares back at me, then slowly nods. "And what if today is all we have?" He takes my hand, pulls me to my feet—kisses me, then tugs my hand, to go with him.

Somehow I walk with him to the door, even as everything is tumbling so much inside that I can't believe I can still put one foot in front of the other.

And up the stairs, into the bedroom we've shared—but not shared, at the same time. Not wanting to be apart, but sleeping—fingers touching—at arm's length.

He stands, just looking at me, then reaches out a hand, clasps mine. He pulls me closer, leans down, and kisses me once, gently.

"I *do* trust you. Go ahead." He holds my hand to his temple.

"Are you sure?" I say.

"Are you?"

To answer, I kiss him again and again, and then, just as our auras deepen, let my mind touch Kai's.

He knows I am here and he is there—that we are separate and together at the same time—and this time, he doesn't push me away.

Shay? he says inside, his thoughts entwined with mine.

Yes?

I love you.

I caress him, inside and out. It's the first time he's said it. Here, in his thoughts, he can't hide the truth.

I can, but this truth I show him:

I love you too.

Love and want and desire for me and only me are clear and shining in his thoughts, in his aura; his hesitation is finally gone. It is tempting—*so tempting*—to give myself to him and have this now, but how can I add that to the list of betrayals?

I kiss him. Then—instead of loving him—I betray his trust and break my promise. I soothe and sing him to a deep sleep like a siren that promises a sailor love but dooms his boat on the rocks.

And then I write him a letter.

I explain it all. That I am a carrier. That it has to be this way. That he should go to the cave and get a boat home—make sure that everyone knows the real cause of the epidemic and how it is spread.

Without me.

I don't know if he'll understand; I don't know if he'll hate me.

I hope not.

I kiss him one last time, and he smiles in his sleep. I put the letter on the pillow next to him, there for when he wakes up. It won't be for a long time.

I stand in the doorway and drink him in with my eyes—something to hold and keep close in my memory, for as long or as short as I may have left. The way his hair curls at his neck. The softness of his features from sleep makes him look younger—a softness the world doesn't often see. But I do. The rise and fall of his chest as he breathes.

Then I slip down the stairs, barriers up as much as they can be. If Callie is nearby, I don't want her to sense me or follow. I know her better now, from living her memories of underground: there is nothing she hates more than being locked up, contained. I can't let her come with me when that is about the best I can hope for once the authorities know I am a carrier. Besides, she belongs with her brother.

And I step out into the night.

I walk fast, the way worked out and memorized earlier.

I'm strangely calm. Or maybe numb?

I know what I'm doing is right. In addition to the letter I left for Kai, I also posted an explanation to Iona on JIT. I had to tell her that survivors are carriers, that she must tell everyone she can in case no one will listen to me.

And that it was my fault that Lochy died. I hope that one day she'll forgive me.

I walk quickly in the dim light, and the miles go by. Soon the sun is on the rise, and this seems somehow surprising. How can it, when my heart is breaking with every step I take away from Kai?

I'm nearly there now; I can see the air force base in the distance.

I force myself to walk forward a step at a time. The numbness has gone, to be replaced by fear: deep, bone-shaking terror that strikes through me and my resolve and makes me want to run, to hide.

There's a bored-looking guard at the entrance to the base, and he's not wearing a biohazard suit. I suppose that as far as they know, they're the only ones on the island, so why would he need one?

He's not very alert. I have to wave before he notices my approach. He looks startled to see someone here.

I keep my hands where he can see them and make myself walk slowly forward when all I want to do is run away.

I stop when I judge I'm close enough to be heard, my trembling hands forward in a gesture of surrender.

He seems to hesitate, then starts to step away from his position. Toward me.

"Don't come any closer!" I call out. "I'm a survivor of Aberdeen flu. I'm a carrier."

He stops abruptly.

"I also know what caused the epidemic. I want to help stop it. Let me help."

His hands are tight on his gun.

Please don't shoot me, please don't shoot me, please don't shoot me . . .

The words go over and over again in my mind like a prayer.

CHAPTER 34

CALLIE

THERE IS A LOUD CRASH ABOVE when I return the next morning, and I rush upstairs.

Kai is cradling his hand. His knuckles are bloody, and there is a hole in the wall.

He's alone, and there is a letter in his hand.

Where is Shay?

I rush around the house, then go outside. I *will* find her, if I have to check the whole island.

So fast that all I am is a dark smudge, a blur. I skim around the edges of the island, then move in, bit by bit.

I cover it all, including the air force base, but she's nowhere. I can't sense her; I can't hear her.

How can this be?

I *always* feel where she is if we are close enough to each other—there's nowhere on this island she can get far enough away that I shouldn't be able to trace her.

Where is she?

Did she trick me? She asked me to stay away to give her and Kai one last night together alone. Did she wait for me to leave and then put Kai to sleep, so neither of us could follow her, and then go and turn herself in?

I head to the air force base again to search in more detail. There's a guard at the entrance. I rush past him and through every part of the base—quarters, meeting rooms, canteen, supplies—and then on to the airfield. Hangars, planes, technicians doing this and that inside them. She's simply not here.

It wasn't supposed to happen like this. I need to be with her! If she told them everything, surely the first thing they'd do is go and find Dr. 1?

I need to be there when they find him.

Horror grows inside me as I realize—it's even worse. Without Shay, no one can hear me. No one can see me.

She said she was my friend, but she tricked me and left; she knew that without her, I might as well be trapped under the island. I'm unheard. Unseen.

Alone.

She lied. She wasn't my friend at all.

Anguish twists inside me, a deep well of pain that grows and grows, and I scream it out as loud as I can. But for all anyone can hear, I might as well be the wind.

Where are you, Shay? I need you!

But she doesn't answer.

She's gone.

CHAPTER 35

SHAY

PLEASE DON'T SHOOT ME, *please don't shoot me, please . . .*

My heart beats so slow I almost think fear has made it stop.

Instead, it is time that has stilled. What should be a rush of blood in my veins pauses, waits.

A bird's cry seems to hang in the sky above me, the notes separating out and then joining back together. If I must measure the rest of my life in these small things, then they will go slow, as slow as possible, to extend my time on this earth.

Please don't shoot me, please don't shoot me . . .

The soldier's horror and indecision batter against me—a kaleidoscope of sensations painted on waves of something like color and sound that make up *him*, as he is now: his Vox, Dr. 1 called it. And his fear is not just of the disease, but of *me*. But this wars inside him with what his eyes see before him: a girl, hands held forward, on her knees in the dirt.

Yet who would blame him if he pulled the trigger?

Please don't shoot me, please . . .

The temptation to attack his aura—to stop his hands and make him fall—almost overwhelms me. But if I did, what would the point have been in leaving Kai and coming here? The authorities *must* listen to me. They have to know that survivors like me are carriers, that the epidemic started here, underground on this island. If I attack their guard, why would they listen to anything I might say?

Though maybe they already know. Maybe the air force base on this Shetland island is part of the cover-up, and this is all for nothing.

Please . . .

His hands tighten on his gun.

My head is swimming. I've stopped breathing but can't bring myself to take a breath until I know what he will do.

His aura shifts; it deepens with resolve. He's made a decision.

Eyes still on me, one hand moves away from his gun as he reaches down for a radio.

I drop—almost collapse—to the ground, filling my lungs with air in a rush. I can hear the murmur of his voice but not the words.

Be brave, Shay. Be brave like Kai would have been if he were here.

Now that my heart is beating in normal time again, it thumps too fast in my chest, and my breathing is shallow and quick. Exhausted from days of not sleeping much and then walking through the night, I lie down on the ground and look at the calm, blue sky above me. My barriers are up in case Callie has noticed I'm missing, is searching for me, and that makes the world around me feel remote.

I focus inside instead, on slowing and deepening each breath. And despite my fear, exhaustion has my mind drifting in that weird place that comes just before sleep.

Does Kai know yet that I tricked him, that I've left?

Maybe he's still asleep.

I imagine his eyes closed, lashes dark on his cheek, breathing gently, a half smile of pleasant dreams on his lips.

And then my dream self is there, fingers in his hair, stroking his bare chest where his heart beats under his skin.

Click.

My hand stills. What is that?

Click. A harsh, jarring sort of sound, like metal on rock.

I'm confused, and then I come back to here, now—to my body lying in the dirt.

It's footsteps. Someone is coming. I push sleep away and sit up.

Walking toward me are two men and one woman, all in head-to-toe biohazard suits. Execution squad or welcoming committee? They're remote, muffled by the barrier of their suits—their auras are still there but half-strangled.

The woman takes the lead.

"Good morning. I'm Dr. Morgan. And you are?"

"Shay McAllister."

"I understand you've told our sentry that you are a survivor of the Aberdeen flu. And that you are a carrier."

"Yes. That's right."

"How do you know you are a carrier?"

"Everywhere I've gone, the epidemic has followed. I didn't know; I realized after. I could show you on a map where I've been and tell you when, and then you'd see."

She listens, nods; what I can see of her face behind the transparent front plate of the helmet of her suit is guarded and giving nothing away, but it is there, in her aura. They knew—or, at least, suspected—as much.

"Why did you come to Shetland?"

"To trace the cause of the epidemic. It wasn't from Aberdeen at all; it came from here. Underground."

They exchange glances. A ripple of alarm passed through them when I said "underground," but I can't read why.

"You'd better come with us," she says. She hesitates, then holds out a hand.

I take hers in mine, scramble to my feet. The suit is cold, metallic, the form of her hand vague underneath its glove. Any warmth her hand may have doesn't penetrate.

"We don't have enough suits to cover the base, so we need you to put one on before we go in. All right?"

I notice then that one of them is carrying a suit over his shoulder. He passes it to me.

"I've guessed the size about right, I think," she says, and shows me how to step into it. When it closes over my head, I have to fight to not struggle, to not push it away. It snaps shut and seals. She explains the controls and how to breathe inside it. The filtered air tastes dull and removed from the island.

We walk down the hill. I feel clumsy, like the earth under my feet is too distant to walk on with any certainty.

As if I'm separate from it and will never be part of it again.

ACKNOWLEDGMENTS

Thank you to my agent, Caroline Sheldon. Thank you to Megan Larkin and Emily Sharratt for their editing wisdom, and to everyone at Orchard Books and Hachette Children's Group for their enthusiasm and hard work. And to all my publishers and readers around the world!

A few years ago I was invited to the Stirling Off the Page festival in Scotland, and combined this with a writing retreat at Lake of Menteith and a school event in Callander. When I started a new story the next year, the places I'd visited were in my mind. The settings puzzle for *Contagion* fell into place with two more trips to Lake of Menteith and then Killin, and finally Newcastle.

Killin and Loch Tay are such beautiful, peaceful places—perfect for dreaming, perfect for plotting. The Old Smiddy in Killin was a lovely place to stay and write, and thanks to everyone there for answering my endless questions about the area.

I needed somewhere remote also, and Shetland, with its oil terminal, seemed perfect. Thanks to Karen Murray and Lyndsay Stone for coming along to Shetland, driving me about, and braving the many and varied hazards of research!

Thanks to Jo Wyton, with her geology hat on, and to Addy Farmer, Paula Harrison, and my writing friends everywhere—it's not a contradiction to say that you're my kind of crazy, and help me stay sane.

Thanks to Iona, Euan, and Duncan for coming to so many of my events, from the very beginning! And for their names.

And first, last and always: thank you, Graham. I couldn't do it without you—I wouldn't be me without you either.